*Out of the crucible of war,
they forged a dream of independence
that would never die.*

Ian McPherson: A proud Scottish warrior exiled to the
Virginia tidewater, he yearns to return home and avenge
the terrible slaughter visited upon his people by the
English army. But now, joining the Virginia militia
under the command of Colonel George Washington, he
allies himself with his hated, ancient enemy—the British
Crown. His true enemy is tyranny in all its forms, and he
will fight with all his heart to find the path to freedom
in this strange new land.

Captain Thomas Shields: A gentleman by birth, a soldier by choice, a man of limitless ambition, he joins
General Braddock's colonial expedition, confident that
fame awaits him in the fields of war. But his dream of
glory is shattered in the horrifying chaos of battle.
Scarred in the flesh and in his soul, he drowns his despair
in rum . . . his only hope for peace and redemption in
the warm embrace of a woman.

Praise for *New York Times* Bestselling Author
Harold Coyle

"Coyle is at his best when he's depicting soldiers facing
death. . . . He knows soldiers and he understands the
brotherhood-of-arms mystique that transcends national
boundaries."

—*The New York Times Book Review*

Megan O'Reilly: Sold into indentured servitude by her mother, the fiery-eyed Irish lass refuses to accept enslavement on a Virginia plantation. Innocent, impetuous, fiercely independent, she looks to the horizon, toward the great western wilderness, and sees a chance to stake her own claim to the future. But the journey will be fraught with mystery and danger . . . and could end in tragedy if the man she loves perishes in the flames of war.

Katherine Van der Hoff: The only child of a wealthy Albany merchant, she is well versed in the subtle arts of social intrigue and courtly seduction—a woman who knows what she wants and how to get it. Now, she has set her china-blue eyes on the captivation and capture of a dashing young British officer. But she must overcome a rival more powerful than any she has faced before: the officer's driving impulse toward self-destruction.

"[Harold Coyle is] the Tom Clancy
of ground warfare."
—W.E.B. Griffin

"Coyle captures the stress, exhilaration,
and terror of combat."
—*Cincinnati Post*

Ensign Anton de Chevalier: The bastard son of a nobleman, the French artillery officer has been robbed of his rightful inheritance by an accident of birth. Now, in the New World, he has discovered a land where a man's character means more than his lineage. Here in this wondrous and savage place, he seeks a nobility beyond the blood—a search that will lead him into the darkest abyss of war . . . and of his own soul.

Toolah: A Caughnawaga native whose tribe has sworn allegiance to the French, the young brave is full of hatred toward the European invaders who have driven his people to slaughter. To lead his tribe back to the ways of their ancestors, he must first find wisdom to match his courage, and restraint to match his strength. But it may be too late, for the bitterness in his heart and the fire raging in his blood have left him with one unquenchable desire: destruction of the white man.

"In many ways Coyle is even better than Clancy. . . . What sets Coyle's work apart is his absolute authenticity."
—*Phoenix Gazette*

"Coyle's examination of individuals caught in the complexities and cruelties of combat is first-rate."
—*Booklist*

Books by Harold Coyle

Savage Wilderness
Until the End
Look Away
Code of Honor
The Ten Thousand
Trial by Fire
Bright Star
Sword Point
Team Yankee

HAROLD COYLE

SAVAGE WILDERNESS

POCKET STAR BOOKS

New York   London   Toronto   Sydney   Tokyo   Singapore

Originally published in hardcover in 1997 by Simon & Schuster Inc

A Pocket Star Book published by
POCKET BOOKS, a division of Simon & Schuster Inc
1230 Avenue of the Americas, New York, NY 10020

ISBN: 0-671-00387-9

First Pocket Books printing April 1998

10 9 8 7 6 5 4 3 2 1

POCKET STAR BOOKS and colophon are registered trademarks of Simon & Schuster Inc.

Map by Rick Britton

Cover illustration by Steven Assel
Cover design by Myles Sprinzen

Printed in the U.S.A.

Acknowledgments

Savage Wilderness is a novel, a work of fiction. And while the major characters in the story are imaginary, the events depicted within this book are real. I have, with very few exceptions, recounted the battles of that forgotten war, as well as the causes, reasons, and events that led to them, as accurately as possible. In this endeavor, I have been helped by a number of people.

First and always, there has been Ms. Ren'ee Chevalier. She has worked on this book as if it were her own. In many ways, she is as much a part of it as myself.

I would like to express my thanks to the staff at the Fortress of Louisbourg for the help they gave my assistant Ren'ee Chevalier while she was doing research on the French and Indian War period. Though I do regret that the sections on Louisbourg had to be cut, I am indebted to the wonderful and caring Staff of Louisbourg. In addition to Greta Cross for her help to my assistant others include:

Ann Colman
Sandi Balcom
B. A. Balcom
Sandra LaRad
Brad
Ken Donivan
Gerry Delanie
Eric Krause

Bill O'Shea
W. A. O'Shea
Roger Wilson
A. J. B. Johnston
Charles Burkle
Andreé Crépeau
Bruce Fry

I would also like to thank Dr. Joyce Thierer of Emporia State University and Ride into History and Ann Birney from Ride into History for their kind help. And Judith Stoll of Topeka Technical College for her assistance and discussion of the historical subjects covered in the book and some of the Indian issues.

Then, there's Frederick J. Chiaventone, an author and certified character in his own right. He helped guide much of my early research and put me into many a good book on the French and Indian War. He also provided a sympathetic ear to hear my laments, as well as a fellow amigo along what otherwise would be a lonely trail.

To all of you, thanks.

H. W. COYLE

To Ren'ee Chevalier

"Oh, call it by some better name.
For friendship sounds too cold."

THOMAS MOORE

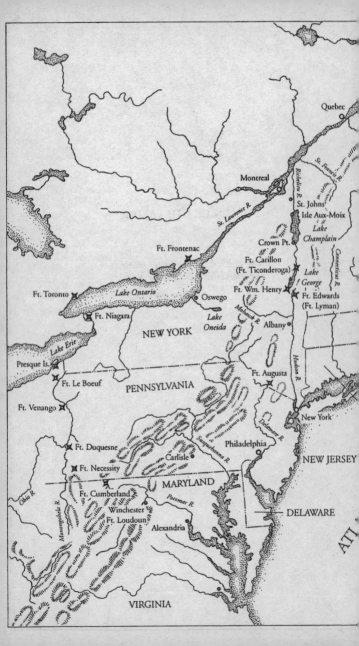

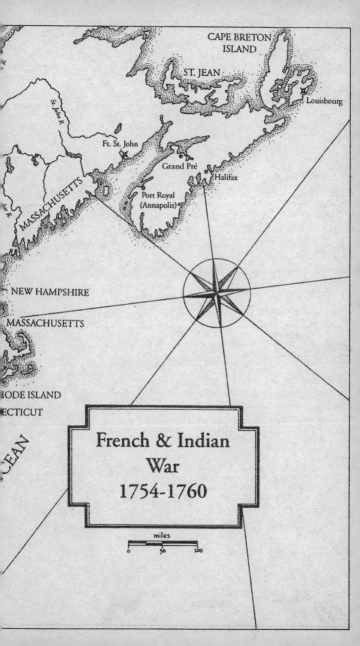

SAVAGE
WILDERNESS

PROLOGUE

Saint Croix Island
Fall, 1604

EVEN BEFORE darkness gave way to the cold, pale dawn, the old warrior was there, sitting on the rocky banks of the island. The only sound that disturbed the early morning quiet was the splashing of the swift, flowing river on nearby rocks. As he had on so many mornings, he peered through the early morning mist, still rising off the turbulent waters of the river, at the camp of the strangers. And as he had on each such occasion, he silently prayed that the sun rising in the east to greet him would reveal that the strangers had gone.

Yet even before he could see them, he knew they were still there. He could smell them. While the smoke from their fires smelled no different than that which warmed the warrior's own lodge, the stench that rose from the squalid living conditions the strangers seemed to revel in marked them as certainly as the white banner of their tribe, adorned with three yellow emblems. Slowly the warrior squatted into a comfortable position on a large, flat rock from which he could watch the comings and goings of the strangers as they tended to their early morning rituals and tasks.

One of the first stirrings that occurred each morning was the appearance of a handful of men dressed in armor that had once been bright and shiny, but now, like the leaves on the trees, had been made dull and lifeless by the passing of time. The stranger who had been at the entrance to their crude log enclosure seldom greeted the group of men as they approached him. Instead, with bowed head, the man left the spot where he had stood watching throughout the night and trudged away to join the others with less enthusiasm than a captive moves when faced with certain death. In his place another man, similarly dressed and looking equally dejected, moved forward to take the first man's place at the entrance. Once he had reached the spot that seemed suitable for him, the new guard lowered the wood and metal weapon he bore, eased it down until one end rested on the ground, and then leaned against the post that the rickety gate hung on.

It was only after he was comfortable that the new sentinel bothered to lift his gaze from the dirt at his feet. Slowly, more from want of ambition than from attentiveness, the sentinel surveyed the island he and his companions had chosen to occupy. The old warrior wondered if the strangers, with skin as white and as fair as any he had ever seen and faces covered with fur, saw the same things that he saw. He liked to think that they did, that the strangers shared more than bodies shaped as his was. But the more the old man watched them, the more he came to realize that this breed of man was unlike any other human he, or anyone he knew, had ever come across. Even the shaman, after much contemplation and consultation with the spirits, was at a loss to explain who these men were and what their coming foreshadowed.

Unable to find answers in the legends of his people or in the wisdom of the elders of the tribe, the old warrior decided to do what he always had done when faced with a new situation or challenge. He would study it, as often as he could and as long as he could. It was important, he knew, to be familiar with the land that surrounds you and all the creatures that inhabit it. This simple prescription, while it had failed to gain him sufficient triumphs to be considered a leader of his tribe, had permitted him to live to an age that none of his boyhood friends ever saw and bask in the warmth of a family that honored him as if he were the greatest warrior chief who had ever lived.

When the eyes of the stranger guarding the enclosure of the settlement on the island finally fell upon the old man, the stranger studied the warrior for a moment. There was no surprise in the man's face, for he and his companions had seen the warrior and others of his tribe, from afar, on many occasions. Only the warrior seemed to show any real interest as the two men stared at each other for several minutes. One question, the same one that always came to mind whenever the old man knew he was being watched, was why the strangers, after all these months, still refused to make an effort to contact them. It was foolish, the old man thought, utterly foolish on the part of the strangers to stand aloof on their isolated island, in the middle of their own stench, and make no effort to come to terms with the world or the people about them.

Suddenly, the stranger's eyes lifted slightly, so that they were now gazing over the old warrior's head. Seeing something behind the old man that aroused his interest, the stranger pushed away from the post he had been leaning on and straightened up. For a moment, the old warrior perked his ears, but he did not turn around. There was no need to, once his tired ears were able to pick up the familiar sound of the footfalls above the noise of the turbulent river before him.

"Why do you come here, my child, and disturb me?" the warrior demanded without taking his eyes from the strangers across from him.

"I come here," the sweet voice of his granddaughter responded, "for the same reason you come, in search of answers."

"Then you are wasting your time," the old warrior responded gruffly, "for men such as those can provide us with no answers."

With a smile, the young girl came up close to her grandfather and settled down next to him. Without a word, the two eased against each other, both for support and for warmth, as they had done on so many other mornings. Together, the old, tired eyes of the warrior, set deeply in the crags of a face that had seen many winters, were joined on their lonely vigil by the wide, eager, bright eyes of a girl on the verge of womanhood.

Across the way, another fair-skinned stranger emerged from the compound with a wooden bucket in each hand. When he came abreast of the sentinel, he stopped and looked across the river at the old warrior and his granddaughter. After a moment, the two strangers exchanged comments. The old man enjoyed listening to them talk. Though he had no idea what they said, their language had a lyrical quality that reminded the old man of a young woman's song.

"What do you suppose they are talking about?" his granddaughter asked in the sweet tones that only an innocent maiden could manage.

From the look in the stranger's eyes, the old man knew full well what they were discussing. Yet he did not tell her. Instead, his response reflected his own feelings and beliefs. "It does not matter what they speak of. People who are foolish enough to settle on an island that has no game, no source of fresh water other than the river itself, and will be all but washed away when the floods come in spring should not be listened to. They are like the rainbow, my child, beautiful to behold, but of no importance. In time, they will be gone."

His granddaughter thought about his words as she watched the man with the buckets move down to the river, fill them halfway with water, then trudge back to the enclosure. Finally, she turned her face toward the old warrior's. "Do you really think that they will be gone soon?"

That was a question that the old man had pondered himself many, many times. His brain told him that they would not, could not, last very long, not if their choice of settlement was any indication of their skill and wisdom. Yet, in his heart, he knew that there was more to be feared from these strangers than their actions to date indicated. As stupid as he liked to try to make them out to be in his own mind, the old man knew that these strangers had a presence about them that was, for the warrior and his people, ominous. In his dreams, these strangers had come to personify all the faceless fears and demons that he had known since childhood. Though they had not done him or his people any harm, the old warrior had lived long enough to know evil when he saw it.

"You fear them, too, don't you?" his granddaughter finally stated as she looked back across the river.

Taking his hand out from under the fur that had been keeping it warm, he grasped the girl's hand. "No, my child, I do not fear these men, for I am an old man that is not long for this life. I believe that my eyes will not see many more winters. But," he said as he squeezed her hand, "I fear these are not men, not as we know. In time, we will be allowed to see inside their hearts, and learn what it is that brings them here, to our shores. And when we do, I fear our people will weep."

The chill that swept across them didn't cut the young girl as deeply as her grandfather's words did. For she, too, had felt the same foreboding that the old warrior now voiced. Unable to think of a suitable response, the girl simply squeezed the old man's hand and sat beside him in silence, watching, studying, and waiting.

PART ONE

Distant Shores

CHAPTER ONE

Culloden, Scotland
April, 1746

STUBBORNLY, IAN MCPHERSON continued to blink in a vain effort to clear the cold drops of rain from his eyes even as the wind whipped more of them into his face. Every now and then, he managed to catch a glimpse of the red-coated Government troops, now arrayed in line of battle some five hundred yards away. Like others around him, he looked sharply for some evidence of a weakness that would be their undoing. But there didn't seem to be one, not one that could be seen from the rear ranks, where he stood with the other warriors of no title or little means. Frustrated, Ian gripped the hilt of the ancient broadsword tightly as he lifted the arm holding the small, round shield, wiped his face on his sleeve, and shifted his weight from one foot to the other to keep his legs from cramping. The waiting, he had found, in the closely packed clan ranks, was almost as unnerving as battle itself.

On this day, the sixteenth of April, the wait was particularly trying. The night before they had been marched about in a vain effort to surprise the Government forces in their camps with a night attack. Confusion, however, prevailed, ending that effort with a retreat near dawn to a soggy patch of ground where they were allowed to catch two or three hours' sleep. Near seven o'clock the pipes called the men back to the ranks. Without having so much as a biscuit to eat, the exhausted Highlanders were marched to Drummossie Moor and deployed for battle. Tired and disheartened, some of the men had failed to heed the call of the pipes that morning while others had gone off alone or in small groups in search of the food that their leaders seemed incapable of providing them. Those who stayed, like Ian, had little else to do but wait with their fellow clansmen, clustered shoulder-to-shoulder, and watch as the English troops of Lord Cumberland deployed from march column and wheeled into line on the boggy moor across from them.

For Ian, watching the British was unnerving. Smartly dressed in baggy red coats faced with a rainbow of colors representing different regiments, they paraded about as if the army of Prince Charles did exist. Contemptuous of their mud-spattered foe, the English units performed their mechanical gyrations without the slightest regard for the massed clans that Prince Charles of the House of Stuart held in check. "We should go forward and have at them," Ian muttered in angry frustration. "Now, before they're all set and arranged for battle. It makes no sense, no sense at all, to stand here like a bloody rock and let them prance about as they please."

From behind him, a low, gravelly voice responded to Ian's utterings. "Be patient, laddie. You'll get your chance soon enough to throw your life away."

Turning his head slightly and glancing over his shoulder, he glared at John McLynn. "You heard me, boy," McLynn growled. "I do not know if Bonnie Prince Charlie or any of those fine Irish and French gentlemen who profess to lead us really know what they're doin', but I do know it'll make little difference for us common sorts whether we go now, or wait a little longer."

"I think," another voice from off to one side chimed in, "they're waitin' for those who went aforagin' to come back."

"I see no sense in that," yet another offered. "It seems to me that the few we get back aren't goin' to matter when the bloody English cannon start firing."

"We have our own cannon, you know," stated a thin wisp of a man who was leaning on a Lochaber ax for support.

McLynn was unimpressed. "Do you think the half-wits they have manning those guns will do us much good?" Not waiting for anyone to answer, McLynn shook his musket at the thin man and thumped his clenched fist on his chest. "This," he growled, "twelve rounds of powder and ball, and our miserable wretched bodies is all we'll have to throw at them, when the time comes."

From somewhere in front of the packed mass of men, a shrill voice rose above the mutterings in the ranks. "All right, lads, settle down now. Have a little faith in Prince Charlie and yourselves." It was their colonel, Charles Stuart of Ardshiel. Lethargic by nature and described by some as being "pretty," Ardshiel was not what Ian had imagined a clan chief should be. In part, that was explained by the fact that Ardshiel was not the clan chief, but only the clan chief's tutor. Since the real Appin Stuart chief was still a child, Ardshiel, who had the reputation as a swordsman, was chosen to go in his stead. "We've seen this all before," Ardshiel stated as if he were scolding unruly students. "They couldn't hold us at Prestonpans and Falkirk. They'll not stop us today."

Their colonel's words managed to quiet the rumblings of the impatient men, for a while. They did nothing, however, to relieve the cold and hunger that gnawed at them. Nor could mere words dispel the growing uneasiness Ian felt welling up inside of him like the bile that his stomach spewed forth every time the order to charge was given.

This war that Ian found himself involved in bore no resemblance to the grand and glorious tales his grandfather had spun for him when he was but a lad. Sitting before the aged, gray-haired warrior on the dirt floor of their Highland hut, Ian would hang on every word that passed from the old man's lips. On occasion, the old man would allow Ian to hold the great broadsword the elder McPherson had carried into battle in 1719. To Ian, those moments had been magical. The squalor of the hut he had been raised in disappeared as he became lost in his grandfather's tales. The back-breaking toil of daily life that consumed every waking hour was forgotten as Ian's imagination carried him away to a place and time where mighty Highland warriors fought under their rightful king to defend their land and their freedom. Those must have been wonderful, glorious times, Ian told himself, times that he dreamed he'd have a chance to experience for himself.

In the beginning, it had been just as he imagined, a grand adventure and a wonderful lark that took Ian away from the mundane chores of tending sheep and the odd head of cattle his father managed to procure every now and then from an unwary herder. As he entered his fourteenth year in the summer of 1745, Ian McPherson felt he was ready to take his place in the world, a world free from the oppressive traditions, feudal obligations, and poverty imposed by Englishmen that bound his family to land that wasn't even their own. "What right," he innocently asked his mother one day as they walked slowly to the village to pay their rent, "does a foreigner have to run our lives?"

Ian's mother was a humble woman whose back was already stooped from the hard work and long hours tending their meager crops, despite the fact that she was only a few years past her thirtieth. With a quizzical expression, she studied her son's face for several moments as they walked, hoping that he hadn't suddenly been struck with simplemindedness. When she was sure he was in good health and serious, the woman shook her head. "Why," she said, half befuddled by the queer question her son had posed, "it's because that's the way things are."

Ian thought about pursuing the matter with her, perhaps even explaining the strange thoughts that he found stirring in his mind as he crossed from childhood into manhood, but he didn't. It would, he realized, be pointless, as he noticed the worried expression that creased her face. Nor would he bother his father with such a question. Like the clan chief himself, his father ruled their small family with a firmness that left no room for compromise, no doubt that any ideas contrary to his would not be tolerated. And though he didn't show any inclination that he had inherited his own father's martial skills, Ian's father was a man who was not to be trifled with.

So, when word spread that Prince Charles had raised the Royal Stuart standard at Glenfinnan in August of 1745, Ian McPherson saw this event as a God-given opportunity that simply could not be ignored. With an ease that his youth permitted him, he turned his back on the only life he had ever known without a moment's hesitation. He was driven by more than a simple desire to seek a measure of freedom that his family and clan did not offer. As inviting as this was, Ian's goal was to make a mark for himself, one that the bards would sing of for generations, just as his grandfather had done. Armed with his family's broadsword and a head full of romantic legends that told of the great deeds of Robert de Bruce, the courage of William Wallace, the cunning of Rob Roy, and brave deeds performed by legions of McPhersons who had sallied forth before him, Ian informed his father that he was going to answer the prince's call to arms.

"You're a fool," the older McPherson bellowed when Ian had announced his intentions. "What matter is it to us if it's Stuart or a German king who claims to be our rightful ruler? McPhersons were here, on this land, long before any of them and, God willing, will be long after all of their miserable bones have gone back to dust."

When Ian explained that it was freedom that he wanted, his own personal freedom as well as that of the Highland clans, his father laughed, then spit on the ground. "Freedom? What do you know of freedom? *Nothing!* I was born here, in this miserable pile of stone and thatch, just as my father was and his father before him. I've tended the herds, following the same dung-covered paths they did from one barren moor to the next since before I could remember. And I'll do so, day after bloody day, till I curl up one day and die, just as my father did and his father before him. Freedom," he repeated, "is a myth, a dream that noblemen wave before our poor, miserable eyes to enflame our passions and make us do their bidding. Only the dead, boy, are free, free from this miserable land and the suffering that this life has condemned us to."

The young McPherson, however, was not to be dissuaded. There was something better, he kept telling himself, to live for, to be achieved. There had to be more out there, beyond the misty moors of his homeland and squalid existence that drained away a man's life and dreams like a deep wound that would not heal. What it was, he did not know. Nor did he know where he might find it. All he knew was that he could not, would not, sit idly, as his father had, in the humble hut that generations of McPhersons had called home, and let his life slip away day by tedious day. So, one morning, while his father was off tending to the daily chores, Ian prepared to leave. Carefully, almost ceremonially, he wrapped himself in the McPherson plaid. With just as much reverence, he dug up the broadsword, the dirk, and the small round metal-studded shield known as a targe that his grandfather had kept hidden under the sod. Not waiting for the McPhersons' own chief to call, Ian struck off alone and attached himself to the Appin Stuart clan regiment, following their Bonnie Prince.

"There's a cheeky bastard for ya," McLynn muttered as he nodded his head toward the center of the field that separated the two armies. Standing on his toes and placing a hand on the man next to him for support in an effort to see over the heads of the front-rank men, Ian McPherson caught sight of the lone English officer riding out from the Government lines.

"Now, what's he after?" the thin man asked as he held firmly to the long pole of his ax and stretched his neck as far as it would go till he looked like a stork.

Ian, though just as curious, couldn't imagine why the Englishman was riding out before his enemy as if he were alone on the contested moor. Still, the image of the English officer, turned out in glittering finery and bravely sallying forth alone, from the safety of his own lines, captured Ian's youthful admiration. Only when a cannon, off to Ian's left, fired a ball that sailed over the lone British officer's head did the mounted Englishman stop. Yet even then, he did so without betraying any fright or concern. For a moment, he stood stone still, surveying the jumbled clans assembled before him. Then, as if he hadn't the slightest concern in the world, the Englishman casually turned his horse's head away and began to ride back to his own lines.

Without any prompting, the men about Ian began to cheer the brave show they had just been witness to. Moments later, the Government troops across the way added their hoarse adorations to salute the feat. Only after reflecting upon the Englishman's recklessness for a moment did Ian begin to question the wisdom of the enemy officer's actions. While it was obvious that most saw this as a brave act, Ian found himself trying to understand the notion of duty or courage that had driven the man to ride out as he had done. It had been nothing more than a fool's errand, Ian concluded, and the English officer had been a great fool for performing it.

Slowly, the cheering died down, and for a moment, except for the ringing of the fading cheers in their ears, there was silence. Then, after standing silent for so long, the three-pounders that studded the long line of red-coated Government troops came to life.

"We'll catch it now," the thin man moaned. "We'll surely . . ."

A sudden shove threw Ian off balance as a series of screams and animal-like yelps cut the thin man's dire warning short. Staggering, Ian regained his balance as he looked about in an effort to see what had caused the sudden shift in ranks. To his horror, his eyes fell upon the writhing figure of the thin man lying at his feet, flailing his arms and hands wildly in the air as yard after yard of intestine and bloodied organs spewed upon the ground from a gap torn through his midsection. Even while the man who had been standing behind the thin man and had been stricken by the small cannonball fell against Ian's back, Ian found it impossible to take his eyes away from the contorted face and bulging eyes of the thin man. No word came from his mouth, no final prayer. Only the rushing out of his last breath announced that death had come.

From the front and flanks of the clan regiment, officers began shouting for their charges to close up the gaps. McLynn gave Ian a shove that managed to break the trance that had held him motionless. "Ye'll see more of that," McLynn barked as he continued to shove Ian into the vacancy made by their dead and dying comrades. "Either that, or ye'll be joinin' the poor wretch."

Stunned by the sudden shock of battle, Ian said nothing. There was, he knew, nothing to say. McLynn was right. Until the order to charge was given, he had nothing to do but stand and wait. He had made his choice many months before, and that was it. There was no running away, no going back to what had been. Deserters were seldom, if ever, welcomed back by their clan with open arms. He could only go forward, into the smoke and flame of the enemy cannon that now obscured the Government line from view. Forward, Ian thought, into that strange land beyond the moor that he had once imagined would be his salvation, his future. Preparing himself, Ian tightened his grasp on the hilt of his broadsword, choked down the bitter bile that burned his throat, and waited.

As if they were of one mind, Thomas Shields and his mount pranced about in nervous anticipation. First the lively bay stomped his front hoofs in one direction, then, with a jerk of his head, he turned the other way, dancing back across the same beaten patch of bog. In unison, and without the slightest hint of effort, Shields, the second son of a minor baronet, swayed to and fro in the saddle, ignoring his mount's antics. Like the other aides and staff officers gathered about the twenty-five-year-old William Augustus, the Duke of Cumberland, Thomas kept his eyes on young Lord Bury, the twenty-one-year-old son and heir to the earl of Albemarle, who was also present on the field, commanding the duke's first line. The young Lord Bury had ridden out between the lines at the duke's request to discover "what, if anything, the Rebels have in mind."

Shields, like Bury, had received his commission at age fourteen in the Coldstream Guards. Unlike Bury, this was Shields's first action. At sixteen he was an ensign who had been hand-picked to accompany the duke's official family, as his personal staff was called, when the duke passed through London in January of that year en route to assume command of the Government's forces in Scotland. For young Shields not only was this appointment a blessing, saving him from the drudgery of ceremonial garrison duty in London, but it also provided him with an unheard-of opportunity to become acquainted with, and known by, the senior commanders of the army, men who would, in the coming years, make or break his career. For while it was possible for his father to purchase a commission for Thomas and provide him with the funds necessary to maintain a standard of living expected of an officer of the Guard, only distinguished and conspicuous duty on the field of battle could secure fame and glory for him.

"I will not divide those holdings our family has managed to secure," Thomas' father had admonished him as he bid his second son farewell at age fourteen. "By right of birth, your brother Edward shall inherit all my titles and estates. You, unfortunately, will have to seek your own. I have provided you with as good a start as I could manage. What you do with that advantage is up to you. Good luck, Godspeed, and be gone." That had been it. No undue sentimentality, no tears shed by either party. Though Thomas would have, in truth, preferred to have gone into the Royal Navy, where service on a lucky ship commanded by a competent captain would have provided prize moneys, Thomas had no love for the sea or the hardships that such a life demanded. So it was the army for Thomas.

Now, after less than two years of service, it seemed as if he had made the right choice. Situated behind the Royal Scots, the duke and his staff, arrayed in scarlet and blue coats, trimmed with yards of gold braid and lace, waited for the Highlanders to charge. The duke, confident of victory, was satisfied to watch the cannon of brevet Colonel William Belford flail and hack at the tightly packed Highland mobs while the guns of Prince Charles did no harm to his own ranks. Behind him, his staff waited to be dispatched to any part of the field, carrying the duke's orders to the lieutenant general, the earl of Albemarle, commanding the first line; Major General John Huske, charged with responsibility of the second; Brigadier John Mordaunt, leading the duke's small reserve; or Lieutenant General Henry Hawley, the army's foul-mouthed cavalry commander.

Most of the staff officers gathered about the duke were as young as the duke himself. There was Charles Cathcart, who at age twenty-five was a veteran of Fontenoy and the ninth baron to bear that name. Next to him stood Colonel Joseph Yorke, the twenty-two-year-old son of the earl of Hardwicke. Behind them was Captain Henry Seymour Conway, at age twenty-five an accomplished man who had received his commission in the Coldstream Guards at age ten. Since then, Conway had served as a member of the Irish Parliament, seen action with the king's army at Dettingen and Fontenoy, and lost an eye to a pistol ball in battle. And, of course, there was the young Lord Bury, returning from his hasty reconnaissance of the Highlanders' line, turned out in regimentals as fine as those worn by his commander. Of them, Thomas was the youngest and, for the moment, the least distinguished, the only star among his peers who had not yet been afforded the opportunity to show how bright he could shine.

Eventually, the duke came to the conclusion that the Highlanders would soon be coming forward, throwing themselves at his silent ranks in the wild, desperate charge that was their hallmark. Not fully satisfied with his earlier dispositions, the duke decided he needed to make several corrections. With a wave of his arm and a few brief remarks, he sent one of his retainers off to Brigadier Mordaunt with orders for him to send two of his three regiments over to the right in order to extend the army's flank. As for his left, the duke tasked young Yorke to ride over to Major General John Huske with instructions for him to detach Wolfe's regiment from the left of the second line and send it forward, where it would wheel inward until it was at right angles with the first line.

Somehow, Thomas sensed that the critical point of the duke's line would be there, on the right, where Wolfe's regiment would stand with its back to a stone wall. If that were so, that's where Thomas was determined to be. Bringing his mount up beside the duke, Thomas asked permission to accompany Yorke. The duke, a young man whose own blood was already aflame from the continuous rolling of the drums and the smell of burned powder that now permeated the air, smiled and gave Thomas a nod without taking his eyes off the butchery that his cannon were visiting upon the Rebels. Whether Thomas returned with Yorke after the new orders had been passed on mattered little to the duke. His line was set, his troops were ready, and the battle had been joined. It was now up to his counterpart, the twenty-five-year-old Charles Stuart, to make the next move.

Freed from the necessity of having to wait in abeyance, the two young officers rode at a gallop between the triple ranks of red-coated soldiers in search of Major General John Huske. They found the leathery old man riding behind his troops, instructing them on what he expected of them when they faced the inevitable Highland charge. "If you have time to load, do so," he yelled so as to be heard above the sound of the cannon. "If not, drive your bayonets into their bodies and make sure work of it."

It was, Thomas knew, the bayonet, and not the famed British platoon volleys, that would make all the difference in this fight. They were not facing the white-coated French today. This foe was not an army that would march to within musket range at a steady, measured pace and stand their ground, trading volley for volley with the duke's men.

The Highlanders, when they came, would dash forward like packs of hungry wolves, closing with their foes as quickly as possible so that they could dispatch them with the naked steel of broadswords and pole axes. To meet this, the duke had drilled his men in the preceding months to ignore the enemy to his front. Instead, each soldier had been instructed to trust his comrade on his left and, against human nature, face to his right and use his bayonet on the enemy facing his neighbor. This action, they were told, would negate the effectiveness of the small round shield the Highlanders depended upon for protection, leaving them exposed to a quick, deadly thrust to the armpit. "Drive your bayonets," Huske continued to yell as he thrust his right arm forward to emphasize his point, "and make sure work of it."

When they were within yards of the old general, Yorke and Thomas reined in their mounts and waited until they had Huske's attention. Yorke, the senior of the pair and the one specifically charged with the task, relayed the duke's instructions as young gentlemen officers, no different than Thomas himself, closed up behind Huske and craned their necks to hear what the duke's messenger was saying. When Yorke was finished, Huske turned to one of his aides and asked the clean-faced nobleman if he had heard and understood the order. With a smirk and a nod, the young gentleman indicated that he had. With a wave of his hand, the old general told him to ride off and see that the duke's instructions were carried out. Not waiting to be dismissed, or bothering to tell Yorke what he was up to, Thomas spurred his mount and followed Huske's aide. If there was to be a decisive point, Thomas concluded, it would be there, with Wolfe's men. And he, despite his assigned duties of tending to the young duke, planned to be there.

IT was fast becoming intolerable as more three-pound cannonballs, solid spheres of cast iron that could carry away a man's limb, continued to rain down around young Ian McPherson. "Close it up," the clan officers continued to shout after each round had finished gouging its way through flesh and bone. "Close it up."

"Close up my arse," McLynn shouted back, half in anger, half in frustration. "Take us forward, or take us away from this place, you bastards."

Too caught up in the jumbling, pushing, and shoving, Ian

had no opportunity to call McLynn to account for his sudden change in opinion. Besides, the mere fact that a hard-bitten type like McLynn would show signs of breaking under the stress and strain of the English fire was unnerving to Ian. Since the beginning of the terrible bombardment, Ian and his companions had seen nothing of the English line, hidden now behind the clouds of dirty white smoke thrown out from the firing of the enemy's cannon. Only an occasional tongue of orange and yellow flame, heralding the discharge of another cannonball and the coming of more death, was visible. "Damn you, man," McLynn screamed as an officer pushed him to one side to fill in the newest gap cut through their already decimated ranks. "Let us go forward and die like men, or lead us away from here."

Swaying to and fro, Ian found himself casting a wary eye behind him to see if anyone was bolting to the rear. Worn from hunger and lack of sleep, left to stand for hours in tightly pressed ranks, and forced to face a maddening slaughter by a foe he could not even see, much less strike at, Ian McPherson began to worry as he felt his own courage begin to waver. If a man like McLynn couldn't tolerate this, what chance did he have?

The sentiment expressed openly by McLynn and felt by Ian was shared not only by many of the clansmen gathered about Ian but by those in the other clans as well. Some of those clans, like those standing under the banner of the Clan Chatten and led by Lady Anne of Moy Hall, collectively acted upon their frustrations. Without orders from the prince or any of his advisers or staff, the Chatten men tossed their bonnets over their heads and surged forward with a collective yell. Few of their officers dared try to stop them, for they, too, had felt that the time for action was long past due. And with Clan Chatten, those of the Mackintosh followed suit, rushing forward into the smoke, yelling tribal cries such as "Loch Moy" and "Dunmaglass." Even one of the pipers, as caught up in the moment as any of his companions, handed off his prized instrument to an attending boy, drew his claymore, and ran for all he was worth to join the frenzied charge.

Like a wild fire, the urge to attack took hold and drove

other clans forward. Next in line after the Mackintosh, Clan Fraser joined the mad rush. After that, it was the turn of the Stuarts themselves. Ian heard no distinct command, no single voice urging them forward. All he knew was that at one moment he was all but pressed up against the back of the man before him, and the next that man was gone, taking great strides forward in order to keep up with the man in front of him. Even their colonel, thought to be a bit lethargic, was caught up by the spirit as he ran four to five paces in front of the nearest member of his own clan.

Ian saw little other than the backs of the men before him and an occasional glimpse of the curtain of smoke that still hid the red-coated foe who waited for him.

WITH the surging forward of the Highland clans, both Thomas Shields and his mount stopped their nervous prancing about. Standing at the juncture where the right of Wolfe's regiment of foot met the left of Barrell's regiment, Thomas watched as the gunners of Colonel Belford ceased ladling scoops of black powder into the hot maws of their guns. Instead of loose powder followed by a single solid shot, the crews rammed home large paper cases containing not only the charge and dozens of small balls but nails, odd pieces of iron, and any bits of scrap that the gunners could find when they made up the cartridges. Grapeshot was the proper term, though one of Thomas' fellow staff officers insisted on referring to it as partridge-shot.

With detached interest, Thomas watched the gun crews go through their drill with hardly a word or a command required to guide their actions. When the case was rammed home and seated at the base of the cannon's bore, an assistant gunner reached over and shoved a pick that reminded Thomas of an oversized sewing needle into the touch hole located near the base of the cannon. When the pick was withdrawn, another gunner stepped forward with a small horn and poured fine-grain powder into the touch hole until a few grains spilled over the side. Stepping away, he cleared the way for the man with the linstock, a long pole measuring better than a yard in length around which a slow burning rope, called a match, was wrapped. At the lit end, the match was attached to a metal hook. When all was ready and the crew had stepped a respectable distance from the gun, the crewman holding the linstock was given the command to fire the piece. With practiced ease, he brought the lit match down to the vent hole and touched it to the powder. With a whiff, a small flame shot from the vent hole a split second before a greater one spewed out the contents of the bore and threw the entire gun and its carriage back like a great bucking horse. Once the gun had settled, the crew went about resetting the piece and swabbing out any burning residue with a wet sponge attached to the end of a ramrod as they prepared to repeat the whole process again. The speed and efficiency with which the gunners went about their tasks, ignoring the howls and screams of the closing Highlanders, made it all seem so easy to young Thomas.

Looking up from the gun crew, Thomas watched in amusement as two clans, still staggering under the brutal lashing Colonel Belford's guns were inflicting upon them, came together and ground to a halt. As they milled about in the open, with clan officers either rushing forward and screaming for their men to follow or pushing their charges from behind, Thomas surveyed the long, quiet ranks of British musketeers to his left and right. No wonder, he reasoned, the duke was so confident. Once those silent muskets were brought to bear, the rabble before them would be swept away like so much trash. Amused by this analogy, a faint smile lit across Thomas' face. Digging his spurs into the flanks of his mount, Thomas let the horse dance about in a small circle as it burned off some the same nervous energy it shared with its impatient rider. Rather than the chaos and confusion he had imagined, Thomas found this battle, and the feelings that were stirring in him, more akin to a hunt, a sport that he much enjoyed and fancied himself quite good at. "Dear Lord," he muttered to himself excitedly, "if this is what it feels like to be a soldier, why have I been forced to wait so long?"

IAN MCPHERSON had no opportunity to raise his voice to his Maker or to anyone else. He didn't even have time to consider what he was doing, let alone what was happening all about him. The sudden halt that caused him to plow blindly into the back of the man before him came as a surprise to him as much as their first rush forward had. Then, as men milled about in an effort to sort themselves out and start forward again, the grapeshot struck them, ravaging their ranks and laying men low by the score with the ease of a great, invisible scythe.

Still, despite the carnage that surrounded him, Ian felt no desire to turn and flee. Nor did those about him, no matter how brutal the punishment heaped upon them grew. Enraged, McLynn threw away his musket without ever having fired a shot, drew his claymore, and pushed ahead until he was beside Ian. Together, the two stepped off as soon as those still standing before them broke forward at a run again. All about Ian, others did the same. Fathers stepped quickly over the writhing bodies of their slain sons, cousins pushed aside the bloody, staggering remains of stricken kinsmen they had known since childhood. Up ahead, Ian heard the hoarse voices of officers who were still on their feet. He could see them waving their broadswords over their heads as they competed with the echoes of cannon fire and the screams of the dying in an effort to implore their fellow clansmen to follow. And forward they went, yard by bloody yard. Those who were still in the ranks howled for all they were worth, ignoring the terrible price they were paying for each foot of ground gained. In their wake, the wounded and broken men left behind added to the terrible roar of battle their own laments, moans, and animal-like shrieks.

WITH steady, measured commands that rivaled those of the gunners, the officers of foot began to take their charges through the drill they had practiced for hours on end. Divided into four grand divisions of two companies each, and further broken down into platoons of about thirty men by the regimental major and the assistant adjutant as they had waited for the battle to be joined, the regiments of foot stood ready to deliver their devastating fire upon the wild men who would soon fall upon them. Most of these men, considered by their own officers to be the dregs of their society, did not share Thomas Shields' lighthearted appraisal of the battle. Most had already stood their ground against the best army in Europe less than a year before at Fontenoy and knew what battle was. Together with rumors whispered about the camps that painted the Highlander warrior as something more than mortal, few in the long, silent ranks had any illusions of an easy victory or enduring glory. Survival and the chance to fight again, somewhere else, was the best they could ever hope for.

Still, they were ready. Unlike their screaming opponents, the soldiers of the British line had slept well the night before and enjoyed a sparing meal and a bit of brandy before marching out of camp. Together with their proven tactics, long hours of drill that created machinelike responses to orders, and special instructions in dealing with the Highland charge, the soldiers' confidence in their commander fortified them. When company officers began to issue their string of orders, bringing them to the ready, the common soldiers in the ranks responded as one, without thought, without hesitation.

Absorbed by the spectacle of battle unfolding at his very feet, Thomas ignored the howling masses closing on him. Mouthing the words as his hand subconsciously worked the reins to control his own mount's excitement, Thomas followed the commands of the nearest captain of foot.

Above the din of battle, Thomas heard the command

"Make ready." Like a string of puppets jerked into action by their master, the soldiers of the front ranks dropped on their right knees while bringing their muskets in tightly at their sides in anticipation of the next command. With the order "Present," all three ranks brought their muskets up, pulling the stock into their right shoulders and laying their cheeks against the cool, smooth wood. With great deliberateness, many of the veterans sighted down the barrel, from the tip of the cocked hammer to muzzle's end.

For a moment, there was a pause, a hesitation, as soldiers and officers watched and waited for their frenzied foes to close on them. Thomas shifted his eyes from the line of waiting foot soldiers over to the masses of frenzied Highlanders. With kilts flying and flapping as they ran waving their assorted swords and axes madly above and before them, Thomas had a momentary pang of doubt. "Can we actually stop them?" he muttered.

As if in response, the company officers of foot gave the command to fire. No one single musket's report could be heard, no single soldier's actions distinguishable from that of his comrades to his left or right. While the cannon issued a roar when fired, the massed volley of musket fire ripped through the air with a series of thunderous, sharp cracks as each rank of each platoon fired in succession. First, those of the front rank let loose their fire. With cool, measured deliberateness, they were followed by the second rank as those of the front rank sprang up and began the tedious process of reloading. Finally, when the men of the front rank were all back down on their right knees, the soldiers of the third rank took a step to the right, brought their muskets up between the heads of the men before them, and added the weight of their volley to the carnage the mass firing was throwing up.

Up and down the line, platoon by platoon, company by company, the ranks issued a devastating fire that was meant to be as physically shocking and overwhelming as it was deadly. With the same satisfaction that he derived when he saw hounds tear at a cornered fox on the hunt, Thomas watched the carnage as three-quarter-inch soft lead balls, weighing one and a quarter ounces each, tore their way into or through the bodies of their assailants. Full-grown men, as big or bigger than the average man in the Government ranks, were thrown back as if kicked in the chest by a horse's hoof.

Through breaks in the great clouds of dirty white smoke generated by the steady discharge of musket and cannon, Thomas could clearly see the faces of some of the Highlanders as they went down. Those killed outright simply dropped in their tracks, falling with arms outstretched as their eyes rolled back into their heads and their faces lost all expression. Others, stricken with mortal wounds, howled or screamed with their last breath as their faces, etched with anger and hatred a moment before, were suddenly twisted and contorted into masks that betrayed the unbearable pain and agony they were suffering. Twisting or staggering in the throes of death, many of these poor souls clutched their nearest companion in a desperate search for aid or comfort. None could be found, however, as those they sought out for succor either pushed them aside and continued to lunge at their assailants or were themselves cut down like ripe wheat at the harvest.

The lethal fire of the British infantrymen, seen by Thomas for the first time applied to real flesh and blood, more often than not broke even the stoutest and most resolute foe. Panic and flight usually ensued after those behind the decimated front rank realized that their own death was a few scant seconds away. No one, Thomas suddenly realized, could stand up to such devastating fire. No one.

THIS was no time for hesitation, no time to stop or even think. Ian McPherson saw what was happening. He knew that where there had been three ranks before him a moment before, there were now but two, and soon, maybe none. Still, oddly, that didn't make any difference to him. Whatever earthly concerns he had struggled with back there, where they had waited so long, were gone. The hunger and cold, the queasiness of his stomach, were forgotten. In their place there was nothing left but a madness that drove him onward, a hatred that was focused squarely on the red-coated puppets before him. He no longer saw them as fellow human beings, he felt no emotions. Nothing but pure hatred and blind anger drove him as those about him fell like the leaves in autumn.

Without regard for those beneath him, Ian climbed over, on his hands and knees, the stacks of bodies, now three deep, that lay before him. He paid no heed to the writhing mass of clansmen as his eyes fell upon a young English musketeer. There was nothing that distinguished that particular red-coated soldier from another. No action or expression to mark him as any more dangerous than the one to his left or right. It was just that this man, by luck of circumstances, just happened to be the one whom Ian's eyes fell upon as he was in the process of navigating the grisly pile of the dead and near dead.

The British soldier, his face betraying little concern for his plight, glanced up from the task of reloading his musket and saw, for the first time, Ian's murderous expression. For the briefest of moments, the Englishman paused and, as his eyes locked with Ian's, he attempted to gauge the sincerity and power of Ian's determination. Then, as if a voice from inside the soldier told him that the wild Highlander bearing down on him was in deadly earnest, the Englishman's hands continued to speed along with the task of reloading his musket with renewed vigor.

Suddenly, the battle for Ian and this one British infantry-man was reduced to the lowest possible denominator. For them, the thousands of other combatants gathered about them and pushing in from all sides disappeared. Any thoughts of noble causes or quests for personal freedom were lost by the time Ian regained his feet and prepared to close with the one foe whose death, in the twinkling of an eye, had become his sole purpose for being. Hatred, unlike anything he had ever felt before, drowned out the crashing din of battle. Raising his broadsword above his head and bringing his targe up from his side to cover his chest, Ian let loose a mighty scream and plunged forward.

It was when he was little more than an arm's length away that Ian witnessed the most incredible thing he had ever seen in his entire life. Without taking his eyes off Ian, the Englishman had brought his musket up to the on-guard position when he realized he had lost the race to reload and fire before Ian closed on him. Ian, with his targe held close to his chest, prepared to parry the Englishmen's bayonet thrust. That he didn't deliver it, at least against Ian, was what caught Ian off guard. Instead, with little more than a sideward glance, the British soldier drove his seventeen-inch bayonet into the side of the clansman on Ian's left. Both the stricken clansman and Ian were shocked, the clansmen by the sudden and unexpected blow that had befallen him, and Ian by the strange disregard that the English soldier had shown in the face of certain death. Even as he felt a burning pain crease his right shoulder blade, Ian simply did not understand what was happening.

Nor did he take the time to sort things out. Regaining his composure, he brought his right arm down with all his might and cleaved through the shoulder straps, uniform, flesh, and bone of the Englishman he had chosen to kill. Honed to near razor-sharpness, Ian's broadsword severed flesh and bone, causing great spurts of blood to spray both victim and assailant as arteries were separated by the single, slashing hack.

Only when he stepped back with his right foot in an effort to finish drawing his sword through the gaping wound of the stricken foe did he realize that the soldier to his right had attempted to drive his bayonet into him, accounting for the sudden and unexpected pain he had felt across his back. Jerking his head in that direction, Ian caught sight of the horrified expression worn by the next Englishman over as soon as he realized that his strike had not been true. Rather than impaling Ian under the arm, as he had been taught, the English soldier had merely run his bayonet through the bundle of Ian's plaid that he wore over his shoulder, biting into Ian's taut skin and along the shoulder blade but not causing a mortal wound. And although he could feel the wound burning as if the cold steel of the bayonet had been heated in a flame, the injury was neither critical nor debilitating. Finished with the man who had, up to that moment, been the sole object of his attention, Ian shoved his targe into the chest of his new foe to throw him off balance as he stepped back and brought his sword up waist-high, making sure that he did not expose his flank to another unexpected thrust.

HAD he not seen Barrell's regiment buckle and give way under the onslaught of the wild men in plaid, Thomas Shields would not have believed it possible. Time and again he had been told by officers who had been there that no foe could stand the smashing weight of English firepower. "We fire on the Frenchies, lay low their front rank, and stop them cold, just like that," a senior captain of the Coldstream had bragged to Thomas with a snap of his fingers. "On occasion, they make a show of it by returning a volley or two, but," the captain concluded with a bored sigh, "like good gentlemen, eventually, they see the errors of their ways and depart peaceably."

These men, Thomas thought, weren't behaving like the Frenchies. Despite the devastating volleys that Wolfe's men were pouring into their flanks with a cool efficiency that surprised even Thomas, the mad Highlanders continued to surge forward. With the same frenzy that carried them over the stacked bodies of their own clansmen, the Highlanders hacked their way into and through the ranks of Barrell's regiment. Thomas watched in utter amazement as one young British officer faced down a howling Rebel by raising his thin sword as if he were preparing to duel the ragged fellow. The Highlander, caught up in the heat of the moment and fury of the charge, simply grasped the hilt of his sword, raised it over his head, and brought it down with all his might, severing the British officer's sword arm in a single, swift motion. Pitching forward, the stricken officer fell to the ground and disappeared from sight under the feet of his screaming foes.

Though he had no command here, Thomas could no longer hold back. The situation was desperate. Most of the officers of Barrell's regiment of foot were down and those men who still had their wits about them were teetering on the brink of panic. His duty was clear, his destiny was at hand. Drawing his sword, he dug his spurs into the flanks of his horse, causing the lively bay to jerk forward, out of the lee and safety of Wolfe's ranks and into the swirling mass of madmen in plaid and soldiers in scarlet.

LIKE a ghostly apparition, the mounted British officer, slashing and waving his sword over his head, burst out of the smoke and pandemonium in front of Ian. With an expression every bit as fierce as those worn by the grim clansmen around him, the Englishman squared up as soon as he laid eyes on Ian, leveling his sword until its tip was aimed right at Ian's heart as he dug his spurs into his horse's side with all his might. For the first time that day, Ian realized that he was going to die. Yet he was not ready to simply roll over and surrender his life or his freedom. He had vowed that he would never bow his head under the yoke like a beast of burden, as his father had done so long ago. Ian's dreams and aspirations, though still as shapeless and distant as ever, were too real, too much a part of him, to give up.

Tightening his grip on the handle of his targe, Ian spread his feet apart, locked eyes with the British officer, and held his sword at the ready in case he did manage to parry the Englishman's first thrust.

THOMAS saw the look in the young Rebel's eye and the upward movement of the boy's shield as he prepared to receive his attack. With a jerk of the reins, Thomas veered his mount over to one side as he prepared to brush the wild-eyed Highlander with the flank of his horse. If he managed to throw his foe off balance, he would have a clear, downward thrust as he rode past. Yet before he closed the pitiful few yards that separated him from his intended prey, things went terribly wrong. For the first time that day, the lively bay did not respond to his wishes. Instead, the animal bucked and reared up on its hind legs. With a scream and whinny that cut through the tumult that surrounded him, the bay tried to throw Thomas and flee the wretched field strewn with dead and dying men. Reluctantly, Thomas turned his head away from the Rebel who stood ready to receive his attack to find out what was causing his horse to buck and rear.

SET to receive the mounted officer, Ian was slow to react to his sudden change of fortune. Instead, he watched as John McLynn leaped over the corpse of an English musketeer and ran his sword into the flank of the officer's charging bay. The reaction was both instant and advantageous for Ian. In pain, the horse reared, throwing the rider back almost onto the animal's rump and breaking the man's concentration.

But the English officer was an accomplished rider, a man of great poise and swift reactions. While still struggling to control his mount as well as maintain his seat, he shifted his gaze away from Ian to search out the source of the unexpected pain his horse was responding to. When his eyes fell upon McLynn, the officer's response was both swift and deadly.

With his own sword driven into the side of the horse almost to the hilt, McLynn dropped his targe and grasped the hilt with both hands in a desperate effort to free his weapon from the bucking and rearing animal. This left him open to the single, neat swipe that the English officer delivered across the top of McLynn's bare head with the sword that Ian had moments before been prepared to parry or receive. Like a pile of sticks that had been loosely stacked, the three of them—McLynn, the horse, and the English officer—tumbled down upon one another.

For a moment, Ian stood rooted to the ground, gasping to catch his breath as he gazed at the squirming mass of horse and men before him. He had survived, his stunned mind announced joyfully. The sour, caustic John McLynn, for whatever reason unknown to Ian, or simply by a fortunate stroke of faith, had saved Ian's life at the price of his own.

There was no time, however, to ponder what lay behind his sudden and timely reprieve. Though his first thought was to leap forward over the kicking and screaming horse now stretched out upon the ground and dispatch the English officer who was pinned beneath the dying bulk of his own mount, Ian hesitated. Instead, he looked around, noticing that the fury that had taken him and the clansmen who followed the yellow and blue silk Appin regimental standard had been spent. Instead of throwing themselves into the solid ranks of the British second line, those who were still on their feet were backing away, taunting their foes but showing no sign that they wished to close with them.

It was over. The same mysterious voice that moments before had told Ian that he could not simply give in to fate and die without a struggle now told him that there was nothing to be gained by staying here or going forward in a futile gesture of defiance. If the other men of the clan regiment, officers included, deemed it was time to leave, that was good enough for Ian. What would come next, after this battle, was beyond Ian's ability to imagine. That there would be a future, he was sure of. All he needed to do, at that moment, was survive till the next. And after that, survive till the next. And then, the next.

Slowly making his way backward, stepping carefully so as not to trip over the bodies of the fallen while facing the enemy, Ian melted into the ragged and tattered mass of beaten and disheartened Rebels who had defied the British Crown. Until he knew what those blurred images out there on the far horizon were, he would let fate be his guide and his master.

THOUGH fate had denied Thomas Shields his first kill of the day, the wisdom of the Duke of Cumberland and the steadiness of the British infantrymen would provide him ample opportunity to make good that missed opportunity. Pulled out from under the heaving mass of his dying mount, Thomas assumed command of the first body of soldiers he found without an officer. Falling into the vacant position of their dead company commander with the ease that a spare part is fitted to a broken machine, Thomas drove his men forward when the order was given to pursue their broken foe.

Grimly, the reformed ranks of Barrell's decimated regiment marched back over the ground that they had been forced to yield moments before. Their dead and wounded comrades lay mixed with those of the enemy. They ignored their own, turning instead to pursue and hound their broken enemy. Those of the enemy, however, were a different matter. The grim-faced men in red coats with yellow facings streaked with blood and grime hardly paused as they twirled their long muskets about and drove their bayonets into the chest of each wounded foe they passed. Some, unable to bring the bayonet to bear in the tightly packed ranks, used the butt of their muskets to smash the skulls of those Highlanders who still showed signs of life.

Even Thomas, a gentleman by birth, had no qualms when it came to dispatching a wounded Rebel. Like the men of his adopted command, his blood was still up. Only the spilling of more blood would quench the burning passions that he felt at that moment. In time, it would pass, as would the sharp, uncompromising picture of hell on earth that filled his eyes wherever he looked. In its stead, the warm, soft glow of glory and honor would fall upon his brow, as it had on the other officers who had followed in the Duke of Cumberland's wake.

With each step forward, the pain Thomas Shields felt in his hip and leg began to disappear as he realized that he had found his place in life. He was to be a soldier, as his father had so wisely decreed. And, he told himself as he reviewed his actions and feelings while they were still fresh in his mind, he would be a good one. The fact was, Thomas had enjoyed the experience. The scent of burned powder, wool uniforms soaked in sweat and blood, and men fresh from a desperate struggle were as intoxicating to Thomas as the most expensive perfume. This, he decided, was where he belonged. From now on, every step he took had to be measured by the fame that he had set out to find.

CHAPTER TWO

Along the Maumee River
(Present-day Ohio)
October, 1751

THE CRISP FALL wind weaved its way through the forest like a tide, never stopping, always in motion. Sometimes its force slackened and receded, almost stopping. But then, without warning, it gathered new strength from some unseen source, swirling its way around the trees, whistling mournfully like a squaw's death chant as it did so. Except for the rustling of dead leaves, pulled loose from their moorings by the movement of the wind and cast adrift, the wind alone provided the only sound. In time, even this would stop as every one of the countless leaves, whether already torn from the branches or struggling to hang on, would be silent. Separated from their homes by a force they could not resist, they would wither, rot, and disappear into the same earth that had once given them nourishment and life. Then only the wind would be left, free to make its way through the barren forest.

The young Caughnawaga brave caught in this quiet tempest wasn't concerned with the subtlety of nature's rhythms. To him, the wind and the scattering of leaves were little more than an annoyance, a hindrance to his ability to hear the return of the two older braves he was accompanying or the approach of an unexpected foe. Even before he had started this quest, he knew that he could not depend on Gingego, his brother, for very much, at least not when it came to matters that were of real importance. Though Gingego was older, and squatting with his back against the same tree Toolah himself was resting against, Gingego had never shown much interest, or aptitude, for the ways of a warrior.

Toolah viewed Gingego with the same contempt that he viewed others of his tribe who found themselves lost between the world of the whites and his own people's past. Lured away from their parent tribe, the Mohawks, by French missionaries generations ago, the Caughnawaga lived in a land the whites called Canada. There they labored under the watchful eye of white priests who worked with great zeal to separate them from their old ways and teach them a way of life that was foreign to the Caughnawaga. First, and always foremost, was devotion to a god whose only son had been a white. Simultaneously, the Caughnawaga were instructed in the ways of the priests' native land, a place located across an ocean Toolah had never seen. Everything, from their language to loyalty to a white king who had never stepped foot in Canada, was hammered into them over and over again, and again. "By casting off your savage ways and embracing the true faith and civilization," the priests admonished Toolah and his peers, "you can achieve true redemption in the next life." The only thing that rivaled their endeavors to teach the Caughnawaga to love the French god were the priests' efforts to encourage Toolah's people to kill the English, another nation of whites who shared the same god as the French.

Unlike Gingego, who spent far too much time trying to reconcile the often vulgar habits of the French traders who frequented their villages and the lessons the priests struggled to convey, Toolah rejected everything any white said out of hand. "Their ways," an older boy who served as Toolah's guide repeated time after time, "can never be our way. Whites will never see us as equals. To them, we are less than beasts. When there is peace, we are treated as women, forced to carry furs taken from land that was once ours to trade with the English for goods and silver they never share with us. And when there is war between the whites, we are expected to do their killing and dying. No," the older boy exclaimed solemnly as he looked across the fire into Toolah's eyes during one of the many secret gatherings of young braves that Toolah attended. "We must close our ears to their lies. We must follow our own spirits, find our way back to our old ways. We must be men again, and live as *our* creator meant us to."

To this end, Toolah sought his guardian spirit, as his ancestors had, by submitting himself to a dream quest. In the late summer, when he felt he was ready, Toolah left his village and made his way to one of the small, uninhabited islands that dotted the Saint Lawrence River. There, with only the trees for companions, Toolah fasted for three days, taking neither water nor nourishment, though both were abundant all about him. He denied his body's urge to sleep, forcing himself to sit before a fire he kept burning day and night, chanting songs in an effort to evoke a response from the spirit world.

During the first three days, his only rewards were hunger and fits of self-doubt. Hour after hour, twin fears, unlike anything he had ever experienced, grew within him, threatened to overwhelm him. Before starting each new incantation, Toolah found himself facing these fears, fears that were becoming as real to him as the bared teeth of a vicious wolf. The first was a sense of dread that the spirits of his ancestors, so long ignored by his people, could not hear his chants. The second, and most disturbing, was a growing apprehension that perhaps he was not worthy of a spirit guide. Perhaps he had lived too long with whites. Perhaps he had allowed himself to be wooed by too many of their lies.

At dawn of the fourth day, as the sun began its arduous climb into the sky, Toolah found that he had reached the end of his tether. Even as the sun bathed all it touched in vibrant shades of crimson, Toolah felt his last bit of resolve slip away. All efforts to stop his body from weaving this way and that failed. Even his parched throat refused to yield up a sound as he struggled to evoke a chant. Closing his eyes, he prepared to meet his failure as best he could.

Then, with a jerk, his body stopped its uncontrolled gyrations. All sounds and smells, even the terrible pangs of hunger that moments before had dominated every fiber of his tired mind, disappeared. Opening his eyes, Toolah was greeted with the image of a forest awash in deep, blood-red shades and shadows. Looking about, his eyes came upon an apparition that emerged from those shadows like a mist rising from the water. It had no discernible form or features that Toolah could make out. Only the image of a hatchet decorated with two red feathers stood out in contrast to the dark, nebulous mass that presented itself before Toolah. Instinctively, Toolah stood and followed the apparition when it began to move away from the fire, for he sensed that it presented no danger to him.

While he followed in its wake, Toolah tried to determine if this spirit were man or beast. He marveled at its ability to move without effort or noise, without leaving a trace or track upon the ground. Whatever it was, Toolah sensed that it had power, real strength that comes from within. Slowly, carefully, the boy crept through the trees behind the apparition, trying hard to make no noise. With each step, he found this task becoming easier, less demanding, allowing him to concentrate fully on watching his guiding spirit.

Then, without warning, the image of a man appeared before the apparition. The man who had come from nowhere stood before Toolah's apparition, tall and erect, showing no fear of either the apparition or Toolah. Without hesitation, the hatchet borne by the apparition flashed before Toolah's eyes, rising high above it before being brought down with a terrible swiftness that struck down the man with a single, clean strike. Strangely, Toolah saw no blood, for the man, dressed in red, was already drenched in the bloody crimson light cast down by the sun itself.

Toolah had no time to reflect upon this strange sight, for

suddenly other men, men without count, leaped before the great black apparition with stunning swiftness. With equal speed, the apparition cut them down, each blow striking true with such force that the body of the new victim was thrown here and there without rhyme or reason. In awe, Toolah watched the horrible execution until, when it seemed as if the very floor of the forest itself could hold no more corpses, the apparition stopped its terrible work. For a moment, the two stood there, Toolah in wide-eyed amazement, and the apparition surrounded by the wreckage of the dead. Then, as new hordes of men appeared, the apparition held out before Toolah the bloody hatchet with the two red feathers. Needing no encouragement, Toolah seized the hatchet and ran forward. With a scream unlike any he had ever issued forth before, Toolah waded into the mass of men in red, hewing them down with the same ease that the village women cut ripened wheat.

When he finally came to his senses, Toolah found himself alone, in the woods, far from the campfire where he had kept his lonely vigil. The sun was well up in the sky. All about him the traces of red that the dawn had greeted him with that morning in his dream were gone. The only red left was that on the end of a stick that Toolah held in one hand. Looking down, he saw the quivering body of a rabbit at his feet. It was bleeding from its mouth and a gash along its side. Looking back at the stick, then up to the sun, Toolah realized that he had met his guide spirit. In an instant, he knew what his dream had meant. Dropping to his knees, he held his bloody stick to the sky and chanted a song of praise.

Then, in recognition of his conquest, he carefully laid the stick beside him, took the rabbit up in both hands, and thrust his fingers into the gash. With one mighty jerk, he all but ripped the rabbit apart, exposing its red, glistening entrails to the harsh light of early morning. In part as a gesture to symbolize what he would do one day to all his conquests, and in part out of sheer hunger, Toolah buried his face in the exposed cavity of the rabbit's side, swallowing the warm blood as he gnawed at the soft, raw flesh in search of nourishment.

The memory of that vision caused Toolah to chafe at the indignity of being left behind while the two older boys tried to find the whereabouts of the trappers they had been stalking. When the four young warriors had left their village, Toolah did so with the understanding that they were doing so as equals, youths untried in battle all seeking their first coup. It quickly became obvious, however, that neither of the two older boys intended to let Toolah do so if it meant that they themselves might lose their opportunities to prove their courage. For even though he was three years their junior and barely beyond the threshold of manhood, Toolah's physical presentation was both intimidating and ominous. His ability to move his lean, muscular body with a grace and speed that rivaled that of a deer amazed all who saw him at play and on the hunt. "He will be a mighty warrior, without equal," Toolah's father bragged after watching him run a buck to ground.

Without hesitation, Toolah's mother, Steyawa, announced, "His skills will be our undoing." Knowing she was a powerful woman, destined to become the chief matron of the Chanters of the Dead, Toolah's father knew better than to cross his wife on such matters. Her skills when it came to dreams and matters of the supernatural were unquestioned, even by the tribal shaman. Rather than attempt to discuss the subject, Toolah's father dropped it. In his heart, a voice told him she was right, otherwise she would have said nothing. Still, he had no intention of allowing her to soften Toolah to the point of ineffectualness, as she had done to his older son, Gingego. Only once had they openly debated the subject of how they would raise their sons. "You may allow Gingego to listen to the priest's words and learn their tongue," he had concluded after becoming frustrated by Steyawa's skilled arguments. "But, you must permit our other son to follow our ways, without challenge. Only in that way can we be sure that we have chosen right."

"Even," she whispered, "if it means one may die before his time?"

Turning his face away, Toolah's father hesitated before answering Steyawa. "I fear soon," he stated calmly as he turned his head and looked into her eyes, "our people will no longer be free to choose as they wish. Even our deaths will be in the hands of others." By others, Steyawa knew, he meant the whites.

•

Jumping to his feet, Toolah drew forth his tomahawk, adorned with two small red feathers. "I will not sit here like a woman," he proclaimed, more in an effort to steel his own nerve than inform Gingego. This outburst came as no surprise to Gingego. If anything, the older boy had been wondering why his brother had been so accommodating and placid until now. Without saying another word, Toolah stalked off in the direction the older boys had disappeared. For his part, Gingego did nothing. To have attempted to dissuade Toolah would have been a waste of time. No one, these days, ruled Toolah. Even his own mother had come to the realization that his soul had been touched by a spirit that she considered evil. As Toolah's footfalls disappeared in the distance, Gingego sighed, shook his head, and went back to watching the leaves before him twirl and flit about as the invisible wind carried them along. They would all need to come back to him, Gingego knew. He was carrying their shelter and food. Even a self-imagined warrior such as his brother would soon tire of war when his stomach was empty.

It wasn't long before Toolah came upon the two older boys. They were lying burrowed in the newly fallen leaves on the crest of a slight rise behind trees. Only their heads, poking fugitively around the trunks of the trees, broke the outline of the crest. The two boys were watching something on the other side. Toolah didn't bother to stop and ask, for he knew what they were studying. He didn't even slow his pace in order to allow them to rise up and join him. His blood was up, boiling in his veins like water held over a fire too long. Drawing deep breaths as he went, he quickened his pace, swinging his un-sheathed hatchet at his side as he pumped his muscular arms to gain speed.

Without pausing, Toolah ran between the trees his companions lay behind. In shock and confusion, both looked up as their young protégé charged past them at a dead run. It took them several seconds before they comprehended that the apparition flying past them was Toolah. By then, it was too late.

Bursting over the crest, Toolah gained speed as he ran

downhill. In a single glance, he took in everything before him. There, down by the creek, a man, a white trapper, was bending over a trap he had just fished out of the water. To his side was a woman, his squaw, waiting to take the dead beaver as soon as the trapper freed it from the trap. Off to one side a boy, ten years of age, Toolah guessed, stood patiently, holding the reins of two heavily laden pack horses as he watched the trapper and the woman.

Even before the trapper looked up, the rhythm of Toolah's footfalls and his panting told him that he was in trouble. Pushing his way past his woman, the trapper reached for a rifle that Toolah hadn't seen leaning against a tree at the back of the creek. It was a race now, Toolah realized, between him and the white man. It was a race, he knew, that would end all matters for him. Either his dream had been a true one, and he would win the contest and kill the white, or his spirit quest, like the words of the priests, would prove to be a lie. In a second, all would be settled.

For the briefest of moments, it seemed as if the trapper would win. No man, white or red, survived in the wilderness long unless he had skill, instinct, and luck. When any one of them failed, even the luckiest of men died.

Redemption came when one of Toolah's older companions realized what was afoot. Leaping to his feet, the older boy yelled to Toolah in an effort to stop him, "No! They are French! Don't, Toolah, they are . . ."

The young man's words were cut short by the discharge of the trapper's rifle. Hearing the shouted warning before he had yet looked up, the trapper instinctively oriented himself and the muzzle of his rifle to where the shouting brave stood. In one swift motion, the trapper brought his rifle to his shoulder, aimed, and fired, hitting the Indian square in the chest. Under other circumstances, such skill would have been laudable and given the trapper the edge in the coming fight. But not now, for it was luck that deserted the trapper. Even before he had started to lower his rifle, the white man realized this as Toolah's frenzied form entered his field of vision for the first time. Now it was he, and not his assailants, who was at a disadvantage.

Still, there was no thought of yielding, either to the Indians or to his fate. Twirling his long rifle with the hand that had held the stock steady, the trapper prepared to use his firearm as a club to deal with Toolah. There was no fear in the man's eyes that Toolah could see, not even a hint of surprise. This pleased Toolah as he raised his hatchet high over his head just as the trapper's right hand came to rest on the warm barrel of the rifle he was whirling over his head with the other hand.

Without a pause, without hesitation, both men went at each other. All their moves were swift, smooth, and sure. In the end, it was the trapper's hasty decision to fire at the most obvious noise that cost him his life, though not by much. Even as Toolah was boring down with his hatchet, the trapper was bringing his clubbed rifle to bear. But the trapper was a second or two off, and Toolah's blow was sure and true. It caught the trapper in the left side of his neck, drawn taut and exposed by the trapper's own efforts to bring his rifle's butt up and over his right shoulder in preparation to strike.

When he felt his hatchet bite into the trapper's neck, Toolah turned his face toward the trapper's. The look of shock in the trapper's eyes and the geyser of blood that spewed forth on either side of his blade told Toolah that this man was dead. The spray of warm blood on his hand and face excited Toolah, confirming for him his first victory in a physical manner that no words could match. Even as he felt the body of the trapper begin to fall away, tugging at the hatchet wedged amid shattered bones, Toolah stood there and continued to stare into the trapper's eyes as all life drained from them and they rolled back into the man's head. This was a moment to be savored, a feeling unlike any he had ever imagined, even in his dream. He was a man now, a warrior, and no one, no lies from the priests or sanctions from his revered mother, would ever take this feeling away.

Only the boom of a musket shot broke the momentary trance Toolah had sunk into. Turning, he looked down at his feet, where the trapper's Indian woman lay on the ground cowering. Then he looked over to where the boy had been holding the horses. The youth was partially obscured by a cloud of white smoke. Only the quivering barrel of the musket he held pointed toward Toolah showed.

With a jerk, Toolah freed his hatchet from the trapper's shoulder, walked past the screaming woman, and resolutely began to march toward the boy. As the smoke cleared and the boy realized that his shot had missed, the boy panicked. Toolah's face, covered with the blood of his father and set in an expression of hatred that was utterly uncompromising, sent the boy backing up until his retreat was blocked by one of the horses he had been holding. This kill, Toolah saw, would be easy.

From behind him, he heard the cries of the surviving warrior. "No, Toolah. They are Frenchmen. The priests sent us out to kill only English traders and trappers. Don't!"

Toolah didn't pay heed to the words of the older boy who had supposedly been his guide. What difference did it make whether they were French or English, Toolah thought as he closed on the trapper's boy, now scrambling with shaking hands to reload the musket. Toolah had never paid much attention to the explanations of the priests as they tried to teach them that the English traders and trappers were their natural enemies and the French *coureurs de bois* were their friends. Both were, to Toolah, evil and vile. Both needed to be destroyed.

From the crest where he had been hiding, the second warrior rushed to the white boy's side. "We will be punished," he shouted to Toolah. "We were sent with the French priests' blessing only for the purpose of killing English."

Toolah heard the words, but paid them no heed. Unlike others of his tribe, he saw no room for compromise, no room for accommodations with the whites, whether they be French or English. The issues before them were clear, as clear as the vision the spirits had presented to him during his dream quest. Without pausing or taking his eyes from the panicked eyes of the boy who stood rooted to the ground in sheer terror, Toolah shoved his companion to one side with his free hand and swung the hatchet he held in the other across a wide arc. With a jar that Toolah's muscular arm barely felt, the blade, still smeared with the blood of the boy's own father, came smashing into the side of the boy's head. Like before, his blow had been true and deadly, though not as gratifying to Toolah. Still, the hot-tempered warrior thought as he watched the corpse before him crumble to the ground at his feet, the scalp, undamaged by his carefully aimed blow, would be just as noble.

Finished, Toolah turned to face his companion, now scrambling to his feet. He pointed to the squaw, still shrieking in hysteria. "Go, bind her. We will take her with us. Tonight, we will deal with her as our people have always dealt with their foes. Her death, and that of these interlopers, will be celebrated by our people and the spirits of our ancestors." Then a smile crossed his lips for the first time. To his companion, the look in Toolah's eyes and his shameless smile were as frightening as his deeds had been. "We shall even win," Toolah added with a note of mockery in his voice, "the praise of the priests themselves for what we have done. After all, French scalps smell no different to a white nose than English ones."

Versailles, France
Late November, 1751

TIRED and depressed, the colonial minister threw down the dispatch from the governor of New France, pushed himself away from his desk, and stormed over to the window that ran from floor to ceiling. Folding his arms tightly against his body, he stared out into the bleak late-afternoon shadows that had descended upon the vast garden below. After standing motionless for several minutes, the minister realized that not even the view of the magnificently laid out and manicured hedges and walks could dispel his anger and frustration, as they so often had in the past. Turning his head, he looked back at his desk. The letter from Governor Jonquière spoke of nothing but troubles and woes. It was as if, the minister thought, Jonquière allowed his own illness and bleak state of mind to permeate every line of his reports.

Returning his gaze to the garden below, the minister pondered the sad state of affairs in New France. The last war had solved nothing, either in Europe or in North America. If anything, conditions in France's colonies on that distant continent had worsened. Before the war, the Indians had been either helpful allies or, at worst, a benign presence. Now, however, it seemed that not a month went by without a new report telling of another cruel depravation being committed against a French settler, trapper, or soldier. Unable to undersell the English traders, who were roaming farther and farther inland, French traders found it difficult to maintain the loyalty of the Indians they had come to rely on. With such serious inroads being cut into the tribes scattered along the long, vulnerable frontier of New France, the minister realized that if nothing was done, it would not be long before that colony became untenable.

That the English needed to be kept in check was without question. How best to do that with state finances in total disarray, the minister asked himself as his eyes traveled along a winding path, was the only real question. The French settlers themselves in both New France and Louisiana were too few, too thinly scattered, and too near the brink of survival themselves to be relied upon for even a partial solution. And the policy of relying on the Indians, it now seemed, was unraveling. They all too often proved as fickle as the king's mistress. It was becoming more and more obvious that sooner or later the waves of English immigrants would burst over the Allegheny Mountains and spill into the river valleys of the Ohio and, if left unchecked, the Mississippi itself. When that happened, the lucrative fur trade, New France's only redeeming quality, would be lost.

Heaving a sigh, the minister let his arms fall to his sides. Eventually, he realized, they would need to sink more troops, and money, into a proposition that, even at its best, was of marginal value. Walking back to his desk, he stopped short of it and stared at Governor Jonquière's report for a moment before deciding to push that problem aside, if only for a while. Instead, he picked up a letter from a dear friend that he had not yet found time to finish. Collapsing into his chair and leaning back, the minister picked up where he had left off when an aide had brought in the Canadian dispatches.

As you know, his friend wrote, *my son, Anton, will soon be finishing his studies at the Royal school of artillery and seeking an assignment.* The minister chuckled. At least, he thought, his friend had had enough sense to pull his bastard son out of the university, where he had been exposed to the worthless babbling of philosophers, and secure him a commission in the artillery. There he would not only learn the meaning of discipline but he might even become an asset to his ambitious father, a man who was wise enough to know that commissions in the infantry and cavalry belonged to the legitimate sons of the cream of French nobility. *While I do wish the best for the young man, and have worked to provide for him as circumstances permitted, I do not want him, shall we say, underfoot. In considering this problem, the thought came to me that perhaps you might be able to find a suitable position for him, in either India or New France. It would be ideal for me as well as the boy, in that it would provide him an opportunity that his situation might not allow if he stayed here, in France.* As well, the minister thought with a cynical chuckle, a wonderful opportunity to die honorably for the king, earning the grief-stricken father the gratitude of his sovereign, while bringing a lifelong embarrassment to an end.

He tossed the letter onto his desk, where it landed on top of Jonquière's report. Seeing this caused the minister to laugh out loud. "Oh, the irony of fate." Leaning forward, he seized a pen from the inkwell and scratched out a note to an aide on a scrap of paper, instructing him to make arrangements for young Ensign Anton de Chevalier to be assigned to the garrison of New France as soon as he had the king's commission in hand.

"There," the minister proclaimed triumphantly as he stood up. "I have responded to Monsieur Jonquière's request for assistance and solved an old friend's problem, all in one fell swoop. Now," he announced to an empty room, "I may dine in peace."

CHAPTER THREE

Alexandria, Virginia
March, 1754

With the first hint of spring in the air, the old cook threw open the windows and doors of the small plantation cookhouse. Everyone, including the new servant girl, reveled in the breeze that carried away the heat of the cookhouse oven. "Enjoy it now while you can, girl," the thin black slave warned the newest member of the plantation's small staff. "Comes April, when the flies thaw out, we'll be shuttin' this place up like a tomb. Miss Agnes Bell don't like no flies lighting in her puddings."

Agnes, the stout old English cook, looked up from the bowl of dough she was kneading and made a face. "I'm paid to feed Master Richfield, not his flies. And your indentureship," she barked at Maggie across the room, "was bought by 'em so I could have some decent help for a change."

Bent forward with her bare forearms resting on the windowsill, Maggie pretended she didn't hear Agnes's admonishment. Instead of paying attention to Agnes and learning the proper English way to cook, her mind, like her eyes, was fixed squarely on the young wheelwright working in front of the carriage house across the yard from the kitchen. "Do you suppose he's thirsty, Agnes?" Maggie mused.

"Well," Agnes snorted as she lifted the dough and slammed it down onto the wooden table in preparation for rolling. "If the effort he's put into his tasks is anywhere close to that which you've put forth since he's come, I seriously doubt he's been able to break a sweat."

"Oh," Maggie replied as she turned and looked back at Agnes. Ignoring the look of anger in Agnes' face that had grown fiercer with every minute Maggie had squandered watching the wheelwright, the young Irish girl leaped to the wheelwright's defense. "But he has. In fact, he's almost finished. T'would surely be a sin if he were sent away without one of us making so much as an offer of our hospitality."

For a moment, the old woman stared into the longing eyes of the lively Irish girl. In a flash, the image of a slovenly servant was transformed into that of a young maiden, poised on the threshold of womanhood. Like Agnes herself, Maggie had been sold into indentureship by a widowed mother with more mouths to feed than her means would permit her. Though charged with running the plantation's kitchen and training a girl who would one day replace her, Agnes could not ignore the fact that Maggie was still a fifteen-year-old child struggling with the trauma of coming of age. Until she got out whatever was in her system, the old cook realized, Maggie would be worthless to her. Turning to the slave girl, called Bessy, Agnes gave a wink, then looked over to Maggie. "You're right, child," she replied with a kindly tone so unlike her usual sharp voice that often reminded Maggie of a dog's bark. "It would be rude of us to do so. Bessy," the old cook commanded, "fetch some of that grog I keep in the storehouse and take it to the poor, hard-working lad."

Before Bessy could say a word, Maggie was up and away from the window, shouting as she flew out of the room, "Oh, Bessy, don't bother yourself. I'll tend to it."

As she listened to the young servant girl stumble about in the storeroom, the old cook smiled. "That one has plans, all right. She's not been here but four months and already she's tryin' to snare the first poor man who'll help her find her dream."

Watching through the doorway as Maggie struggled to wrap her shawl around herself without spilling any of the rum-and-water mix, Bessy sighed. "And what, Miss Agnes, would that dream be?"

Agnes snorted as she slammed the dough down on the table again and worked it out with her hands. "She's Irish. She wants what every Irishman who steps foot off a boat in this colony wants, land. A patch of earth they can call their own to build a house on in which they can dally with their mate till all hours and stuff full with noisy, rude children."

Bessy turned and stared at the old cook as soon as Maggie rushed out the door behind her. "You make it sound as if a dream such as that is, well, wrong or somethin'."

"It's a fool's dream, girl," Agnes barked back. "She knows nothing of this place, nothing of the dangers that wait beyond the mountains, where the only land available lies. She still thinks that the counties west of here are like the tidewater, cleared and peopled with decent folk. What she and the others like her mistake for freedom is nothing more than a sentence to hardships, dangers, and a short, dirty life in the wilderness. She's a fool."

Bessy looked at the old woman for a moment, then out the window where Maggie was crossing the yard. Going west, over the mountains, might be foolish, Bessy thought, but at least in four years she'd have the freedom to try. All the white folks, Bessy knew, even those as low on life's ladder as Maggie, had something that she and most of the black slaves in Virginia would never have—opportunity and, most important, freedom.

The young man, stripped down to his shirt, was nearly done when Maggie approached him. Even from behind, she liked the looks of him. In his early twenties, the man had a good straight frame and powerful arms, arms strong enough to lift the carriage wheel without any undue strain or grunting.

Stopping just short of him, Maggie waited until he had finished aligning the wheel's hub with the refurbished spindle and slid it on. Holding the wheel with one hand, the wheelwright bent down and stretched in an effort to retrieve the pin that would hold it in place. It was then that he noticed her standing behind him. "Well, girl," the wheelwright called out in a gruff Scottish accent. "If you're gonna stand there agawkin', you might as well make yourself useful. Fetch me that pin off the ground there, the one layin' on the cloth."

Looking about, Maggie spotted the black iron pin, already coated in grease. Stooping, she carefully set the tankard on the ground, fetched the pin off the rag it was nestled upon, and handed it to the wheelwright. The Scotsman, watching her every move, took the pin, then went back to his work without so much as a smile. Sliding the pin through the hole in the spindle, he secured it at the other end. After giving the wheel a wiggle to make sure that it was firmly seated, he stepped back a bit, grasped the carriage wheel on the outer edge, and gave the wheel a spin. As it rotated, he watched to make sure that it spun freely and easily about the hub without wobbling. When he was satisfied that his efforts had been good and true, he placed his hands on his hips and nodded. "Well, now, that should hold up so long as the fine gentleman who owns this lovely carriage doesn't take it where it wasn't meant to go." Then he turned and looked at Maggie. "But, then, dear girl, he wouldn't be a proper Englishman if he didn't, would he?"

Not sure how to respond to the man's cutting remark, Maggie wiped the grease off her hands, reached over to retrieve the tankard of grog, and offered it up to the wheelwright. "We were watching you from the kitchen and thought that perhaps you might be thirsty."

Slowly, the harshness left the man's face as he accepted the pewter mug. "From what I could see from here, dear girl, you was the only one doing any watching."

As he took a long drink, Maggie tucked her head down to hide her crimson cheeks and folded her hands in her lap. "I . . . I didn't think I was being *that* obvious."

"*Obvious?*" he roared loudly, throwing his head back. "If you had hung out that window any further, you'd have fallen to the ground flat on your face!"

Embarrassment gave way to anger. Jumping to her feet, she advanced until she was toe-to-toe with him, looking up into his grinning face. "You're a cruel one, you are. Have you no manners, *sir?*"

With one hand on his hip and the other holding the tankard off to one side, he leaned over Maggie, forcing her to lean backward to avoid contact. "And have you no decency, girl? Or is it true what they say about Irish women?"

"And what, dear sir, do they say about Irish women?"

Backing away until she could stand upright, the wheelwright took a sip of grog, wiped his lips with the sleeve of his shirt, and smiled. "I've been told that they are impetuous, hot-blooded, and," he added with great emphasis, "bad-tempered."

"Well," Maggie stammered, "better to be an impet-u-ros . . ."

"That's impetuous, girl," the wheelwright corrected her.

"Well," Maggie continued, becoming more flustered as she went on, "whatever that means, I'd rather be it than a sour, tight-fisted Scotsman interested only in hanging on to his gold."

"Ha! You can rest assured, dear lass, if I had a bit of gold to hang on to, I'd be miles away from this place, workin' for myself."

Suddenly, his words struck a cord. In an instant, Maggie's expression changed from one of fury to an excited, quizzical look. "And if you were doin' your own work, where might you be doin' it mister, ah . . . ?"

Noting her change in demeanor, and having no desire to say anything that would cause this girl with soft, clear skin, fetching green eyes, and flaxen hair to go away, the wheelwright lightened his tone. "McPherson. Ian McPherson."

"Megan O'Reilly of Cavan County."

"Well, Miss O'Reilly of Cavan County, it is my pleasure," Ian responded with a clumsy bow that he had meant to be a mockery of English ways but which Maggie took to be charming. "I'd be as proud of my late home, as I am sure you are of yours, if it were still mine," he said sharply as he turned to give the wheel another spin in the opposite direction.

A slight frown crossed Maggie's lips. "Are you a convict?"

Without facing her, he wiped his hands on his shirt as he watched the wheel slow to a stop. "That, dear girl, is a matter of opinion. There are those who would call me a patriot."

In an instant, it all became clear to Maggie. "You're an exile. You marched with Bonnie Prince Charlie in the '45, didn't you?"

Slowly he turned, looked over at her, but said nothing. His expressionless face betrayed no thoughts as he slowly bent over, set down the half-empty tankard, and began to gather his tools and rags.

Worried that she had said something to upset him, Maggie's brain worked feverishly in an effort to find the right words to get the conversation headed back in the direction she wanted it to go. It was Ian, however, who took up where she had left off. As if struck by a sudden spell of exhaustion, he eased himself down till he was sitting on the ground, resting against the wheel of the carriage with his bag of tools between his legs. After dropping a wooden mallet into the bag, he looked up into Maggie's eyes. "I can't say that I am thrilled to be here, laboring for another man like a Negro. As much as I'd regret saying so, if I had me way, I'd be back in the Highlands tending my father's flocks and land. But," he continued in a sad, mournful tone as he bowed his head for a moment, "I have no ancestral lands to go back to. My kin, and everyone I knew, were swept away during the Great Clearance." There was a pause, after which he looked back up at Maggie. Though there were no tears, Ian's eyes told of a great sorrow that cut him through and through. "I don't even know where my parents went off to." Looking over his shoulder, he nodded as if he were referring to some faraway place. "I have nothing back there." With a slow turn of his head, he looked past Maggie, in the direction of the setting sun. "I have only myself now."

He almost told her of his desire, his dream, of going back to Scotland to reclaim the heritage that was rightfully his, but he didn't. This girl, he realized, wouldn't understand such sentiments. He could see that in her young, wide eyes that betrayed nothing but innocence. Instead, he told her what he told everyone who managed to incite him to speak of his future. "In time, I suppose, I'll go off and start my own place, off to the west, where there's more land than any one person can own and no landlords."

"Is there someone to share this land with you, when you find it?" Maggie slowly asked as she lowered herself down to the ground next to Ian.

Surprised by the girl's boldness, Ian pulled back from her and stared at her for a moment. Then he laughed despite the deep emotions their conversation had brought to the fore. "If it's a proposal of some sort you have in mind, I'm afraid you're sniffing around the wrong tree. I have nothing except the clothes on my back and this bag of tools to claim as my own. And comes two weeks hence, when my indentureship is at an end, I won't even have them. The tools, that is."

"You'll have a trade," she said excitedly as she drew closer. "There is much opportunity for skilled workers in the colonies, or so I'm told."

"Yes," he replied dryly, "if you're of a mind to enslave yourself to another and do their bidding, as we both have had to in order buy passage to this forsaken land. No," he stated solemnly as he looked down at the bag of tools and shook his head. "I've had my fill of working for the benefit of others. In two weeks, when I hand these tools over, I'm done with the craft of mending wheels."

"But how will you earn the cash you need to purchase the land and supplies you'll need to establish yourself beyond the mountains?"

Drawing his knees up to his chin, Ian wrapped his hands around his legs and stared off in the distance toward the setting sun. Resting his chin on his knees, as he had done so many times when he was troubled as a boy, Ian thought a moment before he answered Maggie. His story of going west, so long little more than a ruse to cover his true desire for revenge, was becoming, as of late, his only viable option. There was, after all, no point in returning to Scotland now, since there wasn't even the hint of another rising. And the idea of selling his soul to a foreign army as a mercenary just so that he could indulge in the pleasure of killing Englishmen was quite unappealing, especially since the world was at peace, for the moment.

Finally, he whispered, "I don't know. In the beginning, when I first started working here, I lived like a monk, buying only that which was necessary to sustain life. I had hoped that by doin' so, I would be able to scrape a few shillings together by the time my term of service was over." Lifting his chin from his arm, he looked into Maggie's eyes. "But they never gave me a chance. It was all fixed, you know, from the start. It's no different here than it was back in Scotland." Stretching out his arm, he held his hand before his face, then curled his fingers into a tight fist. "They take you, they take everything you own, and then they squeeze you, till there's nothing left of you, not even your soul."

Though Maggie had no idea who "they" were, she listened attentively to Ian.

"In four years, I've not managed to save a single bloody shilling. A single shilling! Everything, from the moldy straw used to stuff me mattress to the puny tallow I have to light my hovel, I'm charged a fortune for. The sorry old sod doesn't even bother to give me an excuse whenever I make mention of this. When the old skinflint even dignifies me with a response, it is only to remind me of how fortunate I am to have been given an opportunity to learn a trade."

Though she hadn't expected such a response, and felt quite sorry for the man, Maggie's mind was too animated with what she thought seemed to be an obvious solution, one that would serve both her and Ian. "Have you heard about the offer the governor's made to all the men who've joined the Virginia Regiment?"

Lifting his chin off his knees, Ian glared at Maggie, telling her that he'd not only heard of it but disapproved of it, for some reason or another. "Do you think," he all but barked, "that our fine governor and those gentlemen in the House of Burgesses are going to pay up when the bill comes due?"

"They'll have to!" she exclaimed innocently. "It's all part of the enlistment terms. I heard Mr. Thomas and Lieutenant Colonel Washington of the Virginia Regiment discuss it over dinner one night. The governor has set aside over two hundred thousand acres of land for those who volunteer to serve. And that's not to mention the pay."

"Eight pence a day?" Ian scoffed. "And that's before they take money out for uniforms and other such things. Eight pence a day to risk life and limb, not to mention disease and bad food, for any poor sod foolish enough to go. And as to their promise of land, well," Ian added with great scorn, "no one seems to notice that the land the governor is being so generous with is the same land the Ohio Company is setting claim to. No, I've not given the matter a second thought."

"Then you'll be content to sit here in Alexandria and pine away, dreaming about all the land you'll never have while slaving for another?" Maggie taunted.

"You are a saucy lass, aren't you?"

Jumping to her feet, Maggie snatched up the tankard. "And you, sir, are a miserable excuse of a man. I was foolish to think that you'd be worth my time or effort."

Before he could respond, she had turned her back and marched straight back to the cookhouse. For a moment, he watched her as she crossed the yard with great, bold strides. When she was gone from sight, Ian rested his chin on his knees and gazed off at the setting sun. He sat there like that until the cool air of late afternoon became too much for him. With a blink of his eyes, he shut away his dreams and thoughts and returned to the task of taking the repaired carriage off the blocks he had set it upon while he worked on the wheels and prepared to leave. It was a long walk back to his small room in Alexandria, and it would be long after dark when he reached it. But that didn't bother Ian. He had much to think about while he was walking, not the least of which was how best to court the young fiery-eyed Irish girl who had managed to enflame passions he had long thought were dormant.

IAN had been told he would find the man he needed to talk to at the tavern and he wasn't disappointed. He found him straight off, seated in the corner with his back to the wall, slowly sipping his ale while he listened intently to the chatter of two companions.

For a moment, Ian stood just inside the doorway as he turned his decision over again in his mind for the umpteenth time. It was foolish, he kept telling himself, to walk away from one form of tyranny and willingly walk right into another. Foolish to the extreme. His efforts to flee the clan system that had buried his family at the rock bottom of their society had nearly gotten him killed. That he managed to escape with his life was, for the longest time, of little comfort. Rather than earning his freedom, he had become a fugitive, with little hope of returning to a home that was no longer his, though he still entertained the desire to do so, if only for revenge. In the beginning, he never gave any alternative a serious thought. "Better a free beggar," he told a fellow wanderer one night as they huddled together under a blanket in a muddy roadside ditch, "than a slave."

Such lofty thoughts, however, wore terribly thin when Ian was finally caught by English dragoons. Chained and imprisoned with fellow patriots, Ian survived the weeding-out process that sent some to the gallows, some to prison, and others into exile. That he was chosen for transport to the colony of Virginia was of little comfort to him. Like most sons of Scotland's Highlands, he viewed the prospect of being carried away to the savage wilderness of North America little more than a temporary stay of execution.

That he was now standing there, outside the tavern, ready once again to surrender his body and soul to another in the hope of gaining some illusory goal that always seemed to be just beyond his grasp, was troubling. But he had no real choice, or so he kept reminding himself. If he was to survive as a free man, he had no choice. The fiery-eyed Irish girl at the Thomas plantation had planted an idea that had taken root. Like a wild weed, it had grown and spread, pushing aside all other alternatives. Drawing in a deep breath, Ian told himself that the time for thinking was over. It was time to act.

With the same resolve that had carried him away from his ancestral farm, he stepped off toward the man in the corner.

The man he had been eyeing was in his late thirties, but looked older. His eyes were always in motion, peering out from narrow slits as they darted about the room, taking in everything. They had lighted upon Ian while he had stood in the doorway of the tavern and had quickly taken note that Ian was returning the stare. So, when Ian finally managed to muster the resolve needed to advance, the man was ready.

"What is it," the gruff Irishman barked as Ian stopped just short of the table, "that I can do for you, *sir?*"

The "sir," Ian took note, rolled off the man's tongue in such a manner as to leave no doubt that it was added only as a formality, and not as an acknowledgment of respect. "If you are Captain Shaw of the Virginia Regiment, then I think you have need of me," Ian replied as firmly as he could.

For a moment, Shaw looked into Ian's eyes, trying to see if there was any sign of mischief hiding behind them. Though he sensed that Ian posed no threat, Shaw put down his mug of ale on the table, just in case he did need to have the free use of both hands. "I am John Shaw. What is it that I need from you?"

Ian swallowed hard and blinked twice as he wiped his sweaty palms on his pants. "You need men, men who can fight. I've come to offer my services to you, if there's still an opening."

The two men who were sitting at the table with Shaw looked at each other, then began to laugh out loud. Shaw, ignoring them, continued to peer into Ian's eyes without saying a word. " 'If there's an opening,' the lad says," a heavy-set man Ian knew to be a local merchant roared as he slapped his hand on the table and continued to laugh. "Boy," he said, looking up at Ian with eyes moist from laughing too much, "I'm sure my friend here will be able to accommodate you."

With that, the other gentleman at the table, whose laughter was about to die down, broke out in a new outburst. Still, Shaw did not say a word or crack a smile. He looked at his companions straight-faced, then back at Ian. "Don't mind those two. They're easily amused."

"That's right, Jake," one of the men shouted out as he struggled to control his laughter. "And as long as the *Regiment* is here, we'll not have far to go when we need a laugh or two." This statement set the other man off on another laughing jag.

Shaw, clearly tiring of the antics of his companions, stood up. "If you gentlemen don't mind," he growled, "I have business to tend to."

Too caught up in his own laughter, the heavy man waved a hand to Shaw as he eased his way around the table. "If you'll come with me, mister, ah . . ."

"McPherson, Ian McPherson."

Shaw took one last glance at his obnoxious friends. "I think it best if we go outside and discuss this matter. I don't much feel like providing those two with merriment, at least not at my expense."

Ian followed Shaw as they made their way through the crowded chairs and people. Once outside, Shaw paused and looked to the west at the late evening sun, glowing bright red just above the horizon. "What makes you want to join my company?" Shaw asked without turning around to face Ian.

Ian looked into Shaw's eyes for a moment and thought about telling him of his deep-rooted desire to return to Scotland, and to avenge the terrible slaughter the English army had visited upon his homeland. But he decided not to. Such sentiments were, Ian knew, too easily misunderstood. Instead he opted for a lie, one that would easily be accepted by a fellow wanderer. "Land, sir. I have been led to believe that any man who enlists will be entitled to land in the new territories when his service is up."

Shaw glanced over his shoulder, looked at Ian for a moment, then faced the setting sun again. "Aye," he whispered. "That's what we've been told to promise."

"Is it true?"

Shaking his head, Shaw continued to study the crimson hues of the great solar orb as it sank lower and lower in the west. "I'll not lie to you, lad," he finally admitted. "If it's only land you're after, then I don't think the gamble would be worth taking." Shaw paused and glanced over his shoulder. "Are you runnin' from the law?"

"No," Ian stated proudly. "No man has any matter that needs to be settled with me."

Relieved, Shaw looked back at the setting sun. He didn't believe land was the only thing driving Ian to join up. This lad, Shaw told himself, had other reasons, just as Shaw himself did, for risking life and limb. What they were, he could only guess at. "Well, then," Shaw finally stated dryly, "come along, lad, and walk awhile. I'm in need of the company of an *honest* man."

As they made their way through the dark shadows of late afternoon, neither man spoke. Ian wondered if he was being taken for a fool by Shaw. When they reached the edge of town, Shaw stopped, crossed his arms, and went back to watching the sun, now barely peeking over the horizon. "Captain Shaw, what can you tell me about your company? What do you know, for sure? Before I commit myself to the service of another, I must have some assurance that I'll not be wasting my time."

Then, without preamble, Shaw spun about on his heel in the dirt and faced Ian. "I can give you little in the way of assurances, lad. No man who's ever taken the king's shilling can be assured of anything except takin' on all the hardships and misery that goes with a soldier's life. As far as what I know, well, that's simple. I do know, sir, that we're short recruits, have no uniforms, lack supplies of every conceivable kind, and can't even provide weapons for those we already have in camp. Our colonel is a fifty-four-year-old schoolteacher at the College of William and Mary whose only qualifications are, as our dear governor so plainly states himself, that he's a man of good sense and an able mathematician. The regiment's lieutenant colonel is a twenty-three-year-old red-haired surveyor whose only claim to fame is that he's managed to capture the governor's fancy and a commission."

Pausing only long enough to catch his breath, Shaw took a minute to compose himself before he continued. "We've got less than three hundred men in hand at present. With that, and precious little else, we're being asked to make our way to the forks of the Ohio, build a fort, and defend an area almost as large as Ireland itself for the benefit of a group of pompous gentlemen land speculators. Needless to say, the French have the same notion, only they're doing it for the benefit of their gentlemen." Stepping back, Shaw stood with his feet apart, placed his hands on his hips, and looked Ian over closely for the first time. "You're the wheelwright's man, aren't you?"

"As of today, I'm finished with my service with him," Ian responded sharply.

"And here you stand," Shaw stated, half in wonder, "a man, with his freedom and a skill, asking to join an enterprise as shaky as this one. Why?"

"I told you," Ian replied, annoyed. "Land."

Slowly Shaw's eyes narrowed. Taking a step forward, he peered into Ian's eyes. "Have you any idea what you're asking to get yourself involved with? Do you know what it means to be a soldier?"

For the first time, Ian felt himself on sure ground. Though he did not know where Shaw's sympathies had been during the Rebellion of '45, he guessed he was anything but a king's man. "Aye, I know. I stood my ground at Culloden during that frightful execution and followed the banner of the Appin Clan into the jaws of hell. I climbed over the corpses of men whom I had shared many a meager meal with and was hunted down like an animal for my efforts when it was all over. I've begged for food when I was hungry and stole clothing off a dead man when I was cold. I do not know what I'll find at the forks of the Ohio, but I do know that there's nothing here that I much care for."

For the first time, Ian noticed a softening fall across the old Irishman's weathered face. Taking a step back, Shaw gave Ian another once-over. "Then, I take it you can handle a musket," the captain replied.

"And my grandfather's broadsword as well," Ian responded.

For the first time, Ian saw that he had surprised Shaw, as one of his eyebrows rose at the mention of the sword. "How is it, lad," Shaw asked with a hint of amusement in his voice, "that you managed to smuggle the ancestral claymore out of England and hold on to it all these years?"

"I let the passions of youth blindly drive my feet once. That I survived was little more than a simple matter of luck and providence," Ian responded as a mischievous smile crept across his face. "Since then, I've learned to pick and choose my company as carefully as circumstances have permitted. My grandfather's broadsword is with me today thanks to a cowardly lowland jailer with a soft heart and the understanding of a Scottish ship's captain with a weakness for fellow wanderers who could spin a rousing good story."

A smile crept across Shaw's face as he extended his right hand, which Ian grasped. "Well, lad, I hope you'll find no use for your grandfather's sword," Shaw chuckled. "And though I question your choice of occupations, for I've been reduced to recruiting every wretch and malcontent the county sheriff can turn out of his jail, you're welcomed to throw your lot in with my tiny command if you have the stomach for a little adventure." Then, letting go of Ian's hand, Shaw stepped back and took a more formal, imposing stance as he grasped the edges of his open coat with his hands while he masked his face with an official and detached expression. "Tell me now, have you any obligations to your former master or debts that demand an extension of your terms of service?" Shaw inquired.

Drawing himself erect, Ian replied, "No. I no longer have a master, of any description. And though my former employer claims that I am in arrears to him for unspecified sums, I have been more than careful to record all my income and expenses these past four years. I'm confident that I could disprove any and all claims against me before any magistrate in this colony."

Shaw had no doubt that young Ian McPherson would stand before a legal bar to defend his claims. Yet, he was equally confident that if it came to that, he'd lose. It was, after all, a sad fact that many a master, both in the trades and gentlemen who owned the fine plantations for which Virginia was known, took great pains to engineer the terms of his agreement to his benefit. Many an indentured servant, even when the original obligation was fulfilled, found himself so deeply in debt that the poor sod never managed to crawl out from under the master's thumb. In a land where good labor was hard to come by and the draw of lands to the west so powerful that it was always draining away that which was available, few plantation owners and masters were willing to part with what they had, even if it meant occasionally overstepping the bounds of the law, which, conveniently, was administered by their friends and peers. Still, Shaw reasoned, even if McPherson was lying to him, there'd be no time for his old master to bring the matter to trial. The regiment, if the gaggle of men Lieutenant Colonel Washington had managed to gather thus far could be called such, would be marching off in a few days. There would be no time for legal action or reprieves.

"I believe you, lad," Shaw finally stated. "Come by the camp in the morning and make your mark," he commanded. "If you have a blanket, a spare shirt, and a pair of good walking shoes, bring them with you. You'll need them all too soon."

PICKING her way carefully between the rows of tents, stacks of arms, and men, Megan O'Reilly of Cavan County fought the urge to hold her nose. That a group of men could generate such disgusting odors, let alone live among them, was appalling. It wasn't that she was a stranger to such stench. Having been raised on a poor farm in a home that was little more than a hovel, Maggie's trained nose could often distinguish unhealthy creatures, man or beast, by the smell of their bodies or droppings. She could even pinpoint the malady, if the illness were advanced enough. But this stench, an ungodly amalgam of odors that assaulted her nose, was unlike anything she had ever experienced, even during the worst part of her long passage from Ireland to Virginia.

Yet, as bad as the overpowering stink was that reeked from every corner of the Virginia Regiment's camp, it was the sight of the soldiers themselves that gave Megan her greatest concern. She had seen soldiers before, in Ireland, where Government troops served to keep English landowners safe from the occasional resurgence of Celtic unrest that rocked that land every so often. That so many feared the disreputable wretches, whom the king's recruiters were forced to press into service for lack of better specimens, had always been a source of amazement to Maggie. Still, she reasoned, even the most disreputable company of redcoats surpassed, in stature and demeanor, the collection of men that lay about the camp she was making her way through. Perhaps, she wondered, she should have listened to Agnes, the old cook who had tried to dissuade her from seeking out the young Scotsman. "No respectable young woman dares go near that rabble," the old cook warned, "and comes away with her virtue intact. Besides, dear girl," Agnes added in maternal tones, "you're a fool if ya go and fling yourself at a man with so low opinion of himself that he freely gives himself up to be a soldier. Be patient, dear girl. You're young. Every summer brings a new crop of young men in need of a bright young girl who's well schooled in the feminine arts of cooking and managing a home."

Pausing, Maggie pondered the old cook's words as she looked about in an effort to find the Scotsman she had so quickly pegged her dreams upon. Perhaps she was being foolish and far too impetuous for her own good. Her own mother had warned her that of all the temptations a young woman faced in this world, none would lead her to ruin as quickly as giving into her emotions and impulses. Still, Maggie reasoned, caution and a reliance on what had proved safe in the past could be just as damning. Her mother, after all, had been a cautious woman, one who would never imagine doing anything that was not part of the customs of their people or laid out in the teachings of the holy mother church. And look where it had left her, Maggie told herself. Like so many others she knew, her mother had been stuck with a family tied to a tiny plot of land, owned by another, that was too poor to meet their needs, and had been faced with no other recourse but to sell off her own children, one at a time, to a life that was little better than slavery. No, Maggie told herself as she tightly clutched the small sack she carried close to her bosom. "I must stay true," she whispered in an often repeated pledge to herself. "I'll not bring a child into this world till I have a house I can call my own and land enough to feed 'em."

"Have you anyone in particular, girlie," a gruff voice beside her called out, "you're plannin' to do this with?"

Turning in shock, Maggie pulled away in disgust when she laid eyes on a dirty, rough-looking character with stringy hair. Amused by her reaction, the man smiled, displaying a set of brown and yellow teeth that jutted from his raw gums at odd angles. Offended as much by his appearance as she was by his insinuations, Maggie drew away, though she kept an eye on the man, now laughing uproariously. Concerned only with putting some distance between her and the man, Maggie's feet became tangled in a heap of stray camp equipment and several soldiers' personal belongings haphazardly strewn about on the ground. This set her to tottering about as she struggled to maintain her balance, an effort that she failed in utterly. Feeling herself going down, Maggie gave up all hope of preserving what dignity she had left and instead turned her full attention to protecting the bundle she held in her hands. This, of course, only added to her dilemma and awkwardness, not to mention the severity of the impact with which she hit the ground.

Had she fallen on the ground itself, Maggie would have still suffered badly enough, but luck was all against her. The same odds and ends that had ensnared her broke her fall and poked her side and rump at all sorts of angles and degrees. Yet, as bad as the jabs and digs of the scattered equipment were, it was the lusty laughter of the soldiers who had stopped doing whatever they had been concerned with to watch the spectacle of a young girl tumbling over onto her backside that was worse. Even as she struggled to regain the breath that had been knocked from her, Maggie could feel that her cheeks were aglow from anger. Not even the appearance of a hand before her face and a gentle offer of help from a familiar voice was sufficient to soften her growing rage.

With a swipe, she slapped the hand away and sprang to her feet with a dexterity that surprised all those who were gathering about her and set her would-be savior back on his heels. "I'll not be needing any help from your sort, *thank you*," she snapped as she bent over instinctively to smooth her skirt to keep from exposing her legs, or worse.

"Well, now," Ian McPherson responded as he threw his

hands up and smirked. "You'll have to excuse me, *me lady*. From where I'm standin' it seemed like you were in a bit of distress."

When she finally looked up at Ian's face, her green eyes were lit with an angry passion that set her whole face ablaze with shades of crimson and red. Framed by auburn hair struggling to free itself from a tight bun hidden under a white cap set on the back of her head, Maggie's innocent, natural beauty struck Ian like a hammer blow. The half-smile that had offended Maggie disappeared, along with his ability to speak, or even hear, what the young Irish girl was saying. Rather, Ian found himself gazing into her eyes, eyes that were so engaging, so full of life. For the longest time, the only thing that he noticed about Maggie other than her eyes was the manner in which she swayed and weaved about as she unleashed a stream of angry words meant to admonish him and those who had been so crass to her. This motion, Ian realized, was keeping him from holding her eyes with a steady gaze. Without any real conscious thought, Ian took a step toward Maggie and reached out with both hands, grasping her arms gently with his hands and easing her motion, as he often did with his former master's pet when the animal became too excited during play.

The sudden and unexpected feel of Ian's strong hands on her upper arms, and the calm, gentle squeeze that he gave them, shocked Maggie into silence. Like a doe surprised by a predator, Maggie froze and stared into Ian's eyes. This, being what Ian had desired, brought a smile to his face. Neither knew how long they stood there staring at each other like that. Not that it mattered. Not even the crude comments, liberally sprinkled with obscenities and an occasional lurid suggestion, could break the trance that had fallen over the two young people as Ian skillfully led Maggie away from the center of the camp without ever breaking the gaze that had managed to capture her full attention.

The first sound Maggie heard outside of her own thoughts was the quiet splashing of water on the banks of the Potomac River. Forcing herself, she turned her face away from Ian's and looked about her, as much in an effort to gather her scattered thoughts as to determine where they were. As she shook her head, as if awakening from a long sleep, Maggie could feel her cheeks go flush from embarrassment. Slowing, but not making any effort to break the hold Ian had of her left arm, Maggie tilted her head down and stared at the ground. What, she asked herself, had she allowed herself to do? Had she surrendered whatever propriety she imagined she had with her foolish trip to the Virginia Regiment's camp in search of the McPherson lad? Would he think of her now, she wondered, as many men thought of those common women who made a living serving the needs of common soldiers? Befuddled, Maggie didn't know what to do or say. She even began to wish that she had heeded the old English cook's advice and stayed away from the camp.

It was Ian McPherson who finally broke the silence as they slowly walked along the river bank. "I do hope that it was me that you came to see," he stated calmly. "Otherwise, you're makin' a fool of me."

Stopping, Maggie turned to face him, allowing him to fix his eyes on hers, as before. "Oh, no. It was me who was the fool. I should've listened to Agnes, the old cook, and stayed away from the camp. It was a mistake, a stupid . . ."

Sliding his hand down, Ian grasped Maggie's left hand and pulled it up to his chest, where he cradled it between his two callused hands. "I don't know what brought you here, girl, or what you're athinkin'. Nor do I much care what you think of me and my clumsy ways." He paused, hesitating for a moment as he debated whether to press on with what he wanted to say or to hold back. The temptation to hold back was compelling. Yet so was the urge to go on and say what he had on his mind. Time was short, he knew, for as he spoke, the regiment was packing up in preparation to leave in two days hence. If he said nothing now, if he kept it to himself, he might never again have the chance to say what he felt at that moment. He had turned his back on his family in the summer of '45 without saying all he had wanted to say, and he regretted that failure to this very day. No, he decided, he would not march away again with words locked up inside of him unsaid. The young Irish girl with the bright auburn hair and green eyes had plagued his thoughts from the first moment he had laid eyes on her. He knew little of love, and nothing of courting. Yet he knew his heart, and his heart was alive at that moment, like it had never been before, simply because this fiery-eyed girl was there, before him.

"Megan O'Reilly of Cavan County," Ian stuttered and stammered, "I cannot tell you all that I feel right now, or explain with fine words like a gentleman what I hope for. What I can tell you is that when I come back, it is my wish that you be here, waitin' for me. If you're of like mind, and if you see in my eyes what I see in yours, tell me."

As a girl, Maggie had listened with great rapture as storytellers would pass on the ancient Celtic myths of heroes and heroines of her people's past. Often she would dream that she would, one day, find a man who would step from the mist, as so many legendary Irish heroes had in the past, and capture her heart. That her champion was a Scotsman, on the verge of marching to war, mattered little to Maggie at that moment.

Unable to find words that were suitable, and caught up in her own emotions, Maggie responded by bending her head forward as she slowly brought her hand, held by Ian's, up to her lips. Gently, she kissed his fingers. Then she looked up into Ian's eyes and smiled.

In that moment, she crossed the great chasm that divides childhood from adulthood, a girl from the mysteries of womanhood. Like the voyage that carried her away from all she had known before and brought her to these strange shores, Maggie once more found herself venturing into uncharted regions. And like her passage from Ireland to Virginia, she accepted the challenge freely and with all her heart.

For the rest of the afternoon, the two walked beside the placid river, speaking little as they occasionally stopped to watch the moving waters of the river at their feet as it flowed along in search of a home in the distant ocean. Neither thought of how much their lives were like the very waters that shared this land with them. Neither bothered to wonder how, like the river, they were moving along a predetermined course, destined to merge with waters flowing together from other rivers. For the moment, all thoughts of what lay ahead, or what other rivers they might encounter in their travels together, were lost to them.

PART TWO

A Clash of Arms

CHAPTER FOUR

On the Allegheny River,
in Western Pennsylvania
April, 1754

FROM THE PARAPETS of the citadel of Montreal, Ensign Anton de Chevalier had watched, with heavy heart, the departure of Captain Pierre-Paul de la Malgue, Sieur de Marin, and his invasion force in the spring of 1753. He had pleaded to be afforded the opportunity to join Marin. But his requests were denied out of hand, leaving Anton with no other choice but to watch from afar as the grand procession of boats and canoes manned by regulars and Canadian militia departed Montreal. Ladened with supplies, weapons, and munitions of every kind, the flotilla of boats carried everything that an army would need to establish a permanent presence at the forks of the Ohio.

Saddened by the fact that he wasn't with them, Anton

waited high upon the bastion where his cannon stood guard against a foe who was hundreds of miles to the south long after the last of Marin's expedition had disappeared to the west. Bemoaning his fate to a fellow officer, Anton complained, "While the issues of our empire are being settled far off in the interior, I am shackled to this fortress like a prisoner. I am condemned to stand guard on the middle ground, between heaven and hell." If the other officer thought Anton meant Paris to be heaven and the savage interior hell, he would had been wrong. For young Anton de Chevalier, an ensign of artillery with the king's commission, was a dreamer.

Unlike many of his fellow officers, whose lineage would determine their future, Anton could not depend on family or connections for advancement. His father had made this very clear throughout his life, during which he had made the effort to meet Anton only twice. Yet the old fellow did have a conscience, one that drove him to provide for Anton by ensuring that the boy receive a liberal education and a commission. It was the education, his fellow officers jokingly pointed out, that was his undoing. "Of what use, dear Anton," a captain of colonial troops known as La Marine pointed out, "will all your long-winded philosophers be when you come face-to-face with a red savage. It is only for your hair, and not your brain, that they seek you."

While Anton laughed with them in public, he ignored their barbs and continued to study Fontenelle's *The Origins of Myths*, Voltaire's commentaries, and Rousseau's writings. The long winter nights and dull routine of garrison life gave him ample time to do so. It also provided the opportunity for Anton to form his own views, thoughts, and opinions. Though he never fancied himself a great thinker, he realized that his awkward social position afforded him freedoms denied many of his fellow officers, who were condemned to follow the prescribed path of a gentleman. In January 1753 he wrote to a professor of philosophy he had studied under, *I have come to see that I am truly caught between heaven and hell. It is not the heaven and hell, though, that the priests speak of. Rather, it is man made heaven and hell, with the King being the all supreme ruler of our particular French heaven and everyone in his domains ranked somewhere below him. As the bastard son of a noble, I hover somewhere on the fringes of this French heaven, always in danger of falling from this precarious perch my father has placed me upon. Unable to secure my place there by right of birth, I have been led to believe that only by using my wits would I be able to secure a place in Our French Heaven.*

Yet, he continued as he considered the teachings and thoughts of the philosophers of the day and his own observations in New France, *I wonder if the King is truly the ruler of Heaven or . . .* Anton stopped writing when he realized where his thoughts were taking him. He was, after all, an officer of the king. It was his duty to defend what he privately referred to as *"Our French Heaven."* Still, the idea that perhaps it was the primitives, and not the Europeans, who defended the gates of heaven on earth took root in the young man's fertile mind quite early during his tour of duty in Canada. That he would have to find out for himself by venturing into the wilderness became clearer with each passing day. With the departure of Marin's force to the west in the spring of 1753, Anton imagined that his chances of ever being afforded the opportunity had disappeared.

That effort, however, foundered badly. It was defeated not by enemy action, of which there had been none, but by drought, disease, corruption at all levels, and the savage wilderness itself. Anton, condemned to remain with the garrison at Montreal, was there when the dispirited remnants of Marin's army returned in the fall of 1753 without its commander. Remaining at Presque Isle, established to anchor the northern end of the portage that connected Lake Erie and the Allegheny, Marin had died of the same dysentery that had claimed so many of his men along the Niagara and Erie portages.

From his perch at the citadel of Montreal, Anton listened as news of developments to the south were carried through that city en route to the Royal governor in Quebec. In December he listened, as others did, to how one of Marin's subordinates at Fort Le Boeuf, at the southern end of the portage on French Creek, greeted an English militia major dispatched by the governor of Virginia with a letter that lay claim to the same vast Ohio territories that Marin had been sent to secure.

Beneath Governor Dinwiddie's subtle tones of polite diplomatic language, the letter carried a warning to the French that if all their forces and forts were not removed from all lands south of Lake Erie, the Royal governor of Virginia, acting on behalf of the king of England, would remove them by force. Taking great pains to put up a brave and strong front, the French commandant of Le Boeuf's tiny, dispirited garrison endeavored to impress upon young Major George Washington that while he would dispatch Dinwiddie's letter to the governor of New France as protocol required, he had every intention of remaining at his post.

The Marquis Duquesne, governor of New France, wasted no time in renewing his drive on the Ohio. Not waiting for the spring thaw, he dispatched another force of five hundred regulars and militia from Quebec on the fifteenth of January 1754 to take up where Marin had failed. It was the arrival of this expedition in Montreal that galvanized Anton into action. Pleading with the garrison commander to be included as one of three hundred additional troops that would join the small army, he used every argument he could think of to sway his superior. "I have served you faithfully for these past two years without question, without hesitation," he announced with great flourish to his commander. "I have earned the right," he proclaimed, "to serve my king on the field of battle."

Though amused by the young ensign's pompous proclamation, Anton's superior was nonetheless impressed with his sincerity. Faced with the need to detach officers to join the expedition, the commandant at Montreal decided that perhaps Anton's enthusiasm would do more than make up for his inexperience in the wilderness. "Besides," the commander told a confidant, "there is nothing like a tour of duty at a forlorn outpost to make one appreciate the pitifully few pleasures that Montreal has to offer."

Dressed in blanket coats and seal-skin shoes that made officers indistinguishable from any other member of the command, Anton de Chevalier set out on the second of February 1754 on an adventure that would change his life.

The sound of oars dipping into the river, the creak of wood straining against oarlocks, and the soft gurgling noise of placid waters churned into a froth by the efforts of the oarsmen created a rhythm that was almost hypnotic to Ensign Anton de Chevalier. *None of this*, he hurriedly scratched in a journal he balanced carefully on his knees, *is as I imagined*. Looking up, he scanned the pale blue sky, framed closely by the oversized trees of a virgin wilderness that inspired both awe and wonderment in and touched the very soul of the young French officer. Quickly his mind worked in an effort to find the right words that would capture the feelings that this sight inspired. *No palace in Paris can match the beauty of this wildness, nor can any cathedral in that fair city evoke the sense of being at one with our Creator that I have felt since embarking on this wonderful journey. I cannot remember when I have been so alive, so attuned to my own feelings and thoughts as I have been since we turned our backs on Montreal and set out on this grand adventure.*

The grand adventure to which Anton de Chevalier referred was neither a journey nor, as the ensign of artillery imagined, a pilgrimage. It was a military offensive, launched at the direction of the governor of New France in the dead of winter to secure a piece of land claimed by two great empires. Hastening along the frozen banks of the Saint Lawrence River on snowshoes and hauling their supplies on sleds, Anton knew they were in a race with the English. It was their task to establish the French king's rightful claim to all the lands touched by the three rivers that met and flowed from the forks of the Ohio by means of a military presence and, if necessary, by force of arms if the English beat them there.

Still, Anton could not resist the allure that the beauty of this strange and wild land evoked. Liberated from the smoky, claustrophobic confines of quarters shut tight against the ravages of the Canadian winter, Anton found himself in an almost continuous state of euphoria as each day opened new vistas, new scenes, to the young ensign. Nothing, not the bitter cold that stung his cheeks or the labors of trekking through snow whose depth was measured in feet, could dampen his enthusiasm. Mile after mile they trudged ahead through cruel weather across a land where life itself seemed locked away in the ice and snow. On some days, conditions were so severe that they were forced to pitch camp almost within sight of the previous night's resting place. And still, Anton reveled in his childlike delight of seeing sights that defied all expectations. Yet, as excited as he had been by all he had seen and experienced during their advance along the Saint Lawrence and the skirting of Lake Ontario, as frozen and inhospitable as the rest of the land, no description could prepare him for his first view of the great falls that lay along the Niagara portage.

Long before he saw the crashing waters, he heard them. At first, he thought his hearing was playing tricks as he trudged along the trail that had cost Marin so many lives the year before. When it persisted, and he could no longer refrain from asking, he turned to a militia lieutenant. "That sound, what is it?"

The militia captain, with a month's growth of beard coated with specks of ice formed by his own breath, looked at Anton with a quizzical expression for several moments. Then, seeing that the young man was sincere, he cocked his head in an effort to allow his ears to capture the noise that the young ensign was inquiring about. When he finally recognized the familiar roar that was as much a landmark in this part of New France as any land feature, the militiaman smiled. "That, my friend, is the song of the great falls."

Looking down at the river below them, Anton leaned over as far as he dared in an effort to see them. The militia captain laughed at this. "You cannot see them from here. No," he added with a shake of his head. "It will be several more hours before we reach them."

With an expression of guarded disbelief that he had learned to effect after having listened to the many wild boasts and fantastic claims colonists and *coureurs de bois* enjoyed springing on novices, Anton straightened himself up, readjusted his pack, and nodded. "Ah, yes, I see," he responded before stepping around the militiaman.

Only after the serpentine single-file column of soldiers finally reached a point from which he was able to view the magnificent spectacle of the great falls did Anton find, to his utter astonishment, that all descriptions of this natural wonder, like so many others, had been woefully lacking. In awe, he stood before the massive falls, mouth agape. His eyes darted wildly about in an effort to capture the spectacle of ceaseless torrents of water streaming over the precipitous edge of the upper falls. He watched the water cascade downward till it crashed into the churning froth below, creating mist and rainbows, as others in the long column, groaning under the weight of their packs, passed him by with little more than a glance at the falls. Heads bowed under the weight of their burdens and monotony of their labors took scant notice of one of the world's truly great wonders. Most of the soldiers concerned themselves exclusively with the chore of keeping their footing as they struggled to navigate the narrow path strewn with rocks layered with ice that coated everything near the massive falls. Only the bump of a soldier slipping on the treacherous path freed Anton of the trance that the sight of the great falls had lulled him into. Still, the awesome beauty had so impressed him that he found he needed to do something to capture forever the thoughts and feelings he was experiencing at that moment.

Silently cursing himself for leaving his journal in Montreal, Anton tried to think of someone who would have pen and paper handy. When it came to him, he tore himself away from the spectacle before him and took off in pursuit of the materials he would need to record his thoughts and feelings. Ignoring the hazards of the narrow portage, Anton raced toward the head of the column until he found the officer serving as the command's adjutant. Along the way, he slipped several times, crashing into the heavily laden soldiers either with his whole body or with his own pack. Neither the muttered curses that followed him nor his hairsbreadth brushes with stumbling and sliding down the slippery ledge did anything to deter Anton's quest.

Stammering like an excited schoolboy when he finally managed to reach the adjutant, Anton all but insisted that the bewildered officer give him paper, pen, and ink right then and there, without delay. Removing a small jar of ink he kept in a pocket under his blanket coat, the adjutant handed it to the excited young ensign. From another pocket he produced a few scraps of paper, and from still another pocket he laid hands on an old quill pen he had meant to throw away for days. "This is hardly the time, young man," the adjutant complained as he fumbled about his person searching for the various items, "to take up poetry."

Anton, ignoring the remarks, all but grabbed the gifts from the older officer's hands and turned to find a spot where he could sit down and write while looking out at the great falls. Plopping down on the first spot that appeared to be relatively dry, Anton set madly to jotting down the first passage of what was to become a journal of his American adventures. *Today,* he started, *I have seen the hand of God.*

From that point on, Anton became a zealot when it came to recording all he saw. While the expedition enjoyed the halt at Fort Niagara, Anton found he could not rest until he had secured a proper journal. Though the price he eventually paid for a partially used quartermaster's record book would have fetched him a dozen newly bound diaries in Paris, Anton paid the man without complaint.

Nothing escaped his attention. No sight, smell, sound, or thought was too trivial to be ignored. *It is like I have been asleep,* he wrote once when reflecting upon this obsession to record everything he came across. *And now that I am truly awake for the first time in my life, I must ensure that I do not allow myself to be lulled into complacency or ignorance again. I must find the words to convey, to my fellow countrymen, the beauty of this land, and what it means to those of us who have, for so long, been lulled into believing that we, in Europe, had all the answers. For I truly believe that if we, as a people, open our eyes and hearts, we can rediscover the meaning of life here, in this land unspoiled by the corrupt hand of tradition and stagnant beliefs.* Almost without realizing it, Anton, so long an innocent youth adrift in a world that provided him little comfort or safe haven, found what he believed to be his calling. He would, he imagined, become the man who would be the chronicler of this new empire, built in a wilderness free of lords and nobles and all the trappings of the Old Regime.

It was Anton's habit of writing and questioning everything that drew one of the Indians accompanying the expedition to him, a Caughnawaga by the name of Gingego. During one of their night encampments, Gingego boldly approached Anton while he was transcribing his daily thoughts onto paper. "I have watched as you write without tiring each day of our march," Gingego announced without any introduction or preamble. "For many years, I have wished to learn more than what the priests are willing to teach us, for I know there is more to your world than that which the Bible tells us. Will you teach me to read as you and allow me to see the books that tell of your people?"

Astonished by this request, Anton's heart leaped with joy at what he took to be an offer of friendship. With an enthusiasm that knew no limits, Anton launched upon a private campaign aimed not only at fulfilling Gingego's request but also at broadening his own knowledge of the people who inhabited the wondrous lands that had inspired his writing. *As I was blind to the wonders that God has wrought here in this untamed wilderness,* Anton admitted, *I was ignorant of its custodians. Now, through a native by the name of Gingego, I have a key to unlock the secrets of their people and culture.*

Yet as grand an opportunity as Gingego's acquaintance presented, Anton quickly found that it was Gingego's brother, an unruly and thoroughly savage character named Toolah, whom he wished to know more about. *Though Gingego is an invaluable source of knowledge that I would be lost without,* Anton admitted to himself one night as he wrote in his journal, *I fear he has been too badly corrupted by the teachings of the mission priests. His thoughts and ideas do not, I believe, reflect his people and culture because of this. To learn about both of them, to truly understand them, I must learn from a member of their race who has rejected all that has led Gingego away from his own kind. Though Toolah holds any and all whites in contempt, I must gain his confidence so that I can learn what being an Indian truly means.*

Such an effort, however, would have to wait. Returning to boats after completing the difficult Niagara portage, the expedition continued down French Creek. From there they passed into the Allegheny River. After that, the journey was quick. Now, less than a few miles from their destination, shouted orders from the head of the long column of boats came to Anton and other officers. "We are approaching the Ohio," came the announcement. "Prepare your men for action."

Anton looked up from his writing. All around him, the phalanxes of boats and canoes were rocking as men shifted about while they retrieved rifles and cartridge boxes that had been laid aside. Beyond the armada of small crafts, he could see that the river they had been traveling on appeared to broaden where it followed into the Ohio. On the shore where it did, there were several thin, wispy pillars of smoke. English cook fires, he guessed. That explained the sudden excitement.

With the same ease that he closed his journal, Anton's mind turned from all thoughts of the natural beauty that surrounded him to the practical matters of the military arts. Looking about, he located the boats in which the guns, carriages, and crews under his command were loaded. When he was satisfied that they were all present and closed up, Anton looked to the front again, waiting for orders to make their way down to him. That didn't take long.

"The English are still there," a militia officer relayed to Anton. "You are to mount four of your guns as soon as possible to cover the landing and advance to the English fortifications."

Scouts, sent in advance of the main body, had discovered the presence of the English. What was not known was their actual strength, a matter that bothered Anton. "Have the men in the lead boats spotted any cannon?" Anton shouted back.

Without bothering to call back to find out, the militia lieutenant simply shrugged and stared blankly at Anton. Though he was tempted to insist that the man at least make the effort to find out, Anton didn't. He could have used his status as a regular officer to order a higher-ranking militia officer about, but he didn't. It made for bad relationships between the officers and men of the militia companies. Since many of his gun crews were militia, Anton could ill afford offending or alienating them.

Without any idea of what they would find, Anton decided to err in favor of caution. He quickly ordered his noncommissioned officers to concentrate the efforts of all his men to mounting two of their heavier guns as well as two of their four-pounders. "If they have guns," he told one of his sergeants, "I want to be able to at least match them."

The sergeant, a wiry regular who was a veteran of many of the king's continental battles, grinned in approval. "Yes, my lord," he called back. "It will be all the better if our shot outranges and outweighs his."

Anton smiled at the easy confidence that this sergeant displayed. "Yes, quite right," Anton replied in agreement. "Even better if they have none."

Looking up at the sky, the sergeant crossed himself. "Be of good faith, sir. Saint Barbara will see us through."

Prayers before battle to the patron saint of artillery by those who were religiously inclined was one of the quaint, old army habits that fascinated Anton. Still, Anton had been taught that gunnery and tactics were practical and scientific matters, nothing more. Only fools depended on chance and fortune in battles. Drill, discipline, and the skillful use of artillery, he had come to believe, were the keys to success. To this end, Anton's mind mechanically went over each and every step that he and his men would need to perform to unload the guns, mount and secure them to their field carriages, and bring them to bear on the English. Even as the bateaux carrying him and his guns began to turn into the river's bank where they would disembark, Anton calculated the number of shot, canister rounds, and barrels of powder he wanted with each of his guns before he advanced. While he dedicated one part of his mind to these practical matters, he managed to listen to his gun captains as they directed their crews to unlash the ropes, save for one or two, that secured the heavy bronze gun barrels to the boats.

Only the shouting of several Indians interrupted Anton's cool calculations. Distracted by this commotion, he turned to watch as the canoe carrying his friend Gingego and Gingego's brother crashed its way through others in a race for the shore. Even before the prow of the canoe touched dry land, Toolah, with a red-feathered hatchet held at the ready in one hand and his musket in the other, leaped into the water and scrambled to the shore. Ignoring the shouts of his brethren, Toolah scrambled up the river banks and plunged headlong into a charge toward the enemy. Gingego, left in his canoe, made no effort to stop his brother. Instead, he contented himself with steadying the rocking canoe before bringing it into the shore in a rather leisurely manner. He had been right, Anton decided that moment, about the two brothers. If he was to understand these people and their ways, he would have to manage to work his way into Toolah's confidence.

The thumping of his own bateaux's bow against the muddy bank jarred Anton's mind back to the problem at hand. With the assistance of several of the men, Anton made his way forward, over the rows of rough-hewn seats and onto the dry shore. "Quickly now, lads," he shouted at the knots of men laboring to manhandle the bronze guns off the rocking bateaux and into the hands of another group of gunners who stood waiting at the river bank. "Quickly."

Few heard his admonishment above their own grunts and groans. Those who did paid him no heed. They had no need to be encouraged. All knew what was at stake here. None of them wished to allow their opponents an opportunity to fall upon them while they were in such a defenseless state. Not out here, in the vast wilderness, where a defeated force had no place to go, no place to hide from an enemy as implacable as the land itself.

The fear and concern felt by Anton's men as they struggled with their pieces was more than matched by the thirty-six Englishmen defending a pitiful log stockade they had named Fort Prince George. Ensign Edward Ward of the Virginia Regiment had been left by his commander, Captain William Trent, at the forks of the Ohio with orders to hold the place while Trent rode south to Willis Creek in the hope of securing food and supplies for his tiny command. When rumors of the French approach made their way to Ward through the effective Indian grapevine, Ward attempted to solicit support from the company's lieutenant, a trader named John Fraser. Fraser, having no desire to abandon his newly established trading post at Turtle Creek in favor of a questionable military adventure at the forks of the Ohio, rebuffed Ward. "What can we do?" Fraser asked blandly before returning to his business affairs. Like Trent, Fraser sidestepped his responsibilities, leaving Ward and a pitiful band of frontiersmen armed with rifles and muskets they themselves provided to defend Virginia's claim to the vast Ohio territory.

Unschooled in the art of war, yet left with the governor's commission to build a fort at the forks of the Ohio, Ward and his tiny band set about the task with great urgency. Even the Indian warriors under the leadership of Tanacharison, known to the English as the Half King, assisted in this effort. But it was an effort, Ward sadly discovered, that was woefully too little too late.

Dumbfounded, young Ensign Ward watched as the troops under the command of Captain Claude-Pierre Pecaudy, Sieur de Countrecoeur, disembarked, formed into units, and made ready to advance on his position.

Laboring alongside his men, Anton de Chevalier grasped a wheel spoke of one of the guns they had mounted and assisted its crew in manhandling it into position. "A few more yards, men," he exhorted, as he felt he was required to. "Quickly now," Anton commanded between huffs and grunts as he threw his weight into moving the massive gun carriage over the broken ground. "We must move quickly, before the English have a chance to turn on us."

"I would not be too concerned about that, sir," an old sergeant stated as he paused for a moment from his efforts on the other side of the same gun that Anton was striving to wheel forward. "I do not think we have much to fear from the English today."

Calling a brief halt to their labors, Anton stood upright. As he wiped the sweat from his brow with a rag that served him for a handkerchief, he surveyed the scene now laid out before him. The slope they were standing on gave way to a point of level land that was bordered on their right by the Allegheny River, and on their left, not very far off, by another river, known as the Monongahela. Where these two bodies of water met, at the tip of land before him, they formed the

Ohio, a wide, gentle body of water that cut its way through the narrow opening between the forest-covered mountains that rose on either side. Despite his training, Anton found himself, as he had been at the great falls, overwhelmed by the natural spectacle that lay before him. Slowly, the hand holding the handkerchief fell away from his face, now lit with an expression of utter amazement. "Oh, my," he exclaimed out loud. "How beautiful."

The old sergeant, his eyes fixed on the ramshackle collection of logs and earthworks that Ward's men had attempted to fashion into a defensible stockade, smiled and nodded. "Yes, my lord, it is indeed a grand sight. They have no cannon."

With a shake of his head, Anton turned to see what it was that his sergeant was referring to. When he saw the old campaigner's eyes fixed on the chaos that their appearance had thrown the English camp into, Anton again shook his head, as if to clear it of an unwanted thought. With a blink of his eyes, he was able to return his full attention to his military responsibilities. "Ah, yes. I see," he muttered as he tried to hide his embarrassment at being so easily distracted from his duties. "No cannon at all."

Turning his attention to the labors of another crew as they ran their gun up next to the one he and his ensign had been working forward, the sergeant grunted. "I think we will be ready in a few more minutes, sir."

Clear-headed now, and back on task, Anton looked about, taking note of how the men behind the field pieces went about stacking the barrels of powder, shot, and canister. They were well drilled, he saw, and quite eager to get on with their duties. Those men detailed to serve the guns prepared themselves and their assigned gun for action. The tools of trade they wielded were varied and highly specialized, like the art of gunnery itself. There was the rammer, used to drive home the shot and powder brought up from the rear of the piece. Affixed to another pole as thick and as long as the rammer was a sponge. Dipped in a bucket of river water placed near the barrel, the sponge was used to swab out the barrel to extinguish any burning fragments of powder that might remain in the barrel after firing and before the ladle with a set scoop of powder was run down the bore for the next shot. Behind the gun stood a gunner holding a long wooden hand spike, designed to fit into a hole on the gun carriage so that the gun could be aligned with its target. And, of course, there was the linstock, with its twin metal heads holding the slow-burning match needed to ignite the powder when all was ready for firing.

With satisfaction, Anton watched his men go about their duties. He turned to the stockade that passed as an English fort and went about the chore of estimating range. His guns were on ground slightly higher than that where the English fortifications stood. Anton would have to take that into consideration. And they were not that far away, a fact, he had been warned by veterans of previous campaigns in New France, that was a major feature of most battles. He would need to take care that he did not overshoot the target.

When he was satisfied that he had worked out the problem in his head, Anton walked to the rear of the first piece and, with great deliberateness, went about the task of sighting it. This one, he decided, would be aimed left of center of the crude stockade. When all was as he desired, he moved to the next gun and personally aligned its barrel with the center of the stockade. The third gun would be targeted to the right of center, while the fourth gun would be used to shell the log storehouse that stood in the middle of the English works. The old sergeant, always wary of new officers, watched in silent approval as Anton went about his duties in a calm and methodical manner. If the young ensign had any fear about the approach of his first battle, the old soldier thought, he was not allowing it to show.

If the truth were known, the fact that this was his first battle, and that men, both his and English, might soon be dying, had somehow totally escaped Anton's attention. Always the diligent student, whether studying the esoteric thoughts of great philosophers or the black art of gunnery, Anton applied his whole being to the task at hand with a single-mindedness that forced aside all feelings and thoughts not immediately associated with the matter before him. Though he could see the raw recruits commanded by Ensign Ward, Anton's mind didn't allow itself to be cluttered with the fact that these were human beings whom he was preparing to blow to pieces. He, an ensign of artillery, had been presented a problem and was expected to solve it. And that was that.

Ready, Anton stood up and adjusted his vest. "Sergeant," he announced, "please inform Captain Le Mercier that we are ready."

From their commanding position, Anton and his gunners waited with lit matches ready to be applied to their primed and loaded cannon as Captain Le Mercier, the expedition's second in command, marched forward with flags flying and drums beating. Stopping midway between his five hundred soldiers arrayed in line of battle and the English stockade, Le Mercier waited until a lone figure, Ensign Ward himself, ventured forward from his stockade. When the two officers met, Le Mercier saluted the disheveled Virginia officer with great flourish and handed him a written demand for immediate surrender.

Unschooled in the European niceties of war, Ward endeavored to stall. He attempted to convince Le Mercier that he, the third-ranking officer of the company charged with defending the forks of the Ohio, did not have the authority to surrender his post. He needed time, he insisted, to contact his superiors.

Le Mercier was unimpressed with Ward's feeble plea. With measured nonchalance, Le Mercier drew his watch from his vest pocket, noted the time, and informed Ensign Ward that he had exactly one hour to make up his mind.

For a moment, the young provincial officer looked at Le Mercier, the forces arrayed behind the Frenchmen, and the cannon aimed at his motley collection of recruits cowering behind their makeshift defense. He had no need to turn around and survey his own command. Any effort to resist such a host, he knew, would be futile. Besides, resistance would not only expose the men under his command to death in battle but would leave them open to an even worse fate, that of a slow, tortuous death at the hands of the French's

Indian allies, who hovered off to one side of the field waiting for their chance to strike. With bowed head and a broken spirit, Ward muttered his agreement to the French terms. Without a shot being fired, all the vast territories that touched the Ohio River, and all rivers that flowed into it, passed from the English king to the French.

The reactions of those who participated in this brief yet monumental event were varied. Anton, rather then being relieved, was keenly disappointed. Having overcome all the obstacles associated with hauling his guns and munitions this far, and having personally computed the angles of fire needed to destroy the English fort, he was disappointed that he was being denied the opportunity to see if his solution to the problem worked. Sensing this, the old gunner sergeant walked over to him as he brooded over a campfire that night and tried to console him. "This, my lord," he predicted, "is only the beginning. You are young. Our king will provide you with many more chances to earn your pay, as he has done so many times for me."

For Toolah also, the rapid English capitulation was a bitter disappointment. "The English are dogs," he screamed as he tried to control his fury at being denied the opportunity to collect more scalps and coup. "They do not deserve the title of men." Though tempted to ignore the warnings that the English were not to be attacked, Toolah held his anger in check, this time.

Amazed by his brother's display of restraint, Gingego pondered the meaning of the day's events. Though the English colonists were numerous, and boasted of cheaper trade goods that were superior to those offered by French traders, their performance at the forks of the Ohio had not been impressive. The ease of the French victory, not to mention the sheer disparity in numbers and the condition of the troops arrayed on both sides, had been startling. The French, Gingego decided, were going to be the victors in any future wars with the English settlers. His ancestors, Gingego saw clearly that night, had been wise to leave their Mohawk brethren and follow the French. Now it would be necessary to learn more of these whites, people, he saw, who would dominate the lives of his people and all the lands they touched. Whether or not that would be good, Gingego knew, could not be seen, not now.

What was certain, Gingego convinced himself as he stared into the fire while he ignored his brother's ravings, was that he needed to find a middle path. There had to be a place between the extremes where his brother stood and a world totally dominated by whites, such as the invasion that the English settlers promised. The young French officer, perhaps, was the key, a key he had in his hand for the taking.

CHAPTER FIVE

The Great Meadows,
in Western Pennsylvania
May, 1754

NEITHER GRUNTS nor oaths could achieve what Ian Mc-Pherson's skills as a wheelwright and his persistence could not. With a note of dejection in his voice, Ian told Private John Miller, who had been helping him, to step back and let go of the wheel he was holding up. As soon as he did, the heavy wagon wheel slid off the improvised axle Ian had fashioned and down onto the ground with a thump. The clumsy farm wagon wheel, itself damaged through hard use over a forest road that was little more than a winding path, wobbled but a foot or two before it flopped over onto its side, wobbled a bit more, then settled in the meadow grass like a great weight.

From under a nearby tree, Babtist Hasty, who should

have been helping Ian and Miller, called out, "Told ya it won't work. Could see that from here."

Miller, soaked in sweat, took off his hat and wiped his forehead with the sleeve of his shirt. Pulling his hat back on, he glared at Hasty. "Well," he growled, "if ya had spent more time over here, given' us a hand, maybe we would've gotten somewhere."

Hasty smirked, waved his hand at Miller, and took a long sip of rum. Everyone knew Hasty was pilfering more than his fair share of rum from the small stock they had, but no one could prove it. "Well, now," he grunted, "if I was gettin' paid to be a wheelwright, I'd have been glad to join you, lads. But," he concluded, "I signed up for eight pence a day to soldier. Far as I'm concerned, that's all I'm obliged to do."

Miller turned to Ian, who was shaking his head as he stood before the hand-fashioned axle, hands on his hips, staring at it in an effort to decide what to do next. "I wish he'd left with Trent's boys when they up and decided to leave this ragged collection our esteemed colonel calls a regiment," Miller grumbled.

His mind on other things, Ian wasn't following what Miller was talking about. So absorbed by the task at hand, it took Ian a few moments before he even realized that Miller had been addressing him. "Leaving?" Ian asked dumbly. "Who's leaving?"

Angered that Ian hadn't been following his comments, Miller pointed to Hasty. "That worthless clout. I said, I wish he had left with Trent's gaggle of backwoodsmen."

Ian looked over to Hasty, who was starting to doze off with a smile on his face. "I don't see how he could've," Ian responded. "Trent's boys had a legitimate excuse for goin'. Trent had promised 'em two shillin's a day, and I don't think Colonel Washington's obliged to pay them that, seein' as we're only getting eight pence for the same work and duty."

Astonished by Ian's attitude, Miller shook his head. "We stand here, one hundred and fifty souls, pitifully armed, with the barest of supplies and no hope of support, tasked with facing down thousands of French regulars who are sniffing us out as we speak and *you* side with that scum that ran out on us? Are you daft?"

Ian smiled. "They say that there're not even a thousand Frenchies at the forks of the Ohio, so how can they send more after us than what they have?"

"Who," Miller demanded, "told you that rubbish?"

"One of the Half King's Indians. They should know," Ian insisted. "They've been following 'em as they bumbled about in the woods."

With a look of disbelief, Miller shook his head. "Damn, boy," he stuttered. "You know as well as I do you can't trust any of them. An Indian will tell you whatever it is they think you want to hear and go their merry way, laughing at ya behind your back."

For a moment, Ian thought about Miller's comment. Though he hadn't paid much attention to the Indians who followed the regiment about, for the life of him, Ian could not remember seeing anything even approaching a smile on those he had seen, let alone hearing them laugh. Not that there was much to laugh about. Slowly, Ian looked about the field of grass they were camped in. Seeing the whole command gathered there for the first time since leaving Winchester, Ian realized just how few of them there were. Yet as bad as that fact was, even more appalling was their wretched condition. That, together with a near total lack of even the most fundamental training, left little to laugh about. By now, the reign of misfortune that had been the hallmark of this expedition had managed to turn even the most optimistic man in the regiment into a pessimist.

First, there was the problem of supplies, which never seemed to be plentiful. Promised that they would find both wagons and rations at Winchester, Colonel Washington and his tiny band had been disappointed not only by their absence but by the attitude of the locals. Time and again they were told that there wasn't a scrap of food or a wagon to be spared anywhere in the whole of Frederick County, though none of the inhabitants seemed to be lacking for sustenance. Frustrated, their regimental lieutenant colonel had attempted to use his authority to confiscate those wagons he needed. When a warrant for Washington's arrest was issued after an aborted attempt to take a wagon, only the use of armed force and a quick departure of his command kept the commander of the Virginia Regiment from being incarcerated.

Those wagons that had been purchased or procured were, of course, often in a sad state. Knowing of Ian's skills, Captain Shaw offered his services to maintain the regiment's wagons. Though Ian protested, reminding Shaw in a heated exchange that he had no intention of taking up his former trade, Shaw managed to bribe him by offering Ian a promotion to corporal. Since Ian assumed this meant more pay, he took it, though grudgingly. It was along the slow and arduous march to Willis Creek, located on the Potomac River in western Maryland, that Ian came to appreciate his assignment of tending to the wagons. As difficult as it was to keep the dilapidated relics the regiment depended upon for transportation moving, Ian's labors paled in comparison to the task of cutting a road through the dense wilderness that lay between Winchester and Willis Creek. Mile by painful mile, the small band of provincial soldiers hewed a road able to support wagons where before there had been little more than a foot path. John Miller, sent back to help Ian when his hands became too blistered to hold an ax, did whatever he could to keep from returning to the backbreaking work that consumed most of the regiment's time and effort. "A trade," Miller would repeat time and again. "That's what separates honest men from common laborers and slaves. I always knew it to be so. Now all I need to do is find one that fits my temperament."

Unsure of what it meant to be a corporal or to supervise others, Ian simply dealt with Miller as an equal and a friend. This served him well, on most occasions. At other times, however, it failed him utterly. When Babtist Hasty was sent back to Ian, he tried the same approach that had worked so well with Miller. Hasty, a malcontent from the word *go*, could not be won over by friendship or fair treatment. Instead, he used Ian's lack of experience in leadership to cease all useful labors and, as most suspected, rob what little supplies they had.

At first Ian paid no heed to this, since word had been passed down the line that there would be ample supplies awaiting them when they arrived at Willis Creek. If any of the men in the ranks doubted this, they didn't let on. Still, it wasn't that much of a shock when they arrived to find that this promise, like so many of the others, was as hollow as their ranks. "We're on a fool's errand, me boys," Hasty repeated. "And we're all fools if we keep at this."

But keep at it they did. Even when word of Ward's surrender to the French and the very real danger of combat with regulars reached their tiny camp, their lieutenant colonel kept them to task and moving on. "We're to make our way to where Redstone Creek meets the Monongahela, cutting road all the way," Shaw told Ian. "There, we'll cache our supplies and munitions, fortify ourselves, and await the rest of the regiment."

"And then?" Ian asked innocently.

Shaw grunted, cast a wary eye toward the head of the column, where Washington was, and answered Ian's question halfheartedly. "Why, then, my lad, we march to the forks of the Ohio."

Realizing that this meant an open confrontation with the French, Ian asked no more about his commander's plans. Instead, he limited his thoughts and labors to the chore of keeping their few wagons from becoming fewer as each tortuous turn of the wagons' wheels took them farther into the wilderness.

Ian was still working on the wagon axle that had dominated his entire afternoon when a commotion on the far end of the clearing caught his attention. Standing up and wiping his hands on a rag whose every thread was permeated with dirt, Ian looked across the meadow. "Looks like someone's found the Frenchies, John."

Miller, working next to Ian, also stood up. "Well," he mused, "had to happen sooner or later, I guess."

"Yes," Ian agreed as he watched Captain Shaw turn away from a gathering of officers and head over to where Ian stood. "I guess that's why we came all this way."

"McPherson," Shaw called out as he approached. "Put up your tools, fetch your musket, and bring your little band over. We have some troubles we need to tend to."

The troubles, as Captain Shaw put it, were, indeed, the French. As Ian took his place with the other twenty-odd soldiers of Shaw's company, he watched their commander. Lieutenant Colonel Washington seemed excited by the prospect of a confrontation as he stood next to the Indian messenger who had brought him word from the Half King that he had found the French encampment. Ian studied him for a moment, wondering if his skill in battle would match his martial appearance. "I cannot tell," Ian commented dryly to John Miller, "if our young colonel is up to this."

Miller, who was busy adjusting the cartridge box and canteen straps to where they were comfortable, looked up at Washington for a moment, wrinkled his nose, and went back to what he was doing while he responded to Ian. "Can't say that I am," he stated bluntly. Pausing, Miller turned his face toward the threatening clouds that hung low over the meadow. "That's especially true seein' how's it's gonna rain like no one's business before too long."

With little more than a glance at the gray early-evening skies that seemed to trap the warmth and humidity, Ian went back to his thoughts. "Back in the Highlands, you could look a man in the eyes and tell if he was to be trusted or not. Here, it's not so easy."

"That," Miller responded as he twisted one way, then another, to make sure that his equipment was suitably arranged, "is part of being a gentleman." Satisfied, Miller looked up at Washington. "I suppose he means well and, given half a chance, will make something of himself. I just wish he'd be a little less conscious about his social standing. The governor's back in Williamsburg, where I hope he stays. There's no need to impress us, not out here."

"That's just what I mean," Ian replied. "A clan chief was a clan chief. He didn't need any fancy uniforms, nor did he have to go about struttin' like a prize cock to prove his worth. If he had the look, the clan would follow. If not, well, he was a lonely man."

As Captain Shaw slowly walked among his men in the gathering darkness, Miller looked back up at the sky. "Well, if we don't get moving soon, it's gonna be darker than a witch's heart and our colonel's gonna find himself a lonely man indeed."

It was quite dark before the band of forty men, led by the Indian guide, left the Great Meadows. And, as Miller had predicted, the rains came, washing away what little enthusiasm their colonel had managed to whip up in his men. Stumbling forward, they made their way through a night that was as gloomy and miserable as any Ian could remember. At times, he found himself bent over, groping about in the rain in the pitch-black forest in an effort to find the trail whenever he became separated from the man in front of him. At other times, he and the men around him found themselves waiting in the downpour as another of their party searched for the path that someone farther ahead had lost. Reduced to a state of near blindness, Ian eventually contented himself with simply keeping up with the man in front of him. Occasionally he felt a hand reach out and tap his back or grope desperately at his cross belts as Miller groveled about in the darkness behind him. Ian, however, was too exhausted, too wet, and too demoralized to care whether Miller kept up.

It was dawn before they ended their night-long ordeal. Soaked, exhausted, and chilled to the bone, Washington's small band, reduced by the loss of seven men who had lost their way sometime during the night, staggered into the Indians' small encampment. This, too, was a disappointment when it was discovered that the Half King had but seven armed warriors, two of whom were mere boys, eroding many of the men's spirits even before they had a chance to rally. "We're on another fool's errand," Miller moaned as he dropped to the soggy ground. "We break our necks gettin' here and find less than we bargained for. Boys, I'm done in. Wake me when it's over."

Miller and the rest of the disheartened Virginians were not given an opportunity to give in to their exhaustion. Their commander, once launched upon this enterprise, intended to see it through. After rousing his men once more and setting them to the task of drying and priming their weapons, Washington convinced the Half King to send two of his king's men to scout out the French camp. Unable to escape from the inevitability of the coming confrontation, communicated by

Washington's very manner, each of the men set about making himself ready.

It took little time for Ian to put his weapons in order. He had taken great care, despite the adversity the previous night had heaped upon him and his companions, to protect his musket's lock and his cartridge box. Though some of the paper cartridges were wet, especially those that had been on the outer edges of the box near the stitching, most seemed dry and sound. Those that were suspect were carefully set to the side farthest from the side that Ian would start drawing them from. When he was finished, Ian set aside his musket, fished a chunk of dried beef from his pocket, and settled back against a tree to enjoy his meager rations while he waited for the word to move out.

Miller, dabbing a half-soaked rag about the open priming pan of his musket, paused and looked up at Ian. "You've been in a fight or two, haven't you?"

Like Shaw, Ian never spoke of his exploits or experiences during "the '45," as the last Jacobite Rebellion was referred to. It wasn't because of shame, for Ian knew he had done the right thing. Rather, Ian found that he kept to himself all that he had seen and done then simply because he didn't quite know how to deal with it all. His mother had raised him to be a God-fearing Christian, yet the male members of the clan had raised him to be a Highland warrior, ready and able to fight all the clan's enemies. He had been taught to care for the cattle that his family was charged with tending, nursing those that were injured with the same loving care that his mother showered upon his younger brothers and sisters. Yet when he had answered the call of the pipes and followed his officers into battle, Ian had found he could use the same hands that had healed a lame animal to take another man's life. He knew he was no beast, for he saw what beasts men could be as British dragoons rode down the survivors of Culloden with a glee in their eyes that was itself quite terrifying. Yet, Ian also appreciated the fact that he was not innocent. He had spilled another man's blood and had found that there wasn't a hint of regret in his soul. Faced with this great paradox that followed him like a shadow, Ian refrained from sharing these thoughts with others.

"Funny," Miller went on when he saw that Ian wasn't going to answer. "Both you and Shaw fought before, for the same thing I guess, and yet neither of you admit to it."

Carefully setting the half-eaten lump of meat aside, Ian drew the ancient broadsword from his belt. Carefully grasping the tip of its blade with his free hand, he slowly inspected the weapon. "No two men," Ian whispered in quiet, somber tones without taking his eyes from the sword his ancestors had passed down from one generation of warriors to the next, "ever fight for the same thing. Though there may be many a clansman standing under the same banner, the reason that took each of them there is as different as the men themselves. And only they know the reason."

Miller nervously chuckled at Ian's sudden transformation into a philosopher. "I don't believe that, and neither do you. Take you and me. We're both here 'cause we want the land the governor promised us. We're just as anxious to get our share of this country as our dear Colonel Washington and his land-hungry cohorts are."

With great deftness, Ian let go of the sword's tip and swung it until it was inches in front of Miller's nose. "Kind sir," Ian stated in a deep, menacing voice, "if it was only land I was truly after, you can rest assured I'd have found a far safer way to procure it. No," he said as he lifted the blade up and over his head, his eyes following the tip, "there is something else I'm after, I think. Something my heart is keeping hidden from even me."

Miller, confused by Ian's gibberish and a bit concerned that this man he had put his faith into might be a bit soft in the brain, drew away from him. Without another word, he went back to drying his musket as Ian sat there, in the early morning gloom, staring at the tip of a sword held motionless before him.

With the same skill he had used many a time when sneaking up on rival herders in the Highlands of Scotland, Ian cautiously made his way between trees and boulders. Always, as he picked his way forward, he kept an eye on the gaggle of thirty-odd Frenchmen below him, watching, waiting for any sign that they had detected him or another member of Washington's small band. As each second passed, and each footstep took Ian closer to the spot where he would take up position and wait for the command to fire, he lost more respect for the French. They were, he had been told, professionals, veteran campaigners. Yet, Ian and many of his companions marveled at how they were lounging about in a deep, rock-strewn ravine they had bivouacked in without a single sentinel, as if they were still in Canada. They were either totally confident in their concealment and stealth to date or not nearly as dangerous a foe as he had been led to believe. Whatever the reason, Ian thought as he looked about the rim of the ravine, catching an occasional glimpse of another Virginian moving into position, their error will make this enterprise far easier than he had feared.

Still, he noticed, his body was preparing itself for battle. Only through a concerted effort was Ian able to control his breathing as it threatened to outrace his heart, which was pounding in his chest. The familiar taste of bile, rising from the pit of his stomach, burned his tongue like a vile acid. And the sweat, beading up on his face and the back of his hands, formed little rivulets that ran down along his skin, stinging his eyes and making his grip on his musket slippery. Even while his mind soared at the sight of a hapless foe, Ian's instincts prepared his body.

In the end, it was good that his instincts were so keen, so attuned to the reality of the situation. While Ian was still several feet from the spot he was headed to, a Frenchman below threw down the cup he had been holding and let out a panicked scream. As he watched the alerted Frenchman's companions leap for their arms, neatly stacked amid their overnight campsite, Ian heard Colonel Washington's voice bellow out the order to fire. Deciding there was no need or time to take up a proper position, Ian raised his musket to his shoulder, brought the barrel to bear on a tall Frenchman about to lay his hands on his musket, and fired. Though the aim had been quick, and his musket far from the most reliable weapon ever manufactured, Ian saw that his shot had been true. Even before the smoke of his own musket cleared from before him, Ian could see the stricken Frenchman staggering backward, throwing his arms about wildly in an effort to grasp something to arrest his pending fall. Unable to do so before consciousness abandoned him, the Frenchman flopped over backward on the ground, quivered a moment or two, then fell still.

With his head now clear and all prebattle nausea whisked away by the smell of burned powder, Ian settled down to reloading his piece. Not having spent enough time drilling, he found that he needed to divide his attention between his immediate task at hand and keeping an eye open to the confusion all about him. Here and there, along the rim of the ravine, puffs of dirty white smoke marked the location of his fellow Virginians as they took their shots.

The Frenchmen, reeling from their initial surprise, seemed to be doing a great deal of running about and very little firing. In the midst of this pandemonium stood a French officer, clearly dismayed by all that was going on about him and the terrible misfortune that had befallen him. With sword drawn, he looked in vain to find a way out of the trap that was enveloping his tiny command. From Ian's standpoint, it was difficult to tell who was more confused, the attackers or the French. All about him he caught glimpses of fellow Virginians working their pieces as quickly as their fingers let them while searching for something substantial to hide behind. It was a blessing, Ian thought as he brought his musket up to fire again, that the French commander didn't have the slightest clue as to how fragile his assailants' command really was. One full-blown rush, Ian thought, by a handful of determined men wielding bayonets would be all that was needed to scatter Washington's band.

Fortunately, Ian's supposition was not put to the test. Blind to everything but the fact that their companions were being mercilessly cut down all about them, the French turned away from the semicircle of fire that was raining down upon them from the lip of the ravine and began to run. This effort, however, was arrested in its tracks almost as quickly as it began when the Half King and his warriors, who had been encircling the French when the firing began, came rushing, head-on, at the fleeing French. Completely shaken by this, the

French turned and ran, this time straight for the Virginians. Throwing down those weapons they had managed to secure, they waved their hands frantically above their heads in a desperate attempt to surrender to white soldiers.

Anxious to seize his first victory in battle, Washington was up and stumbling down the rocky sides of the ravine as fast as his feet could carry him. Those around him, not knowing what else to do, followed. Ian, not having heard any command, didn't know whether the colonel had ordered them forward or whether they were simply caught up by the same enthusiasm that was driving Washington onward. Whatever the case, he didn't join. Instead, Ian stood his ground and reloaded his musket, watching with a strange detachment as the Indians who had cinched this victory for them went about the task of slaughtering their hapless foe. With grim fascination, Ian watched an Indian warrior grasp the pigtail of a French soldier, still in his death throes, and scalp the stricken man. With one quick, clean cut across the forehead followed by a swift cut toward the rear of the head, the warrior freed the skin and its attached hair enough so that one good rearward jerk was all that was needed to separate the Frenchman's hair from his skull. It was, Ian thought, not at all different from skinning a rabbit.

"Good God, Ian," Miller exclaimed, coming up and bumping into him as he stumbled on a tree root. "Look at those bloody savages have at it! Have you ever seen anything like it in your life?"

The image of a stack of dead clansmen, piled four high and dismembered by point-blank artillery fire, flashed before Ian's eyes. Without a hint of emotion, Ian turned and faced Miller. "Aye, I have." With that, he turned his back on the chaos that was playing out below him as Virginians struggled to save the very men they had just tried to kill from their own allies.

CHAPTER SIX

Fort Duquesne, at the
Forks of the Ohio
June, 1754

STEPPING BACKWARD from the six-pound gun mounted on
the bastion, Anton de Chevalier surveyed the open space that
lay between the newly constructed fort and the woods to the
east. As he did so, it struck him as funny that little more than
two months before, he had been standing out there, in those
very woods, with the very same gun, facing down an enemy
defender who was standing on the very spot he was now preparing to defend himself.

Turning, Anton looked over the compact but well-built
fortification that he, and just about every man on the expedition, had labored so hard to build. Starting the day after the
English had been ejected, Captain Le Mercier had thrown
himself into this task by tearing down every vestige of for-

tification that the Englishmen had thrown up. His, he had bragged, would be a proper military work, built using the same principles that had made so many of Vauban's fortresses in France works of art that were all but impregnable. Though time and monetary constraints prevented him from using stone and masonry, the material Le Mercier had at hand was quite good. Even the walls and bastions facing the river, considered to be safe from a serious direct attack, were made of massive log pickets measuring a foot in diameter and standing twelve feet out of the ground. From firing platforms built inside the fort, French defenders could shoot down and out, through slanted loopholes, at any assailant foolish enough to try the fort from that quarter.

It was in the construction of the curtain walls and two bastions facing east from the jutting tongue of land where Le Mercier and his men had put the bulk of their effort. While still using logs, here they were laid horizontally to build huge cribs that were filled in with dirt that was scraped away from a dry ditch that surrounded the entire fort. Standing fourteen feet on the outside and measuring twelve feet thick, these bastions would not only protect the defenders, they would provide Anton and his guns with elevated, shell-proof firing platforms from which he could resist an English attempt to wrestle back the forks of the Ohio, like the French had so recently done themselves. "When the English come," his sergeant mused as he stood next to Anton on the bastion, "they'll not have an easy time like we had. No," he exclaimed as he slapped the barrel of the six-pounder beside him, "they shall have to shed more than mere sweat."

Leaning up against the wheel of the gun carriage, Anton folded his arms. "You know, they say that those provincial cutthroats who murdered Lieutenant Jumonville in late May are but the lead detachment of an English army numbering over five thousand."

Turning, the sergeant gave his ensign a knowing, fatherly smile. "I do not mean to tell an officer such as you what is right and wrong, my lord, for I am but a humble gunner. But," he said as he looked out over the vast assembly of Indian huts and soldiers' tents that all but filled every open space between the fort and the forest, "any foe foolish enough to venture this far from the colonies on the coast would not last long here, in the wilderness. There is no road or river that will permit the English to haul their guns, munitions, provisions, and fodder to this place as we have done."

"They will come," Anton insisted. "They already have a fort not eighty miles from here."

The old veteran of many campaigns would not be shaken from his convictions. "They are like a leaf, hanging by the narrowest of stems at the end of a long, weak twig." Pointing to the Indians below, the sergeant's smile grew. "While it is true that our savage friends will not stand up like proper soldiers in battle, and they fight only when they choose, I would not want to be faced by them out here, in a forest they claim as theirs. While we clear the forest wherever we go in an effort to protect ourselves, they flow through this savage wilderness with the ease of fish swimming in the sea. When it is their wish, they will break that twig the English are hanging on to for dear life, leaving the English leaf to wither and die."

Though the sergeant's argument was quite compelling, Anton knew better than to allow himself to be lulled into a false sense of security. "Well, perhaps that is all true. But I will tell you this. I will be much more at ease when the English have been thrown back from the place they call the Great Meadows."

With a wink, the sergeant nodded his head. "It would seem, sir, your wish is soon to be fulfilled."

Though he never quite understood how his sergeants always seemed to know what was about to happen well in advance of him, Anton stood upright as he eyes flew open. "An expedition? Are we sending an expedition against them?"

The sergeant nodded. "Yes, my lord. Soon."

Looking about, Anton's eyes darted about the fort's parade ground, searching for his superior. If there was going to be an expedition against the English fort, he told himself, he was going to be part of it. After all, as important as building the fort and defending it were, it was in battle where an officer made his mark. "Ah," Anton stammered, "I must find Captain

Le Mercier. Would you be so good as to finish the work here and release the men as soon as you are satisfied with the sighting of the piece?"

With a salute and a smile, the sergeant acknowledged his ensign's orders and watched him scurry down the ladder in search of Le Mercier. "The young gentleman," a Canadian offered as he watched Anton disappear into the press of men gathered on the parade ground, "is in a hurry to die."

The old sergeant folded his arms and watched his ensign go, too. "No, my friend. He is in a hurry to live. I only hope the boy survives long enough to discover that there is a difference between seeking something which he has not seen or experienced and living."

Fort Necessity, in the Great Meadows
June, 1754

THEIR success over the small French party in April had failed to bring Washington's Virginians any rewards or relief. If anything, the confrontation that had resulted in the bloody deaths of ten Frenchmen at the cost of only one Virginian's life had multiplied the problems Washington and his small command faced. Now there was no question that open hostilities would prevail the next time the two sides met. This thought increased, rather than diminished, the stress of the campaign. "When they come again," Ian dryly commented one day as he posted John Miller as sentinel at the entrance of the small stockade they had built at the Great Meadows, "they'll not be taken so easy. They'll come at us with far more than we can handle. In the end," he concluded as he surveyed the low-lying hills that hemmed them in on all sides, "the only land we'll be left to lay claim to is that upon which our miserable bones will be left to be bleached white in the sun."

This state of affairs in itself would have been cause enough for concern. But it was only one of the problems facing the command. Perhaps of more immediate concern, since it was a matter that faced the men each and every waking hour, was that of food. When the last of the flour rations had been issued in the first week of June, their already dismal diet was reduced to little more than beef and parched corn. The coming of summer, heralded by heat, violent thunderstorms, and the appearance of hordes of black flies, together with the poorly butchered meat rations, filth, and strenuous labors, added sickness to the regiment's growing list of woes. Diarrhea and dysentery, always a soldier's companion on long campaigns, was soon threatening to do what the French had, to date, failed to. Only the speed with which their morale was failing exceeded the rapidity of the declining physical condition of the soldiers of the Virginia Regiment.

The arrival of the first reinforcements did little to reverse this trend. In many ways, it worsened it. For the help that came into the Great Meadows was an independent company of regulars from Charleston, South Carolina, dressed in the brilliant scarlet of English regulars. The disdain and disciplined formality with which the soldiers of Captain James Mackey's company conducted themselves when dealing with the Virginians annoyed Ian and his companions. For, despite the uniform and the quality and quantity of their equipment, most of the rank and file of the Virginia Regiment saw that these men were not much different than themselves. They had been recruited, John Miller pointed out to Ian, like the Virginians, from the idle and unemployed of their colony, by Mackey, a native of South Carolina himself. "Only difference," John Miller scoffed as he watched them go about their routine in a camp they kept separate from the Virginians, "is their officer has the king's commission, and ours, well . . ."

But Ian knew it was more than that. He saw it, his captain saw it, and Ian had little doubt that their young regimental commander saw it. Unlike Washington and his officers, Mackey was a regular army officer, and nothing else. His whole purpose in life was to train and maintain his company. He had no political ambitions, at least none that Ian or any of the Virginians could determine. He was not here, in a place that wasn't even Virginia, intent on securing landholdings for ruthless speculators who would never set eyes on the property they hoped to convert into a neat profit for themselves. Instead, Mackey lived by the king's regulations, followed his orders, and carried out his duties as he saw fit.

This warrant, much to the anger of the Virginians and surprise of Washington, did not include physical labor or participation in foolhardy adventures against a numerically superior foe, which Washington insisted in pursuing despite conditions. "Worse than the meanest of Trent's lot," Miller snapped bitterly on more than one occasion. "The whole lot of them are worse than the lowest scoundrel amongst us. Imagine," he fumed as he made a face and threw away a bit of rotted meat he had picked out of his bowl. "They won't work. Not a one of 'em, unless they're given an extra shillin'. Why, that's three times what we're bein' given a day. Three times! Even their drummer puts on airs and struts about like a lord. I won't be surprised if, when the French come, they insist we load the muskets for them."

Despite their dismal plight, and the lack of support from an officer Washington considered subordinate in rank, the red-haired Virginia aristocrat insisted on pressing forward with their effort to cut a road north from the Great Meadows toward the forks of the Ohio. Washington had his orders, too. Lacking any changes or clarifications from the man who had granted him his commission, Washington turned his faltering command back to the task of marching to the forks of the Ohio.

The results, of course, were predictable. As they slowly inched their way north, mile after grueling mile, the Virginia Regiment staggered on, more from habit than from determination, cutting a road wide enough for cannon they did not have. Each tree felled, Ian grimly noted to himself, marked a further erosion of the regiment's strength rather than progress. Even desertion, despite the omnipresent threat of Indians that haunted most members of the regiment, was becoming preferable to the slow, agonizing death that Ian and his companions seemed to be condemned to.

For the most part, Ian kept these dark, foreboding thoughts to himself. On occasion, however, circumstances overwhelmed his self-imposed restraint. "Can't say that I blame 'em for desertin'," John Miller mused as he and Ian tugged at a stubborn tree trunk they were attempting to move. "If I could find a way out of this that left body and soul together, I'd be gone."

Unable to hold up his end, Ian let the trunk fall between his callused hands. "Then, what's keepin' ya here?" he snapped. "You're moaning more than Hasty ever did on his worst day. Least he did us the courtesy of up an' leavin'."

Angered by Ian's comparison of him to Hasty, a man who had never amounted to anything more than an excess mouth that had to be fed and listened to, Miller let go of his end of the tree trunk. "I'll not stand here and take such abuse from the likes of you," Miller growled. Without another word, he turned and stalked away, leaving Ian with the impossible task of moving the tree trunk and dealing with his growing despair.

Even the normally tight-lipped and stoic Captain Shaw began to buckle under the oppressive weight of his own growing apprehensions and let vent his anger. One evening, while Captain Shaw was in the middle of giving Ian instructions for the work he and his small detachment would be responsible for the next day, Shaw exploded. "Sometimes," he fumed as he crumpled the scrap of paper he had been reading from, "I don't know what that man is thinking!" Without mentioning his name, Ian knew Shaw was talking about their young colonel. "He starts a fracas with the French without so much as a warning, infuriates Mackey's regulars with his pompous attitude, and then drives us like dogs to build a road that'll be of little use to anyone except the French. What," Shaw asked in frustration as he glared at Ian, "is the man thinking?"

Embarrassed, Ian looked down at his feet. "I don't believe any of us are thinkin' clear anymore," he admitted. "I think we're just sort of doin' things hoping that somethin' good will turn up soon. I remember how it was, back in the '45, when we marched south into England after Falkirk. 'Twasn't a man amongst us, I'm sure, who thought we'd beat the English in their own country. But we had to go. We had to try. We couldn't just stand there, like they had us do at Culloden, and let 'em thrash us without tryin', could we?"

Shaw didn't answer. Instead, he shook his head and walked away, leaving Ian to wonder if his captain agreed with him or was simply just frustrated with the impossible circumstances he found himself in. Exhausted by his labors, wrung out from the effects of diarrhea that lingered despite everything he tried, and ever mindful that they grew weaker the farther north they went, Ian shrugged and went about his duties as best he could.

WITH great deliberateness, Ian marched his small detachment through the early summer grass, across the meadow, and toward the encampment of Captain Mackey's regulars. Only when he caught the first glimpse of their bright red uniforms, which stood out in stark contrast to the lush green all about them, did Ian become painfully aware of his own wretched condition.

Casting his eyes downward, he glanced at the shoe on his right foot held together by a thin flap of leather. His pants, worn every day since leaving Winchester in early April, were filthy and shredded with tears that no patch would ever be able to mend. Over them he wore a shirt that had once been white. Now, between the mud, the layers of dried sweat, and the grime of manual labor, it barely resembled the garment it once had been. Even his hat, a smart and very proper tricorner when he had bought it months before in far-off Alexandria, had long ago lost its shape. Its wide black brim now flopped about his head. His only other clothing, a vest and a coat, both equally disreputable and reduced to little more than rags, were wrapped in his threadbare blanket. This he carried slung over his right shoulder, rolled into a small, tight bundle held together by a wide leather strap he had stripped off the cartridge box of a dead French soldier. In addition to the blanket roll, hanging from straps arrayed about his body, were a haversack in which he carried his meager rations, a canteen, a cartridge box, and his weapons. Together with the clothes he wore, these comprised the sum total of Ian's worldly possessions.

Lifting his head took more effort than it should have. In his worst nightmare, Ian could not remember feeling this miserable, this weak. Even after Culloden, with English dragoons nipping at their heels day and night, Ian had never succumbed to the frailties of the body as he now appeared to be on the verge of doing. Perhaps, he thought as his clouded mind struggled with this, the very real danger of English horsemen riding him down had been more than enough to overcome physical hardships that had to have been as overwhelming as the ones he now faced.

Of course, he reminded himself as he labored to lift one foot and throw it out in front of the other, then he had been evading his foes through a countryside that was familiar, open, and friendly. Fortune had smiled on him when no door was barred to his pleas for refuge and succor while others had been cut down while they tried to escape. Yes, he thought warily as he glanced up at the looming hills and dense forests that surrounded the Great Meadows. That had been so different, so very different.

From behind him, John Miller, his voice raspy from exhaustion and thirst, called out to Ian, "You suppose they'll come?"

Another man in Ian's small party, Beverly Low, spit on the ground before Ian could answer. "The bastards haven't done much of anything since they've showed. What makes ya think they'll rouse their miserable bones to help us now?"

"Aye," James McPike replied. "Worthless! The whole pack of them are worthless."

"Ta think," Miller added, "here we are, laborin' day in and out like galley slaves and not a one of them will lift a finger to help 'cause manual labor isn't the business of a soldier of the Crown."

"Not unless," McPike shot back bitterly, "they gets their extra shillin'."

"They'll not come," Low concluded.

Ian led his small party a bit farther before he responded. "If this company from Carolina is anything like their English brethren, they'll come." Then, stopping midstride, Ian turned and looked at McPike. "You, of all people, should know that."

Though he hadn't risen to support Bonnie Prince Charlie as Ian and Shaw had, McPike had been afforded ample opportunity during the Great Clearance to see just how enthusiastic and thorough the king's troops could be. McPike had lost everything as English troops pulled down the only home he'd ever known and turned him and his family off the land that had provided them with their only livelihood. Letting his head drop low, McPike didn't respond. Satisfied that he had made his point, Ian straightened his tired body until it was as erect as he could manage and continued to head for the regulars' encampment.

Stopped at the perimeter of the independent company's camp by a sentinel, Ian and his small party waited for the sergeant of the guard to come forth. A tall fellow, wearing a red sash and the short sword of an English noncommissioned officer, made his way slowly toward the gaggle of Virginians, some of whom had dropped to the ground already. Ian had had a few dealings with this sergeant before Washington had marched his small command north to build the road. On those occasions, their conversations had been short and strained. "I have a dispatch for your captain," Ian called out as he fished in his haversack for Washington's hastily prepared request.

"What's it concern?" the sergeant snorted as he approached Ian. "I trust your *colonel* isn't asking for a detachment to help build his road. We've been over that. . . ."

Without waiting, Ian replied sharply, "The French are coming."

North of the Great Meadows
July, 1754

EAGER to avenge the murder of his brother at the hands of the English, Captain Coulon de Villiers had abandoned his artillery and heavy trains at Redstone Creek on the last day in June and force-marched his command of six hundred French regulars and militia and one hundred Indians in an effort to surprise the English in the open. Arriving at their abandoned camp two days later, de Villiers was disappointed to find that his foe had fled. Exhausted by his drive south, and now feeling very vulnerable surrounded by trackless forests deep in enemy territory, de Villiers came to the conclusion that this task was beyond the means of the seven hundred men he led. Without his wagons, which contained everything from tents to rations, de Villiers could not hope to survive very long. Even if he did manage to make his monotonous and meager rations last, the thought of coming face-to-face with an English force rumored to be receiving more than five thousand reinforcements, with little more than muskets, unnerved de Villiers.

The same thought, apparently, bothered some of de Villiers' Indian allies. The Algonquins were already deserting him. Others, he feared, would surely follow their example if and when it was learned that they were outnumbered by the English. While the Indians made up only a small portion of his force, the loss of their services as scouts would doom his expedition before a single shot was fired. Even nature, it seemed, conspired to dampen de Villiers' already sagging morale, as it started to rain.

While still teetering on the verge of abandoning his mission and returning north in failure, a gift walked into his camp on the northern end of the road blazed by the English. The bearer of the gift was a deserter from the English camp located some thirteen miles south of them. Wretched and demoralized, the Virginian, John Ramsey by name, told of the desperate and miserable plight of his fellow Englishmen. He relayed how, just days before, the Virginia Regiment and

Mackey's independent company had stood, right where the French now stood, preparing to make a stand. But then, fearing the superior French numbers, the Virginians and regulars had beat a precipitous retreat back to the stockade they had built at the Great Meadows. As far as reinforcements, the deserter knew of only one or two additional independent companies coming from other colonies that, as of the time he left, had not yet arrived.

While heartened by this turn of events, de Villiers was too good a soldier to simply take this man's story at face value. Of all the commodities that were needed to conduct military operations in the vast, savage wilderness in which the French, the English, and the Indians battled, knowledge of the enemy was perhaps the single most critical element required for success for de Villiers, as well as for the English. He could not discount the possibility that this man, despite his horrid condition and apparent honesty, was not, in fact, part of a plot to trick de Villiers into hastening his command forward into the waiting arms of a superior enemy force. Without cannon and no hope of relief from Fort Duquesne, those members of his force that were not swallowed up in such an ambush would die alone, in this jungle, either at the hands of the Indian allies of the English or from starvation.

Unable to come to a decision on his own, de Villiers gathered his officers together. No one spoke as they came into the small circle, soaked to the bone as they sat watching the water drip listlessly from their hats. Only when young Ensign Anton de Chevalier made his appearance was de Villiers tempted to smile. Anton, young, energetic, and infinitely curious about every new experience, found something to smile about even now, in the face of such a grave situation.

Dressed in moccasins, leggings, and a gray collarless coat worn over a simple linen shirt, Anton's clothing was indistinguishable from any of the other French officers and men under de Villiers' command. Yet there was no mistaking him with another. While everyone, including de Villiers himself, wore the stress and strain of the last few days' exertions and apprehensions like a heavy pack, Anton still moved about with the bounce of a young lover greeting the coming of spring. "I do not imagine," de Villiers stated blandly as Anton found himself a seat on a log that had been cut down by a Virginian only days before, "that you will be smiling for very long after I start."

Anton's expression changed little as he wiped aside a stray strand of wet hair that hung before his eyes. "Oh, fighting the English," he chirped. "Well, yes, I suppose that is a serious matter."

The innocence of his remarks, and the spontaneity of them, caused most of the officers gathered to laugh or, at least, chuckle. Anton's manner reminded some of the older officers, hardened by long, bitter campaigns in the wilderness, of their own youths and took heart. "Well," de Villiers continued, "perhaps you will soon be regretting leaving your cannon behind with your sergeant when I tell you what we are facing."

To this, Anton did not reply. Though he had little doubt that when the fighting began he would feel naked without a single cannon, Anton was, secretly, glad to have been allowed to continue with the expedition when it had been decided to leave the guns behind. That decision, which de Villiers had agonized over, had liberated Anton from his responsibilities, leaving him free to enjoy the rapid overland journey. Though still charged with duties concerning the night watch, guard, and the handful of one-pound swivel guns they had brought forward, such tasks interfered little with Anton's study of the countryside, his observations of the Canadians and Indians who made up the bulk of the force, or his conversations with Gingego. As with every other aspect of his life, Anton was able to shift his entire consciousness quickly from one matter to another with great agility and completeness. This led some to wonder if Anton was simpleminded, for no sane man, they concluded, could possibly enjoy the trials of campaigning with the zeal that Anton affected. One or two of the seven hundred French, Canadian, and Indians understood Anton, perhaps even better than Anton himself did. "He is a free spirit," Gingego tried to explain to his hotheaded brother, Toolah. "He does not yet know his place or his powers."

Having no use for whites of any nationality or persuasion, Toolah scoffed at his brother's attempt at explaining why he spent so much time with the French ensign. "I do not know where he belongs either, brother," Toolah barked in response. "But I do know that not he, nor any of his kind, belongs here, on our lands. Let him go back, from where the sun is born, and find his spirit there."

"The question I must place before you," de Villiers stated as he opened his council, "is a simple one. Do we accept what this Englishman says as the truth and move, at once, to attack them," de Villiers asked, pausing to allow this thought to take hold, "or," he continued, lowering his eyes and voice as he did so, "turn our backs on the enemy and slither away into the forest?"

Wide-eyed, for it was a novelty for Anton to be included in a council that would decide such a weighty matter, he looked about at the faces of the other officers around him. The faces he saw were grim, dirty, tired, and etched with deep concerns. There was, Anton thought as he looked around, no doubt how de Villiers felt. His choice of words made it clear that he wished to go on. What he was seeking here, Anton guessed, was not a debate, or even a decision. It was support, he deducted, for a decision that de Villiers himself had already made. What he hoped to gain from collective approval, Anton knew, was not a warm, comfortable feeling that he was doing right. Rather, it was collective responsibility. If, after the fact, it was found that the English deserter had been a trick and their expedition met with disaster, de Villiers could, provided he survived, point out that his officers had, during a council of war, concurred with his decision to go on.

When he had allowed enough time for his gathered officers to consider his question, de Villiers called for their views. As was the custom, he turned to the junior officer first. "Well, my friend," he asked Anton, "what do you say?"

Knowing that all eyes were upon him without needing to look, Anton shifted his weight from one side to the other before answering. "It would be," he started in a low, almost hesitant voice, "a sin to turn back now. We have all," he stated as he looked at his fellow officers, "traveled too far, toiled too long, and been afforded too many wonderful gifts from our enemy, such as this road and the deserter's information, to drop the matter here. I believe that we should go forward, if for no other reason than it is what our honor, as soldiers, demands."

From his seat, de Villiers smiled and nodded. Though many mocked the naïveté of this young ensign of artillery, none could fault his dedication and knowledge when it came to the profession of arms. "I am pleased to see," de Villiers commented before continuing his quest for approval, "that we are of like minds." With that as a warning, de Villiers turned to the next officer and asked for his opinion.

Gingego was waiting for Anton to return from the council of officers. The grave, contemplative expression worn by the young French officer told him all he needed to know. "Then, it has been decided that we shall trust the English deserter and attack."

Anton looked up, stared at Gingego with a blank expression for a moment as he cleared his mind of the thoughts he had been pondering, then shook his head. "Yes, we go forward." Then, as an afterthought, he added, "I am sure your brother will be pleased."

Gingego said nothing as Anton came up next to him, stopped, and looked about for Toolah. "He didn't leave with the Algonquins," Anton asked when he did not see Toolah at first, "did he?"

Gingego grunted. "He is off in the woods, together with some of the others."

"Preparing for battle?" Anton asked.

"Escaping, as he claims," Gingego bitterly responded, "the stench of the whites."

When the young French ensign turned to face him, Gingego could see the hurt Anton felt in the Frenchman's eyes. "Why," Anton stammered, "does he hate us so?"

Were it his nature, or that of his people, Gingego would have laughed at the ridiculousness of Anton's question. Why, Gingego thought, indeed. Was this man so naïve as to be blind to what the French had done to his people? Did he not understand that the war that they were embarking upon was between three peoples, and not simply the French and English? And if this was true, Gingego thought as he looked into Anton's eyes as he waited for an answer, how could he possibly explain it to one who had never been faced with the prospect of losing both his own soul and that of his people?

"He travels a different path," Gingego finally stated flatly before turning his back on Anton and heading off to make his own personal preparations for battle.

Bewildered by Gingego's conduct, Anton shrugged his shoulders. It must be, he concluded, that his friend was apprehensive and had no desire to talk. Most of the French and Canadian officers, after all, were feeling that way. That much was to be expected, Anton reasoned. After all, if a man of de Villiers' position, experience, and knowledge could be intimidated by their pending confrontation with an English force they so heavily outnumbered, it only stood to reason that a savage with only the sketchiest of education would also feel the same fear.

That he, himself, did not feel even the slightest twinge of fear never occurred to Anton as his mind turned away from Gingego and pounced on the immediate issue of preparing himself. Shaking his hands, covered with rain that had run down his soaked gray coat, Anton looked up through the branches overhead that all but blocked the sky above. The low, dark, gray clouds rolling along matched the mood of so many of the men about him. While raindrops pelted his face, forcing him to squint, Anton thought about the coming ordeal. It would be a miserable, messy affair, he decided. Perhaps, he thought, the English would see the errors of their ways, as those at the forks of the Ohio had, and leave without a fight. Wouldn't that be grand, he thought. Yes, he concluded. It would be another bloodless victory and an opportunity to enjoy, uninterrupted, his study of a land that continued to fascinate him as nothing had before.

CHAPTER SEVEN

The Great Meadows
July 3, 1754

WORD THAT the French were close at hand served to motivate every able-bodied man in Washington's command to new levels of achievement. Even Mackey's regulars set aside their well-instilled disdain for physical labor and threw in with the Virginians as they hurriedly dug trenches in the mud that surrounded the small wooden stockade mockingly named Fort Necessity.

Yet no last-minute effort, no matter how well directed or Herculean, could overcome the handicaps that faced the Virginians and Mackey's independent company. They were, Washington knew, out on a limb, alone, already reaching the end of their physical tether. Faced by a challenge that few were ready to meet, he had few illusions about his chances of success. Had his men been up to it, he would have preferred to continue his retreat to Willis Creek, where provisions and other troops had to be waiting. Everyone in the ranks expected that. Everyone in the ranks hoped for that.

But it did not happen. Or, more correctly, it could not happen. "I don't know," Ian confessed to Shaw after he had collapsed in the mud at his commander's feet in the midst of trying to throw a shovel full of heavy dirt over his shoulder, "if it's preferable to die here, in this muck and mire, or out there." He nodded toward the wood line to the south.

Shaw, with the measured stoicism that his race was noted for, simply nodded. "Dead, lad, is dead. While I'm not keen on exploring that particular aspect of our miserable human existence, given a choice, I'd rather do it at a place and time of my own choosing."

"Well," Ian replied between breaths, "would you be so kind as to inform me well in advance when and where that'll be so that I can arrange to be elsewhere?"

Shaw threw back his head and laughed. Other men nearby, their consciousness buried deep in their own dark thoughts and exhaustion, paused and looked up at Shaw to see what had caused him to guffaw. "McPherson," Shaw roared, "if the good Lord grants me the foresight of knowing that, I'll be sure to pass the word on to you. Now," he added as he bent down and offered his hand to Ian, "it's time that you put your back into your work and do what you can to make sure that neither of us meets our end in this wretched place."

Though still weak and in desperate need of rest, food, and clean, dry clothing, Ian took Shaw's hand and pushed himself off the ground as his captain pulled. After a futile effort to wipe away some mud from his trousers that only served to spread it about, Ian went back to digging.

Ian was still digging beside John Miller when soldiers on picket duty came stumbling across the meadow, raising the alarm. Looking up, Ian caught sight of one of the three French columns as it poked its head out of the woods and began to deploy. Keeping shovel in hand, for he could not bring himself to cast aside anything that was of value or use, Ian made for the stack of arms where his musket rested with the others of his small mess team. Carefully leaning the shovel out of the way up against the side of the small storage building, he quickly took his haversack, cartridge box, and canteen off the upturned bayonets of the muskets and slung them over his shoulders.

"I did not think him foolish enough to stand here," John Miller stammered as he fumbled with his equipment. "A man's got to wonder why our fool colonel has chosen to stand here and fight, doesn't he?"

Captain Shaw, walking along the line of men with a deliberate slowness, cut off Ian's response. "Come on, lads," Shaw called. "Be quick about it. 'Tis not the time for idle gossip. Take arms and fall in, at the double quick, or the Frenchies will gobble ya up."

With shoes caked with the mud of the water-filled trench he had just been laboring in, Ian made his way as fast as his wobbly legs would carry him to where Shaw stood, like the other company commanders, waiting for their small units to form on them. "Be lively now, lads," Shaw exhorted. "We've not much time."

Looking up after settling into his place in the rear of the three straggly ranks formed by the half-trained and nervous soldiers of Washington's Virginia Regiment, Ian could see over the shoulders of his comrades that the French were doing likewise. Then he glanced to the left and right at the motley appearance of the half-naked soldiers in ranks with him. He took in a deep breath before looking back at the French across the way and muttered, "It's Culloden, all over again."

No sooner had that thought crept into his head than Ian dropped it as he spotted the French's Indian allies beginning to gather on the flank of the well-dressed French soldiers. He knew, at that moment, that this wasn't going to be another Culloden. That battle had been fought in his own country, by men who, despite the passions that bloody battles evoke, eventually managed to regain some semblance of civilized conduct when dealing with their vanquished foe. Defeat here, perhaps a hard week's march from the nearest friendly settlement, would spell complete and utter doom for them. With that thought in mind, he slowly pulled his musket in closer to his side until the muzzle, now exposed to the rain, was tucked under his armpit. With a quick glance down, he made sure that the pan of his weapon's lock was closed and protected, as best he could, from moisture. With the odds so much against them, the last thing Ian wanted was a weapon rendered worthless through his own neglect.

Having done all that he could and left with little else to do until someone issued further orders, Ian turned his face up at the gray sky crowded with dark rain-laden clouds. "We've not shared much time together, Lord, but I've always tried to keep what you've laid down as the law in my heart. I ask you now, not so much for me but for some of these other lads here, to see us through this. Though we're far from bein' your best, I humbly believe even the meanest man amongst us deserves your blessing." Ian paused, trying hard to think of something else, blinking every now and then as a raindrop hit him square in the eyes. Unable to figure out how best to end his impromptu prayer, Ian blinked again and added, "Well, I guess that's all I've got to say."

The word "Amen," whispered only a few inches from his right ear, caused Ian to start and turn to see who had come up while he had been talking to his Lord. He was quite surprised to see Captain Shaw, head hung low and eyes closed, standing next to him. Without opening his eyes, Shaw placed his hand on Ian's shoulder, held it there while he muttered a few words of his own in prayer, then looked up at Ian. "Do your best to keep the lads in line when the fracas starts. There're a few, and you know 'em as well as I, who'll take to their heels given half a chance."

Ian looked at Shaw with a worried look on his face. "How'll I stop 'em if they're determined to break 'n' run?"

Shaw squeezed Ian's shoulder. "Look mean. When a lad turns his head and starts to eye what's behind 'im, move about till your eyes meet his. Then given 'im the meanest stare you can muster. You know, like your father would do whenever he thought you were about to get into something you had no business with."

Suddenly, the image of his father glaring at him flashed before Ian's eyes. A slight smile lit across Ian's pale lips as he recalled how his old man was always on the watch to make sure that Ian stayed away from one thing or another that he had warned him to leave alone. "Aye," Ian responded as he nodded. "I'll do what I can."

"That's all," Shaw replied, "I can ask of any of you." With that, he turned and went back to his post.

When Ian turned his attention back to what the French were up to, he could see that they had thrown a skirmish line that extended most of the meadow. They were advancing slowly, he imagined, so as to keep their alignment. When they were about five hundred yards away from where Washington's small command and Mackey's independent company stood, in three ranks, as required by the king's regulations, the French stopped, raised their muskets, and fired. Shaking his head as he watched the cloud of dirty white smoke hang before the French line, Ian all but laughed. "What are they doin'?" he called out in amazement. Ian didn't even look up and down the line to see if anyone was hit, for he was sure that the French volley had been totally ineffectual. "No man can hit a bloody thing at that range, not without a rifle," he called out in contempt. "These French are fools."

From somewhere in the ranks before him, a voice called out, "Aye, that may be true, but there's a whole lot of 'em and they keep gettin' closer."

Seeing the line of gray-clad French and Canadians emerge from the smoke of their own volley, Ian saw that this was true. Apparently Washington and Mackey had come to the same conclusion. Before the French were able to close half the distance between where the first volley was fired and where the Virginians stood, the order to move into the fort was given. "*Now*, McPherson," John Miller shouted as he made his way past Ian in the press to find shelter, "ya can praise the Lord."

While others were more than ready and willing to seek the protection of the muddy parapets and shallow trenches they had dug, Ian hesitated. The idea of holing up behind the pitifully small berms of dirt, knee-deep in mud and water, while the enemy surrounded them and picked them off one at a time, was not very appealing. Clutching the hilt of his broadsword, Ian found himself suddenly yearning for the swift, decisive rush of the clan, when all one's fears and apprehensions about the pending fight and death were consumed by the mad passions ignited by a wild charge of desperate men.

"In ya go, lad," Shaw admonished Ian as he went by. "We'll not be paid any more for givin' the Frenchies a better target to shoot at."

Ian turned and faced Shaw. For a moment, he wondered if his captain knew what he had been thinking. He wondered if Shaw, the last man in the company to enter the works, was thinking the same thing. The shouts of French officers closing fast broke Ian's concentration. Lifting his musket from the ground and carrying it at trail arms, Ian preceded Shaw into the trenches, found himself a spot, and prepared to wait for the battle to unfold.

AFTER watching the English break their ranks and flee into the confines of the pitiful stockade that passed as a fort, Anton followed the line of his own infantry until they were within sixty paces of those works. After unleashing one last volley, which didn't seem to have much of an effect on the English, the line and militia officers ordered their men to the right, into the protection of the woods southwest of the fort. Just as quickly as they had formed into a skirmish line from the march columns in which they had approached the English fort, de Villiers' mixed force of regulars, militia, and Indians melted away into the forest. Each man, without being told further, found himself a tree or a fallen log that offered suitable protection, took up position, and began to fire on the English works at his own pace.

Though he also carried a musket, as most officers did, Anton did not join in this general engagement. Instead, he hung back several paces in the wood line, to a spot from which he could observe a goodly portion of his own men and, through breaks in the trees and branches, the enemy works. From them, flashes and puffs of smoke, followed by the faint noise of distant discharges from enemy muskets, appeared to match, at first, the volume of fire being laid down by his French and Canadians. Already Anton could see that these English, unlike the ones they had faced at the forks of the Ohio in April, were ready and more than willing to offer up a fight. Whether this was good was difficult for Anton to decide. On one hand, as a soldier, he felt obliged to accept battle gladly when situation and circumstances dictated. Yet, his classical education, and reading the popular philosophers of the day, left him forever hoping that a better, less sanguinary, way of solving differences between nations and people could be found. That none of his fellow officers would admit to sharing such ideas didn't bother Anton. It wasn't, he knew, that they were lesser men. It was just that they, like the savages who served as their auxiliaries and allies, had not yet been enlightened.

With his head full of such weighty concerns and thoughts, and the spectacle of a protracted firefight between several hundred men before him, Anton didn't notice how exposed he was. Neither the zip of a near miss zinging past his ears nor the fragments of leaves riddled by high, wild shots falling all about him alerted Anton to the hazards he so mindlessly was exposing himself to. Only when de Villiers came up to him and ordered him to seek cover was Anton able to shake his thoughts clear of greater issues and concentrate on their present plight. "No one will be erecting a statue here," de Villiers admonished Anton. "So there is no need to strike a noble, sangfroid posture."

It took a moment for Anton to understand what his commander was talking about. When he did, he smiled. "Oh, sorry. I didn't realize that . . ."

"No need," de Villiers replied dryly. "It is easier to deal with one who is a bit too cavalier than prying one from the ground after his fears have glued him to it."

Anton laughed, then glanced at the fort. "One cannon, a

four-pounder, would have made short work of this." When he looked back, de Villiers' expression had changed. Now it was streaked by the exhaustion of the long forced marches and the strains of command. "Yes," de Villiers sighed. "I should have . . ."

Realizing what he had done, Anton tried to correct his error. "Oh, I didn't mean anything by what I said, other than idle speculation."

De Villiers nodded, though he did not smile. "I know that. Yet, it is true. I should have brought at least one gun."

"If I leave now," Anton offered, "with a few dozen men . . ."

"You wouldn't be back for a week, if that," de Villiers replied before Anton finished his thought. "No. This battle will be won or lost here, today, with what we have on hand."

The idea that his commander was even entertaining the notion of losing startled Anton. For the first time, the fact that the issue at hand was one of simple life or death became real. For a moment, as the gunfire behind him kept up its irregular rhythm, Anton looked into his commander's eyes and saw the concern, mixed with exhaustion, that he would soon learn were the first seeds of defeat.

"Stay here," de Villiers finally told him, "and keep an eye on this part of the line. Keep the men to task and don't let them slip back, even if they feign doing so to help a wounded comrade. Now that we've started this, we must finish it. The sooner, the better."

Without another word, de Villiers was gone, moving farther down the line to see that his men were fighting and his officers were doing all they could to maintain order and discipline within their own ranks and pressure on the enemy.

NOT satisfied with merely snipping at the cowardly English, Toolah took to joining in the general slaughter of the unprotected cattle, oxen, and horses left to fend for themselves in the open meadow or crude corrals. With tomahawk drawn and held aloft, Toolah sallied from the cover of the woods and leaped across the open in great bounds toward the bewildered beasts. Though there was fire directed against him, Toolah, caught up in his own self-generated blood lust, didn't even take note of it.

The first animal he came upon was a cow. Like many of the others, it had lost interest in the sudden disturbance that had rent the late-morning air of the meadow and, finding that it was doing her no harm, had returned to her lazy grazing. Only when Toolah was but a few yards away did the animal bother to raise her head and study the wild figure rushing toward her with the same dumb, uncomprehending stare she would have used to watch a harmless rabbit scurry through the field.

Toolah, however, was far from harmless. Using all his might, magnified by his own forward motion, Toolah brought his hatchet down in a single, killing blow that cleaved clean through the animal's skull. Stunned, the beast shook, staggered a step or two, then flopped over onto her side. With the exception of a quivering of the legs, jutting out stiffly, the hapless cow showed no more signs of life.

Though it had only been an animal, it had been an Englishman's animal, a beast owned and prized by a white man. Its destruction, to Toolah, was almost as good as the death of one of the foes himself. Holding his bloody hatchet up, he let out a terrible cry that he renewed as soon as he felt the warm blood of the animal curl its way down the handle of his weapon and flow over the hand clutching it. By the time he was able to regain his composure, the other animals within easy reach were dead or about to fall under the hatchet of another brave. Though disappointed that he had just one kill, it was enough for now. There would be more, and better game to slaughter, Toolah knew, when the English dogs broke. Turning his back in contempt on the random shots from the fort that sought him out, Toolah returned to the tree line, where his brother, as always, waited for him.

"That was a foolish act, brother," Gingego admonished him.

Toolah stopped just as he was passing his brother. Turning his head, he stared into Gingego's condemning eyes. "We have deprived the **Engl**ish of their meat and transportation. If our *noble* white allies, the French, fail to subdue them, hunger and the inability to haul away their stores and wounded will."

"It was not with your head that you chose to strike down those creatures. It was with your heart," Gingego stated flatly with a voice that rose with each word. "*Always*, brother, with your heart, a heart that knows only hate."

Unable to bear his brother's taunts, Toolah responded with fury. "If it is hate that is driving me, it is a hate that I learned from the whites. *They* are the ones who have come to our lands. *They* are the ones who have separated our tribes. And it is *they* who bring misery and suffering to our people. Never forget that, brother of mine. *Never!*"

Without another word, Toolah turned from his brother and stalked into the woods, where he would wait until the English and the French finished playing at war and the real killing could then begin.

KEEPING some of the men to task, Ian found, was far harder than he had expected. Though the narrow confines of the crowded trench and the straggly picket wall of the stockade limited the abilities of the halfhearted to flee, nothing seemed to be able to keep them from slithering down into the muck and mire of the crude trench in an effort to hide from the withering French fire. "My bloody musket's fouled!" was the popular excuse given whenever Ian, moving about the trench, roused a soldier who seemed to be spending too much time between shots. While taking care to lay his own musket aside to keep it from falling into the water, Ian would snatch the skulker's weapon from his hands, then check the flint, hammer, primer pan, and flash hole to ensure that all parts of the lock were functional.

As a lad, he hadn't been trained in the use of firearms.

The men of Ian's family had always been too poor or too wed to the old ways to part with the broadswords they hid from the English. Everything Ian knew about small arms had come from Shaw. "Their accuracy past fifty, sixty paces is laughable," Shaw pointed out. "At a hundred paces, the best shot could fire away at a man-size target all day and never hit it. Too much play in the barrel. No way of knowing which way the ball's gonna come out as it bangs about from one side of the barrel to another. So you see, McPherson, it's nigh impossible to compensate for its erratic flight. Only way to make up for the miserable performance of one piece is to mass 'em and train the lads to load and fire as fast as they can."

Not every man in the company took this simple lesson to heart. Deprivation of almost every human want, together with exposure and long hours of hard labor, had sapped the strength and motivation of even the strongest of them. "I had it better," Jim Stone, a freed black man, moaned daily as he trudged next to Ian on the march or at work by his side, " 'fore Master Morris freed me. Never thought I'd long for my slave days. Never."

The next lesson Ian had learned was that it was easy to judge a man's motivation and dedication to the task of the regiment by how well he kept his musket. Those, like himself, who knew that one's survival in battle was directly tied to his arms went to great extremes to ensure that, if nothing else, their muskets were clean and serviceable. Even when he was shaking so much from the effects of the diarrhea that his legs wobbled and threatened to give out, Ian took the time to wipe down his musket and make sure the lock was covered and his powder was kept high and dry. Most of the men Ian was charged with needed reminders to do so. "McPherson," John Miller growled every time Ian reminded him, "you're worse than a mother hen. A man would think you had nothin' to do all day but lay 'bout and think of ways of makin' life for us more miserable than it already is." Still, though he complained, Miller took care and kept his musket in reasonable condition.

Others, however, could not be bothered. And now, as he made his way along the trench, it didn't surprise Ian to see those men squatting in the muddy brown water, cowering with their useless weapons tucked between their knees like tails. "What's wrong with your piece?" Ian shouted at one man, who was leaning with his back against the forward wall of the trench.

Slowly, the man rotated his head until his wide, unblinking saucer eyes met Ian's. The blank stare, framed by a pale complexion streaked with drops of water that cut small rivulets through the dirt and grime of his face, told Ian all he needed to know. He was scared, to the point where he could no longer function, no longer raise a finger, even in his own self-defense. Looking down at the man's musket, Ian noticed that there wasn't even a piece of flint locked down in the hammer. "Don't ya have a spare flint, man?" Ian barked. As French bullets whistled overhead and smacked into the logs of the stockade, Ian stood towering over the man, staring into the blank, unblinking eyes. He felt his anger raising. "I said," Ian shouted again, "don't ya have a bloody flint?"

A hand on his shoulder caught Ian off guard. Turning away from the cowering soldier, Ian turned his head, just as a near miss whizzed past his ear, to see who was behind him. It was Shaw. "Save your breath, lad," Shaw advised in a calm voice that seemed out of place. "Even if he had a workin' musket, he wouldn't use it."

Blinking his eyes in an effort to shake off the raindrops that were gathering on his eyelashes, Ian looked at Shaw, then back at the man squatting at his feet in the water. "Get on to the others," Shaw ordered in a tone that made it seem more like a suggestion.

Though he realized Shaw was right, Ian found it difficult to walk away from the man. He stood there for a moment longer, and glared down at the miserable figure. How, Ian thought to himself, can a person, faced with the choice of life and death, simply sit here idle in the middle of all of this and do nothing? Only a scream from a familiar voice managed to distract him.

Looking up, Ian saw John Miller thrashing about in the knee-deep water that covered the length of the trench. "Oh, God," Miller yelled as he struggled unsuccessfully to keep his head above water. "Help me, dear God. *Help me.*"

Pushing his way past the cowering soldier, Ian made his way to Miller. Though in a hurry to reach his friend and help him, Ian still took great care as to where and how he rested his musket. Once both hands were free, he grabbed Miller by the straps of his canteen and cartridge box, pulled him up until his head and shoulders were out of the water, and dragged him over to the side of the trench, taking care to ensure that his head stayed below the level of the parapet. He didn't need to ask Miller where he'd been hit, for the blood from the wound in his arm gushed forth and mixed readily with the muddy brown water that soaked the stricken man. "Oh, lordy, Ian," Miller howled, "It burns bad, real bad."

Though he meant to be gentle, the awkwardness of working in the close quarters of the trench, together with the crowded conditions and Ian's own haste to help his friend, negated any tenderness. The result was that Ian virtually slammed Miller against the back wall of the trench. To make matters worse, he lost his footing in the slick, causing him to fall forward on top of Miller.

"*Aheee*," Miller howled as Ian tried to regain his footing and get off his friend. "You tryin' to finish me for the French?"

"I'm sorry, John," Ian muttered, "I was . . ."

"If me arm wasn't half shot away," Miller shouted, his expression of pain now turned to one of anger, "I'd beat you ta within an inch of your life."

Finally composed, Ian shouted back, "Well, you're shot, you old fool. And I'm gonna take you to the surgeon. Now, shut your trap and quit fussin'."

With a blink, Miller stared at Ian for a minute, then smiled as best as his pain would let him. "God bless you, boy. Now, let's get this over with and, for God sakes, do take care. I don't think this body of mine can take much more."

Reaching up with his hand, Ian laid the muddy, wet palm on Miller's cheek. "I'll stay with you, Johnny. I promise."

AFTER the initial rush and excitement of the opening encounter with the English, the contest settled down to an irregular fire, with the English cornered in their pitiful earthworks and the forces under de Villiers holding positions in the nearby woods. With little need to exert any direction or supervision over the small band of soldiers in his charge, Anton was free to study the battle. Early on, the young French ensign had found himself at wit's end, trying hard to make any sense out of the random shooting that everyone seemed to be engaged in. Rather than being fired up with the passions that he had always been told dominate men in battle, these Canadians and soldiers of La Marine units were going about their task of killing the enemy in a rather casual, almost lackadaisical, manner. *It is*, Anton scribed quickly in his journal, *as if these people do this every day. They load their muskets, take aim, and fire as mechanically and unemotionally as would a cobbler working on a shoe. It is nothing, nothing at all, like I would have suspected.*

Were it not for the growing concern that etched new lines in de Villiers' face every time Anton saw him, he would have felt totally comfortable despite the occasional hiss of the odd shot that flew overhead. Perhaps, Anton wondered, his commander was concerned about the foul weather in which they had been forced to fight their battle. After all, whenever the rain increased in intensity, the firing from both sides slacked off and all but stopped. Anton could not tell for sure whether it was because of the soldiers' desire to protect their paper cartridges from the rain or that the fighting men of both sides, feeling the misery of nature in an equal measure, took pity on their opponent and decided to lessen the others' suffering. If it were the latter, Anton could find no fault. He found that even he, an officer, had a tendency to huddle up under his tree and draw his coat a little closer about himself.

It was during one of these lulls, late in the afternoon, when de Villiers came by and found Anton about to fall asleep. "I see," de Villiers announced to the officer accompanying him, "that our young officer of artillery has grown tired of our little battle."

Realizing that he had dozed off, Anton scrambled to his

feet. Wide-eyed and blushing, he pulled on the lapels of his soaked gray coat in an effort to make himself more presentable. It was growing dark, he noticed for the first time, as his eyes began to focus. The day was about to end, and still the sound of random firing told him that the battle dragged on. "I . . . it was the firing. It had . . . ah . . ." Anton tried to explain.

For the first time in hours, a hint of a smile lit across de Villiers' face as he held up a hand. "No need to explain. I admire a soldier who can manage to take advantage of any circumstances and, well . . ."

"It will not happen again, I promise," Anton volunteered.

In the twinkling of an eye, the slight smile disappeared. "I did not seek you out to chastise you for doing what many of us wish we could. Rather, it was to present you with a new mission."

AFTER spending the entire day, from just before noon until the light began to fail, pushing and prodding others to get up and out of the mud and fire, Ian found himself unable to do anything more than that which he had admonished others not to do. With his musket cradled in his arms, he fell against the back wall of the trench and allowed himself to slither down into the cold, muddy water that he had been standing in all afternoon.

When he finally came to rest, Ian closed his eyes and craned his neck back. When his head came to rest, he opened his mouth, allowing the cold rain that had been pelting them on and off all day to fall lazily onto his parched tongue. He was beyond exhaustion, beyond feeling, and, worse, almost beyond caring. While it had been true, Ian thought as he felt the raindrops cascade across his face and make their way down his throat, that the clan charge had been bloody and brutal, it had been quick. Judgment had been swift. It was either victory or defeat, life or death, not at all like this slow, agonizing punishment that the men of the Virginia Regiment had been subjected to all day.

Swallowing what water remained in his mouth, Ian opened his eyes, lifted his head, and looked about. Next to him, lying facedown so that only his shoulders and upper back broke the surface of the dirty water they shared, was a dead man. Ian thought he knew who the man was. He should have known, he thought, seeing that he had been sharing this small stretch of trench with him for most of the day. He was sure that sometime during the long afternoon he had seen this very man standing, alive, like the others, fighting side-by-side with them. When he had gone down, Ian had no idea. Nor did Ian know if the man had been wounded when he was knocked back from his position and drowned, like some of the others, simply because he had been too weak or was in shock. All he knew of this man now was that he had become one of the many bodies littering the trench, making walking its length more difficult.

"Ah, McPherson," Shaw's voice boomed out through the failing light of early evening. "I'm glad you're still with us, lad. I've been worried about ya."

Without changing expression, Ian looked up at his captain. With him was his colonel, dressed in his regimentals, which now looked as disreputable as that of any of the privates in the regiment. "Do ya think the Frenchies are gonna wait till it's dark 'fore they rush in here and slit our throats, clean and proper?" Though he addressed his question to Shaw, Ian's eyes were glued on Washington's long face. Though his colonel's face showed no reaction, and he didn't answer one way or the other, Ian could tell that the man who had led them there was deeply troubled and quite worried.

"We've held on this long," Shaw replied. "I imagine we can hold on a bit longer. Perhaps the French are just as beaten up as we are. Without cannon to pry us out of here," Shaw added in an effort to boost the morale of his tired corporal, "he may up and slink away in the night."

"Or," Ian added in a flat, even tone, "he might let his savages loose on us."

Shaw smiled. "It's not their way, lad. The Indians don't much care for the white man's way of war." Nervously, Shaw turned his head and looked up over the edge of the parapet toward the French positions. "They save 'emselves for when they have us, in the open or deep in the woods, where . . ."

Stopping in mid-sentence, Shaw fixed his gaze on something that he saw beyond the edge of the trench. With one hand he touched Washington's sleeve and then pointed out in the direction he was staring. Like Shaw, Washington poked his head up over the edge of the trench, searched the distant horizon for what Shaw was watching, then stopped when he had caught sight of it.

From his position, Ian watched the two officers. Though he was curious as to what they were so intently studying, he felt no great urge to pick himself up out of the mud and water to find out. Instead, he simply let his head fall forward, closed his eyes, and waited for whatever came next.

ANTON stepped out of the tree line and made his way across the muddy field toward the English works to greet the two approaching Englishmen. The slick, sticky mud made this difficult. Rather than worrying if the English would respect the truce he had called for and hold their fire, Anton found himself very concerned about keeping his footing. It would be a great embarrassment to the entire command, not to mention himself, if he fell flat on his face in the mud right there, with all eyes of both armies watching him. He found he had to force himself to lift his eyes off the ground before him and look out, straight ahead.

The two Englishmen, he thought, were having the same difficulties. Anton stopped only a few paces out in the open when he judged that he was far enough to show that de Villiers' offer to parlay had been made in good faith. Let the English, he decided, brave the mud and fear of embarrassment.

When they were in front of Anton, the young ensign pulled himself erect in the best parade-ground form he could manage before asking, in his native tongue, "I trust one of you gentlemen speak French?"

The older of the two responded with a disheartened *"Oui,"* to which Anton smiled and replied, *"Bon.* If you gentlemen would follow me." Leading the English officers into the woods, Anton took them to where de Villiers and his senior officers were waiting. Stepping aside, Anton let the two Englishmen present themselves as he stood back and watched the proceedings.

It was, for Anton, almost as entertaining as it was instructional. It was clear that the exhausted Englishmen were quite surprised by his commander's offer to allow the English to quit the fort, with their arms, possessions, and full military honors. Anton wondered if the English had, by this generous offer, guessed how desperate de Villiers was to end this affair right here and now, before he was forced by lack of provisions and ammunition to break off the stalemated contest and slink away, back north, in defeat. Perhaps that was why the English emissaries were asking that de Villiers write down his demands for their colonel's consideration. It would, of course, be logical, now that they had seen the plight of the French forces, to go back to their own commander, inform him of this, and hold out until their enemy broke.

But then Anton changed his mind. The more he studied the English officers, the more he became convinced that it was they, and not the French, who were closer to the end of their rope. Haggard faces and nervous eyes watched every move and took in every word spoken as an officer recorded de Villiers' terms under the light of a single flickering candle held by another officer and shielded with his free hand from the wind and rain.

So, this was how it was, Anton found himself thinking. This was how great empires were created and lost. Frightened, exhausted men, grappling with each other in the dark wilderness just beyond the fringe of civilization, served as the midwives or pallbearers of the grand designs of their respective sovereigns.

Looking about, Anton took note of several militiamen, leaning on their long muskets for support, watching the proceedings with detached interest. For a moment, he studied the face of one of the bearded soldiers. Anton could not tell, by the militiaman's bland expression, if he was pleased with how the affair was playing itself out. Instead of joy, this part-time warrior looked on with only a calm, almost serene expression. Why was it, Anton wondered, that no one wrote of moments such as these in terms that reflected such monumental events as they really were, and not as others thought they should be? Why was it that no one ever noticed there was as much nobility in a man taken away from his farm and family in Canada and asked to serve the king as there was in a general, adorned with sliver and gold lace, leading a charge in Flanders? If anything, it was the common man, often left to fend for himself and his own provisions while on the march, who endured the unbearable hardships and misery that senior officers often claimed for themselves in dispatch after dispatch. Was the military history that his instructors had taken great pains to inoculate him with little more than heroic mythology that differed little from Homer's *Iliad*? Turning back to the gathering of French and English officers, Anton wondered if this drama, coming to a close before his very eyes, and not the heroic legends of Comte de Saxe, Jeanne d'Arc, and Charlemagne, was the truth.

Then, despite the haze of exhaustion that clouded every thought, Anton wondered if this episode, to which he was more than a simple witness, belonged in his journal. Until now, he had been little more than an impartial observer, a simple soul chronicling his journeys through the wilderness. Now, however, he was a participant, a warrior whose actions were making a mark upon this pristine land. Did he need to include his role as a soldier in his story? Did the people of France need to know the true story of what he was seeing and feeling now, regardless of possible consequences? Or should he, as so many others who had gone before him, perpetuate the myths of New France that spoke of men and women who, despite great hardships and sacrifices, served their king and Church out of loyalty in this savage wilderness? As troubling as such questions were, even more disturbing was the fact that he was even considering them.

WORD of their capitulation and pending departure spread through the English and colonial ranks like wildfire. In the close confines of the crowded fort and water-filled trenches, there was no hiding the comings and goings of their officers out to the French and back throughout the early evening. It was, as best as Ian could determine, near midnight when Captain Shaw finally announced that they would surrender the next morning. "We'll go out under arms, with full military honors."

With every stitch of clothing he owned soaked, his face and hands turned black from the firing of his musket all afternoon, and hunger gnawing at his stomach like a ravenous wolf, the word *honor* seemed strangely out of place. "What of the wounded?" Ian asked. "We've no oxen or horses to pull the wagons for 'em. I don't see how we're gonna manage to haul 'em back to Willis Creek, not with the Indians nipping at our heels."

"Aye," Shaw responded dryly. "It'll be a challenge. But," he added with great deliberateness, "we can't leave anyone behind. *That*, lad, would surely be their end."

Ian lowered his head, then nodded. "You're right, Captain." Then, after thinking about it for a moment further, he began to stand. "If ya don't mind, I'll go along to the surgeon's and see how John Miller's doin'."

Shaw said nothing. Instead, he only laid his hand upon Ian's shoulder, gave it a firm, fatherly squeeze, and went on to check the remainder of his small company.

Ian found Miller outside the small storage shed, propped up against the log walls. "What are ya doin' out here?" Ian demanded incredulously. "You should be in there, out of the rain."

Ignoring Ian's question, the haggard man slowly, painfully turned his head and looked up at the figure of his friend as he knelt down beside him. "They took me arm, Ian. Took it all," Miller replied with a weak, broken voice.

"All the more reason for ya to be in there, out of this horrid weather."

Miller, with great effort, shook his head. "No. Much worse in there. Much worse. If I'm to die, let me do it out here, away from that hell."

Having been deafened to a large degree by firing all day and too concerned with the immediacy of the tasks he had been confronted with, Ian hadn't paid much heed to the shrieks and howls of pain that issued from the storage shed. As he looked around the corner into the open door, the scene before him and the noises reminded him of the butcher's slaughter shed. All about the table where the surgeon still worked, ill lit by a couple of candles, lay the bloody carcasses of wounded already tended to and those waiting their turn. Yes, Ian thought, it was much better out here.

Turning his attention back to Miller, he carefully took the collar of the wounded man's shirt and pulled him closer to his mouth. "Listen. We're surrenderin' in the morning. Marchin' out of here and headin' back to Willis Creek. You need to rest, save your strength. I'll be back in the morning to help you. I'll not leave you here for the savages."

Barely able to speak now, Miller leaned his head forward and whispered, "Stay with me, lad. I beg you to sit here with me, if you will, till it's time to leave."

Suddenly, without having to be told, Ian realized that John Miller would never leave this place. Pulling back a bit, he thought about fleeing to the trenches, away from this terrible place. But then, in the darkness, he saw the eyes of his friend staring into his, unblinking as they pleaded for comfort and companionship that only he could now render.

Letting go of Miller's collar, Ian laid his musket off to one side in the mud. Carefully, he moved around till he was sitting with his back against the wall next to the stricken man. With as much tenderness as he could muster, he reached over and gently pulled Miller's head down till it was resting on his shoulder. For a moment, he sat there still and silent. Only after he felt Miller relax did he do so. "God bless you, lad," the dying man whispered. "God bless you."

The Great Meadows
July 4, 1754

UNDER gray skies that continued to sprinkle cold rain upon both victor and vanquished, Anton de Chevalier watched the wretched remains of the English force march out of their water-filled trenches. There were about 250, maybe more. While some wore smart, if somewhat dirty, red regimentals, most were clad in what could only be described as rags. "On our worst day," a Canadian officer bitterly commented to Anton, "even *my* men can make a better turnout than that."

"Ah," responded Anton, "but this is not your worst day. It is theirs."

As if to underscore that point, Anton caught sight of some of the Indians, who had been hovering off to one side, slowly making their way closer to the ragged column of Englishmen. "Trouble," the Canadian murmured.

Turning away from the Indians, Anton looked back at the Canadian, who was eyeing the approaching Indians. "What trouble?" Anton asked innocently.

"Our wild friends," the Canadian replied without taking his half-closed eyes off the Indians, "are not going to be pleased if they are not permitted their due."

Looking back at the Indians for a moment, then at the Canadian, Anton shook his head. "But Captain de Villiers has granted the English full honors and permission to leave. How could he permit the Indians to do the English any harm?"

The Canadian glanced sideways at Anton, folded his arms across his chest, then looked back at the Indians, who were now eyeing the English column for plunder that they wished to take from their hapless foe. "It is not a question, my young friend, of being able to stop them. Rather, how long will your captain allow the Indians to have their way with the English, and what, if anything, will he do to stop them? You see, this isn't Europe. Formal terms and honors of war mean nothing to those savages. Nothing."

Anton was about to rebuke the Canadian for his callous remark when he saw an Indian, Toolah to be exact, break from the pack and rush forward to a downcast straggler bringing up the rear of the column. "I," Anton declared as he began to rush forward to intervene, "will not permit the honor of France to be sullied in such a manner."

The Canadian, amused by the noble innocence of the young ensign of artillery, said nothing as Anton charged off to place himself between Toolah and his intended victim. Instead, he stood back with the others and watched the Indians go about their business with detached amusement.

Dejected and exhausted after a sleepless night leaned up against the wall of the storage shed, Ian dragged one foot after the other as he trailed the straggly column. He had spent the better part of the morning digging a grave for his friend, and the rest searching the strewn contents of the storage shed for something to eat. His mind was not on what was going on about him, much less where they were headed. Too tired to think clearly, Ian was satisfied to follow along dumbly, in the wake of the men in front of him. In his sorry state, he did not notice the sound of running feet approaching him. Only when the Indian adorned in bright red war paint let out a piercing screech did Ian look up.

Instinctively, and with a quickness that belied his pitiful physical state, Ian raised his musket up over his head just as the savage was bringing down his hatchet. As the blade of the hatchet bit into the stock of the weapon fouled beyond use, Ian let go with both hands, jumped back and to one side, and let the forward momentum of his assailant carry him by. Though he saw that this quick maneuver had saved him, it quickly became obvious that the Indian had no intent of letting things go at that.

Regaining his footing, Toolah staggered to a halt, spun

around, and stared at his disarmed foe. Having lost his hatchet, whose blade was now hopelessly wedged deeply in the wooden stock of the Englishman's musket, Toolah reached down and drew his knife from the sheath on his thigh in one quick, easy motion. He was about to lurch forward to renew his aborted attack when, to his surprise, Toolah watched the Englishman draw an incredibly long and wide sword from a sheath he had not noticed before. Though it was not like anything he had seen before, it was not the size of the weapon that gave him pause. Rather, it was the keen look of hatred in the eyes of his intended victim that held him in check. From the wretched, disheartened weakling Toolah had originally singled out, this man had suddenly become a deadly adversary, ready and willing to trade blow for blow.

Realizing that not only the Englishman but every other Indian in sight had seen him flinch, Toolah felt he had no alternative but to risk all in a single rush or walk away in shame and dishonor. Steeling his nerve, Toolah let out as fearful a scream as he could muster and started forward again. Only a hand grabbing his arm from behind and spinning him about kept him from closing with the Englishmen.

"*No!*" Anton screamed after he seized hold of Toolah's arm and twirled him about. "They have surrendered. I will not allow you to dishonor my king by killing helpless men like this."

Though it was obvious that the Englishman was far from helpless, standing with feet spread shoulder-width apart, bent over, and broadsword held at the ready, Anton didn't care. He was incensed that such depredations were permitted and had no intention of allowing them to happen, if he could help it.

Regaining his footing after a second unexpected turn of events, Toolah glanced at the Englishman. When he saw that his foe was foolishly making no move to take advantage of the situation, Toolah turned his complete attention, and anger, against Anton. "How dare you?" he hissed. "How dare you deny me the honor of the kill?"

"And, you!" Anton snarled back. "How dare you profane my king's honor by attacking an enemy who has surrendered according to the traditions of war?"

"Your king is not my master, just as this land is not yours," Toolah barked. Stepping closer to Anton with his knife held closely at his side, Toolah stopped only when his chest bumped into that of the French ensign. "Do not imagine," Toolah whispered menacingly, "that I shall forget this." Then, without another word, he turned away and stalked off, stopping only long enough to bend over, grab the handle of his hatchet, and jerk it free of Ian's musket.

When he saw that the danger had passed, Anton straightened up, shook his head, and walked as calmly as his excited state permitted him to the Englishman, still standing at the ready to repel any and all attackers. When he was a few feet away, Anton raised his right hand, palm out, in a sign of friendship. Only then did Ian lower his broadsword. Though he had little doubt that he could have held his own against a second attack by the savage, Ian still felt compelled to nod his head and utter a curt "Thank you" to the young French officer.

Taking Ian's words as an acknowledgment of gratitude, Anton stopped, came to attention, bowed, and, in French, replied, "You are welcome." When he straightened up, the two men stared at each other before Ian, with sword still drawn and on guard, backed away. Turning, he hurried to rejoin the rear of the column as it staggered out of the Great Meadows. With little more to do, Anton stood there for the longest time and watched until the Englishmen were swallowed up by the dense wilderness that surrounded them.

"And so," Anton muttered to himself, "we bring this matter to a close."

But, of course, like so much else, Anton had much to learn. Though beaten and bowed, the red-haired colonel marching at the head of his disheartened command was far from defeated. If anything, the experience of this awful embarrassment served to strengthen a character that would, in years to come, serve him and his nation well.

PART THREE

Braddock's Road

CHAPTER EIGHT

Alexandria, Virginia
April, 1755

STEPPING OUT of the doorway of the tavern where he was billeted, Captain Thomas Shields stopped for a moment and looked up and down the muddy street that passed for a main thoroughfare. People were already coming and going past, tending their daily business without paying him the slightest bit of attention. Most of them were heading for, or returning from, the town's market, located right next to the house of John Carlyle, which General Braddock was using as his headquarters. The people, like the town, were a poor excuse for a settlement. Incorporated barely eight years before, much of its center was still occupied with corrals and pens where residents kept cows, pigs, and horses together, each of which added its own peculiar stench to the already loathsome atmosphere that permeated the whole place. Some of the residents even buried their dead in the garden adjoining their house. It did not take long before Thomas came to the conclusion that the worst street in London was far better than the best one this colony could boast of.

With a sigh, Thomas shook his head and smiled. Though this was a far cry from the delights of London, the gain he expected to reap from joining this expedition would, in the end, more than compensate for this journey to the colonies.

When word of General Edward Braddock's expedition began to spread about London in the fall of 1754, few of his fellow officers of the Coldstream Guard showed any interest in the undertaking. This was especially true when it was learned that the two regiments selected to make up the bulk of the army were the Forty-fourth and Forty-eighth Foot. Both, garrisoned in Ireland, had been raised in 1741. Both had fought in the Jacobite Rebellion of '45. And both had a reputation as being the two worst regiments in the British army. Even worse, when called to gather from their scattered billets from Limerick to Dublin and muster at Cork, their combined strength didn't even equal the authorized strength of a single regiment.

To remedy this last deficiency, drafts from other regiments, the Twentieth from Exeter, the Eleventh from Salisbury, the Tenth and Twenty-eighth from Limerick, as well as the Twenty-sixth and the Royals from Galway, were called on to bring the two departing units up to at least five hundred men each. Those unit commanders, seeing an opportunity to purge their ranks of their least desirable soldiers and their troublemakers, gladly sent as many malcontents along to the Forty-fourth and Forty-eighth as they dared.

This massive reshuffling of personnel also afforded outstanding opportunities for those who were astute enough to appreciate them. For Thomas, the expedition was heaven-sent, an escape from a posting that, while prestigious and fashionable, had turned out to be restrictive and costly. The purchase of further promotions within the Coldstream Guards was expensive, well beyond Thomas' means and the charity of his father. And even if he had the money needed to advance himself, the cost of existing in London in a manner befitting a gentleman was becoming quite exorbitant. Since the Guards never seemed to deploy to places where a man with ambitions and skill could further his own fortunes and career, one had to leave its ranks and seek fame and fortune elsewhere. It was, Thomas slowly came to realize, not the plum that he had once thought it to be.

An expedition to the colonies, where many a soldier had achieved both fame and fortune, was an opportunity too good to ignore, even if it was with a unit such as the Forty-fourth. With a deftness that he had learned from serving in a city known for able politicians and astute businessmen, Thomas was able to convince his father to advance him the sums necessary to purchase him a promotion to captain in the Forty-fourth Foot. The elder Shields took advantage of this chance to place his son in a position from which he would be able to establish himself financially. "It is," Sir Shields confided to his business agent, "a prospect far too rich with all sorts of possibilities to ignore. Even if the boy doesn't gain me anything in America, he rids me of a financial burden I have borne far too long."

Finding himself a good spot in the Forty-fourth was Thomas' doing. In this, he used all his charms and connections to secure the post as commander of the Forty-fourth's company of grenadiers. He joined his new command at Cork, Ireland, attired in his new regimentals faced in bright yellow, without the slightest regret or apprehension. "It's rather like dice," Thomas told one of his friends in London before departing. "You have to be willing to take a chance if you expect to gain, don't you?" The idea that his life was part of the bargain never seemed to enter into the equation.

The expedition arrived in the Virginia colony in the dead of winter, 1755. For Thomas and his fellow officers, their first sight of the New World came as a shock. After taking a stroll along the muddy, rutted paths that passed as streets in Alexandria, Lieutenant Clarence Holmes of the Forty-fourth shook his head and moaned to Thomas, "If this is what they consider the populated region of this colony, I shudder to think what we'll find once we set off for the interior."

Thomas, ever mindful of his purpose, didn't allow the inconvenience to bother him. "We're on the fringes of civilization, Clarence," he countered with enthusiasm, "where fame and fortune lurk. If you're sharp, the king," he reminded Holmes, "is not the only one who'll find his domains and fortunes enhanced by this adventure we're undertaking."

That adventure, however, had to wait until other, more practical matters were tended to. Before a single man made his way into the wilderness they had been sent to conquer, the tons of supplies needed to sustain an army in the field needed to be gathered. Transportation to haul this, as well as the army's munitions and cannon, also needed to be marshaled. Since only sixteen specially built ordnance wagons had been brought over from England, some two hundred wagons, with all the horses and harnesses required to pull them and the army's cannon, had to be procured and gathered. And then there were the colonial levies, men recruited from the surrounding communities who would be needed to bring the regiments of foot up to full strength.

None of this, of course, went off as planned or promised by the colonial governors or their miserly legislatures. Even more reluctant were the very people whom Braddock and his small army had been sent to defend. Rather than embracing the expedition, General Edward Braddock's demands were met by halfhearted compliance or, in some cases, downright rejection. Among the complaints that the general leveled against his colonial comrades to the foreign secretary was the charge of trading with the enemy. Instead of selling the meat and flour badly needed by the army, the merchants of New York and Pennsylvania were trading it to the French at Louisbourg in exchange for rum, sugar, and molasses. The elected government of Pennsylvania, controlled by the Quakers of that colony, even went so far as to request that they be "excused" from providing any sort of provisions to Braddock's gathering army since they were "not a fighting people."

Time and again, Braddock and his procurement officers were stymied by the failure of governors, colonial legislatures, and the colonists themselves to act in unison for the common good. In frustration, Braddock informed the British secretary of state, after meeting with the governors of Virginia, Maryland, Pennsylvania, New York, and Massachusetts, of "the impossibility of obtaining from the several colonies the establishment of a general fund agreeable to His Majesty's instruction." To deal with this reluctance, Braddock had his own ideas. "I cannot but take the liberty," he went on in his report to the secretary, "to represent to you the necessity of laying a tax upon all His Majesty's dominions in America, agreeable to the results of the Council, for reimbursing the great sums that must be advanced for the service and interest of the colonies."

.All this, of course, was of little concern to Thomas Shields. He tended to his company of grenadiers, ensuring that they were both well turned out and drilled in accordance with the king's regulations. And, of course, he pursued those diversions, no matter how pitifully few they were, that time and circumstances permitted. With little to do this day, Thomas strolled about the dusty streets of Alexandria in search of something to occupy his time. Pausing when he reached the marketplace, Thomas stood off to one side to watch the merchants and shoppers go about their daily business. Like many of his fellow officers, he was quick to develop a true and unbridled dislike for these colonists. While claiming to be His Majesty's subjects, to a man and woman they seemed to shun any obligation to support the Crown with the same disdain that one avoided a leper. Even those who ran the colony from its legislative house, named the House of Burgesses, hesitated to lend their support until they were sure it was to their advantage. It seemed to Thomas that they were content to come and go in peace, trading and bargaining with each other with no other thought than to advance their own personal fortunes and well-being, often at the expense of someone else. No one was immune to the shenanigans of these sharp Yankee traders. One of Thomas' fellow officers, after being wined and dined by the wife of a rich local planter, whom he described as being anything but beautiful, bought from her a horse that turned out to be "dog lame and moon-blind." Though Thomas had fared far better in finding a suitable mount for himself, the price he eventually paid was so exorbitant that it prohibited him from purchasing a second, "bat" mount, had one been available. Thomas wondered how they would be able to achieve the king's directives under such adverse conditions.

Still, Major General Edward Braddock, an officer for forty of his sixty-one years, had his orders from the king himself, orders that he intended to execute to the letter, colonials be damned. Through sheer will and perseverance, Braddock danced the delicate minuet of intercolonial politics, extracted promises of aid and support from the Royal governors, and pushed ahead with his plans to march to the forks of the Ohio with overwhelming force.

Thomas was still standing across from the marketplace, watching with mild amusement the comings and goings of the Virginians and pondering the prospects of the entire expedition, when a woman's voice interrupted his thoughts. "Excuse me, sir, but you'd be one of the general's aides, would you not?"

Blinking his eyes, Thomas looked down at the plainly dressed green-eyed serving girl. Even with her auburn hair piled up on top of her head and hidden under a crisp, white cap, she was, Thomas thought, quite alluring. Still, he had to remind himself, she was little more than a servant girl. "Ah, no, I am not. I am an officer with the Forty-fourth Foot."

His response brought a bright, innocent smile to her face that was highlighted by her sparkling eyes. "Oh, I was hoping to find an aide of the general, but perhaps," she pleaded, "you would do me a favor." Without explanation, the girl placed the overladen basket she had been holding on her forearm on the ground, reached into a hidden pocket in her skirt, and pulled out a folded, crinkled paper, which she held out at arm's length. "There's a boy, well, he's actually a man, with Captain Shaw's company of rangers. They marched out with that bunch of soldiers the other day 'fore I could come in and say my proper good-byes. I was wondering, seeing as you're gonna be going to join 'em soon, if you'd be so kind as to see that he gets this?"

Not quite sure whether he should be amused or appalled

by this affront, Thomas looked at the scrap of folded paper for a moment.

"I wrote it all myself. Master Richfield has a tutor for his children who's taken on the task of teachin' me and Betsy, the Negro cook's helper, how to read and write."

The mention of the planter's name reminded Thomas of where he had seen the girl before. This brought a slight smile to his lips, a smile that the girl assumed to be a yes to her rather forward request. Beaming an even wider smile, she all but shoved the letter into Thomas' hand. "Oh, thank you, sir. I told Betsy that one of you gentlemen would be kind enough to see this letter delivered safely."

The touch of the girl's hand against his caused Thomas to recoil. This time, however, it was not because of the affront that he had suffered at the hands of a mere servant. Rather, the physical contact, mixed with the sweet smell of cooking vanilla and her engaging smile, were beginning to make Thomas quite uncomfortable. Leaning back noticeably, Thomas opened his hand, took the letter into it, and mumbled something that the girl could not understand. To divert his attention from his own growing arousal as well as from the girl's piercing green eyes, Thomas held the letter up before his face and tried to read the name upon it. The oversized, squiggly letters, which reminded him of a child's handwriting, were hard to understand. "McPeter, McPeterson . . ." he mumbled as he tried to match the letters he could identify with a name that made sense.

"McPherson," the girl volunteered. "Ian McPherson, of Captain Shaw's company. He's a corporal, don't you know? Fought with our very own Colonel Washington last summer 'gainst the French."

Though Thomas had no regard for the provincials who had been recruited to complete the filling out of the Forty-fourth and Forty-eighth's ranks, he had even less for the independent companies of rangers sent by the various governors. "Well, yes," Thomas replied, being careful to avoid the girl's eyes as well as to hide whatever telltale passions might have been tainting his cheeks. "I, ah, will see to it. Yes, as soon as practicable."

Stepping back, the girl gave a shallow, if somewhat awkward, curtsy. "I'd be much obliged if you did."

Coughing as if to clear his throat, Thomas held his hand up to his mount and waved the girl off. "No problem, no problem at all."

Without further ado, the girl pivoted on her heel, recovered her basket, and skipped across the muddy street to a spot where a wide-eyed Negro girl was standing, watching her. From behind him, a familiar voice caused Thomas to jump. "Consorting with *ladies* in broad daylight, I see," Captain Robert Ohme sneered.

Turning, Thomas made no effort to hide his embarrassment or surprise. "That, sir, was no lady."

This caused Ohme to laugh.

"Most extraordinary people, these Americans," Thomas went on as he held up the letter to show Ohme. "That girl just pranced right up to me, shoved this letter in my hand, and asked that I deliver it to her lover, who's with the first column."

Ohme snickered. "And what was it that you charged that spirited young thing for postage?"

"Robert!" Thomas started to protest. "I am astonished that you would suggest that . . ."

Ohme put his hands up. "Oh, please, don't bore me with your feigned protests. I'll be the last man on earth to deny a fellow officer his pleasures. I'd just suggest that in the future, you be a bit more discreet when you're consorting with 'ladies.' Gentlemen simply do not go about, in public, doing that sort of thing."

Seeing an opportunity to throw in a barb of his own and put Ohme on the defensive, Thomas smiled. "Oh, yes. And I suppose you, a gentleman with vast knowledge of such affairs, are speaking from personal experience."

Ohme smiled and winked. "We're supposed to be gentlemen, not saints. Now," he added, changing his tone and the direction of the conversation, "there is much to do before the general is ready to leave. We need to be off and see what we can do to speed our departure from this place."

Finding no fault with Ohme's logic, since he was equally pleased by the prospect of getting on with the campaign,

Thomas nodded and stepped off smartly, taking up station to Ohme's left. It would be a blessing, Thomas thought, to be back on campaign dealing with something that he thoroughly understood and, more important, enjoyed: war. Without another thought, he took the serving girl's letter, crumpled it into a small ball with one hand, then shoved it into his vest pocket. As soon as he had done so, Thomas forgot about it, leaving it for his laundress to remove and dispose of, as she did all such worthless scraps of paper the captain had a habit of stuffing in his clothing.

Western Maryland, on the Road to Fort Cumberland April, 1755

IN silence, the soldiers of Shaw's company of Virginia Rangers watched the well-ordered ranks of Sir Peter Halkett's Forty-fourth Regiment of Foot march by. Every now and then, one of Shaw's men who had served in the Virginia Regiment recognized a man in the red-clad ranks who had also been part of that now disbanded unit. "I'll tell you straight, Ian," James McPike mumbled when he spotted one of their former comrades go by, with eyes fixed to the back of the man's neck before him. "It gives me the willies."

Ian McPherson, watching as they went by, nodded. "Tell me, James, what part worries you the most? Seein' a man like Frederick marchin' along with the English, or just the sight of that bloody damned uniform?"

McPike surveyed the long ranks as he considered the question. "I guess a little of both," he finally volunteered. "I came here in the hope of puttin' as much space between them an' me as I could. And now see what's become of us. We're marchin' side-by-side with the bastards as if the '45 never happened."

Shifting his weight as he leaned on the muzzle of his musket, Ian shot a quick glance over at McPike. "Now, don't you be feedin' me a lie like that. Ya came here 'cause they threw your smelly ass on a prison brig and hauled it over here."

Drawing in a deep breath as his face reddened, McPike lifted his musket and turned his back on the passing column. "Well, that may be true," he snorted, "but it was their loss, and my gain."

With a friendly pat and slight shove on McPike's pack, Ian motioned him toward the front of their own column, now forming on the side of the road under the eyes of their captain, John Shaw. Shaw was glad to see Ian in a cheerful mood and good health. Both, he knew, were due to his efforts. After the debacle at the Great Meadows and the long, grim march back, Ian was at the end of his tether. With no place to go, Shaw took him back east while those fit enough stayed at Willis Creek to build a proper fort. With the help of the Negro tenants who tended Shaw's small farm outside Fredericksburg while he was off on regimental business, Ian recovered from the effects of malnutrition and finally shook the debilitating diarrhea that had clung to him for so long. By the fall of 1754, Ian was recovered sufficiently to help take in the harvest. "Stay with me, McPherson, through the spring," Shaw would bellow halfway across the field as they and the freed Negroes worked under the fading autumn sun, "and I'll teach ya to be a proper Irish peasant."

Ian did stay with Shaw, but it was not farming that they were pursuing when the hard winter began to give way to the hot, sultry days of Virginia's spring. With the threat of the French still hanging on their frontier, the need for a provincial force was as compelling as it had been the year before. And though the British army would supply the bulk of the force being dispatched to deal with the French, each of the colonies affected by this foreign incursion was expected to provide both troops and support.

In Virginia, Governor Dinwiddie was more than willing

to do what he could to both please his sovereign and advance his personal fortunes. When it came to fulfilling the need for manpower to serve as part of the expedition, it came in three forms. The best of the survivors of Washington's disbanded regiment who could be induced to do so were offered up to Braddock to finish fleshing out the ranks of the two regiments of foot that had accompanied him from England. Others, to include many new recruits, were formed into several independent companies known collectively as rangers. In addition, companies of carpenters, needed to cut the twelve-foot-wide road Braddock required for his train of artillery and supplies, were recruited.

Though Ian could easily have either joined a company of carpenters or signed on as a wheelwright with the supply column, and thereby avoid the risk of combat all together, he chose to follow Shaw. "The way I see it, Captain," Ian told his host, "if I stay out of this, I stand to lose the land that the governor promised us last year. Besides," he added with a sincerity that touched Shaw's heart, "I figure I owe you for what you've done for me." And though Shaw protested profusely that he had done it out of kindness for a fellow expatriot, he was far too practical a man to turn down Ian's officer. As he had last year, Shaw would need good, reliable sergeants and corporals to both train his recruits and, when the moment came, provide the backbone needed to keep his green volunteers from becoming a useless rabble easily swept aside by a determined foe. "I don't see the English making all this effort just for show," Shaw cautioned Ian. "There'll be a fight this time. A proper, stand-up European brawl that'll make last year's fracas look like a Quaker prayer meeting."

With determined eyes that told Shaw all he needed to know, Ian responded dryly, "Aye, I've seen what those lads in their smart red coats and lace can do." Then, resting his hand on the hilt of the broadsword he had symbolically strapped on when he had come forth to offer his services, Ian added, "I've also seen what good men, well led and with a cause they believe in, can do. With a little help from Providence, we'll be a match for 'em, this time."

A former foe of the very men whom they now marched alongside, Shaw knew that Ian was speaking of both English and French soldiers, for he was of a like mind. "Few believe," Shaw cautioned, "the French are the danger our governor and the gentlemen of the colonial legislature claim."

"We'll take what we're given," Ian stated without undue bravado, "and make do. If our cause is just and our leaders fair, all will come out in the end."

"And what cause," Shaw asked bluntly, "is powerful enough to drive you, lad? What brings you back into the wilderness, to risk life and limb again?"

For a moment, Ian glanced back down the well-trodden road they had taken from Alexandria. "It's no great secret that except maybe for Maggie, there's nothing binding me to this place." Then he looked at Shaw. "My home's in Scotland, where the bones of my ancestors lay covered by the same sod that they farmed and lived on. In time, God willing, another will come to those troubled lands and raise his banner. When he does, I'll be there, ready this time, to fight like a proper soldier. I'll be able to do more than dumbly follow a clan chief into the slaughter. The next time I come eye-to-eye with those red-coated bastards in a fight," Ian stated in tones that left no compromise, "I'll be ready."

"And what," Shaw countered, "will you do till that day comes?"

Ian smiled. "Like you, I'll find myself a small plot of land I can call my own, farm it, and, God willing, raise a family."

While Ian's plan seemed to Shaw scant justification for his determination to sign on for another campaign against the forks of the Ohio, he didn't pursue the matter. But the conversation stayed with Ian as he trudged along the muddy trail churned up by the feet of the Forty-fourth and the wide, heavy wheels of their ordnance wagons. Again and again, Ian found himself reliving long-forgotten memories. As McPike had been, Ian was affected by the sight of the redcoats in ways he could not have predicted. Recollections and images, long left dormant by time and the immediacy of day-to-day living, were reawakened, stirred, and brought to the surface like the mud underfoot. First at Alexandria, where Braddock had mustered his force, and now, again, along the length of the army's line of march. The only other thoughts that passed through Ian's mind were those of Maggie and the renewed romance they had shared during the winter. Only the necessity of living side by side with the very same soldiers who had crushed the last hope of freedom for his ancestral homeland dampened the growing love he felt for the fiery young Irish girl.

Ever attuned to the shifting moods of the man she had chosen to be her mate, Maggie O'Reilly had done everything in her power to keep Ian from dwelling on this. "Though I cannot say for sure that I fully understand what yer feelin', Ian," Maggie claimed one evening, "I do know that you've got to let go of the demons from your past that are drivin' ya. What happened back there, in Scotland, is over and gone, for good, just as my dear family is. We've got to shut our eyes to those ghosts and live our lives, as we see fit to live 'em, in the here and now."

Ian, however, would not allow himself to be dissuaded from the uneasy feelings that crept forth from his subconscious memory every time he laid eyes on a British soldier. "You've got to understand, girl," Ian countered with a steadfastness that unnerved the young girl. "What they did over there can never be forgotten. If there is to be a future for us, I want it to be a real future, for our children as well as for us. I tell you, so long as we're in the shadows of those people," a term he used liberally when referring to the English, "we have no future we can claim for ourselves. I've seen 'em, with me own two eyes, come down on innocent villages like hungry wolves and consume all before them."

"Then, why on earth," Maggie protested, "did ya make yer mark to march side-by-side with 'em to fight the French? Why, man, do you persist in exposin' your body and soul to such miseries and dangers?"

When she posed that question to him months before, Ian had been unable to answer in a manner that would make sense to her. And now, as he followed in the footsteps of the very men he hated and despised, he wondered if he would ever be able to do so. That there was an emptiness in his soul that needed to be filled could not be denied. While learning to mend broken wheels under the firm hand of his former master, Ian had endeavored to find a way to mend the wounds that scarred his past. He had hoped that he could learn from the working people and artisans of Alexandria. Far too many of them, however, were themselves on the move, in search of something new, something better both for themselves and for their children. Besides, Ian had learned quickly for himself that simple monetary gains, regardless of the pleasures they brought, were, in and of themselves, hollow and fleeting.

Looking up from the muddy furrows of the road before him, Ian saw the back of Shaw as he led on his small command. That man, Ian had decided long ago, provided him with something that the master wheelwright had never been able to. Though skilled and articulate, his old master viewed everything in his life, including all those whom he associated with, as credits or debts. Whatever spirit and soul the man had once possessed had been replaced long ago by the allure of profit and gain.

Shaw, on the other hand, was different. He was, for Ian, both a substitute father and as near a clan chief as could be found in these colonies. He had the rough, pragmatic view that made Scottish leaders respected among their own people. He was kind without being condescending, firm without being rough, demanding without being cruel. He had, as Ian recalled, all the qualities that he had admired in his father but had never permitted to mature in himself under the watchful eye of the elder McPherson. Perhaps, Ian thought, he needed Shaw as much, or more, now, to help him through to the maturity and manhood that his youthful adventures had postponed so long ago.

Or maybe, Ian thought as he looked up at the blooming buds exploding from every branch that covered their way, there was more to his simple desire to return to Scotland, something his soul perceived yet kept concealed from him for now. Whatever the reason, he concluded, deep down inside he knew that this was where he belonged, for now. He was needed here, not only by Shaw, who saw him as a reliable noncommissioned officer, but by those lads marching side by side with him who were new to the art of soldiering. To Shaw, he was a son. To them, he was an older brother or, in a few cases, a father. Though Shaw's company was raised to be a band of warriors, for Ian it had become a home.

CHAPTER NINE

Fort Duquesne, Western Pennsylvania
May, 1755

ANTON WATCHED the latest arrival of Indians from the safety of one of the fort's eastern bastions. As with all bands of natives arriving for the coming campaign season, the fort's commandant, Captain Claude-Pierre Pecaudy, Sieur de Contrecoeur, made a great show of the affair. Standing before the fort's main gate, in the open space between the fort and the forest to the east and across the river, Contrecoeur greeted the newcomers. Gifts from the fort's meager stock were provided to the leaders of the band, salutations of admiration and mutual respect were heaped upon the warriors, and the obligatory pledges of fidelity in pursuit of a common cause were exchanged.

Such affairs were neither foreign nor unusual to Anton

and the officers of the garrison. In Europe, similar shows, accompanied by great pomp and martial displays, were very much a part of the military fabric. Even the arrival of a new commander to an army in the field was celebrated with ceremonies not unlike the one unfolding before Anton's eyes. "Those are little more than dress parades," commented a provincial officer who had served with the French army in Europe before immigrating to Canada as he pointed out some of the subtle nuances to Anton. "Here, it is a matter of life and death for us. In order to cement the loyalty of such a fickle race of people to our cause, we must assure them that we are the stronger, more 'just,' of the antagonists. We must," the provincial officer stated as he puffed out his chest until his eyes bulged and threw back his shoulders in an exaggerated manner in an effort to make himself appear larger, "demonstrate our power." Letting the excess air rush from his lungs and slouching his shoulders forward, he glanced down at the gathering below. "Otherwise," he muttered in a soft tone, "they go home, or worse."

"Go over to the English?" Anton volunteered.

With a slight nod, the provincial officer replied. "We have little to offer them," he mused in a soft voice. "Regardless of the king's proclamations, this is their land. We are but visitors, interlopers, passing through their forests and along their rivers like predators. Were it not for the fact that they are just as unreasonable as we Europeans when it comes to living in peace with their neighbors, they would sweep both us and the English off of this continent."

"You often speak, Jerome," Anton replied thoughtfully, "as if you wish they had."

The provincial looked into Anton's eyes and chuckled. "My name may be Pepin, but not all my blood is French. My grandmother was Huron. As a child, I spent much time among her people when my father was away trapping." Then, looking away and out over the assembled mass of Indians below them, he added, with a hint of regret in his voice, "She tried hard to teach me the ways of her people, but I never paid attention."

Anton's eyes grew in size. "Why?"

The slight smile that had been on the provincial officer's lips disappeared as his brow furrowed. "Because I am a Canadian, as will be my children." Lifting his eyes, Pepin looked out beyond the clearing before them at the river and mountains beyond. "The days of my grandmother's people are numbered. Even as a child, I saw that. Perhaps she did, too, which is why she tried to teach me. Like a swollen river, we, the white race, will sweep all before us and make this continent ours," Pepin announced with a wide sweep of his hand. "God has ordained that, Anton," he stated flatly, as if it were an immutable fact. Then, looking back at Anton, he smiled. "You are a dreamer, one of those who believes that these savages are God's children, closer to Him than we because they have been left unspoiled by our wicked European ways."

Anton bowed his head and gestured vaguely with his hands. "Well, I . . ."

Pepin laughed now. "Oh, please, you have no need to fabricate excuses. I understand. I suppose all of us have looked into the eyes of a young Indian maiden and seen something that we all wish we could understand, that we desperately wanted to embrace. But it is not ours to have and hold, my friend," Pepin now added as his voice grew whimsical. "They are of a different blood, the Indians and we. No matter how many years a white may choose to live with them, no matter how much time he spends trying to learn their ways, we will never, can never, be one of them."

Again, he looked over at the rivers and the mountains. This time, he held his arms outstretched and open, and closed his eyes as he gestured in a manner Anton had seen many an Indian do when giving praise to spirits he believed in. "They are as much a part of this land as the trees and the mountains. The winds that whisper through the forests are the spirits of their ancestors." Then, dropping his arms, Pepin stepped up to Anton and looked him squarely in the eyes. "We will make this our land, you can be assured of that. But we will never possess it, not as they do." Without any further explanation, the provincial officer turned and made his way down the ladder into the bustling parade ground in the center of the fort.

Left alone, Anton looked back into the crowd of Indians, listening attentively to his commandant's exclamations and praise. He was still pondering the words of the Canadian when his eyes fell upon a familiar face. It was his old Indian friend, Gingego. For a moment, Anton's heart skipped a beat as he searched frantically for the Caughnawaga's brother. Not finding him, he turned his attention back to Gingego, who was, as if summoned by his attention, staring intently at Anton.

In the evening, when his duties for the day were finished and he was relieved of his post, Anton boldly strolled into the camp of the newly arrived Caughnawagas. Though he never regretted coming between Toolah and the hapless Englishman Toolah had singled out for death, Anton was uneasy about the consequences of that affair. The harshness in Toolah's voice, and the anger he had seen reflected in that young brave's eyes, had haunted Anton throughout the long, hard winter. Privately, he had hoped that neither of the brothers would return in the spring, that they would find other adventures or pursuits.

But the sight of Gingego had crushed that hope. As he eased up to one fire after another, searching for either of the two brothers, Anton repeatedly tried to convince himself that he was no coward, that he could deal with whatever came to pass when he found himself face-to-face with a man he had convinced himself he had saved from certain death. Yet, as he made his way through the darkness, deep down inside Anton felt a terrible apprehension that slowed his steps and heightened every sense in his body as he subconsciously prepared himself for a confrontation he dreaded.

After making his way through most of the campfires, a warrior caught Anton's gaze and locked stares with him. Though Anton did not recognize the man he was looking at, there was no doubt that the Caughnawaga knew him, or at least who he was. With a flick of his head and a slight glance, the Indian broke his stare with Anton, looked at another warrior whose back was to Anton, and indicated that there was someone behind him he needed to turn to. With a deliberate slowness, the warrior with his back to Anton turned his head.

By the time Anton could see which of the brothers it was, all eyes that had been watching the dancing flames of their fire were riveted on him.

"It is good to see you well," Gingego stated in a flat tone that conveyed neither emotion nor sincerity.

Clearing his throat, Anton mustered up enough moisture in his mouth to respond with a voice he hoped hid his apprehensions. "I am glad to see that you have chosen to join us here, for another campaign."

To this, Gingego did not reply. Instead, he sat, his body twisted about so that he could see Anton behind him, and waited, like the others, to see what Anton would say next. Knowing that something was expected of him, Anton drew himself up a bit straighter. "I did not see your brother, Toolah. Is he well?"

Though his lips didn't move, Anton detected a hint of a smile in Gingego's eyes. "He goes to Crown Point," Gingego announced matter-of-factly, "with the German who leads your armies in Canada."

Though he tried hard to conceal the relief he felt, Anton's face betrayed the joy this announcement brought him. It was several seconds before he could regain control of his voice in order to respond. "Ah, well, that is too bad," he managed. "We will have a great challenge to face this year."

"Greater," Gingego replied, "than that which you came here to face?"

For a moment, Anton wasn't sure whether Gingego was referring to the English or to his own personal feud with Toolah. "Perhaps," Anton finally replied cryptically.

Satisfied that he had prolonged Anton's misery as long as he could, Gingego turned to his fellow braves and muttered something in a low voice that Anton could not hear. Then he stood, turned, and left the circle about the fire, joining Anton in the shadows. "I had not expected to see you here when I returned," Gingego stated in French as he approached Anton.

"This is my post," Anton responded boldly. "I am a soldier and I have my duty."

Gingego smiled. "What passed between you and my

brother has not been forgiven. Before all to see, you prevented him from counting coup on an enemy. You admonished him as if he were a child, not a man."

"I probably saved his life," Anton countered in defense. "That Englishman was no stray, ready to surrender his scalp so that your brother could go back home with a trophy of war hanging from his belt. Given half a chance, it would have been your brother's blood, not the Englishman's, that would have stained the ground."

Gingego shook his head. "You do not understand, do you, my innocent French friend. Though I was ashamed that my brother chose to fall on a weak and wounded soldier in an effort to enhance his standing as a warrior, it was his right to do so."

"But the English had surrendered," Anton protested. "We had an understanding. They were to go in peace. It was my duty to see that no harm came to the Englishmen."

"Perhaps you had made a peace, but," Gingego stated sharply, "what passes between you and the English is of little concern to us."

"When you march with us," Anton announced in a voice that reminded Gingego of the French missionaries who had beaten their foreign teachings into his head, "you are obliged to do as you are told, and obey my commanders, as I am expected to."

To demonstrate his displeasure with this attitude, Gingego drew himself away from Anton by folding his arms and leaning backward. "We do not understand the arguments between your king and the one who the English call George. We follow you because we choose to, because the English come to our lands, in numbers that cannot be counted, taking what they please in return for goods that my people have come to depend upon. We do not fight for you. This war we fight now is for *our* land, for *our* people. The laws you use to govern the conduct of your people in peace have never been used when dealing with my people. Never! How, then, can you expect us to obey those laws in war?"

In disbelief, Anton drew away from the Indian he thought he had once understood. "What," he exclaimed, "has become of you, Gingego? Last year, you were so anxious to learn all that you could of my world, so ready to embrace what even you considered a future that neither you nor your people could escape. Have you forgotten what we talked about all those months?"

"No," Gingego replied bluntly. With great deliberateness, he looked over at the fort, where he could see the dark silhouette of sentinels, highlighted by watch fires from within the fort, maintaining a vigilant watch over their gathered allies. After a moment or two, he turned and looked back at his gathered companions, all of whom were watching, with great interest, the discussions between him and the young French officer. Finally, Gingego faced Anton again. "I have not forgotten what I learned from you. Nor have I forgotten what the missionaries taught us."

"Why, then," Anton asked, "are you speaking as if we were enemies?"

Gingego replied with a firmness that left no room for doubt as to his sincerity. "You have chosen to make yourself my enemy by making an enemy of my brother. Though my heart tells me you did not mean to, your action reminded me that our people can never live as one, as equals, in peace. So long as you and the English insist that your laws and your God be the only ones that are to govern this land, we can never be brothers."

Without waiting for a response, Gingego turned and started to head back to the fire. But before he took more than a few steps, he paused, turning to face Anton. Standing fully erect, Gingego allowed his arms to relax and the blanket he had wrapped over his shoulder to fall away, exposing his glistening bare chest. "One thing that you have taught me well is who I am," Gingego added. "You reminded me, monsieur, that I am a Caughnawaga."

Braddock's Line of March,
Western Maryland
June, 1755

THE red-coated Irish lad glanced back and forth between Ian and James McPike in an effort to catch any hint of a grin or smirk. "I know," he finally stuttered when he couldn't detect any outward sign that they were having fun with him, "what you say cannot be true. No man could survive havin' his scalp lifted an' live to tell of it."

Ian straightened up and contorted his face, as if insulted. Turning to McPike, he slapped his companion's arm. "I think he's callin' us liars, James."

McPike, also sitting upright, folded his arms and glared at the young soldier. "Yer know, I think you're right, Ian. I think our friend here is bein' downright rude."

With a shake of his head, Ian stood up, took his musket from the tree it had been leaning against, and looked down at the worried expression the Irishman was now wearing.

"I didn't mean to offend you," the lad volunteered in an effort to make amends. "I mean," he stammered, "I'm sure the stories about the Indians and all you've been tellin' us are quite true. It's just that, well, I find it hard to believe that any human being can be as cruel and savage as you make the Indians out to be. I mean, I've heard some say that the red men are God's chosen children, put here to live in a natural state of grace."

Leaning forward until his face was only inches away from the Irish soldier, even after the lad had backed away some, McPike gave him a devilish grin. "Grace, you say? Aye, they've got grace, for sure." With his hands making the motion, McPike told how an Indian brave could slit the throat of his victim with one, clean motion, and in the next, peel away the poor man's scalp before the unfortunate soul had a chance to faint away. "You'll still be tryin' with all your might to figure out what happened as your life oozes away," McPike warned.

Bowing his head until his mouth was covered by the

crook of his arm, Ian hid the laughter he could no longer hold back. Though both men knew what they said was, for the most part, true, they, like many of the provincials, took great care to embellish the stories they passed on to their English brethren with as many gory details as their fertile imaginations could conjure up. Pulling away from the Irishman and standing up next to Ian, McPike thumped his chest with his thumb. "I'm here to tell you, lad, I've seen it with me own eyes. And it was a terrible sight, to be sure."

Still unsure as to whether to believe the cocky Scotsmen, the soldier took a deep breath and went back to glancing from one blue-coated provincial soldier to the other. Ian, who by now was reduced to tears by the strain of trying to conceal his laughter, had turned his back and, in an effort to disguise further the purpose of this move, began fiddling with his musket. "I do not think," replied the young Irishman, who was barely past his eighteenth birthday, "that we'll need to worry about that. The officers in my company are all of the opinion that as soon as they see us coming on, they'll just melt away into the woods."

McPike gave the Irishman a leery smile. "You'll stop thinkin' that way, lad, the mornin' you wake up and find the man next to you in your cozy little tent a layin' in a pool of blood with his throat cut from ear," McPike stated as he ran his finger along his own throat, "to ear."

Having had enough, the Irish lad finally stood up and prepared to return to where his comrades were gathered. "Well," he said in parting, "when I see that, I'll believe it."

"I just hope, fer your sake," McPike shouted as the soldier wandered away, "that it's not your throat and blood ya'll be findin'."

Now unable to restrain himself any further, Ian broke out in laughter that caused his shoulders to quiver. "James," he called out between sobs, "you're a cold-hearted bastard, you are. You've got a heart as black as the devil himself."

For the first time, McPike allowed himself to grin. "Aw, I'm just havin' some fun with the lad, you know. I did not mean him any harm."

With a shake of his head, Ian turned and started to make his way up the crowded road. "Come on, you blaggard," he called back to James, "before the rest of the company gets too far ahead."

McPike, lifting his bedroll and haversack from the ground, didn't move any faster. "We've no need to rush, Ian. What, with Braddock's aim of cutting down every tree between here and the Ohio, this army hasn't moved more than four miles on any given day and isn't likely to do any better today." Pausing as he adjusted his equipment until it was comfortable, McPike watched an overloaded wagon being pulled by a team of jaded animals that were more skeleton than flesh. "And even if the carpenters were a bit quicker at their task," he added, "we'd never be able to move with anything even close to resemblin' a crawl. Not with all this stuff that our dear cousins from across the sea are draggin' with us."

An English sergeant, overhearing McPike's comment as he marched by with his detachment of soldiers, glared at McPike. Sensing that the man was about to say something, McPike threw out his chest, jutted his chin, and returned the sergeant's stare. Convinced by this show that the provincial would meet any challenge in kind that he hurled at the man, the sergeant hesitated, then let the matter drop with no more than a mumbled something to a soldier next to him that McPike couldn't hear.

From his location a few yards down the road, Ian had been watching the passing confrontation, ready to intervene had it been necessary. Since nothing had come to pass, Ian contented himself with greeting the annoyed English sergeant as he went by with the broadest, toothiest smile he could manage, evoking another string of muttered comments from his red-coated counterpart. "Now, now, Ian," McPike chided his friend when he caught up to him, "don't go causin' trouble with our dear brothers in arms."

Ian dropped his smile and looked over his shoulder at McPike. "I'll tell you straight, James," he stated flatly in a tone that was both sincere and troubling. "When the shooting starts, I'm gonna be hard-pressed to remember they're on our side."

Slapping his friend's back, McPike laughed. "Are they, now? And who told you that?"

The dark thought that had clouded Ian's mind drifted

away as he looked his friend in the eye and grinned. Then, without a word, he turned and leisurely started to make his way forward to catch up to the rest of the company.

Their progress was slow, excruciatingly slow. Braddock's army was, by European standards, a small, trifling affair. But the North American continent had never seen such an assembly of power before. The king and his advisers were intent on ending, once and for all, the French threat to the Ohio territory. To this end, General Edward Braddock assembled overwhelming power at Willis Creek in May 1755. There was, to start with, the two regiments of foot. The Forty-fourth, under Sir Peter Halkett, with bright yellow facings and cuffs adorning their long-tailed red coats, marched to the beat of twenty drums and comprised the bulk of the first division of the army. The Forty-eighth, commanded by Colonel Thomas Dunbar, wore the same red coat and brown marching gaiters that extended above the knee as the Forty-fourth but had distinct buff regimental facings on the collars and cuffs. Added to these regiments of the line were two independent companies from New York, one of which was commanded by Captain Horatio Gates, a twenty-seven-year-old whose father was the housekeeper for the duke of Leeds. Like Mackey's company the year before, these were colonials who were mustered into the British army, serving under officers holding the king's commission. Clad in red like Braddock's men, they added to the spectacle that impressed the Indians scouting for the French at Fort Duquesne, who watched from the cover of the surrounding forest.

To augment this powerful force of infantry and rain destruction on the French fort at the forks of the Ohio was a train of artillery consisting of eight twelve-pound guns, six six-pounders, four eight-inch mortars, and fifteen small cohorn mortars along with the crews needed to man them. The last element of Braddock's main force was not soldiers at all but a group of thirty sailors under the command of Lieutenant Charles Spendlow of His Majesty's ship *Norwich*. They were charged with assisting Braddock with ferrying the army over rivers along the line of march that proved too deep to ford.

Mixed in with this impressive force trained in the fine art of European warfare were the provincials, organized into what were called companies of rangers. The majority of them, five total, came from Virginia. Dressed in smart blue coats, vests, and trousers, they were a far cry from the motley collection that had set out along this same trail just one year before. But they were still, much to Braddock's disgust, far from being the best the colony could offer. Braddock was most charitable when he referred to them as being "very indifferent men." In plain fact of truth, the companies of rangers, and those drafted into the ranks of the Forty-fourth and Forty-eighth Foot, were drawn almost exclusively from the idle and destitute of the colony, riffraff who had few, if any, prospects short of jail.

The other ranger companies, one each from Maryland and the two Carolinas, were little better. After watching them but a short while, Braddock's aide-de-camp, Captain Robert Ohme of the Coldstream Guards, pronounced the provincials "languid, spiritless, and unsoldierlike in appearance, which, considered with the lowness and ignorance of most of their officers, gave little hope of their future good behavior."

Still, it was felt they were needed, since there were so few Indians willing to throw their lot in with the English. The fact was, through blunders, mismanagement, and an attitude that could only be described as arrogance, Braddock had but fifty natives to do his scouting and reconnaissance for him. "It's not at all a healthy sign, Ian," Shaw had pointed out at the very beginning, "that we have so few Indians with us. It's not so much the scoutin' that we'll miss. It's their fighting. If French up and fight us in the woods, instead of the proper European siege that everyone's expecting, it'll be mayhem the likes of which those regiments of foot have never seen. The savages and the Canadians will take one look at the fine drill of the regulars, duck behind the nearest tree, and laugh their fool heads off while they're sneakin' around to our rear. I tell ya, lad," Shaw concluded, "it's a bad sign, one that no one seems to be paying heed to." Ian, in his short time, understood well his commander's concern.

Still, the column blazed ahead through the wilderness

with the help of two companies of carpenters, all Virginians, guarded by Lieutenant Colonel Thomas Gage's advance guard. Under the command of Braddock's chief of engineering, Harry Gordon, a Scotsman who had served under Cumberland in Flanders, these carpenters were charged with the task of cutting a road twelve feet wide over the mountains of western Maryland and Pennsylvania with axes and hand-saws. Where necessary, they built bridges over those streams and gorges that could not be forded or bypassed. Still, try as hard as they might, they had neither the time nor the where-withal to make the road a proper one. Instead, large stumps and the long, thick roots of primeval trees studded the road-way that was both the pathway and the lifeline of the army.

In manpower alone, this army consisted of almost twenty-two hundred effectives, not counting laundresses and teamsters. To sustain this host, as well as carry the munitions for the artillery and reserve cartridges for the troops them-selves, close to two hundred wagons and several hundred packhorses trundled up and down the bumpy road. These were all driven by colonials, many of them farmers driving their own wagons, but some were professional teamsters, like the rough and profane Daniel Morgan, or young men, still in their teens, taking part in their first great adventure, such as a boy named Daniel Boone. Together with cattle on the hoof, the number of four-legged members of the army came close to equaling that of the two-legged variety. It was, therefore, not unusual, given the slow pace of the advance, for the rear elements of the column to camp where the lead units had pitched their tents the night before.

As they made their way along its fringe, both Ian and McPike studied the equipment and men that made up the great host. "We're a great bloody snail, Ian," James McPike sneered as the two Virginians made their way along the line of march. "With all the tents and private camp beds for the officers, and the cannon we're draggin' along, it'll be a miracle if we make it to the Great Meadows before the first snows."

Ian, equally frustrated by the slow pace, nevertheless took heart in the undertaking. "At least," he countered with a smile, "we're not gonna starve like we did last year. And if we ever do find the French," he added as he patted the brass barrel of a cannon they were passing, "we'll not have to do our fighting knee-deep in water."

McPike looked at the gun as he went by, giving one of the sweating gunners a nod and a smile as he did so. "Aye, you've got a point there, laddy. You've got a point. Now," he added, as he always did when things were looking up, "let's hope the Frenchies see it our way and oblige us by waitin' till we're all together, lined up, and ready, like Bonnie Prince Charlie did at Culloden."

With a shake of his head, Ian sighed. Though he shared some of his companion's apprehensions, Ian was convinced that this time there would be no retreat. This time, they would be the ones watching the French march away. Though he hated the sight of the bloody red coats worn by his new comrades in arms, he had the greatest admiration for what they could do.

Also making his way along the column, on the opposite side of the road from Ian and McPike, was Thomas Shields. He, too, was fretting over the slow pace of the army's advance. Catching sight of an officer of artillery, he turned his horse's head toward his friend, dug his spurs into the animal's side, and plowed his way ahead through the rank of men in front of him. "Richard," Thomas called, catching the young officer's attention. "Still enjoying the natural beauty of His Majesty's far-flung dominions?"

When the artillery officer looked up at Thomas, his face showed little joy. "Yes, of course," he responded dryly, looking up and down the slow moving column that had moved less than a mile in the last three hours. "Seems our rather extraordinary pace is affording me more than ample time to partake of it."

Chuckling, Thomas and Lieutenant Richard Steele moved off the road and the tree line that confined the lumbering column of men, horses, wagons, and cattle. Stopping, the two officers turned and looked back at the column. "Hard work, Thomas," Steele volunteered. "Far harder than anything I've ever been involved in before."

Thomas didn't respond. Instead, he swung his leg over the horn of his saddle and slid down off his mount. As he did so, the horse gave an audible sigh of relief. "Go ahead, you bloody nag. Huff and wheeze all you want, you miserable nag," he chided the horse. "You're as stuck with me as I with you."

Removing his hat, the artillery officer mopped his brow with a handkerchief he had pulled from his breast pocket. "You can't blame the poor animal, Thomas. Not after we work them to death all day and do little more than turn them out into the woods, to nibble at whatever leaves they can manage to find. Even my best shire horses back home would be a wreck by now if I treated them like this."

Looking over at his friend, Thomas thought about the poor conditions both they and their animals were laboring under, then nodded as he drew a silver flask from a pocket inside his coat. "Do you suppose anyone back home truly understood what they were demanding of us?" he asked before taking a long sip from the flask.

Finished wiping away the sweat, the artillery officer looked up at the trees above them. Their branches, as thick as most of the trees he remembered from his home in Yorkshire, merged to form a canopy that all but blocked the sunlight above. "I don't see how. Even the most pessimistic of our company never imagined we'd be faced with mountains the likes of which we've seen to date." Then, looking down at Thomas, his expression dissolved into one that was so forlorn, it sent a chill down Thomas' back. "And it's so barren, Thomas. So empty and barren of human life. It's almost as if we're marching clear off the face of the earth itself. And the pace is so bloody *slow*."

With a nervous chuckle, Thomas offered his flask to his friend before turning his face back at the column. "Well, that's about to change," Thomas replied. "The general's splitting the column."

Not sure he heard right, though the silence of the forest was little disturbed by the ponderous movement of the mass of men and their materiel on the road before them, Steele blinked and asked incredulously, "Split the column? Did you say the general's going to split the column?" before taking a long sip from Thomas' flask.

Looking back over at his friend, Thomas nodded his head. "Yes, it seems so. The general, as anxious as the rest of us, has apparently decided that it would be best if he went on with a lighter force and left the bulk of the wagons, and some of your precious guns, to follow as best they could."

"And whose bloody brilliant idea was this? Not General Braddock's?"

Thomas smiled. "Seems our friend Mr. Washington has more influence over the general than we thought."

Steele rolled his eyes. Neither he nor Thomas could bring himself to use *Colonel* when referring to the provincial officer who had attached himself to Braddock's personal staff as an unpaid aide. And though all agreed that his knowledge of the area was useful, since he had cut the original road up to this point less than a year before, most of the officers of the line considered him to be little more than an amateur when it came to military matters. "I do hope," Steele finally volunteered, "that the division of the force has been entrusted to, ah, more capable hands than Mr. Washington's."

"Oh," Thomas replied, "quite. It seems St. Clair is to lead off with the advance guard to cut the road. The best of both regiments and the provincials, with only a few wagons, most of the packhorses, and your twelve-pounders and mortars, will follow. The rest will come up with Colonel Dunbar as best they can."

Leaning against a tree, Steele looked back over at the slow-moving column. After clawing away at his arm in a futile effort to kill some of the chiggers tormenting him, he nodded. "We can do it, I imagine, with that. So long as the French don't come out after us, we can make a show of it."

"I was hoping," Thomas responded, "of doing more than simply making a show of it."

Steele waved his hand as his face betrayed his annoyance. "You know what I mean. They've no regulars there, at least no European troops. The best they can throw at us is La Troupe de la Marine. Once we're settled into a formal siege, the entire affair will be over, if it ever comes to that."

Thomas nodded. Like most officers, he subscribed to the prevailing opinion that once the French commander at Duquesne saw that the British would, in fact, reach his fort, he would withdraw the garrison, blow up his stores of powder along with the fort, and beat a hasty retreat back to Canada. "Well," Thomas mused as he accepted his silver flask back from Richard and slipped it back into his pocket, "I do hope you're right."

"What's the matter, Thomas? You sound disappointed."

"I am," he replied as he gathered the reins of his mount. "I was hoping for more from this expedition than a tour of His Majesty's American possessions."

"I shouldn't worry about that," Steele laughed. "We're just beginning. I imagine once things get started, there'll be more than enough war to satisfy even your ambitions."

With a heave, Thomas boosted himself into the saddle, then looked down at Steele, smiling broadly. "Don't be too sure of that. My ambitions are limitless." Then, letting the smile fade, he added, "Still, it seems a pity to waste all of this just to occupy a pile of ash left by a nervous French commander." With a tip of his hat, he bid his friend good-bye and made his way forward, through the line of wagons and men inching their way over the twisting road that took them deeper into an endless wilderness.

Fort Duquesne, Western Pennsylvania
June, 1755

THE confidence expressed by Captain Thomas Shields and the officers marching with Braddock that the fort at the forks of the Ohio was doomed once the British reached that point was shared by the occupants of that fort itself. With little more to do than watch as June faded into July, Anton became more and more convinced that he was seeing French authority in this part of America coming to an end. *We all despair of the day,* he wrote in his journal, *when Captain Contrecoeur will be faced with his fateful decision.*

That fateful decision, as Anton described it, was whether to make a stand and defend the fort or to cut his losses, blow up the fort, and withdraw up the Allegheny. Both would be a defeat, Anton, and any officer even vaguely familiar with the mathematics of siege warfare, knew. "If our commandant decided to make a fight of it, the English will start here," Anton indicated to one of the young French cadets assigned to his guns while standing at the tree line east of the fort. "Just inside these woods they will dig their first trench. A battery of guns will be deployed with it to cover the approach works and isolate us on the tongue of land where the fort is located. If they are wise, they will build a small redoubt at each end of this trench, just in case we sally forth from the fort and assault their trenches or attempt an end run at night, via the river. Once established here, it will only be a matter of time."

Walking out from the tree line toward the fort, along a line he himself would use if attacking the fort, Anton traced a line in the dirt. "Each night after that, the English will dig their approach trenches, possibly along these lines. They will zigzag, back and forth, like this," he pointed out with his stick as they slowly paced off the distance, "so that we, in the fort, cannot fire down the length of them and injure the working parties."

"But," the worried young cadet interrupted, "we will fire on them, won't we?"

Anton stopped his count, looked down at the beardless face of the youth, and smiled. "Yes, but of course we will. We will attempt to do as much harm as we can from our bastions. But," Anton added with a sadness that both his expression and his voice conveyed, "we will fail."

Then, with the authority of a master of his trade, Anton went back to his lecture. "Depending on how industrious the English are, and how many risks their commander is willing to expose his sappers to, they will reach this point and build their first parallel, a line of trenches and gun platforms, where he will mount his heaviest batteries and set up his mortars. From here, they will be able to bombard every corner of our works, almost with impunity. If our commandant is to make a sortie against the English, it will be against these works, after the guns have been emplaced and before they have opened fire."

"Why then?" the cadet asked as he looked around, trying hard to visualize the works and the terrible fighting that would take place on the open plain between the woods and the fort where curious Indians now camped. "Why not when the enemy sappers were still busy working and the trenches shallow?"

"We are not interested in killing a few laborers, men easily replaced from the ranks of their provincial militia," Anton countered. "No. We want to seize the guns, if only for a few minutes. We will then either spike them, so that they could not be used, or blow them up by stuffing their barrels with as much powder as we can lay our hands on followed by mud or wadding. The assault party will then beat a hasty retreat back to the fort while a number of brave men, probably some of our gunners, stay behind to touch off the fuses. Then, *boom*," Anton exclaimed, throwing out his arms to mimic an explosion, "the valuable guns that the poor Englishmen labored so long and hard to haul so far will blow up."

"And the men assigned to set off the explosions? What of them?" the cadet asked.

"With luck," Anton responded after making a quick estimate, "half will return."

For several moments, Anton stood silent, turning this way and that, looking at the land he expected the English to occupy and then back at the fort, where his guns were mounted and waiting. Seeing that his superior was busy making calculations in his head, the cadet stood beside him, in silence, occupying his worried mind by studying the comings and goings of the Indians who passed them by with little more than a glance. Only when Anton announced that they had seen all they needed to there did the young cadet put forth his next question. "What if the sortie fails, monsieur?"

Anton stopped, turned, and looked at the cadet with a puzzled look, as if he had not understood the question. Then, after a shake of his head, he regarded the cadet with an expression that one would use when addressing an idiot. Finally, Anton managed to muster a response. "Well, we would surrender, of course. What else would you have us do, wait and be blown to bits for no good purpose?" Turning away from the cadet, Anton continued. "You must understand, once the English are here," Anton announced, thrusting his stick into the ground with as much force as he could, "with their guns, further resistance is all but pointless. We will, of course, resist for as long as practicable, thereby fulfilling our duty to our Sovereign. To resist any longer, however, and die here for nothing would bring neither France nor ourselves further glory," he stated, his voice becoming harsher as he continued. "On the contrary, our commander would be considered an idiot and we fools if we chose to carry on with a pointless defense. And the English, forced to endure the hazards of battle, would be far less charitable when we finally did choose to negotiate." Anton added, lowering his voice as he stepped closer to the cadet so that he would not be overheard by the Indians all about them, "In that case, we would find ourselves at the mercy of both our enemy and those who, today, are our friends, but who would quickly change allegiance once we were seen to be the weaker of the two European powers."

With real fear in his eyes, the cadet glanced from side to side, looking at the Indian braves as they went by. As they did with all newcomers to the wilderness, the veterans of frontier warfare had filled his head with the most gruesome stories they could recall from past wars or conjure up in their fertile imaginations. His sudden apprehensions and weak response of "Oh" told Anton he understood.

With nothing more to teach his young pupil there, Anton turned and started back toward the fort. The cadet, after standing where he had been left for a moment, took off at a hasty pace and managed to catch up to Anton before he had gone too far.

"You said, monsieur," the cadet asked after coming up alongside Anton, "*if.* Do you think that Captain Contrecoeur will choose to blow up the fort and retreat before the English reach here?"

Anton stopped at the gate of the wooden palisades that

served as an outer perimeter to the fort itself. Turning, he faced the wood line they had just left and the Indian huts they had passed through. As he considered his answer carefully, Anton looked about at the mountains that lay just across the river on either side of the narrow tongue of land they stood on. Absentmindedly, he swung the stick he had been carrying up onto his shoulder and rolled it around the back of his neck. Unlike the previous discussions, which had been purely technical, the young cadet's latest question was one of tactics, always an area that was subjective. "To respond with a worthwhile answer," Anton slowly stated, "we must first consider the enemy and his capabilities. Then we must examine the abilities of our own forces. Finally," he added, carefully choosing his words, "we need to take into account our own commanding officer. What," he asked his attentive pupil, "do we know of the English force sent against us?"

"Well, now," the cadet replied nervously, caught off guard by Anton's demand that he take a hand in answering his own question. "There are two regiments of infantry, regular infantry from Europe, augmented by a number of provincials. Indian scouts continue to put the number at three thousand, but this could be an exaggeration."

"Let's assume it is an exaggeration," Anton countered sharply. "Even at two thousand, it is still a considerable force to be reckoned with. Go on."

"Their guns," the cadet continued, remembering the lecture he had just received from Anton. "Their largest are twelve-pound field guns and, I'm told, eight-pound mortars. In addition, they have some six-pounders and an unknown number of cohorn mortars."

"Yes?" Anton asked, cueing his young student that he expected more.

"Their column has split. Most of the regulars and all the artillery is with the lead column, and the bulk of their wagons and some forces trail one to two days' march behind. This is a mistake, I am told."

"Why do you say that?" Anton asked with an innocent tone that did not fool the cadet.

"Well," the youth replied defensively, "even the dullest

cadet knows one does not divide an army in the face of the enemy. It is foolish. It leaves it open to defeat in detail."

"But," Anton replied, quickly bringing his stick down to his side so that it made a whooshing noise, "it allows one to move more swiftly, with your main force, to strike before your enemy can be reinforced. Do you think the English general has left any of his best troops behind to guard wagons? No, of course not. Now, that, my dear sir, would be foolish. No," Anton stated as he went back to looking at the surrounding mountains, imagining that they, like the English, were slowly, inexorably, closing in on him. "They have shed their excess baggage, as well as their lame and lazy, and are coming on with all they need to execute the task that has been handed to them by their king." With a shake of his head and a blink of his eyes, he brushed aside the image of the ominous mountains that overshadowed them. "What have you forgotten?"

The cadet stared at Anton, his mouth opening as if he would speak, but then closing again when no answer came.

"You must always remember, despite what you have had pounded into that young head of yours, that the British infantry is without peer. They are the finest foot troops in the world. Just one of those two regiments will be more than a match for the four-hundred-odd Troup de la Marine and militia our commandant has at his disposal. And with the rivers running as low as they are this year, and other British incursions aimed at breaking up our American empire, we cannot expect any help from anyone. Which," Anton stated, raising his stick until he held it upright between him and the cadet, "brings us to our last factor, our commander."

Anxious to impress his mentor, the cadet replied before Anton. "It has been said that if Captain Beaujeu were in command, he would use our superiority in Indians to ambush the English either deep in the woods or as they crossed the Monongahela."

"Monsieur Beaujeu, however, has not yet relieved Captain Contrecoeur of his command. Until that happens, the question we must consider is what will Contrecoeur, and not Beaujeu, do."

Suspecting he already knew the answer, the cadet's optimistic smile disappeared as he lowered his head and stared at the ground at his feet. Only now did Anton realize how hard he had been on his young charge. In part, this was due to the fact that he, just as much as the cadet, was frustrated by the sense of impending doom that was smothering the entire command, snuffing out even the faintest ray of hope. Reaching out and placing his left hand on the cadet's shoulder, Anton gave him a slight shake and a smile in an attempt to restore the lad's flagging spirits. "This is not the end of the world, you know. We are both young. There will be many battles ahead, in this war we are about to see open before our very eyes as well as others that are as yet waiting for a reason. France will need us both to defend the rest of the empire, as well as France itself. Far better, young man, to survive this, an event that will soon be forgotten by all save but a few chroniclers, and serve France another day."

Whether the cadet's smile was an acceptance of Anton's logic or merely an effort to put forth a brave front didn't matter to Anton. Their spirits, for at least the moment, were restored, leaving them free to go about the other duties both needed to tend to in preparation for the pending battle, now only days away.

CHAPTER TEN

Western Pennsylvania,
Two Miles West
of the Great Meadows
June, 1755

THERE WAS no middle ground when Ian McPherson crossed from sleep to consciousness. One moment, he would be lost in the great darkness that swept over him after each day's labors, and the next, he was wide awake, fully aware of all around him. Sitting upright, Ian blinked his eyes, then covered his face with his hands, rubbing his eyes as he gently massaged the stubble on his cheeks. The scents that his nose drew from the hands held too close to it told much of Ian's previous day's activities.

There was, as always when on campaign, the dry, dull smell of earth. Even when he took the time to wash his hands in a stream they were passing, dirt stayed on them. It was everywhere, hidden under Ian's nails and ground into every crack and crevice of his knuckles and the calluses that covered the fingers and heels of his hands. Another omnipresent odor was that of smoke. Like the dirt, it permeated every fiber of clothing and every inch of skin and strand of hair. Ian had a knack for cooking over an open fire, a skill he had learned from an old man whom he had marched with under the Stuart banner during the '45. Unwilling to trust his stomach to the comrades who pretended to prefer uncooked meat to hide their ignorance of cooking, Ian spent a great deal of time seated in front of the cook fire, preparing meals for himself and his mess mates. Inevitably, this chore included fighting clouds of smoke that seemed to follow him no matter where he shifted his body to.

While the smells of dirt and smoke were always there, they never dominated like the pungent reek of gun oil. As a veteran on his third campaign, Ian tended to his weapons every night with a mechanical thoroughness that put the "regulars" of Braddock's Irish regiments to shame. Even now, before taking his first step of the day, Ian reached out with one hand and, without looking, laid it upon the stock of his Brown Bess musket, which was leaning in the lee of a nearby tree. With the same gentleness that he would use if handling a fine porcelain statuette, Ian placed the musket across his legs. Carefully he removed the patch of leather he used to cover the lock and trigger. For a moment, he looked the piece over, from one end to the other, searching for obvious signs of rust or damage. With the exception of a deep furrow on the upper stock and a nick in the barrel, caused by the impact of an Indian's hatchet, the musket was as clean and shiny as the day he had been issued it. Satisfied that all appeared to be in order, he proceeded to work the mechanical parts of the lock. Ian pulled back on the hammer with his thumb, jiggled the trigger with his index finger, opened the pan to ensure that no moisture or dirt had gathered about the touch hole, and checked the snugness and sharpness of the piece of flint needed to ignite the priming charge.

Satisfied, he replaced the patch of leather over the lock, put the musket back against the tree, and took his ancient sword in hand. As he had with his musket, Ian took his time as he inspected this weapon for cleanliness and readiness. On more than one occasion, a curious English officer had made inquiries into why Captain Shaw permitted one of his rankers to carry such a weapon. Shaw, ever contemptuous of the British regulars, and fully aware that they recognized the distinctive Scottish basket hilt, would smile as he responded to his imperial counterpart. "Well, now," he'd say with a wink, "I, myself, have never had the nerve to ask the lad how he'd come upon that fine, awful weapon. Nor have I been foolish enough to inquire as to why he bothered to haul it about, seein' as he's more than once demonstrated to my satisfaction that he not only had the will but the skill to use it for its intended purpose. I do, though, imagine that he'd be more than happy to explain anything you wish to know about that particular subject, provided, of course, you ask him." To date, no British officer, including Thomas Shields, bothered to do so. Like Thomas, they knew the answer without having to ask.

Ian ignored the bayonet that hung in its scabbard alongside his cartridge box. It was, he thought, a silly, useless weapon in these parts. Though he had seen what well-trained and determined infantry could do with them, Ian placed greater faith in the effectiveness of his musket as a club rather than as a pole, for the eighteen-inch triangular blade wasn't honed to any degree of sharpness.

Satisfied that all was in order, Ian prepared to rise up from the blanket he had wrapped himself in during the night. While many of the men in the ranks of the English regiments complained of the cool, almost chilly mountain air and their lack of protection from it, Ian found the climate of this new land invigorating. Raised to spend weeks on end tending flocks of sheep with nothing more than his homemade kilt to fend off the bitter cold of the Scottish Highlands, Ian could make do with next to nothing while in the field. "To think," Ian often commented to James McPike as he watched the soldiers of the Forty-fourth and Forty-eighth Foot climb from their tents every morning and huddle together for warmth before the first beat of the drums, "we let ourselves be beaten by the likes of them. It's enough to make a grown man want to cry."

As he stretched his limbs and took a few steps away from his blanket, Ian looked up at the trees above. He could see, here and there in an occasional break, the tops of the trees brilliantly illuminated by the rays of the sun, still partially hidden by the mountains to the east. While some of the more precipitous mountains and hills they were traveling over did manage to rival those of his homeland, Ian couldn't remember ever seeing a single stand of trees in all of Scotland that could rival even the scrawniest patch of forest that blanketed this entire country. A man, he told himself as he looked about him, ignoring the intrusive presence of the army rousting itself from slumber, could find himself in worse places. Looking around, he could see others moving about. Some were tending to personal chores that would not wait until later. Others, like Ian, took advantage of this calm, quiet part of the day to collect and reflect upon private thoughts that noise and activity would later drown out.

Ian was watching an officer's batman move deeper into the woods in search of his master's horse when the roll of the Forty-fourth Foot's drums, erupting like an unexpected thunderstorm, ended his quiet morning reflections. Without another thought, he turned his face back to the road, where soldiers were scrambling from their neatly pitched tents. The once tranquil scene along the length of the road was now a sea of soldiers, regulars and provincials, moving about in haste in various states of dress. The barks of corporals and sergeants, hurrying the slow and despondent, mingled with the idle chatter and grumbles of men freshly woken from a sleep most felt was too brief. They had but a few minutes to be fully dressed, accoutred, under arms, and in double ranks, each facing outward as if to repel an attack.

Drawing in a deep breath, Ian steeled himself for the day ahead. Taking his time, he folded and rolled his blanket, tied it off using the same strap he had salvaged from a dead Frenchman's cartridge box better than a year before, and carefully began to put on his equipment. It would be another long, hot day with little progress, he thought. Not much different than the day before, or the day before that. They still had many miles to cover before they reached the French fort. Despite the army's separation into two parts, it was still slow and cumbersome. So Ian felt no need to scurry about, just to impress the English. Placing his hand on the hilt of his sword, he smiled. No, he mused. He would save any extra effort for the time they came face-to-face with the Frenchies. That this would happen, and that he would perform well, was never a question in Ian's mind. Only when it would happen was still in doubt.

THE slow, cautious creeping through the woods along the flank of the long English column in absolute silence in the still, predawn darkness had given Gingego much time to think. Perhaps too much time. Crouching low to the ground as the darkness gave way to the eerie early morning light, Gingego watched two of his companions, scouting out ahead, move closer to the road cut by the Englishmen. Since the English avoided leaving the road, the scouts would have little trouble getting close to the long column of soldiers and animals. What was difficult was attempting to determine, with any degree of accuracy, the number of Englishmen there actually were. "It is easier to count the minnows in a stream," one of Gingego's companions lamented, "than to find the number of soldiers the English general has brought to this place."

Yet, as impressive and ominous as the spectacle of the moving mass of men and material was, it was of little concern to Gingego. Instead, his mind kept turning to the issue that had troubled him for much of his life, and had left him and his brother at odds. Without even needing to close his eyes, he could see his brother's face distorted in anger. "You have shunned our ways in favor of the whites," Toolah had screamed after Gingego stepped between him and the French officer the night after the Virginians had been sent away from the Great Meadows. "I have stood by while I watched you turn your back on our people. Must I now do nothing while you turn on your own blood?"

While Gingego never feared for his life, the conflict he

had allowed to open between himself and Toolah brought into focus a conflict he'd thought he would be able to avoid. Though he knew he would never be accepted as an equal, Gingego believed adopting the ways of the whites would somehow help his people learn to live with them and share the land they so coveted in harmony. Others, he knew, shared that belief, a belief that had become, in their eyes, the only hope for their future existence. "If we choose to stand like the oak," an old chief stated at council during the long winter, "we will be swept away, roots and all, from the land that belongs to us by the flood of those who come from where the sun is born. We must learn to bend."

From across the fire, angry voices shouted back. "We have learned to bend," detractors clamored. "We have followed the French priests who have led us away from our brother Mohawks to the south. We have allowed them to douse our heads with water and open our hearts to their God. Must we now turn our backs on our ancestors? Must we let their memories fade forever in the hope of finding a moment of peace for our miserable bones?"

Such arguments had always been intriguing to Gingego, even before he was allowed to sit at the council fire as a warrior. So long as they had remained abstract, simple discussions that little affected his daily life or that of his family, he had found it easy to walk along the middle ground between the two worlds. Unlike Toolah, he had taken every opportunity to learn the French language and their ways. He had even entertained the notion of going to one of their cities and attending school. "Given time," he would tell his brother, "perhaps we can find a way that allows us all to realize our dreams."

Time, however, simply was not there. The crisis of the previous summer between the English and the French had led to another, greater crisis that was now unfolding before his very eyes. Rather than being free to search for a path that would lead to a safe future that might not even exist, Gingego, like many other Indians, found himself having to make a stand. For him, this became a very personal stand when his brother threatened to kill the French officer who had checked his quest for an Englishman's scalp. "If you take his life, Too-lah, they will cut yours short with no more thought than they would if they were killing a dog."

Whether Toolah's anger was deliberate and well reasoned or Gingego was merely the most immediate target, Toolah's words nevertheless haunted him every waking hour since that moment. In the presence of the other Caughnawaga warriors, Toolah had admonished his brother. "If you no longer believe in our ways, if you cannot do that which the memories of ancestors demand, then go, go now, and wipe us from your thoughts and bother me no more."

Not having the same singleness of purpose or courage that his older brother possessed, Gingego hesitated. In the end, it was his inability to choose that made the decision for him. By searching for a reasonable solution, Gingego lost the freedom to decide. As winter gave way to summer, and warriors began to prepare for another season of war, Gingego found himself swept away to war. "To stay behind, my son," his mother advised him, "would be to lose all hope of being able to find a place in either world. There are times when all paths lead you away from where you wish to go. If your head is unable to tell you where to go, then trust your heart."

In the end, Gingego did neither. Instead, he followed the first band of warriors who left his village, seeking safety in being part of a group rather than going against his people, regardless of what he believed. Now, with danger less than a stone's throw away, Gingego found himself admiring the simple single-mindedness that drove his brother. It didn't matter that the power behind that drive was a hatred for the whites that knew no bounds. It didn't matter that Toolah's urge to fulfill his dream led him to kill without remorse or thought. The fact that his brother was at peace with himself, who he was, and what he was doing caused Gingego to admire him, even if it turned Toolah away from him and, perhaps, his own people.

These thoughts, and the mental image of his brother's face, dulled Gingego's senses. It wasn't until the English soldier wandering about the woods in search of a horse stumbled over Gingego's outstretched leg that Gingego realized he was in trouble. Looking up from where he had been leaning against the tree for support, Gingego beheld the man's face, now as pale as the white shirt the English soldier wore. Stricken with fear and shock, the Englishman stood as frozen as a statue, mouth open but unable to utter a single sound. Recovering first from the surprise that took them both, Gingego saw his only chance and took it.

With a speed that he would later find amazing, Gingego sprung up from the ground and reached out with his hands. With one he grasped the Englishman's throat, and with the other he covered the poor soul's mouth. Bowling over the Englishman with his weight and momentum, the sudden impact of body on body and the resulting tumble onto the ground worked against Gingego. As the two figures hit the forest floor, Gingego's hand slipped into the Englishman's mouth, allowing the hapless victim the opportunity to bite it. And bite it he did, drawing blood and causing Gingego to pull his hand away as soon as he could.

The resulting howl from his enemy, reverberating through the woods like a trumpet, panicked the Indian. Realizing that he had made a fatal mistake by withdrawing his hand, Gingego reached down to his belt, seized the handle of his tomahawk, and, in one, clean motion, raised his arm as high as he could. It was during that brief moment in time, as he stared into the eyes of his helpless foe, that the Englishman's face disappeared and, instead, magically transformed itself into that of his own brother. It was an illusion, Gingego knew, for the face looking up at him was laughing, laughing like his brother had never laughed before.

With all his might, he brought the weapon crashing down into the face of the terrorized Englishman, ending the Englishman's scream and obliterating the image of a man who had, like a mythical spirit, driven Gingego to commit his first murder.

WORD of attacks by French Indians didn't rattle Ian McPherson. Like many of the Virginians, he had been expecting them. Nor did the markings on trees along the route, made by their unseen foe, cause him any great concern. Those signs left by Indians were almost always taunts or warnings aimed at their brethren. And the crudely carved French words left by the *coureurs de bois* who accompanied their native allies meant nothing to Ian. Neither he nor any of the men in his charge took the time to have a British officer translate them. "Words thrown about like that," McPike pointed out to one of the new lads who stood before a tree, looking quizzically at the markings, "generally are the sort you don't want ta hear."

These physical manifestations of the unseen, evil presence that the provincials had spoken of finally drove home the reality of their situation to those who had till now been able to delude themselves that they had little to worry about. For Thomas Shields, the sight of his batman, his face caved in by a single, awful blow, weighed heavily on him. He had seen death, but not like this. "The savage was in a hurry, for sure," the provincial officer pronounced as he looked over the botched job Gingego had made while taking his first scalp. "At least, Captain," the provincial said with a smile that was as sincere as his sentiment, "you can take pleasure in the knowledge that your man's scalp, or what the bastard got of it, will bring that savage no great praise."

The provincial officer, of course, was wrong. Even as they ran through the woods with the same speed and lightheartedness they had as children, the braves in Gingego's small party took turns running alongside him, reaching out to touch the scalp, still moist from the dead soldier's blood, then cutting loose with a yelp of celebration. They were truly joyous, for not only had they made good their threats, all of which had been little more than symbols till now, but they had regained a brother they had all feared they had lost.

Bravely, Gingego endured the horror of carrying the scalp he had virtually ripped from his stricken victim's head. With sickening regularity, the bloody patch of flesh slapped against Gingego's hip, splattering driplets of blood until there was no more and the scalp had finally dried and hardened. Yet even then, Gingego's imagination provided what his trophy could not. It was truly a curse, he told himself over and over as he forced himself to turn his attention away from the scalp, to have the ability to think and reason. A true curse.

Western Pennsylvania, the Great Meadows
June, 1755

THAT day, as if intentionally orchestrated by the French and the Indians, General Braddock's advance column passed through the Great Meadows, made famous throughout the Western world by Colonel Washington's stand the previous summer. And though there was more grass available for grazing than they had seen during their entire march from Willis Creek, the army did not stop there. Instead, Braddock, who hardly gave the place a second look, choose a spot a few miles beyond, not at all far from where Washington and his Virginians had fired a shot that was destined to start a world war.

Leisurely making his way across the tall grass of the glade, fighting to keep his horse from stopping and gorging itself on the lush green grass, Thomas Shields studied the site. Though the efforts of the French, the weather, and nature itself had eradicated most traces of the previous year's battle, there was still enough to make Thomas sneer at the military wisdom of his colonial brethren. "I can't imagine," Thomas mused to a fellow officer who shared his views, "how our general could take any of *Mr.* Washington's advice after seeing how poorly that gentleman selects his battlefields."

Standing at the edge of the partially filled trench, Thomas' friend looked at the charred remains of the circular fort, then up at the surrounding heights that hemmed in the meadow. "Can't say I blame the French for allowing Washington safe passage back," he finally concluded as he looked over at Thomas with a grin. "Perhaps they were clairvoyant enough to see that it was to their advantage to have such provincial officers fighting on our side."

"Yes, quite," Thomas replied dryly. "Fortunes of war have indeed cast us a wicked hand." After slapping a particularly annoying insect that had chosen to dine on his neck, Thomas looked around the field once more. "Forests that stretch on without end, mountains that follow no rhyme or reason, savages who sneak about in the shadows like the cowards they are, and pompous gentlemen who take on military airs. God, what a wretched land this is."

"Be of good cheer, Thomas," his friend called out as he turned his horse's head back to the lumbering column. "We'll soon be finished here and free to go back to Europe, where the art of war is taken seriously."

The prospect of finishing this campaign and returning with glory cheered Thomas. He had to keep his mind focused, he told himself, on the essentials. He had to maintain his poise and bearing if he was to achieve the notoriety that would earn him new and substantial opportunities for personal advancement. Turning his back on the dismal site of another man's lost opportunities, Thomas rode on to that night's selected bivouac, a spot that would soon bear the name of the commanding general.

When Shaw's company passed through the meadow, an unusual hush fell upon the normally noisy Virginians. Though most of that company had never laid eyes on the spot, all knew its story, and all felt the uneasiness that overcame those who had been there. While the British officers looked to the military topography of the landscape, the eyes of men in the ranks, provincial and red-coated regular alike, fell upon the bleached white bones of dead horses and cows. Even the dullest-witted among them could make the connection between that morning's events and the scene before them.

Slowing his pace, Ian McPherson looked out toward the spot where the fort had been. Two mounted officers, casually chatting as they looked around, stood where he had spent that horrible day. What his eyes could not see, Ian's mind did. "Do you suppose," Ian asked James McPike as he scanned the horizon, "that the savages dug up the remains of our dead and . . ."

The same chill that ran down Ian's back made McPike quiver as his eyes searched for the spot where they had laid John Miller to rest. He didn't answer Ian. Nor did he suggest that they venture out of the ranks to go and find out. It wasn't out of fear of the lurking enemy, for the relative openness of the meadow offered no concealment. Rather, it was a fear of what they would find if they did choose to seek the answer to Ian's question. So, like Ian, James McPike allowed the question to go unanswered. With another fight looming before them, perhaps one more vicious than the one they had fought here, McPike felt it was better not to know the truth than to realize his worst fears and then be forced to relive them for the rest of his life.

Without a word being spoken, the Virginians suddenly quickened their pace. What lay ahead, while ominous, was not as fearful as what lay behind.

CHAPTER ELEVEN

Western Pennsylvania,
Fort Duquesne
July, 1755

THE TIME of waiting was over. With the English pitching camp on the east bank of the Monongahela little more than ten miles from the fort, the decision that Anton de Chevalier had been waiting for, the one that would determine whether a battle would be waged for the forks of the Ohio or not, was at hand. Yet, even with the enemy virtually at their gates, the commandant of Fort Duquesne still hesitated. Like a man condemned, Captain Contrecoeur paced within the constricted confines of his fort, a structure that seemed to grow smaller and weaker with every league the English neared.

Anton, of course, knew what had to be done. "We must strike," he muttered as he shook his head in an effort to refute a companion's vehement insistence that Contrecoeur would be wise to save the small force of regulars and militia by withdrawing it immediately. "Our honor as soldiers," Anton insisted, "demands that we resist."

"Honor?" the Canadian lieutenant bellowed. "This is not Europe! We are not dealing with gentlemen for the possession of an obscure outpost of a mighty empire," he exclaimed loudly with a wide, sweeping gesture of his arm. "This, my friend, has become a matter of life and death itself. A defeat, either here or in the forest, would be catastrophic. If we go out," he stated as he turned and thrust his arm in the direction of the Indian camp, "with that horde, those who are struck dead in battle will be the lucky ones. Win or lose, our Indian friends will return to their families with scalps. If not English, then French. To them, it makes little difference."

Recalling the incident with the Indian Gingego, Anton suspected that there was a great deal of truth to what the Canadian was saying. The mass of nearly one thousand Indians, from many different tribes, would make up the majority of any force marching out to meet the English. They were, as one officer put it, "a very delicate weapon."

Yet there were officers such as Captain Daniel Hyacinth Beaujeu, who still believed victory was possible. Like Anton, he saw no other alternative but to strike. Beaujeu, who had arrived in June with reinforcements and orders to relieve Contrecoeur as the fort's commandant, possessed a fresh, combative spirit. Beaujeu, however, was left in limbo when Contrecoeur, deciding that the English threat was too near at hand, retained command. And though Contrecoeur did dispatch a number of raiding parties to snipe and raid the long, slow-moving English column, the vigilance of Braddock's flankers and their overwhelming power thwarted these feeble efforts. Maybe, Anton thought, it was the failure of these parties to delay, for even a single day, the English's progress that left his commandant despairing of their future prospects. Or perhaps his captain was one of those commanders who was bold and confident when the enemy was over the horizon but flinched when he came face-to-face with the decisive moment. What a pity, Anton thought, if that were the case. To lose a territory that was as large as France itself simply because one man's nerve failed him. Such a thought, to Anton, was mind-boggling.

"If," Anton asked his Canadian friend, "we do sally forth and meet the English at the river, as Beaujeu suggests, will you go?"

The Canadian shrugged. "Ah, yes. But of course. What," he concluded, "would be the point of waiting here, in this little box of wood, with nothing to do but wait to be knocked about by the English guns. No." He shook his head. "If I am to meet my end, it will be out there, in the forest. There, at least," he stated solemnly as he looked over at the forested mountains on the other side of the Monongahela, "I would be able to see my enemy as he comes at me. And, God willing, I will extract my pound of flesh before I go down." Then, with one eyebrow cocked, he looked over at Anton. "Will you be with us, should we go?"

Nervously, Anton looked down at his shoes. "Yes, God willing."

Southeast of Fort Duquesne
Along the Monongahela
July, 1755

WITH their drums beating out the "Grenadier March," Braddock's favorite tune, the combined companies of grenadiers under the command of Lieutenant Colonel Thomas Gage stepped off. Today they were finally beginning the last leg of their journey, long before the sun would make its appearance in the eastern sky. Before it set again, they expected to be standing before the gates of Fort Duquesne.

But there was still much work to be done. The route selected for their final approach to the Ohio was a roundabout one. A direct approach through a patch of land known as The Narrows was broken, heavily wooded terrain. Since it would require many hours of hard labor to forge a passage for the army, it was decided that they would backtrack across the Monongahela, march along its west bank a few miles, and then recross to the east bank where the forests were more open and the land less restrictive for the final approach to Duquesne. Not a word of protest was uttered by Thomas Shields when Gage, commander of the army's van, informed him of this. Had they been ordered to march through the gates of hell itself, barefooted, Thomas felt that every man in his command would have done so, gladly. Anything, he concluded, just to be done with this accursed campaign.

Accompanying the grenadiers was the New York independent company under Captain Horatio Gates and two six-pounders. Together with a handful of guides and a dozen or so light horsemen, they were responsible for clearing and securing the two fords over the Monongahela. These crossings were considered the most dangerous parts of the march. "If we're to be ambushed," Thomas informed his officers and senior sergeants, "it will be there, at one or the other ford. So be sharp. Keep the men closed up at all times, and be ready to deploy on my order." When asked by his first lieutenant what would happen after they were across and the army was closed up again, Thomas chuckled. "Well, now. It's all rather quite simple. Once we've planted ourselves firmly on the east bank of the river again, with all our guns and troops in hand, all that we'll need to do is wait for the French to blow up their fort and scamper off back to Canada. Perhaps if we're quick enough, we'll be able to catch a few before they disappear."

Though his troops universally shared his optimism, not a man dropped his guard, not yet. When they reached the first ford, Thomas' company took the lead while the Forty-eighth's grenadier company stood ready, on the near bank, to unleash their deadly volleys if the French or any of their Indian allies dared to contest Thomas' crossing. Due to the severe drought that had so complicated the efforts of the French to reinforce

Duquesne, the crossing was easy, with water barely reaching his men's knees as they moved steadily toward the far bank to the uninterrupted sound of drums and fife.

As if they were on parade, Thomas' company made its way up the steep bank on the far side of the river without incident. Once they were reassembled and deployed, the ranks of grim-faced grenadiers stood ready to repel the hordes of savages they expected to sally forth from the woods before them at any moment. But nothing happened. They heard no war cries, no rattling of enemy gunfire. Only the sounds of unseen creatures, scurrying about somewhere to their front, broke the nervous silence while the Forty-eighth's grenadiers came up in the wake of Thomas' command.

As the specter of danger faded with each passing minute, Thomas allowed himself to relax a bit and take in the scene before him. Though not nearly as awe-inspiring as Cumberland's army had been nine years before at Culloden, his grenadiers, clad in freshly brushed red coats trimmed in bright yellow, set off by the crisp white vests and pants, were nevertheless impressive. With the raw beauty of the lush green forest that had been their home for these many days as a backdrop, and the bright sun shimmering off the muddy brown water behind them, the sight of his grenadiers arrayed in line of battle filled Thomas with pride and excitement. Now, he told himself, all that he needed to erase all the memories of the hardships and discomforts that he had endured since arriving in America was the chance to lead this fine company of men forward in a bayonet charge. Pulling himself up into the saddle of his horse that his batman had brought forward for him, Thomas scanned the impenetrable woods before him. "If only," he muttered as he gave his horse a pat on the side of its neck, "the bloody Froggies would oblige us and make a show of it."

Fort Duquesne
July, 1755

As their Indian allies gathered about at the gate of the fort, hooting and yelping as they helped themselves to open barrels of powder and shot, Anton knelt in the fort's small chapel and joined the other officers selected for the foray against the English in prayer. Throughout his life, he had dedicated very little time to the faith of his king. He was, of course, quite familiar with it, having been drilled in all its rituals and beliefs. All the great philosophers whom he had studied devoted much time to the discussion of God, the theory of religion, and its place in the modern world. But he, like many of his age, seldom practiced the rites demanded by the mother church. In the fashionable cafés of France, or the safety of the barracks in Montreal, religion had seemed unimportant to Anton and, somehow, trivial. It wasn't until this moment, and this place, in the midst of the savage wilderness that he was preparing to defend for his most Catholic Majesty, Louis XVI, that Anton understood his faith's proper place. Like his fellow officers, he was overcome with a passionate desire to bow his head and ask a God that he had neglected for so long to forgive him of all his past sins.

While Captain Beaujeu, clad only in a loincloth with nothing more than the silver gorget hanging about his neck to show his rank as an officer, accepted the sacraments from the priest, Anton prayed. He thought of asking God to see him through this battle, a fight that even the most seasoned veteran approached with a gravity that was unnerving to Anton. Yet, he found himself unable to do so. It did not seem appropriate to Anton to ask such a favor from a God he had ignored for so long. Still, he did have the need to make amends while he could, as best he could.

Against a backdrop of screaming and howling Indians, Anton repeated his rosaries as he had been taught while still a child. For the moment, he found that he could forget the sight of heathens whipped up by Beaujeu in an all-night dance about the great council fire. Both they and the English column drawing closer with every passing moment seemed distant, totally unassociated with the quiet reflectiveness that held every man in the chapel in its grasp. All about him these things faded from his conscious thoughts. For a few moments more, Anton shed his duties as an officer, those weighty obligations that his commission from his king demanded. As he mechanically passed the beads of his rosary between his fingers, he could imagine himself as a boy again. As clearly as if it were yesterday, Anton could picture himself kneeling in the old stone chapel as the priest looked on. Then there had been nothing more pressing to occupy Anton's mind than a nagging fear that his friends would not wait for him before heading off to play. How different, he thought, the world that those memories came from was from that which he was about to be hurled into. How very different, and very far apart.

Yet, in a few moments, the two worlds would come together again. Along with the other reverent officers of France surrounding him, he would rise up off his knees, step out of this place of silent contemplation and prayer, and reenter the turbulent secular world that was about to be torn by war. Together with men who paid homage to spirits of which he had no understanding, Anton and his fellow officers would sally forth to kill fellow Christians in the name of a king he had never met who ruled a country that lay thousands of miles away from land that was, in truth, not really theirs.

Six Miles Southeast of Fort Duquesne, Along the Monongahela July, 1755

WITH the same slow deliberateness that had characterized the entire expedition, Ian and the others of Shaw's company waited patiently while St. Clair's carpenters and pioneers tore away at the steep banks of the Monongahela with picks and shovels. For while it had been quite easy for Gage's vanguard to scramble across the shallow river and make their way up the river banks unaided; the movement of heavy guns and wagons hauling tons of munitions from one shore to the other demanded a roadway. So the army waited, as it had for nearly two months now, while a few more miles were added to the twelve-foot-wide roadway that now stretched from Fort Cumberland to this spot.

Feeling himself to be in tolerably good shape, Ian discovered that he was in no hurry to see this march come to an end as he watched the sweat-soaked pioneers throw themselves into their labors. The marching and the danger of imminent attack in the vast forests beyond the frontiers of civilization, he found, were far preferable to the tedious duty and boredom that characterized garrison duty at Fort Cumberland. There, amid squalid conditions that bred despondency and loneliness, not to mention disease and sickness, there was little to occupy a man's time. Many of his companions, accustomed to a life of poverty and laziness, took to this aspect of military life without any problem. As they had before being dragooned or bribed into joining Shaw's company, they fell into their old habits of drinking as much as their pay would permit and conniving to do as little real work as the officers and noncommissioned officers allowed them to.

Ian, with a work ethic that bordered on manic deeply ingrained in him, found it all but impossible to tolerate such habits, let alone slip into them. Of the many sayings of his father that he still carried about with him after all these years of exile was the one concerning idle hands being the agent of the devil. At Fort Cumberland, he was greeted with daily reminders of this truism. So, even without Shaw's prompting, Ian endeavored to do what he could to save his companions from themselves.

Such missionary zeal, of course, was far from appreciated. Jeers that he was worse than an officer were ignored as he sought whatever work needed to be done. When not involved in pursuits directly related to improving the fort's defenses, Ian tried his hand at farming. Though the start of the campaign condemned the small garden he had started to languish untended under the hot summer sun, the Scotsman was, nevertheless, well satisfied with his efforts.

It was his little garden that he was thinking of when the cacophony of drums and fifes announced the recommencement of the march. "The damned drums," James McPike muttered as the column lurched forward. "I'll tell you plain, Ian, of all the things I find detestable about our British cousins, those damned drums rank quite high."

Ian chuckled. "McPike, you moan and groan about everything. Why, I'll wager that you'd find something to complain about even if a Frenchy shot you with a clean bullet."

James McPike shot Ian a dirty look. "Don't you go gettin' so high and mighty with me, lad. I'm not cut from the same cloth you are. I'll be glad when all this is over and we're free to squander our petty little lives away as we see fit."

Though he laughed, Ian found himself wondering if he, too, would be satisfied with returning to civilian life. Were it not for the fact that the only women who followed the army were the wives of other soldiers, laundresses who could not find honest men to marry them, or prostitutes struggling to earn a living the only way they knew how, a military life wouldn't be such a bad thing. While the idea of service in a regular unit was as abhorrent to Ian as it was to every other man in his company, soldiering under an officer such as Captain Shaw had its appeal. It was like being in a clan once again, where every man was taken for his worth and the officer shared the trials and hardships of his men. Not every provincial company was fortunate enough to be blessed with a man of Shaw's caliber. But even those officers who yearned for a king's commission found themselves unable to lord over their subordinates with the same aloof indifference as the red-coated British officers. Whether it was out of necessity or habit, those provincial officers still conducted themselves in a manner befitting the circumstances and, most important of all to Ian, the men they led.

As if conjured by Ian's thoughts, a party of officers rode up from behind. A gun carriage, lumbering down the center of the freshly cut road, left little room for the officers to pass, forcing the file of soldiers Ian was marching in off the road into the forests. Pausing, Ian looked up into the face of his old regimental commander, who was looking down at him. Without hesitation, Ian lifted his hand to the edge of his hat and gave the brim a slight tug as a gesture of greeting to Colonel Washington. The colonel, clearly uneasy in the saddle due to the bloody flux that had laid him so low for so long, could manage only a sickly smile and slight nod in return.

Watching Colonel Washington and his gaily clad English companions press their way forward, Ian found he couldn't decide if he liked the man or not. While the colonel was one of those officers who craved a king's commission and did everything he could to obtain one, he was, nonetheless, very much like his fellow Virginians. He had a strong, stubborn streak of independence, self-confidence, and pride that was born from the trials of making something of one's self in that restless young colony. No, Ian decided as he trudged along and watched the blue-clad Virginia gentleman trail obediently behind the British officers. The two of them had far more in common with each other, despite their backgrounds and views on the world, than the young colonel of twenty-three had with his English riding companions.

AMONG the soldiers of the vanguard, something approaching euphoria swept the ranks once they had started moving forward again. Thomas could feel it as he rode at the head of his company of grenadiers. He could see it in the manner in which St. Clair's carpenters and pioneers, following his company, threw themselves into their labors. Whenever he paused and looked back to check their progress, he could see the enthusiasm with which the Virginians cut and hacked away at those trees marked to fall in order to make way for the oncoming army. This task, mercifully, wasn't nearly as demanding as it had been on previous days. Here, Thomas noted, there was a goodly amount of space between trees, with little underbrush cluttering the forest floor. Those trees that had to be felled gave way quickly, making way for an army that Thomas could almost feel coming up quickly behind them. He fancied it was gaining momentum and strength with each step that took them closer to the French fort.

Coming up beside Thomas' horse, Lieutenant Clarence Holmes caught his commander's attention. "Do you think, sir, we'll attempt to storm their works tonight? I certainly hope so," he added without even allowing Thomas time to answer. "The men are all quite keen and it would be a pity to stop, even for one night, and lose such an edge."

With a patient smile, like that of a father, Thomas looked down at his subordinate and shook his head. "General Braddock is too good an officer to allow himself to be caught up in the moment and swept away by sheer bravado. He's brought us this far by being steady, deliberate, and adhering to the king's regulations. He'll not throw it all away now. You can wager on that, sir."

Holmes, however, was as persistent as he was enthusiastic. "Well, with the entire column closed up, sir, it seems that if General Braddock saw the chance to seize the place with an immediate attack from the march, don't you think he'd risk it? You saw how every man and gun are stacked up behind us, like a great battering ram. With the French not daring to show their faces outside their works, I believe all we need to bring this thing to a close is one gallant rush. Every man, sir, I assure you, is ready."

As he listened to his young subaltern jabber on, Thomas felt his smile fade away. Such enthusiasm, he realized, while commendable, could be dangerous if it was not properly controlled. Without responding to his lieutenant's optimistic assessment of their situation, Thomas sat upright in his saddle and began to make a careful survey of the ground and woods all about him. When his head came about to the right, Thomas cast his eyes on the commanding high ground that rose precipitously along their flank. And though the forest was relatively open and clear, there were still sufficient gullies and fallen trees out there, along their line of march, that could cause them problems if the French chose to contest their advance. Even when he caught sight of his flankers moving along the side of the massive hill whose top he could not see, Thomas found himself unable to shake the uncomfortable feeling that began to dampen his previous enthusiasm.

After a few more moments of reflection, Thomas finally took his eyes away from the ominous hill that so dominated their flank. It was foolish, he told himself, to think that the French, after having thrown away so many wonderful opportunities to ambush them when they were most exposed or strung out during their long march, would dare strike now, when they were drawn up and all but ready for battle. With some effort, Thomas pushed aside his nagging doubts and finally responded to Holmes. "Neither of us, I am afraid," he said slowly, halfheartedly, "will be afforded much of an opportunity to see the enemy. I expect," he added as his eyes made one more sweep of the hill that so dominated them, "the French commandant will be firing his magazine anytime now. With the exception of a few stray savages looking to vent their frustrations for having been troubled for no good end, we'll not find anything of value when we reach the Ohio."

Sensing that his commander was right, Lieutenant Holmes took in a deep breath, sighed, and then removed his hat. "I imagine you are right, sir," he acknowledged while blotting the sweat from his brow with a fine linen handkerchief. "Still, I would rather we see some action, no matter how trivial, than go down in history as nothing more than an escort for a road-building detail."

Thomas wasn't given a chance to respond. To the front, he saw the woods come alive with motion. Before he could make out clearly what exactly was going on, the shouts of the army's guides and light horsemen, streaming back toward them pell-mell, alerted them to the presence of the enemy. "It seems," he calmly stated to his startled lieutenant as he reined in his horse and began to search their front for the French, "we're not going to be disappointed. Now, sir," Thomas snapped, "bring the command into line and make ready to engage the enemy."

PANTING, Anton paused to catch his breath. It was taking everything he had to keep up with the band of Canadian *coureurs de bois*, or voyagers, he had been assigned to. The sure-footed frontiersmen, having no need for an officer of La Marine, swarmed through the forest with the ease of natural-born natives. Dropping all pretense, Anton simply kept his head down, held his loose cartridge box tightly against his side to prevent it from banging repeatedly against his sore hip, and ran as fast as he could. Like the Indians, there seemed to be little organization to the ranks of the voyagers. Each man pretty much did as he saw fit, expressing a freedom that was as wild and as varied as his dress. Some even stripped themselves down to their waists and dabbed black, brown, and dark blue war paint all over their faces and naked torsos.

Yet there was a discipline among them that was as iron-clad as that of any regular that Anton had ever encountered. He had seen it the previous year, when they had chased away the bumbling little band of Virginians, and he could see it again now, in their eyes and in their actions. Like a school of fish, they flowed through the open forest with a speed and grace that no French unit could rival. The heavily burdened marine and militia units, struggling with their equipment and massed formations, had difficulties keeping up. No, Anton told himself as he paused and leaned against a tree to catch his breath, it is far better to be with such men in battle.

Before starting off once more and picking up the exhausting trot that was carrying his small band of voyagers forward, Anton looked up toward the head of the long column. He could clearly see Captain Beaujeu, leading the motley collection of French regulars, militiamen, voyagers, and Indians. His pale skin glistened with sweat as beams of sun found their way through the overhead foliage, making his figure stand out even more against the vibrant greens and deep browns of the forest. He was a leader, Anton thought, born to lead men into battle.

Heartened by this sight, Anton began to go forward when suddenly he saw Beaujeu come to a complete halt just as he crested a slight rise in the trail he was following. The men closest behind him, unable to stop, all but piled up on one another as they, too, came to a sudden, jerky stop. For a moment, the noble young French captain stood there, motionless, staring into the distance at some unseen threat that Anton was as yet unable to see. Then, having decided what needed to be done, Beaujeu reached up, grabbed the lace-trimmed tricorner hat from his head, and waved it to the left and right. This was the signal, Anton knew, for the column to divide itself and flow around the flank of the enemy force he had yet to see.

Suddenly reinvigorated by the presence of danger, Anton rushed forward to catch up to the men who were supposed to be following him. Before he reached them, the silence of the forest was rent asunder by the clap of musket fire. Glancing up, Anton could see Beaujeu still standing on the rise, watching the enemy as his own men began to sort themselves out and deploy. A second thunderous volley did little to move the man, convincing Anton that their leader was charmed and had nerves of steel. A third volley, however, fired just as Anton was coming up parallel to Beaujeu, shattered this belief.

As if struck by an invisible hand, Beaujeu was hurled back, almost into the arms of the marines and militiamen forming the line of battle behind him. Like all those who witnessed the sudden death of their leader, Anton slowed his pace. Some of those in the center, closer to Beaujeu and obviously the target of the enemy gunfire, even began to give way and turn to flee. For one long, critical moment, Anton felt the fate of their entire attack resting in the balance. Were it not for the immediate appearance of Captain Jean Dumas, Beaujeu's second in command, Anton felt that a rout would have ensued. Dumas, though, managed not only to halt the faltering line of marines and militiamen but, with the same reckless abandon that had just cost Beaujeu his life, drove the men in his command forward.

Satisfied that all was not lost, Anton turned his attention to the enemy and his men. Surprisingly, the enemy, some 150 to 200 yards away, was far more visible to him, at first, than his own men. Taking advantage of the massive trees and folds of the earth that broke up the forest floor, his voyagers had, each on his own, sought cover before contributing his fire to a steady fusillade that was beginning to flail the massed ranks of red-coated foes before them. Finding a tree of his own, Anton leaned against it, concealing as much of his body as he could, and turned his full attention to the ranks of his enemy. Already, he could see that they were struggling to maintain their cohesion as a telling fire from the voyagers and Indians began to find their marks. The well-drilled volleys that had announced the opening of the battle had ceased. Now some of the English soldiers, tormented by their unseen foe, could be seen drifting away from the firing line. It pleased Anton to see that they were grenadiers, the best soldiers the enemy had, and that they were in serious trouble. If these troops could be so easily cowed, Anton thought, then, perhaps, a victory was possible.

STANDING to the flank of his shredded ranks of grenadiers, amid the hailstorm of gunfire that poured upon them from every direction, Thomas Shields could also see that they were in trouble. For a few minutes he had allowed himself to believe that their opening volleys had succeeded in scattering the enemy before them. The growing volume of fire across their front and along their flanks, as devastating as it was consistent, soon crushed that hope. With a sickening steadiness, as if someone were counting cadence, the men of his company were flopping down on the ground in front of the firing line or being knocked backward, out of ranks. Amid this carnage, his orders, like those of his surviving officers, were either no longer being heard or intentionally being ignored. Far too many men, perhaps as many as half of those still on their feet, were simply standing there, wide-eyed with fear, waiting for a chance to flee.

More from anger than from fear, Thomas continued to

raise his voice and shout out his orders as prescribed by the king's drill. "Make ready to fire!" he shouted, his hoarse voice already cracking from the strain. Glancing sideward, he saw that only a few dozen muskets had been raised in response to his command. He felt like leaving his post, trooping the line then and there, and beating each and every man who wasn't ready to fire with the flat of his sword. But there was no time. Of those who had responded to his order, a number had already discharged their pieces rather than hold the heavy weapons aloft, waiting for the proper order. And there was, of course, the enemy. Even as he debated with himself, the sickening thud of French lead hitting the body of one of his men reminded Thomas of their precarious situation.

With a roar, he yelled, *"FIRE!"*

The resulting spattering of a handful of muskets trained at a clump of bushes in the distance was, to Thomas, disheartening. Not only was his company being chewed to pieces but many of those who still stood were doing nothing. Even those who were, he saw, were having no visible effect. Nervously, he glanced to the rear as the screams and shrieks of his wounded filled his ears. He needed to order a retreat. He needed to move his company back with the main body, which, by now, should be ready and deployed in the line of battle. What little good they could achieve here had already been accomplished. They had blunted the enemy attack and warned General Braddock of the danger. He could leave here now, and do so honorably.

Ignoring the growing number of dead, wounded, and dying littering the forest floor, Thomas turned his head back to the front, searching the woods for any sign of the enemy. When he did manage to catch sight of one or two of them, it was little more than a fleeting glance of a shadow. Only the dirty gray puffs of smoke betrayed the location of foes who were firing on him and his dwindling command with a steady, deadly rhythm. Yes, Thomas' logic told him, if ever there was a time to retreat, *this* was it.

Yet, he couldn't bring himself to give the order. He had no difficulty singing out the orders to reload to those who still chose to listen. But he could not bring himself to mouth that awful word, *retreat*. The glorious stories of whole units of the

British army standing their ground, nobly, until the last man was stricken, raced through his mind. As a soldier, he had always been aware that he might someday die. He had already been witness to the terrible carnage that his trade dealt out and, in return, suffered. When he had long ago opted to stay with such a hazardous occupation, he had committed himself to accept this fate.

But in his dreams, even in the darkest, bloodiest nightmare that his mind could conjure forth while he slept, he had always seen himself cut down while leading a gallant charge, or fighting to the last man to hold the most critical point of the line against advancing waves of enemy soldiers. He had never imagined that he would be faced with such a horrible dilemma as now lay at his feet. The idea of losing a battle, not to mention his life, to a faceless foe who refused to stand up and fight in the open was abhorrent to Thomas. So much so that he found he could not, in the end, give the order that would save those men still on their feet.

As it turned out, he didn't need to. While he struggled with his own thoughts, his men decided for themselves that they had had enough. Though most were good men, and their discipline was about as good as one could expect of soldiers in a line regiment, they were still only mortals. And all mortals have a breaking point. Ten minutes after firing their first volley, and after losing nearly half their number, the Forty-fourth Foot's grenadier company broke and ran. Neither Thomas nor his single remaining subordinate officer could do anything about it.

For a moment, Thomas stood rooted to his spot on the ground, alone between the French and Indians moving ever closer and his fleeing command. Bowing his head, he let the tip of his sword touch the ground. Already the noise of his panicked soldiers, pushing their way past St. Clair's work parties and the lone New York company behind them, was being swallowed up by the whoops of hidden savages and the ever-expanding battle. Were it not for a loyal corporal, Thomas would have stayed there and joined so many of his men. Taking his captain's arm like a parent of a lost child, the corporal led Thomas away.

CHAPTER TWELVE

On the Banks of the Monongahela,
Western Pennsylvania
July, 1755

B Y THE TIME the first distant clap of gunfire reached Ian, Shaw was already making his way up the slope of the hill that loomed menacingly to their right. With his left hand, Shaw signaled Ian and those who had been following him to hold fast while he craned his neck to look down the length of the column in the hope of seeing what the vanguard had encountered. As a precaution, Ian brought his musket down from the jaunty position he had been carrying it in, and began to check the lock and pan. When he saw that his piece was ready, he turned his head and called down the line to those who still stood idle in the road. "Check your pieces," he growled. "Trouble's ahead."

The expressions on the faces of Shaw's men foretold how

they would react when the battle, crawling down the length of Braddock's column, reached them. Those like Ian and McPike, who had faced the fire, wore bland expressions, hiding whatever emotions or fears the coming battle was stirring within them. In sharp contrast were those new to the frontier and war. Like the mortals they were, few made any effort to conceal the very real concern that the tall tales of Indian atrocities and depravations told by veteran soldiers might, in fact, be true. A few, gripped by this fear, stood wide-eyed and motionless, watching as if they were waiting for some terrible beast to leap from the forest around them and consume them whole.

With his musket cradled in his arm, Ian began to make his way through the ranks. To his friends and those trusted veterans in the company, he gave a nod while looking into their eyes. Though no words passed between these men, all accepted this as both a wish for good fortune and, failing that, a farewell. When he would come to a man unable to control the shaking of his hands, Ian did what he could to steady the man's nerve and help him prime his piece. "There's nothing to this, you know," Ian would say as he fiddled with the soldier's primer pan or hammer. "Just stay up close to Jack and do what you've been told." Though few believed him, they acknowledged Ian with a sickly smile. If nothing else, Ian's words reminded the new men that they were not alone in this time of trial.

After finishing with one of the more nervous men, Ian turned to help the next one. Instead of finding a man in distress, however, he found himself facing a fair-haired man in his mid-twenties, standing perfectly still, his bare head tilted up and his eyes closed, muttering. At first, Ian thought the man was mad. But then he realized that he was praying. Though hardly a religious fanatic, Ian didn't hesitate to remove his hat, bow his head, and seek whatever comfort he could from the Almighty. As if their prayers had been one, both whispered "Amen." Ian, bringing his eyes up, and the fair-haired man, dropping his down, looked at each other for a moment. Then, with a nod, Ian pivoted and continued to make his way among the men of Shaw's company until he reached the end.

When he was finished, he made his way back to where Shaw still stood on the rising ground to their right. "We're about as ready as we can be," Ian announced with no preamble, no salutations. Shaw, his eyes darting about, didn't acknowledge Ian at first. He, like many of those farther back in the long column, was trying to make sense of the growing chaos that was threatening to overtake them.

Finally, Shaw's eyes narrowed and his face betrayed a look of disgust. "Look at that, will you," he barked without taking his eyes from the head of the column. "It's an absolute muddle. I can't make sense of what's going on up there." Then, turning to Ian, who was now peering into the distance, catching fleeting glimpses of flags, smoke, red-coated soldiers, and gleaming bayonets and musket barrels, Shaw added, "And I doubt if anyone up there knows what's going on, either."

Confusion, Ian knew by now, was to be expected in battle. Looking around him, he grasped the importance of the sloping ground to their right. "Best we move the men up the hill some, before the Frenchies come thunderin' down on us."

Looking to his right, Shaw nodded in agreement. "Aye, that's about the wisest thing we can do. Bring the lads up and have them take cover amongst the trees and whatever cover they can find. Just make sure they stay together." Then, as Ian was about to turn and make his way down the hillside, Shaw grabbed his arm, causing him to halt and face about. "And for heaven's sake," Shaw warned Ian, "tell the lads not to fire till they have something to fire at, preferably the enemy."

Though Shaw's admonishment was in deadly earnest, Ian smiled. "I'll do that, Captain. You can be sure of that."

"Good!" Shaw snapped, then went back to watching the growing ring of smoke and fire that was consuming the column before him.

BY the time Anton had caught his breath and primed his musket, the English grenadiers had been swept from the field.

With whoops and screeches of joy, the Indians who had kept themselves concealed during the fight poured forth and raced for the cluster of dead and dying enemy soldiers. Though he knew he needed to keep up with his stalwart voyagers, Anton couldn't resist the urge to stay a while and watch their savage allies at work.

While the spectacle unfolding before him filled him with horror, there was a morbid fascination that kept Anton from turning his eyes away. With ruthless precision, the Indians fell upon their fallen foe and began the bloody process of relieving them of their scalps, weapons, and possessions. Using the same sure, swift motions that Anton had seen used by butchers dispatching pigs and cattle, the Indians scalped officer and soldier alike. Grabbing a handful of hair, the victorious warrior would jerk the unfortunate soul's head up and back. Then, with a single, swift slice, the knife would cut a clean red line across the victim's forehead until the weight of the lifeless body itself started the process of separating the scalp from the head. When he was ready, all that was needed was a single, quick jerk to complete the job.

Though his stomach was churning and threatening to heave forth its contents, Anton continued to stare. Some Indians, he noticed, were quite adept at collecting large pieces of hair, while others, through bad luck or lack of skill, walked away with little more than a small patch of skin and hair. Regardless of the amount they recovered, all seemed satisfied with the results of their efforts and anxious for more. When they concluded that they had wreaked all the damage they could upon the fallen soldiers of the British vanguard, the Indians moved off. Tucking the fresh scalps into their belts, they followed their comrades and the French voyagers in search of more.

Having seen more than enough, Anton turned to follow his voyagers, but found that they were nowhere to be seen. All the faces about him, except for one Canadian officer of La Marine, were totally unfamiliar. That officer, seeing Anton standing alone looking forlorn, called out to him as he went by, "If you wait for the ranks to reform and dress, you'll miss the fun, dear boy."

Though Anton found it hard to understand how anyone

could consider what was happening fun, the Canadian was right. The battle, finished here, had moved down the newly cut road and had already, by the sound of it, slammed into the enemy's main body of troops. Grasping his unfired weapon and hoisting it to his side, Anton placed one hand on his cartridge box to steady it and took off running toward the deafening sound of battle.

THE shock of losing his entire company so quickly without having inflicted even the slightest visible damage on the enemy was slow to fade from Thomas' mind. Befuddled, he stood among the growing chaos his fleeing grenadiers created when they ran head-on into the advancing body of troops General Braddock had ordered forward. Just how long he was oblivious to the chaos about him was impossible to tell. Time, it seemed, lost all meaning to those about him who were struggling to establish a line of battle while others, fearing for their lives, sought to escape from it.

The sound of the struggle around him finally managed to penetrate the numbness that had all but paralyzed Thomas. Slowly, anger began to burn away the hazy stupor, allowing Thomas to rouse himself enough to take in all about him. Like a spectator in an audience, he watched as an officer on horseback nervously paced to and fro behind a formless mass of men that stretched across the road and disappeared into the forest on either side. This pathetic line of battle, Thomas saw, was neither straight nor arrayed in three ranks. Instead, it was curved, bent back upon itself and the road like a great horseshoe. In the center, nearest the road, men stood, huddling together like a gaggle of geese trying to escape a storm. There, and elsewhere, men stood six to eight deep, with few making any effort to bring their weapons to bear upon the enemy.

With a shake of his head, Thomas cleared his head. An

officer, one of Braddock's aides, rode up next to him. *"Damn you, man!"* the young officer shouted. "Get yourself back into the ranks. Move," he screamed, "or I swear I'll run you through where you stand."

Shocked, Thomas looked up at the aide, not knowing exactly what to expect. To his surprise, he saw that the man whom the officer was bullying was a soldier wearing the buff facings of the Forty-eighth Foot. Relieved that it wasn't he who was being chastised, Thomas was just beginning to take stock of his own condition and circumstances when the aide turned to him. "Sir," the fresh, bright-faced officer on horseback called down to Thomas, "are you all right?"

With a smile, Thomas nodded. "Yes, I believe so." Then his face went blank. "What's all this about?" Thomas asked as he waved his arm toward the muddle of soldiers.

The aide straightened up in his saddle and grimaced. "I don't know how this happened," he replied, as if Thomas were holding him responsible. "We tried to deploy into a proper line. The general was quite clear, I think, about what needed to be done. But . . ."

The officer interrupted himself, turning his full attention on a hatless soldier of the Forty-fourth Foot who was making his way to the rear. "Back you go, you bloody scoundrel," the aide roared as he lifted his boot in an effort to kick the wandering soldier.

Pulling back, the soldier made no attempt to block the aide's boot. "But sir," the soldier whined in protest, "I'm wounded, I am. Look." Twisting his body while keeping a leery eye on the enraged officer, the soldier made an effort to hold the arm that had been hidden from the officer's view. Blood oozed from a hole in the left sleeve that measured nearly three quarters of an inch. "Some savage has done me good and proper, sir. See," he said, moving his arm about as much as he could. "I'm no good to you anymore. Please, sir. May I go?"

Angry at being corrected by a common soldier, the officer snapped, "Go, damn you."

Then, changing his expression and tone in the blink of an eye, he returned to his conversation with Thomas. "We tried to separate the two regiments after they sort of ran together.

The general himself ordered the king's colors to one side of the road for the Forty-fourth to rally about and the regimental stand of the Forty-eighth for them to follow to the other side. But it did no good. It's all a muddle, all a terrible mess."

While still listening to the officer, Thomas looked about. It was a mess. Here and there, red-faced officers moved about, shoving and screaming as they bullied men forward in an effort to salvage some semblance of order. In some cases, Thomas could see that, rather than helping the situation, these officers were making matters worse by compacting the useless mass of men in the rear ranks and keeping those in front from functioning properly.

He was about to ask why this was being allowed to happen when a loud thud, followed by a sharp exclamation of pain, caused Thomas to look up at the aide. Standing bolt upright in his stirrups, the aide's face was frozen in a wide-eyed expression of shock. Not knowing exactly what to do, Thomas stood by helplessly as he watched the color of the man's face drain away. After a few agonizing moments, the aide began to waver until, like a tree being felled by a pioneer, he finally toppled dead from his saddle.

As Thomas looked on, he felt no feeling of remorse or sorrow for the stricken officer. Bad luck, he thought as he reached out and seized the reins of the frightened horse. Moving around to the side of the animal, Thomas raised his foot, found the stirrup, and pulled himself up. Though he felt his legs riding a bit too high in the stirrups, Thomas saw that this was no time to mess with them. Much needed to be done. Without making even the slightest effort to avoid the body of the fallen aide, Thomas yanked the reins of his new mount in the direction of the confused line of battle and made his way forward.

IT didn't take the Indians very long to make their way down the length of the column to where Shaw and his men were waiting. Only the hiss of a near miss and the smack of another soft lead round in the tree that partially concealed Ian served to announce that they were within musket range. Instinctively, Ian pulled behind the tree, cocked his own musket, and crouched till he was as close to the base of the tree as he could get. When he was ready, he snaked the upper part of his body around the tree, scanned the foliage that covered the high ground above them, and searched for a target. Were it not for the telltale puff of smoke that accompanied each discharge from an enemy's weapon, this task would have been all but impossible. Even at that, it was difficult to draw a decent bead on a foe once he had found one close enough to shoot at. Only Ian's patience and nerve allowed him to even come close to the mark when he did fire.

The fair-haired man whom Ian had joined in silent prayer lay behind a fallen tree that was as thick as his own chest, not far from Ian. "Do ya suppose we'll hit anything, firing like this?" he asked after pulling his long-barreled musket back behind cover to reload.

Ian stuck his head around the tree, squinting as the acrid smoke of burned powder swirled around him, stinging his eyes and irritating a throat already dry from nervous tension. Slowly, he scanned the cluttered forest to his front for any sign of the enemy while his practiced hands went about reloading his own weapon. The whine of a passing bullet caused Ian to pull his head back behind the tree. While his fingers worked the lock of his piece, he looked down the slope just as a mass of British soldiers unleashed a volley blindly into the empty woods before them. As he watched he saw a number of the red-clad soldiers topple over, struck down by the same invisible hand of death that was persistently searching him out. One poor English soul, struck by a ball in the face, dropped to his knees, throwing his musket away as he grasped his wound. Ian was unable to tell if the man was reacting or truly attempting to stop the blood that flowed freely through his fingers and down his arm, staining his white vest and collar. If the man was screaming, his cries of pain were drowned out by the howls of others, nearer to Ian, who were facing their own gruesome demise.

"I imagine," he finally responded in answer to the fair-haired man's question, "we're doin' better than them down there."

The fair-haired man didn't bother to look. "I can't imagine comin' all this way ta die."

To this, Ian said nothing. It had not been his intent, when he had set out on this expedition, to die here or, for that matter, anywhere else. He couldn't imagine anyone, regular or not, entertaining such thoughts. It just didn't seem to make any sense that a man would intentionally place himself in mortal danger for the purpose of ending his life. Yet, as he finished priming his piece and preparing to fire, he looked around and saw hundreds who, like himself, had placed themselves in danger. Down on the road, among the gaggle of men struggling to find safety somewhere in this green hell, Ian watched as officers rode about on their mounts, ignoring the whine of near misses as they struggled to thrash some sense of order out of the chaos that surrounded them. His own Colonel Washington, barely risen from his sick bed, was one of them. The red-haired Virginian, Ian knew, was a rational man, a man with boundless ambitions and dreams of greatness. He had no more desire to throw away his promising life than the lowliest private in the ranks. And yet there he stood, tall and erect in the stirrups, using his sword to direct the fire of a group of Virginia Rangers huddled off to one side of the road.

Ready to fire at the same instant that his fair-haired companion was, Ian pushed aside all concerns other than those that would assist him in preserving body and soul. In unison, Ian swung around the tree while the fair-haired man rose from his concealed spot behind the fallen tree. Pausing only long enough to find a close target, the two fired, then pulled back. For their efforts, they drew a hail of enemy fire from Indians and Canadians who, like them, were playing a deadly game of cat and mouse.

UNABLE to find any trace of his Canadians, Anton was becoming concerned. Had they all been killed? he began to wonder. Maybe they had broken after running into the main body of the British column. Such thoughts, and the idea that he might have been left out here, alone with the Indians, began to worry Anton. Would he, he asked himself, be able to find his way back to the fort? Though he knew some Indian words, what, he wondered, were his chances of finding a savage willing to help him back? Even more important, would the Indians, if they suddenly took to flight, leave him alive?

With his mind consumed by such concerns, Anton was oblivious to the rattle of musketry that echoed through the woods and filled them with dense clouds of smoke that crept along the forest floor. Wandering aimlessly, his eyes darting from place to place in an effort to find a friendly white face, the young French officer paid no heed to any of the shouts or screams, in English and French, that mingled with the snap of musket fire and the occasional report of an English cannon. He was too busy seeking someone to give orders to, or take them from, to notice an English officer, not fifty feet away, taking forty or so frightened English soldiers through the precise drill of reloading and preparing to fire. Had it not been for a hand that reached up from a gully, grabbed Anton's ankle, and pulled him down, Anton would have been cut in half by the volley of musketry that erupted when the word "Fire" was bellowed.

Unprepared for the sudden jerk, Anton tumbled down on top of his savior, an Indian, a fact Anton realized even before he was finally able to arrest his fall. As bits of leaves and twigs, severed from trees overhead by the wildly inaccurate English volley, floated down on him, Anton pulled away instinctively, his hand madly searching for the musket that he had dropped. "Here," a familiar voice spoke in a calmness that contrasted sharply with Anton's own racing mind. Looking up, his eyes fell upon Gingego, kneeling only inches away from him in the narrow gully, holding Anton's musket out before him.

For a moment, Anton did nothing as his eyes darted about, first to see if there were other dangers he needed to be aware of, and then for an exit. Sensing the Frenchman's distress, Gingego pushed the musket forward, almost into Anton's hands. Only now, for the first time, did Gingego understand how much this man, whom he had once tried to make a friend, distrusted him. There was, of course, some justification for this. Still, it hurt Gingego to think that another human being, French or not, could be so suspicious of another at a time like this.

A frown creased the sad Indian's face as he realized that his brother was right. He had spent far too much time listening to the words of the French priests and not heeding the song of his own people that struggled to emerge from the bonds of his heart. His skin was different, as different as the cultures that raised the two men facing each other. Nothing, Gingego realized, would change that. Nothing.

Saddened, he lay Anton's musket next to the frightened Frenchman, picked up his own, and made his way down the gully to find another spot from which he could kill whites.

Left alone in the midst of a battle that all but drowned out his own thoughts, Anton finally managed to catch his breath, calm himself, and decide what to do next. Carefully lifting his head above the lip of the gully, the young French officer looked out over the confused landscape before him. While his own comrades, if any were still out there, had all but been swallowed up by the forest, the British and some of their colonials stood in a small clearing or in the middle of the road they had so laboriously cut. They were in great disorder, so badly jumbled up and confused that they were unable to use their considerable numbers to overwhelm those Indians, Frenchmen, and Canadians still holding to their tasks. These, well hidden and marked only by puffs of dirty white smoke, ringed their English foe.

That his comrades' fire was having a telling effect was in great evidence wherever Anton looked. English soldiers, most of whom were doing little more than huddling in the roadway shoulder-to-shoulder with their comrades, toppled over dead or sank wounded to the ground with a sickening regularity. Those who were not killed outright were, writhing in pain, forgotten, or ignored by their former mess mates except when, in their throes of agony, they kicked someone who was still standing in the ranks.

Looking about him once more and seeing no one who even vaguely resembled the men he was supposed to be commanding, Anton came to the conclusion that his rank was, at that moment, of very little consequence. There was no one who needed to be led. As far as providing motivation or encouraging any of the men near him, Anton's logical mind ruled that out without any trouble. He would never be able to make himself understood by any of the nearby Indians, even if they took the trouble to pay him any heed. They followed their own leaders when they chose, and did what they pleased when they didn't.

Inevitably, Anton came to the conclusion that there was nothing left for him to do but fight. He was, after all, a soldier. In France, it was a matter of faith that a proper officer of the line never profaned his station by handling a musket. This, Anton had been told many times by veterans of many a fight, was not France. Here, everyone fought, with firelock and hatchet.

Easing himself down into the gully, Anton checked his weapon, inspecting it as his old sergeant had instructed him to. It dawned on him as he did so that he had used the same musket the previous year when he had gone with de Villiers against the Virginians. Pausing, Anton corrected himself. He had carried the weapon, but he had yet to actually use it in battle. The terrible truth, he thought, was that until now, he had never truly actively participated in a battle. He had come close with his small artillery section early the previous year, and again at the Great Meadows, though he had not actually done much of anything there either. While he poured the powder from a freshly opened cartridge, which he had torn open with his fingers rather than his teeth in an effort to keep from tasting the bitter black powder, Anton wondered if he was being of any use to his king. To date, it seemed that he had been acting less like an officer and more like one of Voltaire's ineffectual characters, wandering the world and seeing much, but doing nothing.

When the musket was ready, Anton took several deep

breaths as he listened for a moment, waiting until he was sure there wasn't an English platoon about to cut loose with a massed volley. As he sat there, his eyes turned up toward a sky hidden by foliage and branches. Above him the leaves and branches quivered every time he heard the snap or zing of a bullet passing harmlessly overhead. Except for the random motions, and the torn bits of leaf that floated gently down upon him, the deadly missiles were never seen. Satisfied that it was as safe as it was going to be, and finally galvanized into action, Anton pulled himself up with the aid of his musket, poked his head over the lip of the gully, and scanned the desperate scene below him for a target.

He had been told by one of his instructors at the school for artillery that chance is often as important in battle as good, proper planning. That this was true became quite evident when he saw, just scant paces away, a mounted English officer waving his sword madly over his head and pointing it in Anton's direction. The poor officer on the ground, commanding the group of frazzled soldiers who had almost ended Anton's life moments before, was trying desperately to hear what the mounted officer was saying. There, Anton told himself, is my target.

Bringing up his musket in one swift motion, Anton brought the weapon to bear on the Englishman. He ignored the near misses and rounds passing close to his own head from a group of concealed English provincials to his left. All conscious thoughts were centered on the deadly task at hand. Sighting down the long barrel, as he had been instructed by his most faithful sergeant, Anton waited till he was sure the muzzle was aimed properly. Taking in one last deep breath, he closed his eyes, squeezed the trigger, and waited for the weapon to discharge.

"DAMN you, sir!" Thomas thundered, his voice almost breaking. "Can't you see them up there?" he screamed as he leaned over his horse and waved his sword up the hill at a cluster of smoke puffs now drifting lazily away.

Not knowing whether to ignore this officer or get back to directing the efforts of the pitiful remains of his shattered command, the young ensign tried to think of something appropriate to say. He was the last officer within his company and, as far as he could see among the chaos about him, his regiment who was still standing. Though he doubted he was doing much good, firing volley after volley blindly into the brushes and scrub around him, he could think of nothing else to do. Nothing, and no one, had prepared him for such a fight. And though he knew there had to be something else he could do, his training and discipline prevented him from doing anything else, just as it kept him from ignoring the officer on horseback.

Luck, though it was bad, saved him from having to respond. Just as his mouth began to utter the first sounds of a response to Thomas, a ball found its mark. Ripping into the young ensign's side, the three-quarter-inch lead missile cut a path between two ribs and tore through both lungs, and finally stopped as it smacked into the rib cage on the far side of his body. Shocked and surprised, the dead man gazed, for one last time, up at Thomas' face, then fell forward against Thomas' boot and sank to his knees.

With the same disinterest that he had felt while watching the former owner of his current horse pass away, Thomas looked past the man dying at his feet and searched for the senior sergeant of the ensign's command. "You," he shouted when he saw a corporal, "get those men back into proper ranks," and he pointed his sword at a gaggle of men who appeared ready to give way and run. Then, to the entire formation of twenty, perhaps thirty, men, he began to issue orders. "Prepare for volley fire," he bellowed as he turned his face toward the side of the hill where the French and Indians were hidden and pointed his sword to the location he intended to pelt with fire.

Before anyone could respond to Thomas' orders, the front legs of his horse buckled and collapsed, sending him flying over the stricken animal's head. Only by ducking his head, a glancing blow to one shoulder on a tree he passed while in flight, and his landing on the strewn bodies of dead and dying men on the roadway saved Thomas from serious injury.

Struggling to catch his breath, Thomas scrambled to his feet, oblivious to the thud of a round that tore into the lifeless body his head had been resting on a mere second before. Once on his feet, he scanned the hillside before him, struggling to contain an anger that dyed his face a shade of deep, passionate crimson. "There!" he screamed as he pointed to a cluster of white puffs rising from a jumble of fallen trees off to their right. "Prepare to fire by ranks. Front rank kneel."

Grim-faced, the men in the ranks went about their task, happy just to have someone in command directing their actions. The corporal whom Thomas had shouted at before, positioned at the far end of the small formation, hesitated as he brought his musket to the ready when he saw that the men they were preparing to take under fire had their backs to them. Squinting in an effort to see through the haze of smoke that had settled around them, the corporal was soon able to make out clearly the blue color of the coats their targets wore while, without missing a beat, he responded mechanically to Thomas' orders. They were, he suddenly realized, provincials, probably the company of Virginians who had been following them on the march. Though he jerked the hammer of his piece back when the command to do so was shouted, the corporal turned his head and tried to catch Thomas' attention. "Sir!" he called out, his hesitant voice all but drowned out by the rattle of musketry all about. "Sir, they're colonials out there, sir."

With his ears still ringing with an anger he did little to contain, Thomas didn't hear the warning. And even if he had, it was doubtful that he would have hesitated to give the order. Like most officers of the line, Thomas was not attuned to paying attention to men in the ranks. They were simply there to follow his orders. *He* was the officer. *He* was in charge. And *he*, by God, was determined to use his authority to wreak vengeance on the miserable cowards hiding in the woods who had tried to make him look like a fool.

With every ounce of strength he could muster, Thomas screamed, "FIRE!"

THE volley that Thomas unleashed ripped through Shaw's company. With their entire attention riveted on the enemy close at hand, and postured to protect themselves from the cruel enemy fire to the front, none of the Virginians was prepared for the terrible execution that Thomas' misguided volley wreaked upon them. Ian, in the process of pulling back around the tree that served as his shield, was stung by the flight of a ball that creased his scalp. Stunned, the young Scotsman dropped to his knees, loosing his grip on his rifle, and instinctively brought both hands up to cover the wound.

For the longest time he knelt there on the ground, teetering on the brink of passing out without the ability to do anything, including seeking cover. Slowly, the sharp pain gave way to a dull ache that worked its way throughout his entire body. Accompanying this all-encompassing agony was a rising wave of nausea that churned up the bitter contents of his stomach. Thus stricken, Ian found it all but impossible to concentrate on what was happening around him. Only vague, scattered, and totally disassociated images that had no meaning to him managed to penetrate the veil of haze caused by a throbbing pain in his skull that struck with the same brutal regularity of an axman working to fell a tree.

As he stared listlessly at the ground before him, a pair of feet raced past him. From his other side a musket, discarded by its owner in an effort to lighten his load, flew by for the briefest of moments before disappearing from sight. Only slowly did Ian come to realize that his companions were fleeing as his tortured brain began to make sense of what his eyes saw flashing before them. Raising his head, he fought the agony that moving caused and looked around. He was all alone, as best as he could tell, given that his vision was still horribly blurred. Only the fair-haired soldier whom he had been fighting side by side with was clearly visable. Turning his full attention toward him, Ian looked down on his lone comrade. Any thought that Ian had entertained of seeking aid or comfort from that soldier, however, disappeared as soon as he saw a dark red stain that spread in ever wider circles from a large hole torn in the man's back.

Ian turned away from the lifeless form that lay draped over the log that had done nothing to protect him from the brutal effects of English fire. His efforts to avert his eyes brought him no comfort, however, as they fell upon others who shared the fate of the fair-haired man. Unable to concentrate any longer, and wishing to shut out the horrors that surrounded him, Ian lowered his head, clasped it between his two hands, and doubled over.

CHAPTER THIRTEEN

On the Banks of the Monongahela,
Western Pennsylvania
July, 1755

JUST HOW LONG the battle had been raging was hard for Anton to judge. Surely, he told himself as he busily reloaded his musket, it has been two hours, perhaps three. That he had spent the better part of the first hour in a vain attempt to find his company of voyagers was almost certain. And the incident with Gingego, he was sure, couldn't have taken more than a minute, perhaps two. But after that, how much time had elapsed was all but impossible to tell.

Of course, Anton told himself as he rose and brought his musket to bear on the English below, time did not matter here. Only perseverance, holding to the task at hand until the English finally saw the futility of their predicament, was of importance. That they had to be close to that rationalization,

Anton told himself after squeezing off another round at the mass of men that had become his favorite target, was only logical. The number of men still left standing had by now been reduced to well below half those who had been there to start with. Just how much more punishment they could take was, in Anton's mind, the only question that remained to be answered.

Then, catching sight of the officer he had unhorsed with his first shot, Anton amended his last thought. From where he sat, it seemed to Anton that every other enemy officer was down, lying scattered about the bloody roadway mixed in with the corpses of the men they had led into this hell. That this one gentleman, persistent in his efforts to hold his dwindling band of soldiers together, was still healthy amid the terrible carnage about him amazed Anton almost as much as the fact that he was still able to hold his men together. All around the small island of resistance, refugees from the main body of troops, farther up the road, flowed by while they fought on. Some of these stragglers, holding bloody limbs or staggering about as if drunk, were seeking safety and help somewhere down the column. Others were merely looking for a way out, an escape from the fate that had consumed so many of their comrades.

While Anton could understand their desire to escape, he also found himself despising them. Had it not been for the need to direct all his efforts against those still resisting manfully, Anton would have turned his musket on the shirkers who put self-preservation over their duty to their king and country. That such feelings and thoughts sprung forth unsolicited did bother Anton. Like an onion being peeled, layer by layer, Anton's true self was being laid bare by the experience of war.

THE throbbing of his head, the rattle of musketry in the distance, and a thirst that was overwhelming finally managed to rouse Ian from a state of unconsciousness that bordered on death. Opening his eyes, the light of late afternoon, filtered by branches and leaves overhead, greeted him. About him he could faintly hear voices speaking in hushed tones. Occasionally, a sharp scream that was more animal than human silenced some of the talking, but only for a moment.

It took Ian several minutes before he was able to organize his scrambled thoughts. When he finally did, the first thing he was able to appreciate was the fact that he was still alive. Just where he was, and exactly what his circumstances were, were still quite hazy. But that he was alive he was sure. Were he dead, Ian told himself as he tried to ignore the terrible pain that wracked his brain, he would be in heaven or hell. God would not have picked such a place for heaven, he reasoned. And hell could not be this cruel.

With a choking sound that passed for his first word, he roused the attention of soldiers nearby. "See," a familiar Scottish voice cried out, "I told ya he was alive. Takes more than a silly knock on the head to kill a Scot." Suddenly a head appeared in front of Ian's eyes. "Ian, lad," James McPike asked in a cheerful manner totally inappropriate for the circumstances they were in. "Are ya doin' better?"

"Than what?" Ian managed to choke out. "The dead?"

This tickled McPike. "Hah!" he shouted as he bent down, grabbed Ian by the shoulders, and hoisted him into a sitting position. "Here, lad, have a drink. It'll do ya good."

Though the sudden jerking and pulling caused a spasm of pain to work its way from one end of his body to the other, Ian was too thirsty to protest. Like a child receiving a drink from a caring mother, Ian reached out with shaky hands, clasped the tin cup, and guided it to his mouth. The watered-down rum was warm and sweet. Its taste more than made up for the burning sensation that the alcohol caused as it made its way down Ian's dry throat. Though he gagged and sputtered a few times, Ian held tightly to the cup and kept it pressed to his lips. "There, now, lad," McPike finally cautioned as he pulled the cup away. "Don't want a drown ya, do we?"

Dropping his hands, Ian let drops of rum dribble down

his chin as he looked about. Not more than ten paces from where he sat, a surgeon, assisted by two men splattered with blood, worked on an English soldier who thrashed and kicked while they took his arm. Next to him, another provincial, with his upper body and face indifferently covered by a dirty blanket, lay motionless. Here and there, some of the women who had been allowed to stay with the column moved from man to man, helping them as best they could. McPike, sitting before him with a wide grin, wore a tightly bound bandage that ran from just below his right knee down to the ankle. "Captain Shaw had me drag your miserable bones back here, down the column to the wagons, after we took that terrible thumpin'," McPike offered without being asked. "We lost near to half the company, though most of 'em ran instead of goin' down with a clean wound, like you an' me."

"Shaw?" Ian asked slowly.

McPike jerked his right thumb over his back, down the road. "Back up the column, somewhere. A lot of officers are down, not to mention a good part of the army."

Without a word, Ian placed his left hand on the ground, twisted his body to that side, and slowly pushed himself up.

"And what," McPike asked without rising, "do you think you're about?"

Ian did not answer. Slowly, as the warmth of the rum helped to take the edge off his pain, the memory of the terrible carnage on the hillside came back to Ian. Before his eyes, as if he were still there watching it, Ian saw the circle of red growing ever larger about the ugly hole in the fair-haired man's back. With each passing second, as the image grew more vivid and real, a feeling of anger welled up inside the young Scotsman. Shutting his eyes, Ian forced himself to forget about his dead comrade. Instead, he turned his entire concentration on getting himself up off the ground and steady on his feet.

While McPike watched in silence, Ian managed to rise up. Even before he finally managed to stop rocking to and fro, Ian reached over to his side with both hands to grope about in search of the hilt of his ancient broadsword. When they finally came to rest upon it, he lifted his chin, turned his head, and stared down the long road, drawing the sword from its sheath as he went.

"Now, hold on, lad," McPike protested from where he sat. "The captain told me to make sure that you was taken back to safety and that nothing happened . . ."

Ian glared at McPike. "I'm goin' back," he snapped.

"And do what?" McPike demanded.

With a look that was frightening even to an old hand such as McPike, Ian growled, "To kill Englishmen."

WHEN the end came, it was quick. Thomas suspected that eventually it would come to this. In his heart, he knew his small group of soldiers could take only so much.

This bit of logic, however, didn't make it any easier for him to accept the final collapse of the army that had set out so confidently only hours before. For the second time in the same afternoon, Captain Thomas Shields had failed to hold the line. Men under his command were breaking and running, without any shame, without a single glance back. This time, Thomas accepted his fate. Doleful, without a single conscious thought, he tucked his sword under his arm, turned his back on the unseen enemy that continued to fire at them as they fled, and walked away.

Down the road he went, stepping over the bodies of men cut down where they stood. Thomas closed his ears to the sounds of their screams and groans of agony that echoed like a chorus of death throughout the forest. Even when a wounded man grabbed his ankle and pleaded for mercy, Thomas ignored him as if he were no more than a bothersome gnat. It was all a great disaster, he realized as his eyes fell upon abandoned cannon and wagons without seeing them. Only the thrashing of a horse, shot down but not yet dead, caused Thomas to alter his slow, mournful pace. Not even the stench of battle, a weird mix of burned powder, sweat, fresh blood, and human waste, elicited a response from the man. For the moment, the captain who had given up a commission in the Coldstream Guards in pursuit of a dream of fame and glory on a foreign battlefield was now as dead to the world and all about him as the lowliest corpse his tired legs passed over.

EVEN before the last of the enemy to their front had given way to their fears and broken for the rear, the Indians all around Anton rose as one and rushed forth to claim their spoils. With whoops and shouts that quickened the pace of men already fleeing and announced the doom of those who could not, Gingego and his companions ran down to the road. Whatever civilization the priests had instilled in Gingego fell away like a tree shedding leaves as he joined the mayhem all about him. Without the slightest hesitation, in a manner that would have made his brother proud, the once quiet Indian drove his hatchet into the back of a wounded Englishman who had been crawling away.

Still standing in the safety of his gully, Anton watched the Indians go about their work, killing those who needed to be dispatched and scalping every man they came across. He found nothing amusing as he witnessed the discovery and capture of an English private, who had been feigning death, by Gingego. The Englishman had been doing quite well with his ruse until he felt the tug of a brave's hand on his hair. Not knowing what else to do, the soldier jumped up and faced his would-be scalper. Equally surprised, Gingego jumped back, raising his knife high over his head in preparation to deliver a true death blow.

The Englishman, too terrified to flee or even raise a hand in self-defense, stood frozen in place as he watched and waited to be struck down. Recovering his composure, and now conscious that he had displayed fear in the face of an enemy, Gingego was determined to redeem himself. With a single, quick step, the Indian came forward and ran his knife across the man's chest, cutting through his vest and shirt and opening a terrible gash. Whether his legs gave out from fright or he dropped to beg for mercy, the soldier fell to his knees, saving himself from a second slash that would surely have cut his throat open from ear to ear. Deciding that there would be no honor in taking the life of a foe so paralyzed by fear, the brave brought the hand holding the knife down and slapped the Englishman in the head with the back of his hand. To announce his victory and draw the attention of other braves, Gingego let out a scream, then took the Englishman captive.

Shaking his head, Anton dismissed the scene below. Climbing out of the gully that had for so long been his refuge, the young French officer straightened up for the first time in hours and brushed himself off. There would be abandoned cannon and ordnance, he reminded himself as he searched for something to take his mind off the atrocities being played out before him, that needed to be collected. It was once again time to revert to his given profession, that of an artilleryman, and his position as an officer. The victory was at hand, he told himself. Now it needed only to be cinched.

POSSESSED by an anger the likes of which he had never imaged, Ian McPherson made his way down the road in search of a suitable target upon which to wreak his vengeance. Few paid any attention to him. Unlike Ian, they were anxious to escape the carnage that had consumed Braddock's proud army. All the refugees he encountered went out of their way to avoid Ian, lest he hinder their flight.

For his part, Ian quickly discounted those who scurried from his path like quail taking to wing when flushed from hiding. Though most were English, his tormented mind rationalized that such miserable wretches didn't deserve an honorable death. Let the devil take them, Ian told himself as he decided to cut down the first English officer he came across. They, he told himself, were responsible for this. They and their bloody contempt for everything and everyone that was not of their cut or class. With each step, Ian drove the heel of his hand holding the sword into the side of his thigh, as if marking cadence. Only when the number of panicked refugees became too thick to avoid did he slow that terrible pace.

Then, before he realized it, Ian found himself face-to-face with a live English officer. As easily as he had dismissed the poor privates who continued to file by in unchecked flight, his eyes fixed upon the gold braid and sharp tailor-cut uniform of an English captain coming his way. Without hesitation, Ian placed himself squarely in the path of the officer who continued toward him as if he were blind to what was happening all about him. Taking a stance from which he would deliver a good, solid blow, Ian raised his sword, holding the hilt waist-high with the blade held upright so that its tip was level with his eyes. As if he were sighting down the barrel of a musket, the bloody-minded Scotsman looked over the sharp point directly into the eyes of the Englishman, waiting for him to draw nearer. One blow, Ian told himself, was all he wanted, all he needed. One swift blow, and all his anger, all his vengeance, would be released.

But Ian wasn't given the chance to strike that blow. The officer, his face as pale as the white linen shirt he wore, staggered as he grew nearer Ian. Finally, when he was but a yard or two away, the officer stopped, looked Ian in the eye, then fell to the ground.

For a moment, Ian didn't quite know what to do. Keyed up and ready to dispatch the man, the Scotsman's sanguinary mind took stock of his predicament for the first time. Feeling the effects of his own wound, Ian was befuddled. Surely, he told himself, the man hadn't passed out from fear of the fate that was about to befall him. He couldn't possibly have known about the evil intent Ian had been harboring. Slowly, lowering his sword, Ian took a furtive step forward and leaned over the crumpled body to investigate.

In an instant, the cause of the man's sudden demise was obvious. In his right shoulder there was a hole, much the same size as the one that had been bored into the back of the fair-haired man Ian had marched and fought with by an unknown English soldier. All about the hole, blood stained the scarlet coat. Letting his sword's tip fall to the ground, Ian could not but think how ironic this all was. He didn't feel cheated, nor did he feel vindicated. Despite all the hatred and anger that still lurked below the surface, the one distinct emotion that he now found welling up in him was that of pity.

Bending down on one knee, Ian laid his hand upon the man's back in an effort to see if he could feel some sign of life. Surprisingly, despite the man's terrible pallor and the amount of blood that stained the red coat, the English officer was alive. "Well, lad," Ian said as he moved about and sheathed his sword, "it seems that you'll be saved, least till a surgeon has a whack at ye. Now, be a good lad and try to help if ya can."

Though the officer was thin and frail compared to Ian, it had been a long and most trying day. The effort necessary to pull the officer up from the ground reminded Ian of that. Though his new charge hadn't responded, except for a moan or two, while being jostled about, Ian persisted in talking to him. "Now, be a good gentleman and do what ye can to help us hurry along 'fore the savages lay claim to our hair for their lodge poles."

As if to underscore his last point, a series of yips and screams echoed down the now deserted road to where the unlikely pair struggled to get started. Some of the screams belonged to the dying, those left by comrades to be dispatched at the hands of expert executioners who knew how to prolong their victims' fear and final agony. Others were cries of victory and joy, which were both numerous and quite near. Struggling, Ian attempted to increase his pace, half dragging and half carrying the English officer. "Come on, lad, ye gotta do somethin' ta help, don't ye know?" Ian pleaded. But there was no help from the officer, not even a moan. Only the sound of pursuing Indians and a few random shots, always growing closer, could be heard.

Then, as if he appeared from nowhere, another person hustled past Ian, almost pushing him and the wounded Englishman over. Stunned, Ian stopped, ready to let go of his charge if the stranger proved to be a foe. To his surprise, he found himself staring at the back of another English officer, marching absentmindedly away with his head bowed low and his sword tucked tightly under his arm. Taking a deep breath and recovering his composure, Ian shouted out to the man, "You, sir. Stop."

At first, the blundering Englishman made no effort to comply with, or even acknowledge, Ian's command.

"You bloody bastard!" Ian shouted with all the force he could muster. "Stop or I'll strike you down before you can take another step."

This time, the officer responded. Stopping in an instant and spinning about all in one motion, the man lifted his head and stared at Ian. "What," he snapped in a tone that was more of a demand than a question, "did you say?"

Dragging the wounded man along with him a few steps closer before answering, Ian saw that the man's eyes were enflamed with rage. That he needed help to save this one officer was all that overrode his desire to forget his sudden found humanitarianism and return to his original objective. In an effort to disarm the other man's anger, Ian leaned over to one side and pulled up the wounded man a bit higher. "He's one of yours, and he needs help if he's ta be saved. I cannot do it alone."

For a brief instant, Thomas Shields took his eyes off the cur who had so brazenly challenged him and considered the condition of the officer he held upright. The man, with a ghostly complexion, already seemed well past help. "Is he alive?" Thomas asked, the sharpness in his voice betraying the anger he still harbored.

"Aye," the provincial replied, betraying a deep Scottish brogue.

"Well, it doesn't look like he'll be alive for very long."

Angered at the indifference of this new officer, Ian lost his temper. "Damn you, man. Haven't enough of your bloody kind died today? What harm would it do your damned stiff-necked pride to lend a hand and save a life for a change instead of takin' 'em?"

Unable to restrain himself, Thomas flew forward, bringing his sword up from under his arm. The Scotsman, seeing the danger, was about to let go of the wounded man but stopped when his charge threw his head back, looked around, and started to shout out orders in a sudden, feverish fit. "Stand to your duty, men," the stricken captain screamed. "Rally on the colors," he bellowed as his burning eyes looked past Ian and Thomas at men who were alive only in his tortured memory. Then, drained of all energy by the sudden spasm, the wounded officer's head dropped back over as unconsciousness brought an end to his torments.

Startled by the antics of the wounded man, both Ian and Thomas stood silent for a moment, watching to see if more would follow. When it was evident that the man was again blissfully unconscious, Ian pulled the wounded man's arm a little farther around his neck, shooting a dirty look at Thomas as he did so. Then, without a word, he started to drag his charge past Thomas, back toward the Monongahela and safety.

Like a house of cards knocked over by the flick of a finger, Thomas felt all his pent-up anger and frustration come crashing down. As tears welled up in his eyes, he looked at the sword in his hand. He had failed, failed miserably. With all his might, he lifted his arm and threw the symbol of his office blindly into the brush. He didn't wait to see where it fell. Nor did he pay any heed to the approaching enemy, now clearly in sight just a hundred yards or so down the trail. Instead, he turned his back on those who had been so instrumental in bringing his plans to a dismal end and hurried down the trail to where Ian continued to struggle with his heavy load.

When he came up next to Ian, Thomas took up the wounded officer's free arm, hanging limply at his side, and wrapped it around his neck. Both men, without pausing, looked across the bowed head of their charge into each other's eyes. There was no approval or sign of gratitude. They simply exchanged the hard stares of two men, from different backgrounds, with different dreams, who shared nothing else but the poor luck of having participated in a disaster that never should have happened.

THOUGH he was tired, Anton paced along the parapet of the fort that night for as long as he could. It was more than the horrible screeches and the stench of burning flesh that drifted into the fort from English prisoners being roasted alive by Indians celebrating their one-sided victory that kept him from seeking the peace and quiet of sleep. In part it was nervous energy. In part it was the troubling images flashing before his eyes that were called forth by his overactive memory. But most troubling of all, Anton realized, was the terrible realization that he, for all his trappings of civilization, culture, and education, was, in truth, no better than those whom he and his fellow officers called savage.

Reluctantly, Anton made his way to the solitude of his room. In his dark, cramped quarters that habitually reeked from a smoky fireplace, wool blankets and uniforms, and dampness held in by the log and dirt structure, Anton found no escape. Even as he lay on his bunk in the quiet darkness, lit only by a single tallow candle that flickered every time an unseen draft passed over it, he could not escape terrible images that continued to race through his mind. Random sights that his eyes had been witness to but his mind had paid no attention to during the day now floated before him in a slow, unchoreographed procession of horror, pandemonium, death, and tragedy. Events that had been ignored that day as soon as they had occurred now entertained him as he lay on his bunk, staring vacantly at the log ceiling, with his mind in a slow, grotesque dance that no amount of wine could stop.

Unable to rest, the troubled French officer sat up, swung his legs over the edge of the bed, and buried his face in his hands. Though he tried hard to force all thought from a brain enflamed by such images, the reek of gun oil and black powder that permeated his hands refused to let him. Lifting his face, his eyes fell upon the tattered journal in which he had continued to keep his personal thoughts. After standing up, it took him only half a step to reach the chair already pulled away from the desk and waiting for him.

Mechanically, he took quill in hand, dipped its sharp point into the splattered bottle of ink he kept ready at all times to record his thoughts, and systematically began to chronicle the events of the day as he saw them. For a while this occupied his mind, keeping the troubling thoughts at bay. They would not, however, be denied. They were too powerful, and vague feelings that he could not quite grasp brought a halt to his orderly train of thoughts and writing. In mid-sentence, without putting any conscious thought to what he was doing, he began to scribble.

Perhaps, Anton wrote, *what troubles me most is not what I have done, for I am a soldier and have long expected to be called on to do my duty for my King. No. It is, I think, the casualness with which I went about taking another's life. It was, once I started, nothing more than a repetitious drill of load, aim, fire. Load, aim, fire. There was no rhyme or reason as to who I shot at and which shots struck. There was no orderly ebb and flow of battle as the books which I have read described. It was nothing more than slaughter, given less thought than a butcher does when he selects a calf to be killed.*

Pausing, Anton eased himself back into his seat, looked up, and organized his thoughts. Then he bowed his head and resumed his writing. *Surprisingly,* he found himself writing, *as terrible as all the physical horrors of the day were, a feeling of equality with all about me, savage and foe alike, consumed my thoughts at the strangest times. It was, I think, like a great leveling took place out there. Officer and soldier, white and savage, regular and militia, all fought and suffered, side by side. For all my presumptions about the superiority of European culture when compared to that of the Indians whom we use as cannon fodder when it pleases us, none of my education, appreciation of art, or cultivated tastes made me any more important, or any less valuable. Any one of a hundred balls hurled at me could have ended my life as quickly as those I fired which ended the life of the rawest English recruit. If God were there, he was blind to a man's station in life or the knowledge he held in his head. All were equal. All were brothers.*

Again, Anton stopped writing. This time, his hesitation was not because he needed to find the words to fit his thoughts. They were there already, burning in his mind like a piece of metal too hot to hold. Yet before he committed them to paper, he vacillated. To think treasonous thoughts, he knew, was a crime, yet one that could not be held against a man simply because it could not be proven. Once recorded, however, the treason was real, as real as if the act had been committed. Men, he knew, had been hung for doing so.

His thoughts, however, and the driving desire that propelled him to record them now, while they were still fresh and clear, could not be denied. *All I have been led to believe in,* he wrote without hesitation, *is wrong. If I was no better, today, than a savage who could not utter a single word of French, and the soldier in the ranks can be the equal, in battle, to his officer, then why can't they be equals at other times? And if a soldier who has no education can equal the most highly trained and educated officer, does that not make an officer without noble birth equal to the highest nobles at court, or even . . .*

Having reached the limit of his courage, Anton stopped. Sitting back, he looked over what he had just written. Though the word *king* was missing, the thought was complete and, to Anton, the logic inescapable. The images of that terrible day, hailed by all in France as a great victory, would remain with him. But it was the train of thoughts that those events triggered in the young French officer's mind that would trouble him the most in years to come.

As he made his way back north in the company of his companions, no such weighty thoughts troubled Gingego. Rather, the events of the battle along the banks of the Monongahela had been quite liberating. For the first time, the young brave thought, he was at peace with himself and, even more important, with the world he lived in. He wore the scarlet coat of a vanquished foe, stained with blood he himself had spilled. In his haversack, taken from the battlefield along with other trinkets that had caught his eye, were half a dozen scalps. And, best of all, behind him he pulled a captive who had been thoroughly cowed and broken. When he entered his village, any doubt as to his value and manhood would forever be erased.

But that day was still quite distant. There were many long days of travel, by foot and canoe, before he could bask in his hard-won glory and begin the task of finding a mate. More by mutual consent than by order, the band of twenty other braves he traveled with gathered about the spot the file leader had selected for that night's camp. Gingego and others who had prisoners in tow came together and tied their wards to trees in close proximity so that they could be easily guarded by others. Some of the braves, hastened by the pangs of hunger gnawing at their stomachs, gathered wood for the fire upon which a brave placed a pot that he had found in an abandoned English wagon. When all was set, and there was nothing more to do in preparation for their long-awaited evening meal, the braves gathered near the fire and studied their prisoners.

It would be, Gingego knew, a hard choice to make. He, for one, wanted badly to bring his back whole and in good health. Those who had been too old or too young to join a war party would experience enormous pleasure running his gift to them through the gauntlet. If the Englishman survived that, the women of the tribe would find his staked body, bruised, cut, and bleeding, a tempting object upon which they could freely heap whatever scorn and torture they felt moved to inflict upon him for days on end. And each time one of them gouged, kicked, cut, or spat upon the prisoner he had brought back from the Ohio, he or she would be reminded that it was he, Gingego, who had brought them such a wonderful gift.

Eventually, the choice was narrowed down to one of the two English women who had been left behind by their cowardly men. While one was still strong and defiant despite the trials of the long trek and the terrible ordeal she had been witness to, the other had been reduced to a whining pile of rags that was fast becoming a hindrance. Though the two braves who took equal credit for the capture agreed that they could, perhaps, prod and drag her farther, both realized that she would never finish the journey. Without much debate, the whimpering woman was selected.

Too hungry and tired to make any great fuss over ceremony or show, one of the pair of braves pushed himself up off the ground, walked over to where the sobbing woman clung to the rope that tied her to the tree, and grabbed her ankle, the first part of her body that his hand could reach. With a jerk, the brave pulled the woman out, away from the tree she was tied to and pushed her dirty and tattered skirt up her thigh while the other captives looked on in horror. Unschooled in the ways of the wilderness, all thought they were about to witness a rape. None was prepared for what followed.

Once he had the woman's leg fully exposed and in hand, the brave pulled his tomahawk from his belt, raised it above his head, and brought it down as hard as he could as close to the hip as he could reach. Even before he managed to disengage the blade of his weapon from the bone in which it was wedged and take another whack, the other prisoners let out a howl of fear and panic that reminded Gingego of a pack of dogs baying at a full moon. Only the profuse vomiting of some, too repulsed by what they were seeing, reduced their wailing as the brave finished his amputation, lifted the severed limb to inspect it, then walked over to the pot of water and threw it in to be cooked.

Ignoring the antics of the surviving prisoners, and turning his back on the brave as he went back to fetch more meat for the pot, Gingego curled up into a comfortable position before the fire and watched the flames as they licked the bottom of the well-made English pot. Suddenly, he realized as he sat there that while it was true that a live prisoner might be entertaining for a while, and do much to boost his image as a war hero, a pot would have been a much more practical trophy. The Englishman would die within days. A pot, Gingego reasoned, would have lasted many seasons and served his long house well. Perhaps, he thought as he looked over to the owner of the pot, he would find the right words that would convince him to trade prizes. The pot, though a great trophy, could not make the long walk back to Canada.

IT was a small gathering, in part out of the desire for secrecy, and in part simply because there were so few officers still alive. Ian McPherson was there because someone was needed to dig the grave. Colonel Thomas Dunbar, the surviving senior officer and current commander of the expedition, was there, though he wished he were miles from that terrible place. George Washington, by virtue of his position on Braddock's staff and solid service in the days following the great debacle, was there, too. It had also been his idea to bury the general's body in the center of the road over which the surviving troops and wagons of the decimated army would pass. "The colonel," Shaw informed Ian when asked about this, "feels such an indignity is far better than giving the Frenchies or their savages a chance of finding the man's corpse, digging it up, and desecrating it. Besides," his captain added in a hushed tone so as not to be heard by any Englishman who might be within earshot, "I think it's appropriate, given all the time and effort he put into building this bloody road. If we're lucky, both them and the fiasco at the Monongahela will pass into obscurity and be forgotten."

But those gathered about the grave of General Edward Braddock knew that what had transpired would not soon be forgotten. And if there was mourning being done that evening, it was not for the general, who had passed on less than three hours before. It was for themselves. This was particularly true of Thomas Shields, commanding the small guard that kept the curious away from the gravesite. As he looked on, he realized that it was more than a general they were burying. He had gambled much when he had volunteered to follow that man. He had mortgaged his future. And now both the general and his dreams were being laid to rest.

Thomas turned away from the solemn assembly of grim officers whose eyes were red and swollen from lack of sleep accentuated by concern over what would come next. If any had shed a tear that night, it had not been for the dear, departed commander. It had been for themselves. Thomas knew this, for he himself had done so. Even now, as he stared into the dark forest that seemed to engulf them all, a veritable jungle made even blacker and more ominous by the flickering light thrown off by torches held by those at the grave, he felt new tears welling up. "Dear God," he muttered as his eyes searched for the heavens, which were blocked by the ever-present trees of the American wilderness, "what now?"

Though he didn't hear Thomas' pitiful plea, Ian McPherson knew the answer. "We'll soldier on," he told McPike, "as we did after the '45. This fine little war our British cousins seemed so intent on starting isn't going to go away an' neither will the savages." Though his friend reminded Ian that it had been their own Colonel Washington who had ordered the first round to be fired, at a site not very far from where they now stood, Ian ignored him. "This fine bloody road is like an arrow aimed right at Virginia, you see. Just 'cause we won't be needing it anytime soon doesn't mean the Frenchies won't."

"And," McPike smirked, knowing before he asked what the answer would be, "I suppose if they do, they'll find you waiting?"

"When they do," Ian replied with a grin, "they'll find us both, waitin' for 'em."

"And why," McPike challenged, "would we be daft enough to do a foolish thing like that?"

Serious now, Ian stared into his friend's eyes. " 'Cause, lad, the likes of us have no where else ta go. They chased us from Ireland, and made sure we knew we weren't appreciated in this colony's tidewater, where the plantation owners dream of makin' another England for themselves using our sweat and labors. This," he pronounced with a sweep of his arms, "is ours to make of as we choose. It's not them I'm fightin' for, don't you know. It's for me," he snapped as he thumped his chest. "Me, you, and others who have no place else to go. It's not about them," he stated as he pointed at the silent gathering of officers burying their general and their dreams of glory. "It's never been about them. It's about us. Don't ever forget that, James McPike. It's about us."

McPike lowered his head, thought about it, then nodded. "Aye, I'm with you on that," he finally replied when he looked up into Ian's fiery eyes. Without another word, the two men, with nothing more to do, waited patiently in the shadows until the assembly of officers was finished, and carried their own respective thoughts and fears into the darkness that engulfed them all. Together, Ian and McPike stepped up and, without a word, shoved the fresh American dirt into the grave of England's dreams and hopes.

PART FOUR

Love and War

CHAPTER FOURTEEN

*Along the shores
of Lake Champlain, New York
March, 1757*

I
IT WOULD BE light soon, and the small band of rangers
would be moving, if they were smart, before that happened.
So far, everything they had done showed that they were, in
fact, the best the English could send against their foes. Their
trek up Lake George had been cautiously made under the
cover of darkness. Their movement across the patch of land
that separated Lake George from Lake Champlain kept them
away from the trails frequented by the garrison of Fort Carillon. Whenever they halted to study the movement of French
forces up and down the vast lake that served as a conduit of
invasion between Canada and the English colonies, they did
so from secluded, inconspicuous spots and not a picturesque
promenade. Otherwise, the rangers made it a point to keep

oving until well after dark, when they finally established their camp, hidden deep in the woods.

Under ordinary circumstances, rangers sent out by Major Robert Rogers operating in this manner would have had no trouble accomplishing their assigned tasks, for they were the best when it came to what the Europeans called irregular warfare. Unfortunately for this patrol of one officer and nine men, their trail had been detected even before they turned their backs on Lake George. It was on their second day out when a small band of six Caughnawagas found their tracks and took up the pursuit. Had the rangers known they were being shadowed, it would have been an easy matter to turn and annihilate their unwanted guests, since each of them was every bit as good as a native when it came to fighting man-to-man, in the great forest of upper New York.

The leader of the stalkers, however, had no intention of allowing the rangers to discover that they were being hunted. For he had the one thing that often mattered the most when it came to fighting in the forest: knowledge. He knew where the rangers were, while the rangers, totally ignorant of the Caughnawagas, felt protected by the vast wilderness through which they moved. This knowledge meant that the Indians would be the ones who would pick both the time and the place for the fight. For, unlike the rangers, who were only after information, the Caughnawagas were hunting for them.

It wasn't that Toolah needed to prove his skill and courage in battle, or add more scalps to his considerable tally. Already his name and the deeds associated with it were familiar to all the eastern tribes who sided with the French. His ruthlessness and reckless abandon in the face of the enemy had even been acknowledged by the French commander at Fort Carillon, who, while courting the Indians relentlessly to aid in the defense of his fortress, preferred to keep them at arm's distance. It wasn't the pursuit of greater glory that drove this warrior to leave the comforts of his winter lodge and company of his wife in the waning days of winter. It was a new quest that drove him and, conversely, restrained him as he stalked his prey.

"You are denied the full honors and privileges accorded

to a warrior of your ability," said his cunning wife, "because you are considered too rash, too impetuous. In battle you have no equal. But others consider you too reckless. While you are protected from harm by the spirits, others around you are not so fortunate. They want to return to their lodges after the fighting is done, where they can brag of their deeds and adventures, as you do. Most of the men of this tribe do not feel they will be granted this simple pleasure if you lead them."

Toolah was not surprised by his wife's blunt assessment. She was a strong woman, a woman whom few men could tolerate. Toolah, on the other hand, had nothing to fear from her. Rather, he found her a challenge, an excellent mate who would produce children as strong-willed and fearless as they were.

"Those who would not follow me are dogs," Toolah snapped back. "Nothing but cowards and dogs."

"No," his wife countered. "They are only humans, jealous of their lives." After pausing a moment for this thought to sink in, Toolah's wife continued. "When you can prove to the elders of the tribe that you have wisdom and cunning that is as great as your courage and strength, all that you desire will come to you."

After Toolah had reflected upon his wife's words, he concluded that she was right. Leading others in battle required abilities that were far different from the individual courage and skills that were so natural to him. The question that troubled Toolah was how best to go about gaining the experience of leading others while proving his competence as a leader. It was during the late summer of 1756 that Toolah solved this problem and set out on his campaign to achieve this end.

"Who among you," he challenged the young men of the tribe, those standing on the verge of manhood, "is brave enough to follow me to where others dare not go? Who will come with me deep into English territory and show the Iroquois that we are as great as they?" At a time when every man of age, to include Toolah's own brother, once thought to be a coward, was out covering himself with glory, this challenge was too tempting.

Encouraged by the response to his challenge, Toolah

showed his wisdom by selecting only those young men who were the most promising and belonged to the most influential families of the tribe. "When you return with them in victory," his wife advised him, "their families will have to look upon them as men, and listen to their stories, as they have had to listen to their fathers. And when they tell their stories, they will speak of how you, Toolah, led them and brought them across the threshold of manhood."

And that was how it began. First, Toolah took but two young men of all those who clamored to go. Advancing past Fort William Henry, guarding the southern shore of Lake George, Toolah and his companions marched to the very gates of Fort Edward itself. There, they watched and waited until a patrol of provincials left that place and started north for the lake. Stalking their prey like the predators that shared the forest with them, Toolah and his tiny band followed and watched. When the provincials took to canoes at William Henry, Toolah and his warriors followed along the shore of the lake, running just inside the woods as fast as the Englishmen paddled. When the Englishmen camped, Toolah was there, hovering just outside the light of their cook fire, watching, waiting. And when his enemy was most at ease, when he was sure that only the trees about them knew of their existence, Toolah struck.

Not every foray was a success. At times, especially when his prey was a patrol of rangers, the English would discover their danger, and it was Toolah, not they, who would be surprised. Yet even when this happened, Toolah's careful planning and caution always paid off. "I always keep one eye behind me," he confided to his wife after one such failure. "Only a fool builds a lodge with one entrance."

"You have learned well, my husband," his wife replied as she prepared to bestow upon her man his just reward for following her advice.

Now, in the late winter of 1757, Toolah's patience was paying off. No longer did he need to go to the children of the tribe and bully them into following. Now he had the pick of the best and most skilled warriors. He merely had to lift his musket and blanket roll, both kept ready for his immediate use, and walk into the middle of the sleepy lodges of his village, where he would announce, "I am going." Impatient braves, tired of the tedium of the long winter, would hasten to follow Toolah. Often, he found himself sending most back. "Too many," he told those unfortunates not chosen, "is worse than too few."

When the dull gray sky was beginning to lighten, Toolah once more accounted for all ten rangers. While eight slept on the ground, curled up in their heavy fur coats and blankets, two stood guard. Neither was very attentive. One, sitting on a log in the center of his sleeping comrades, gave in to his struggle to keep his wry head from bowing low between his legs. The other, with his blanket wrapped about him and his musket cradled in the crook of his arm, leaned against a tree at the edge of the sleeping circle of men, staring vacantly out into the forest without bothering to look about.

Ready, Toolah turned, nodded to his impatient warriors, and then stood up. With great deliberateness, he walked into the center of the enemy camp, stepping silently over the bodies of rangers lost in a deep, hard-earned sleep. Only when he stood before the ranger sitting on the log did Toolah stop, raise his hand containing his hatchet, and pause. Behind him, he knew there were five pairs of eyes watching his every move. Though they, too, had their weapons out and ready to strike, all held their breath as they intently watched their leader in awe.

As he did on such occasions, Toolah did not strike first. Instead, he let out the most ferocious scream that he could summon from the pit of his soul. Startled, the ranger's face turned up, toward Toolah, while his hands automatically went to seize the musket he kept between his legs. Even before his eyes were open, the ranger's hands were groping about in an effort to find his weapon. But it was already too late for that. Without ever having a chance to defend himself, Toolah's death blow had fallen.

Abandoning his hatchet, now lodged deeply in the ranger's skull, Toolah grabbed up the dead man's musket before it toppled over with him. Turning quickly, he brought the musket up, cocked it, and jerked back on the trigger just as the form of the other sentinel appeared at the end of the long barrel. Though the ranger he had just killed had been a miserable guard, Toolah was confident that he had been wise enough to have his piece primed and ready. In this, the Caughnawaga warrior was right. The flash and discharge was followed by the howl of the stricken ranger as the impact of Toolah's ball knocked him away from the tree that had been such a comfort to him.

By now, the others in Toolah's party were falling on their chosen victims, each of whom was scrambling madly in an effort to escape or defend himself. Most did not have any more of a chance than did the first sentinel on the log whom Toolah had dispatched. Some, however, did have a few seconds to react. One, grabbing Toolah's ankle, gave it a jerk in an effort to throw the warrior chief off balance while he scrambled to gain his own feet. Toolah, however, reacted instinctively to the feel of another's grasp. Letting his leg go with the direction of the pull, Toolah spun about and brought down the butt of the musket he held as hard as he could where he thought his assailant's head might be. For the second time in almost as many seconds, Toolah's luck held. Rather than smacking frozen ground, Toolah heard the crunch and snap of bone as his weapon found its mark. Instantly, the hand on his ankle let go, leaving Toolah free to plant both feet on the ground and turn to meet the next challenge.

But there were no more, not that night. With a frenzy equal only to that of Toolah himself, his fellow warriors had quickly disposed of the other rangers before they had even managed to rise from the ground that had become their final resting place. For a moment there was silence, as Toolah looked about to ensure that it was all over. Then, when he was pleased with what he saw in the growing light of dawn, he drew his knife, let out another scream that reverberated through the woods, and got down to the task of collecting scalps. He would personally present to the commandant of Fort Carillon three ranger scalps for breakfast.

Albany, New York
March, 1757

WITH measured grace, Katherine Van der Hoff paused at the entrance to the well-lit ballroom and took everything in at a glance. Like everything else Katherine did, her hesitation was purposeful. For not only did this provide her an opportunity to see who was with whom, but everyone in the room had an opportunity to see her, alone and unfettered by the clutter of another's presence. The only child of a widowed Albany merchant who was second to none when it came to fortune and power in the Royal colony of New York, Katherine was used to being the center of attention. That and a habit of defying her father's wishes were considered the only serious shortfalls of an otherwise marvelous and most charming feminine creature. "Were she mine," one rather rotund gentleman smirked to another as the two watched Katherine scan the room for one worthy of her company, "I'd take her across my knee and spank her till she came to her senses."

The rotund gentleman's friend laughed out loud. "Ah! I imagine," he said in a lower voice, "that you might find she enjoys it."

With a knowing smirk, the rotund gentleman leaned his head forward and replied, "Well, can't say that I wouldn't mind finding out."

Across the room, Katherine's eyes fixed upon the object of her search. He was an officer of the king, standing as he always did, within easy reach of the table where punch and decanters of wine stood at the ready. Watching his movements for a moment, Katherine judged that he had not yet consumed enough, as was his habit, to impair his judgment or his ability to carry on a decent conversation. Determined to make her interests known before he had a chance to do so, the young woman moved quickly across the room toward her unsuspecting prey.

"Ah," she stated breathlessly as she came up next to him. "I am so glad that you found the time to join us tonight. It is always a great source of pleasure to be afforded the opportunity to entertain the servants of our most Royal sovereign, King George."

Lost in dark thoughts that the brandy had not yet had time to hush, Thomas Shields was caught off guard by the woman's bold advance. "Well," he muttered as his eyes darted about the floor at his feet in embarrassment, "it's, I think, a great pleasure, I mean honor, to be invited here, as always, to partake of your, ah, bountiful hospitality and warm, ah . . ."

Enjoying the floundering of this flustered officer, Katherine reached out and lightly touched his arm. "Oh, please, sir. You pay us too great a compliment."

It was as if he had been shot. His eyes immediately ceased their aimless wanderings and fixed upon the delicate white hand that now rested upon the scarlet cloth of his uniform's sleeve. Not sure exactly what to do, Thomas slowly raised his eyes until they met hers. Composing himself as best as he could under the circumstances, he waited for her to speak.

"I was hoping to have an opportunity to meet you earlier," she stated in a soft tone that hinted of disappointment, "but it seems your duties have never seemed to permit me to do so." Actually, circumstances had afforded Katherine many other occasions to do so, but Thomas' habitual inebriation kept her from following through. "I know," she continued as she gave Thomas' arm a slight squeeze so that he would feel the presence of her hand, "I am being quite forward, and perhaps unladylike, but in these times of war, one must seize the moment, mustn't one?"

Lost in the bright china blue eyes that glistened like tiny jewels set upon a white satin pillow, Thomas didn't respond at first. And while he found the smile that adorned her face charming, he had no idea that it was being driven by Katherine's knowledge that her presence, and her touch, was having their desired effect on Thomas. Already she could see the crimson tones of passion coloring Thomas' cheeks as he stood there before her, in silence. "Perhaps," she finally volunteered, "this is not a convenient time for a visit."

"Oh, no," Thomas stuttered as he forced himself to break his stare. Stepping back, he gently pulled his arm free of her grasp and placed it behind his back. Clearing his throat, he bowed his head as he attempted to hide his embarrassment. "I, ah, am not at all bothered by your manner. In fact . . ."

Realizing what he had just said, Thomas looked up at Katherine, his face contorted in horror. "Oh, dear madam, that's not what I meant. I didn't mean to imply that you are a bother, or anything like that. What I meant . . ."

Stepping forward to close the space that he had so skillfully opened between them, Katherine again touched her hand upon the upper sleeve of his coat. "Oh, Captain, please. There is no need to apologize," she said with a hint of laughter in her voice. Then, in an effort that Thomas took to be conciliatory, Katherine made an offer that he snapped up without thinking. "Perhaps it would be better if we were to meet under other circumstances?"

"Well, yes, madam," Thomas replied. "I think that would be best."

Not wanting to give him an opportunity to collect his thoughts, she pushed the point. "Then tomorrow afternoon, for tea. Would that be satisfactory?"

The fact that he had been skillfully maneuvered into a corner from which there was no escape suddenly dawned on him. Damn, he thought to himself. After evading involvement with any of these bloody provincials for better than two years, he now found himself at a loss as to what to do. Looking into the eyes of the young, beautiful heiress, Thomas concluded that there was little that he could do but submit. Snapping his heels together, he took Katherine's hand in his. Slowly bringing it up to his lips, Thomas lightly kissed her fingers. "Madam, I am at your service."

From across the room, the rotund gentleman nudged his friend and tilted his head toward Thomas and Katherine. "Now," he asked, "what do you suppose that's all about?"

The friend smiled. "My dear fellow, need I explain everything to you?"

"Well," the rotund man replied, "it's just that with all the English officers about, I'd have thought young Katherine would have, well, picked someone who at least showed some promise."

His friend smiled. "Captain Shields may indulge too often, but, take my word, he's no fool. He's one of the quartermaster's brightest assistants. He's keen, thorough, and quite good with numbers. Despite the fact that he's been raised a gentleman, he has the makings of a first-rate businessman."

"But he's drunk," the other protested.

"Oh," the friend replied as if to discount that fault, "I won't much mind that. Once he's managed to put his past behind him, he'll straighten up and be as proper and respectable as his father."

The rotund gentlemen would not give in. "It'll soon be two years since Braddock's disastrous expedition. You'd think by now Shields would have put that sad affair behind him and pulled himself together."

The other man didn't answer at first. Instead, he watched as Katherine, moving about the room from one person to another, kept an eye on Thomas. With a smile, the man finally replied. "Some need a bit more help than others when it comes to closing a sorry chapter in their lives. Perhaps," he mused, "our little Katherine plans on providing that assistance."

The rotund gentleman grunted. "If that's true, then he'll have the devil to pay for that kindness."

SATISFIED that he had done as much as he could given the terrible headache that throbbed like a drum beating a slow, mournful march, Thomas leaned back in his seat and stared out the window. Though soon it would be April, it was snowing again. This revelation served only to heighten the discomfort that wracked his body. In England, spring would be making its first fugitive presence known. While there would still be the odd chilly night, winter's cruel grip would have by now been shaken.

But not here. Here, it would be another month, perhaps two, before the first blooms could make their appearance without the threat of a killing frost or snow. Carefully placing his quill down upon the pile of papers before him, he looked across the room that served as his office at the decanter of wine that sat on a shelf within arm's reach.

He was still staring at the bottle when another officer blew through the door. "There you are," he announced in a voice that was far too cheerful for the likes of a day like this. "I've just finished telling the colonel that you've already packed it in for the day."

After taking one more longing look at the waiting wine, Thomas turned to face Captain Lewis Fenton. "Why," Thomas asked, "would you make an absurd assumption like that? I've not yet cleared away yesterday's reports and returns," he responded bitterly as he swept his hand across his cluttered desk, "let alone touched those that were dumped on us this morning. What, with all this and the colonel wanting me to go up to Edward tomorrow, I'll be here till well after supper."

With a wave of his hand, as if he were a conjurer attempting to make the papers that so troubled Thomas disappear, Fenton dismissed his fellow officer's protests. "They'll wait, you know. Always do. No one much pays attention to most of that rubbish anyway." Then, with a sly grin, Fenton added, "Now, Miss Van der Hoff is, how shall we say, an entirely different matter. I don't think she's the sort to wait. Do you?"

Pausing, Thomas stared at Fenton. "How did you find out about that?"

Charmed with himself for evoking such a response from a man who made it a practice to keep his thoughts and emotions to himself, Fenton grinned. "Not everyone goes about this town with their head in the clouds. People do talk. In this case, Miss Van der Hoff's girl let it be known that her mistress was entertaining a British officer for tea today while chatting with the colonel's cook at the market this morning. After your smashing performance at the Van der Hoffs' last night, I naturally put two and two . . ."

Thomas' expression turned to one of anger. "She came up to me," he snapped, "and made a total spectacle of herself. I had nothing to . . ."

Sensing that he had touched a raw nerve, Fenton smiled, raised his hands as if to fend off Thomas' verbal attack, and stepped back. "Oh, please. No need to explain yourself to me. Everyone knows about Miss Van der Hoff's, shall we say, directness?"

"No, damn you, you should not say. It is a matter that is of no concern to you or anyone else."

"Yes, well," Fenton continued, "that's exactly what I told Brian when he asked if you were still here. He was almost willing to wager that you wouldn't grace madam's presence with your company. I told Brinny . . ."

Standing up, Thomas pushed the chair he had been sitting on out of the way so quickly that it toppled over. "Lieutenant Hackworth is an idiot," Thomas pronounced sharply. "And so are you for going on about matters that are of no concern to you as if you were nothing more than an empty-headed regimental laundress." Then, not knowing what to say, Thomas turned, grabbed his hat and cape off a peg, and started for the door. "If all we're going to do here today is swap stories and rumors, I'm leaving."

With a quick step to the side, Fenton made way for Thomas and watched him go. "Give the dear lady my regards."

Thomas neither responded nor looked back as he stormed past the sentinels posted outside. When the two soldiers were sure that Thomas was well out of earshot, the left snickered. "Can't say that I care for that one much when he's sober."

The other sentinel grunted as he reached up with his free hand and pulled the collar of his thin cloak tighter about his neck. "Can't say that I give a damn for any of 'em. Far as I'm concerned, both they and this Gawd-awful collection of colonies can rot till hell freezes over."

The soldier on the left, shuffling his feet slightly to keep them from going numb, smirked. "Well," he sneered, "you won't have long to wait. If this place ain't hell, it's as close as ya can get. And lordy, it's freezin' already."

THE house was very different in the daylight, uncluttered by officers with ceremonial swords, overweight gentlemen in large, finely made coats, and ladies sporting imposing wigs and wide, ornate ball gowns. Or perhaps, Thomas thought, it was because he was sober. He'd been to this place before. Twice at least, as far as he could remember. Maybe more. But never while he was sober.

As he waited to be announced and escorted to where Miss Van der Hoff awaited his company, he looked around. It was a rather humble affair, like most colonial homes. Far less ostentatious than the residences of some of the Dutch merchants who dominated Albany and the New York colony. Definitely small, almost trifling, when compared to his own ancestral home in England. After taking a couple of precise steps this way and that, Thomas calculated that the entrance hall of his father's "small" estate could easily gobble up at least a dozen, maybe more, rooms of this size.

Still, he thought as he slid off his cape, this room was, in a word, comfortable. Even the color of the wallpaper, a soft dusty-rose, was warm, inviting. The windows and mirrors, elegant in their simplicity, provided just enough light, even on a forbidding day like this, to dispel the gloom of the world outside. The furniture, eminently practical and made to be used, was inviting, upholstered in colors and materials selected to contribute to the feeling of warmth and ease.

Captivated by the simple beauty of the room, Thomas didn't notice the approach of the servant girl. "My lady is waiting for you, sir, this way."

With a shake of his head, Thomas smiled, draped his wet cloak and hat over the girl's arms, and made his way in the direction she pointed. As he did so, his eyes darted about from side to side, taking everything in, from ceiling to floor. Though the color of the rooms and the nature of the decorations changed, the compelling, almost sensual feeling of hospitality that had greeted him in the entry hall flowed smoothly throughout the house. How much of this, he asked himself, was the doings of the widower's daughter?

"Captain Shields, how pleasant to see you." Her words, like the house itself, were warm and inviting. Looking up from his careful study of the well-groomed floor, his eyes fell upon a sight that was well staged for the impact it had. Seated next to a small table upon which the tea service was set, Katherine Van der Hoff graced her chair as a flower would a fine china vase. Her dress, a pale yellow affair judiciously trimmed with fine lace, brightened up the entire room, just as all the decor and furniture he had seen so far complemented the house. It contrasted nicely with her dark hair, worn in fashionable curls that cascaded smoothly, gracefully, down her back and about her shoulders. Yes, Thomas told himself as he smiled and looked into her warm brown eyes, all of this, from top to bottom, was her doing. "Please, be seated," she offered, making it appear an invitation and not an order.

With a nod and a smile, Thomas moved over to a seat opposite hers. Flipping the tails of his regimentals, which still bore the yellow trim of the Forty-fourth Foot, a unit he had not served with in more than a year, Thomas found himself, as he settled across from Katherine, wanting to tell her how lovely she was.

Not that Thomas needed to express his thoughts in words, for his eyes and expression, totally unguarded, were easily read by Katherine. "I am so pleased that you were able to find the time in your busy day to indulge a foolish girl such as myself."

"Oh, please," Thomas protested. "It is, I can assure you, a great privilege for me to be invited to spend a peaceful hour or two with someone as lovely as you." There, he said to himself, he had said it. And from the coy diversion of Katherine's eyes and the slight blush, he knew his compliment had achieved its desired effect.

With practiced ease, Katherine poured the tea, offered cakes from an assortment of gaily colored pastries, and played the perfect hostess. All the while, she did so in a manner that took her closer, for slightly longer periods of time, to her guest. "The Van der Hoffs," she informed Thomas as she chatted during the course of the tea, "owe their fortune to commerce and the fur trade. My ancestors were among those who established Fort Orange, the first settlement here in the upper Hudson River region. We have always enjoyed friendly relationships with the natives and, as a result, have prospered."

Thomas smiled and nodded, thinking as she spoke that her father, like many of the others, also enjoyed very, very cozy relationships with the French to the north. Whom they traded with, he knew, made no difference. Commerce and profit was their nationality. Still, this sinister thought did nothing to spoil his enjoyment of Katherine's company. Like a child being sung to by his mother, he listened attentively to her sweet voice as she told him the story of the region, her family, and the business that had outgrown the small-town world of Albany and spread to New York City. "Dear father was lost when mother died. Though I was just coming of age, I had no choice but to assume the duties and responsibilities as the mistress of the house. I dare say, had I not, he would have simply been swallowed up in his grief and sorrow."

"I understand that you have a home in the city of New York that dwarfs this one," Thomas volunteered.

"True," Katherine sighed. "But it is a showpiece. In order to escape his grief, father threw himself into commerce with all the fury of a berserker. This house," she stated tenderly, "was too much mother's. To this day, he pines so every time he's here."

"You don't seem to mind it," Thomas observed.

The melancholy expression that had darkened her expression disappeared as her voice resumed a sweet, cheerful pitch. "It is my home, dear sir. While I do enjoy my stays in the city and the gayness of life there during the season, I am at ease here, comfortable."

It was as if she had read his mind. Her words confirmed his feelings and thoughts.

"Will you be going north, to William Henry, this campaign season, or following the army making for Louisbourg?" she asked as Thomas' mind dwelt on the feelings she had so casually stirred in him.

"No," he stammered as he tried to catch up on the conversation. "I'm to remain here, with General Webb. I'll be overseeing the provisioning of the militias when they gather here and move north. Though I expect to follow them, it'll be a dull summer for me."

"Oh," she replied with a hint of satisfaction in her tone. "I would have thought you would have been following the main army. Everyone speaks highly of you. Why, when Colonel Gage was staying with us in New York, he mentioned on more than one occasion his wish that he could have had you with the regiment of light infantry he is raising throughout the colonies."

For the first time, Katherine's words stung Thomas. Though she hadn't meant to, she had reminded him of his failure to overcome the oppressive melancholy that had haunted him since the Braddock disaster. "I'd love to make you my adjutant, dear boy," Colonel Gage had himself told Thomas. "But I'm afraid I simply could not tolerate your drinking. God knows," he sneered, "we have enough drunks about camp when the provincial officers come staggering in every year. As servants of His Royal Highness, bearing his personal commission, I must insist that my officers set the highest possible standards." Though justified, Gage's words stung, now as they had then. And despite his best efforts, Thomas had found himself unable to escape his sad pattern of drinking. In the beginning, it had been nothing more than an effort to drown the remorse he felt over the horrible failure of the expedition in 1755 and the end of his dreams of glory. But then, as time softened those feelings, the nightmares began. Though they didn't come often, when the images of his grenadiers, stacked in bloody heaps at his own feet, visited him at night, Thomas found escape from them only through glass after glass of strong spirits.

Sensing that she had lost him, though she knew not how, Katherine quickly tried to regain his attention. "Does your busy schedule permit you the luxury, Captain, of a ride every now and then?"

Shaking his head in an effort to dispel the grisly images that haunted his mind, Thomas looked at Katherine for a moment. "Ah, well, I haven't really taken the time to do so, but . . ."

Seizing the opening, Katherine cut in. "Oh, splendid. I must take you about and show you some of the wonderful countryside. Though it's still quite cold and damp, this part of New York has a charm that defies the ravages of nature's most horrid seasons."

For a moment, Thomas studied Katherine's face. How much, he wondered, was an act. She was interested in something, he knew, for his reputation as an officer who indulged himself far too much was well known throughout the community as well as the army. And she had to know he was not in line to inherit anything from his father that he didn't already have. So, the game she was dragging him into was a mystery, just as compelling to Thomas as the feelings that stirred in him as he stared into her deep brown eyes.

"I must make a trip up to William Henry in the next few days to settle some outstanding accounts with a provincial unit. But, when I return . . ."

Again, she took over before he could finish. With a smile that brightened the room, she rose from her seat and offered him her hand. "Then, it's agreed. As soon as you return, we'll go riding."

Unable to resist, Thomas rose, took Katherine's hand, and slowly lifted it to his lips. "It will be," he added after pressing his lips to her soft, warm fingers, "a pleasure."

CHAPTER FIFTEEN

Fort William Henry, on the Southern
Shore of Lake George, New York
April, 1757

"H E T'AIN'T HERE," the gruff ranger sergeant barked when Thomas asked where he could find the officer who served Rogers's battalion of rangers as quartermaster.

"Well," Thomas responded, refusing to be put off, "where can I find him?"

"Ah," the sergeant replied, "he's about somewhere in the woods."

"And how," Thomas continued, trying to control his temper, "might I be able to contact him?"

The ranger sergeant's weather-worn face that hadn't seen water since the last rain twisted itself into a smile. "Ya might try yellin'."

A pair of rangers who had gathered on either side of

Thomas as he tried to converse with the sergeant laughed. "Good one, Hank." A tall, skinny ranger who smelled of bear grease and body odor snorted.

Ignoring the comment, Thomas persisted. "Listen, Sergeant," he snarled. "I am an officer of the Crown here on the king's business."

"Well, now," the ranger sergeant replied. "Ever think that the lieutenant is out there, in the woods, doin' the king's business?"

This quip brought howls of laughter from the two uninvited rangers.

"Listen, *Sergeant*," Thomas demanded as his temper began to melt away under the ridicule, "I came here to settle some accounting problems with your lieutenant and I demand that you either bring him here, right now, or take me to him immediately."

Rather than being offended or angered, the sergeant smiled. "Well, now. I guess since it's an order, then we've got no choice but to take 'im," the sergeant stated, winking at the rangers on either side of Thomas. "Go get the canoe ready, will ya, lads?"

Pleased to have provoked a response that appeared to be fulfilling his demands, Thomas didn't bother to ask where they were going or how long it would take when he stepped into the frail canoe on the shore of Lake George. Neither did his mind, preoccupied with other thoughts, take note of the three bundles secured in the small craft. Seated between the ranger sergeant, who took up his place at the rear of the canoe, and the tall, lanky ranger who had made fun of him before, Thomas turned his attention to matters he had left behind in Albany that would need his attention when he returned.

Slowly, smoothly, the frail craft slid through the still waters of Lake George. On either side of the serene body of water, mountains covered with dense stands of pines and hardwood trees sprouting their buds rose precipitously into a pale blue sky that sported an assortment of overstuffed clouds lazily making their way overhead. Allowing his eyes to wander wherever they fancied, Thomas was awed by the beauty of this majestic parade of earth, sky, and water. Within a half hour of leaving the overcrowded fort that reeked of dirty men, smoke from dozens of wood fires, and the stench of civilization, all concerns relating to his weighty duties had given way to other, more enjoyable thoughts.

Like the fluffy white cloud that he found himself staring at, the image of Katherine Van der Hoff floated into his mind. Without realizing it, a slight smile cracked the frown that he wore like a badge of office. That she was up to something was obvious. Unable, and unwilling, to curb his drinking, Thomas seldom found himself the guest of the local gentry. Not that he minded. Many of Albany's social elite were, in Thomas' opinion, pompous, overbearing, and rather boring. He found their efforts to mimic what they considered the trends being set in Europe ludicrous for the most part, comic at best. Perhaps, he mused, that's what fascinated him about Katherine Van der Hoff. Everything about her was refreshingly understated. Both her manner and her home were warm and inviting, as inviting as a spider's web to a fly.

There was little to disturb his thoughts other than the rhythmic dipping of the rangers' paddles into the calm lake and the gurgling noise generated each time they took a deep stroke. It had been a long time, Thomas realized, since anything had managed to capture his attention and keep his mind so focused as thoughts of Katherine Van der Hoff were now doing. It was a game of some sort she was playing, no different than the kind the girls in England played. In the past, Thomas had not permitted himself the luxury of being drawn into trifling affairs with a girl who had little better to do than lay snares for men with all the skills of a French trapper. He had had a future then, a bright one. Now . . .

Perhaps that was the most interesting part of the whole idea that drew Thomas to accept Katherine Van der Hoff's invitation into social intrigue. He had nothing to offer, other than a name, while she was poised to inherit all from a doting father. An interesting puzzle, he thought as the serene calm lulled him to sleep while the canoe propelled by the two vigilant rangers moved farther north, toward the French and Fort Carillon.

IT wasn't until the prow of the canoe scraped the rocky bottom just a few feet from the dark shore that Thomas awoke. Startled, his eyes flew open, yet failed to see anything that made any sense or helped him regain his orientation. "What the . . ." he started to exclaim.

"Quiet, lad," the ranger sergeant whispered as he leaned next to Thomas' ear from behind, "or you'll get us all killed." Though still badly confused and upset at being at such a gross disadvantage, something in the ranger's voice told Thomas that he was serious, deadly serious.

Fully awake now, and seated upright between the two rangers, Thomas watched and waited in the darkness that engulfed them. With hardly a noise to betray their movements, both the ranger sergeant and the tall, lanky ranger hopped from the canoe, almost simultaneously, into the shallow water. With their muskets in one hand and the other holding on to the canoe still occupied by Thomas, the two rangers guided the craft closer to the shore. "You need to get out now," the ranger sergeant whispered. "Just watch your footing and fall in behind me. Hold on to my belt if ya need to."

For a moment, Thomas hesitated. This was not at all what he had expected when they had started their journey earlier in the day. In fact, he hadn't even expected a journey. Yet, despite his growing concern, not to mention his natural dislike of being in a position of having to follow the instructions of a provincial, Thomas felt compelled to do as he was told, without question. There would be time, he was sure, to deal with these men in an appropriate manner, later. If not when he met their superior, wherever in the devil he might be, then back at William Henry, when this wild adventure was at an end.

Having resolved himself to this course of action, Thomas cautiously eased himself out of the canoe, into the knee-deep water, and followed the rangers as they lifted their small vessel from the water and carried it several yards into the dark forest that swallowed them as effectively as it did all light. Though he knew that he was but a foot, maybe two, behind the ranger sergeant, Thomas could not see the man. He could hear his breathing, even smell his pungent odor. But Thomas was completely unable to distinguish him from the trees they crept past, even though he knew he was staring straight at him.

It was this overwhelming dependence on his sight that caused Thomas to ram into the back of the sergeant when that man stopped and set the canoe down. Instinctively, Thomas mumbled a halfhearted "Sorry."

For his troubles, the sergeant turned and hissed at him. "Shush!" the ranger warned as he leaned closer to Thomas. "We're not more than four, four and a half miles from Carillon. The Froggies may be about."

Though he had been confused and badly disoriented before, Thomas was not overly concerned, at least not until the sergeant gave him this last piece of information. Though he felt like screaming, or shouting, or doing something, Thomas managed to remain silent as he regained his composure and waited for whatever happened next.

This took a while, not to mention a considerable march that seemed longer than it was by virtue of the fact that it was pitch-black and Thomas had no idea where he was. The ordeal was made worse by the broken terrain and usual hazards associated with traveling through forests. When he was not tripping over tree roots, Thomas found himself being swatted in the face by small branches that were bent back by the ranger sergeant in front of him and then released, like a spring, when the sergeant passed the tree the branch was attached to. On top of these hazards, the physical exertions of marching were having their effects. Not having participated in anything resembling active campaigning for better than a year, Thomas was sadly out of shape, with every muscle in his legs screaming out in pain while he huffed and puffed to catch his breath. More than once, the ranger sergeant stopped and asked Thomas if he could quiet down. "I know it's tough on your kind," the sergeant said mockingly, "but we do need to keep from alertin' every savage to our presence." Though it took all his effort, not to mention his patience, Thomas managed to comply.

After what seemed like hours, the ranger sergeant came to a sudden halt. Used to Thomas' stumbling and ramming him from behind, the sergeant ignored Thomas, crouched, and cupped his hands over his mouth. The sound the man generated didn't sound like anything that a human could produce. Intrigued, Thomas stepped back and squatted, careful to keep within arm's reach of the big sergeant while he listened for whatever came next. From up ahead, a cry very similar to the one the sergeant had generated echoed through the woods. "Ah," the sergeant whispered back to Thomas, "we're here."

The joy Thomas felt was incredible. While he had no idea where "here" was, the mere thought that his travels were over, at least for the moment, was enough for him. Following the ranger sergeant as soon as he was sure that the man was up and moving again, Thomas realized that he was entering an encampment. He sensed, rather than saw, the presence of others gathered about, since there were no campfires or light of any sort. The thick branches overhead prevented even the slightest glimmer of light from an otherwise dark night sky from aiding Thomas.

"La-tennent?" the sergeant called out in a soft, hushed voice.

From somewhere close at hand, Thomas heard a response, equally guarded, though defiantly surprised. "What in blue blazes," the gruff voice barked, "are you doin' here, Emmit?"

For the first time, Thomas realized that he had never asked the sergeant his name. Here he had been, in the care of this man for hours, and he hadn't even bothered to find out something as common as that.

The ranger sergeant, without the cockiness in his voice that he had used when addressing Thomas, responded, "Well, er, this English captain, up from Albany, ya know, came up to the fort lookin' for ya. Said it was important and needed to see you, right away, on an important matter."

"Which is?" the impatient voice of the lieutenant inquired.

"Ah, well, Lieutenant, ya see, I don't rightly know. All he said was that he wanted to be taken to ya, straightaway. Well, seein' as he was an officer, one holdin' the king's very own commission, I did exactly like he said and . . ."

There was movement that Thomas couldn't follow in the dark. Only when the lieutenant spoke did Thomas realize that the ranger officer had pushed his sergeant out of the way and stepped forward so that he was now only inches away from Thomas. "This had better be damned important, *sir*, or someone's gonna be skinned, *alive*."

Clearing his throat and drawing himself fully erect, though he knew these gestures were a waste in the darkness, Thomas started to explain. "Well, you see . . ."

"I'd appreciate it, sir," the ranger lieutenant snapped, "if you'd be so kind as to keep your voice down. No need to let the Frenchies hear this before they need to."

The reminder that they were in proximity to the enemy served to take the edge off the anger that Thomas had felt welling up within him. Starting over, though in a lower voice this time, Thomas went on. "I'm with General Webb's headquarters. There were a number of irregularities concerning the ranger companies at Fort William Henry. I came up here personally in the hope that, perhaps . . ."

A sudden move caused Thomas to draw back a step. Still, when the ranger officer spoke, he was so close to Thomas' face that Thomas could feel the lieutenant's breath. "You risked these men's lives, not to mention your own and those with me, just because some Goddamned accounts don't balance? Are you out of your mind?"

"I had no idea," Thomas shot back, "that you were here, so near the French, when I told the sergeant to take me to you. I thought . . ."

Again the ranger officer didn't allow Thomas to finish. Not that he needed to. By now it was painfully obvious what had transpired. Turning on the sergeant, standing off next to the ranger officer, the lieutenant ripped into him as much as he could in a whisper. "Of all the hare-brained stunts! How could you have thought that I, or anyone else, would be amused by such an idiotic prank?" When, after a suitable pause, no reply was forthcoming, the lieutenant continued. "I'll deal with you later. Now get out of my sight and find someplace to curl up."

Facing back to Thomas, the ranger lieutenant offered no excuse, no apology. "There's no way I'm goin' to send you back down the hill in the dark. Nor do I intend to jeopardize your life or the lives of my men. You're gonna have to make yourself as comfortable as you can till morning." Then, without another word, the ranger officer turned and stepped away, swallowed up by the same darkness from which he had emerged.

For a moment, Thomas didn't know whether to be angry, worried, or thankful. While he was totally unprepared to spend the night in the woods, he was also equally convinced that he would be unable to retrace his steps, even with a guide, until after he had gotten some rest. Heaving a great sigh, he stumbled about until he found what appeared to be a relatively clear patch of ground covered with dead leaves. Pulling his cape closely about his exhausted body, Thomas threw himself down onto the ground, curled up, and tried to sleep. Only his exhaustion permitted him to ignore the cold, the hard ground, and the frightful circumstances he found himself in and fall asleep.

SLOWLY, Toolah backed away from where he had been watching the ranger camp. The addition of three more men was not in and of itself enough to concern the warrior. He and his six companions would, under ordinary circumstances, be more than enough to take on eleven foes. What did concern Toolah was that if there were three who had been out there, beyond the circle where the main body had made camp hours before, there might be more. Perhaps, he wondered, the Yankees were setting a trap for him. Perhaps the men in the camp were nothing more than bait, intentionally making their presence known so that he would be drawn out into a position where they, and not he, would be the ambushers. Not willing to take a chance when he didn't need to, Toolah pulled back to where he had left his band of followers and signaled that he was not ready to strike, but wanted to find a place where he and his party could rest, wait, and watch.

WITH a single shake, Thomas was wide awake. Looking up in the still dark woods, he sensed a large form hovering over him. "Come on, Captain. We're movin'." It was the sergeant who had brought him there, the one named Emmit. Though he knew his night had been far from restful, alternating between shivering from the cold and tossing about in an effort to shift from one painful position to another, Thomas didn't realize how badly his body ached till he stood up. "Oh, God!" he moaned as he straightened his back. For his troubles, three men nearby turned and hushed him with a quick "Shush" or whispered, "Quiet."

Pausing, Thomas looked about. Taking care to keep his cape from opening, he stretched his arms and waited where he was until someone came up to him and whispered, "You follow me." Without another word, the apparition was gone, headed uphill and away from the lake. For a moment, Thomas stood there, wanting to demand that he be taken back to Fort William Henry immediately. But the man hadn't given him a chance. "Don't lose the lead," someone whispered. Not knowing where the lieutenant was, let alone where he himself was, Thomas resigned himself to the fact that he was an unwilling captive of the rangers and moved out.

Slowly, reluctantly, like Thomas' own footsteps, the darkness gave way to a cold, gray dawn. They were moving now along the side of a steep mountain. Thomas, wearing boots that were not at all made for this type of country, often found himself hanging on to trees to keep from losing his footing. Muscles weakened by too much sedentary work and what now seemed to have been a steady diet of wine made the going far worse than it should have been. Still, Thomas had his pride, the pride of an English gentleman and an officer of the Crown. He would not, could not, permit himself to give in. So, despite aches and pains that tortured just about every part of his body, Thomas marched on.

At their first halt, shortly after daylight, as Thomas sat listlessly on the ground, a man, gnawing on a chunk of hard bread, came up to him. "My name's Fergusson," the man announced in a normal tone of voice. "I'm the officer who spoke to you when you came into camp last night."

When Thomas looked up at the man, the lieutenant was offering him a chunk of the bread he had been chewing on. Not having eaten since the morning before, Thomas abandoned his pride and took the bread. "Thank you," he managed, though there wasn't a hint of sincerity in his voice.

"Can't blame you for bein' out of sorts with us," the ranger lieutenant replied while chewing on his bread. "If I were a vindictive type, I'd surely thrash Emmit Smith."

Thomas glared at the ranger. "You mean you're not?"

The ranger officer smiled. "Why, of course not. He was just having some fun. A man's entitled to a little bit of fun every now and then, isn't he?"

Had he not heard all the wild stories about the undisciplined rangers, and had he not been afforded the opportunity to see their misconduct in Albany himself, Thomas would have thought the provincial officer was joking. But he knew that was not the case. Far from being punished, the ranger sergeant who had dragged him all the way here would, in days ahead, be hailed a hero by his companions for making a fool of an English officer.

"So, tell me," Thomas asked, deciding to drop the matter until later, back at William Henry, where it was safe and the king's regulations prevailed, "what are you and your men doing this far north?"

"Lost a patrol hereabouts the end of last month," he replied in a matter-of-fact manner as he stuffed his mouth with another chunk of bread. "Our captain thinks they're dead. Well, he's pretty sure they're dead, but he wants us to make sure. That," he added as he looked about, "as well as extract a little revenge."

Waiting till he finished choking down the dry bread, wishing that he had a glass of sherry to wash it down with, Thomas looked up at the ranger officer with an incredulous look on his face. "What makes you think you'll find the same people who killed your men, assuming they are dead."

"Oh," the lieutenant responded as his eyes continued to scan the forest all about them, "they're dead all right. Otherwise, at least one or two would have made it back to the fort by now. Naw, it'll be the same ones, if we can manage to find them. They've been raising hell with our boys, and just about everyone they can get their hands on, since last fall. They've been good, real good about trackin' us and . . ."

His head stopped turning the moment he stopped speaking. Stepping out in front of Thomas quickly, the ranger lieutenant threw down what was left of his bread and dropped the shoulder over which his musket had been slung, allowing the weapon to slide down into his waiting hand. He was about to let out a scream when a thud, a sound burned into Thomas' memory after Braddock's defeat, knocked the lieutenant backward. A split second later came the report of the musket that had fired the fatal ball.

Unable to believe that the ranger had stepped in front of the scarlet-coated officer just as he fired, Toolah uttered an oath. Having no way of knowing he had struck down a ranger officer, he frantically began to reload his weapon before one of his companions claimed that prize.

Already, to either side, his followers were unleashing their fire on the other rangers below them. Having decided not to strike until he was sure there were no more, Toolah rushed ahead and set an ambush where he thought the rangers would most likely go. Though a few of his followers doubted they would be able to catch their foe in such a manner, once again the Caughnawaga's luck held. "A great chief," his faithful wife had told him, "must be as lucky as he is skilled."

Stunned by the suddenness of the attack, Thomas stared at the body of the ranger officer as it toppled over at his feet. The ranger, his eyes wide open and staring at the gray sky above, made no movement other than a spasmodic twitching. Except for the cut and color of the uniform, the dead man at his feet was no different from those who paraded nightly before his eyes. The first coherent thought that crept into Thomas' mind was the terrible realization that it was happening again. Though far smaller in scale, and of little consequence except for those who were involved, this fight was, for him, no different from the one that had ended his promising career.

The whine of a near miss, followed immediately by the smack of another bullet as it bored its way into the tree he was still sitting up against, brought an end to Thomas' passivity. "By God," he yelled as he turned his face to where he could see smoke rising from his foes' muskets. "You'll not have me! Not without a fight."

Leaning forward just as a ball passed by where his head had been but a split second before, Thomas grabbed the ranger officer's musket. After prying it from the dead man's hand, he seized the cartridge box, then made a dash for a dead tree where two rangers were firing from. With a leap that surprised even himself, he cleared the obstacle, turned as soon as he felt his feet touch on the ground, and dropped between the rangers.

"Glad to see ya decided to join us," Sergeant Emmit stated with a cheerfulness that belied the seriousness of their plight.

Thomas said nothing as he stripped off his cape, opened the cartridge box, fished out a paper cartridge, and began to load his piece. He said nothing as his fingers set about priming the pan, feeding the powder and the ball, and wadding down the muzzle. He then withdrew the ramrod to stuff the whole mess down. All the while he kept his head just inches above the top of the log, scanning for the enemy. When he was ready to fire, he brought the piece up, laid the long barrel on the log, and aimed at a spot where he had seen a whiff of smoke. Patiently, he waited until a head, followed by a shoulder and torso garishly painted in red and black patterns, came popping around the tree. Guessing the range as best he could, Thomas elevated the barrel just above the target and squeezed. As soon as he felt the musket kick back after discharging, he dropped behind the log to reload.

"Not bad," Emmit volunteered, "for an officer of the Crown. I thought you boys didn't think it sporting to aim."

Thomas, realizing that he had just earned a compliment, looked at the ranger. "A trick I learned from you provincials," he stated with as nonchalant a voice as he could manage.

"Well," Emmit replied, "whoever did, he sure did teach ya pretty well. That's one less Indian we'll need to worry 'bout."

Peeking over the log, Thomas was able to make out the head and shoulder of the Indian he had fired at, lying motionless on the ground. He was given little time to enjoy the sight, for a near miss threw a cloud of splinters up and into his face. Pulling his head down, Thomas finished ramming the next round home and withdrew the long ramrod. "How many do you suppose there are out there?"

Lifting his head over the log, the ranger sergeant looked this way, then that. "Oh, half a dozen or so. Not many."

"Do you intend," Thomas asked as he prepared to take his next shot once he found a good target, "to stand and fight it out?"

Pulling his head down, the ranger sergeant looked at Thomas. "I'd love to recover the lieutenant's body and all to save it from those savages. But," he added with a note of regret, "can't take the chance there ain't a herd of Frenchies beating feet this way to join the fun."

Pausing to fire, Thomas pulled his head down and started to reload again. "Agreed. We'll fall back," Thomas ordered without even having stated his intention to take command. Not that he felt he needed to. He was, after all, the senior officer present. The idea that the rangers around him might not follow him never occurred to him. And the fact was, had Thomas not managed to hit the Indian he had dropped with his first shot and shown that he could handle himself under fire, they wouldn't have. So, without ever realizing it, Thomas had been tested and accepted by men he never would have considered his equal, let alone his judges.

"All right," Emmit stated after he finished taking his shot. "You take half the boys and make a break while I hang back and keep these folks busy. When you're back there a ways, where you can cover us, we'll hightail past you, find another good spot, and give you the chance to hold 'em off a bit. We'll just keep doin' that till they give up."

The manner in which the sergeant addressed him, assuming that he had an equal say in what was going to be done, didn't come as a surprise to Thomas. He had been in the colonies long enough to know that there wasn't a provincial in the ranks who felt he didn't have the right to speak his mind. Of course, given the quality of the officers picked to lead the provincial units, this wasn't all bad. Few had little more than political connections to justify their rank. That he himself and the system that he hailed from was no different never entered Thomas' mind. Somehow, there was no comparison.

"That," Thomas announced, "is what we'll do. Only," he added, "I'll lay back here and you lead the first group back. You see, I have no bloody idea where we are."

The ranger sergeant looked up at Thomas and smiled. "Then you'd best pray I don't get myself shot or anything like that."

Despite his dislike of all provincials, Thomas found himself smiling. "You lead us back to William Henry," Thomas said, "and I'll have a mass held in your honor."

Emmit flashed every brown-stained tooth in his mouth as he nodded. "All right, then. I'll be takin' some of the boys and movin' out now." Without another word, he turned and sprinted back to the rear, dodging and weaving as he went. "Clyde! John! Michael! Grab Karl and drag him along! Follow me. The rest stay with the captain!"

With the one wounded man they had sustained up to this point, the rangers took off, leaving Thomas and the others to hold back the Indians.

When he heard the shouts and saw the sudden movement to the rear, Toolah understood what was going on. Now, he thought, was the hard part of being a leader of fighters. Had he been alone, he would have trusted his soul to the spirits of his ancestors and gone forward without hesitation, to claim as many of the foe as he could before they made good their escape. But he couldn't do that, not without losing one or more of his followers. It was bad enough he had already lost one brave.

Still, to give up after taking down only one of the foe and wounding another was too bitter to contemplate. If only for show, he would have to pursue the enemy for a while. Perhaps as he prepared to lead his followers forward, the rangers would back themselves into a cul-de-sac. Or maybe a French patrol would hear the firing and rush to their assistance. Either event would, with luck, turn events back to his favor.

Luck and fortune, not to mention skill, however, favored the rangers that morning. Hanging back just far enough to keep within striking distance yet at the outer fringes of effective range, the Indians followed Thomas and the small band of rangers for hours without drawing any further blood. Yet, as morning faded into early afternoon, Thomas began to worry that they would run out of ammunition before they shook their pursuers. Besides, the danger of Frenchmen sallying forth from Carillon became more and more real as they made their way back toward that post. Though their route would bypass it by miles, no one could be sure if the sound of their firing wouldn't alert the garrision.

"Sergeant," Thomas called as he made his way back after breaking contact and scurrying for the rear.

From behind a tree, a head popped out. "Over here."

Making his way over, Thomas settled down on the ground and leaned his back against the tree to rest until the Indians managed to catch up. "We can't keep going like this."

Emmit, watching for the approach of their pursuers, nodded, though Thomas couldn't see his head. "Agreed. Got any ideas?"

"If we had bayonets, we could rush them. There're more of us than there are of them. By the time . . ."

"Captain," Emmit interrupted, "these are brave boys, not fools. We aim to make it home alive. And though they be good, they're not professionals, not like the pretty soldiers you push about like so many sheep to the slaughter."

"Exactly," Thomas responded with a twinge of regret in his voice. "So, here's what we'll do. They're keeping just beyond range, hoping to corner us or draw out the French. What we need to do is trick them into coming closer so we can hit two or three of them quickly. Maybe then they'd break off the pursuit."

Emmit leaned back from where he had been watching, looked at Thomas, and nodded. "If nothin' else," he added, "might give them pause an' allow us to make a clean break."

"Exactly." What Thomas didn't tell the ranger sergeant was that he could no longer maintain the awful pace they had been maintaining since their first contact with the Indians. Somehow, Thomas had to rest, or at least slow their march rate, even if it meant risking his life. "Now," Thomas went on, "I want you to leave me your three best men. We'll lay low while you and the others fall back, like before, one group after another. Hopefully, they won't count heads as each group goes back, and they'll come on before they realize some of us are still here."

"You fixin' to take them on in hand-to-hand?"

"No. I'll wait till they're within twenty paces, stand, and fire at point-blank range. Perhaps the shock and surprise will scatter them, giving us a chance to turn and run."

The ranger sergeant smiled. "What's so funny?" Thomas asked.

"Oh," he replied, "it's just I never thought I'd hear a British officer advocating running as a tactic."

Thomas thought about the sergeant's statement, then found himself chuckling. "Well, you see, even we can learn. Now, pick your men and let's get ourselves ready."

With each footstep, Toolah became convinced that his plan was going to succeed. The wind was slight, and coming from the west. He would not need to depend on luck. The sound of their firing would surely find its way to the French fort no matter how far they passed it to the west. Alerted, the French garrison would send out patrols to investigate it. And when they did, the rangers would find themselves in a trap. Though they would turn to the French and try to surrender to them, once they realized all was hopeless, he, Toolah, would not let those who called him friend deny him his prey. He would return triumphant after meeting the rangers, face-to-face and outnumbered, in a hard-fought battle in broad daylight. This, he realized, would be his greatest coup.

Thoughts of glories to come were clouding Toolah's mind when, less than twenty paces to his front, a group of men rose from the ground like a covey of quail taking wing. There was only time enough to pause, draw back in surprise, and realize what was happening before the officer he had missed earlier leveled his piece and gave the order, "Fire!"

The surprise that Thomas had hoped for was achieved. Of the braves who had been trotting through the woods in pursuit, two went down, dead or wounded. Two turned and fled without hesitation. Only one, who had somehow managed to dodge his shot, remained when the smoke thrown up by the discharge of his piece cleared from Thomas' vision. Far from panicking, the brave stood erect and defiant. Wearing a mask of anger disguising any fear that he might have harbored, the Indian threw down his musket, pulled a red-feathered hatchet from his belt, and hurled himself forward.

With no time to draw his sword, Thomas shifted his right foot back, brought his empty musket down, and held it diagonally across his chest as he prepared to meet this wild, desperate charge. The other rangers who were with him, caught off guard, could only watch in amazement as the two combatants collided. Thomas, with an upward thrust of his musket, managed to parry and deflect the hatchet aimed squarely at his head. Toolah, his first blow frustrated, reached out with his other hand as Thomas fell over backward and grabbed for the white officer's neck.

In a moment, the two were on the ground, with Toolah hanging on to Thomas' throat with a death grip while trying to bring his hatchet to bear. Thomas, pinned to the ground, was pushing up with his musket, now firmly planted across Toolah's chest, in an effort to shove his assailant off him. As the two men struggled with every ounce of strength they could muster, they glared at each other, eye-to-eye, exchanging murderous stares. In the midst of this mortal deadlock, Thomas caught the downward movement of Toolah's free arm from the corner of his eye. Though he didn't see exactly what was being brought to bear, he reacted to the threat. Toolah, having thrown as much force into the blow as he could, and missing, literally by a hair, found himself off balance for a moment.

That was all Thomas needed. With one last shove, he managed to roll the Indian off him and over to the side. This not only broke the grip his attacker had on his neck but also allowed Thomas to regain his footing. Though gasping for breath and dizzy, Thomas had enough strength and presence of mind to use the momentary advantage he had gained. With a single swipe of his musket's butt, he smacked the Indian brave in the side of the head, putting an end to the melee.

Relieved and overwhelmed by exhaustion, Thomas staggered backward till he backed into a tree, keeping his eyes on the motionless figure before him. For several moments he stood there, along with the admiring rangers, looking down at the helpless foe at his feet. Then Emmit came forward, offering Thomas a knife, handle first. Looking up, Thomas asked innocently, "What's that for?"

Emmit paused, then looked at Thomas with a questioning expression. "Well, ain't you gonna take his scalp?"

A look of horror fell across Thomas' face. "Good God, man! No."

The ranger, with a shrug of his shoulders, looked over at Toolah for a second, then back at Thomas. "Then you wouldn't mind," Emmit continued as he dropped to one knee over the unconscious Indian, "if I did, would ya? He's got quite a good crop of hair there. Be a shame to waste it."

Shocked by the sergeant's eagerness to mutilate a hapless foe as much as by the idea that a soldier in the king's service would do such a thing, Thomas kicked the ranger's hand just as Emmit lay his knife on Toolah's temple. "You'll do nothing of the sort," Thomas shouted. "Now," he commanded as he looked over at the other rangers, "gather up your things and get moving. We need to clear out of here before the French come."

At first there was no response or reaction while Thomas bent over the unconscious Indian, retrieved his musket and hat, and collected himself. When he was ready, he turned to see the rangers still staring at him, as if they hadn't understood his order. "Is there a problem? I gave you an order."

Emmit stepped toward Thomas and was about to say something when he hesitated. What was the use, Emmit concluded before speaking. Eyeing Thomas from head to toe, the ranger knew that this gentleman, standing between him and the dispatching of a mortal enemy, would never understand their ways. With another shrug he slid his knife into its sheath, turned, and signaled the other rangers to follow. Only when they were on their way did Thomas follow, satisfied that he had asserted his authority over this provincial riffraff and kept them from defiling the reputation of British arms.

CHAPTER SIXTEEN

West of Winchester, Virginia
May, 1757

Long before he came within sight of the farmstead, Ian McPherson knew they had arrived too late. The wind carried the sad news of death to him and the others. Without having to be told, a hush fell over the party of one officer and twelve men who were following in Ian's footsteps. Slowing their pace almost to a crawl, the file of soldiers moved on. When they were nearing the edge of the wood line, just short of where they would be able to see the cabin where a farmer by the name of Richardson and his family of five lived, Ensign Ezra Flemming drew closer to Ian. "You don't suppose . . ."

Ian didn't bother to respond. Instead, he kept his eyes riveted to the front, scanning ever so slowly to the left and right as he reduced his pace even more. Only when Flemming tried to get his attention a second time did Ian take one hand from the small of his musket's stock and hold it up behind him, almost in the ensign's face, as a sign for him to be still. Far too nervous and inexperienced, Flemming complied without hesitation. Now that they were in harm's way, their captain's advice that he had best follow Ian's lead proved unnecessary. "I've been told you're a fine lad, comin' from the best sort of family," Captain Shaw had stated bluntly as he gave Flemming his instructions in Ian's presence. "And I expect you'll make a fine officer someday. But for now you'll listen to the likes of Sergeant McPherson, or I assure ya, you'll never see that lovely family again, not in this world."

Ignoring the sweat that ran down his face and neck, forming rivulets that soaked his shirt until it could absorb no more, Ian inched his way forward. Finally, he halted, then lowered himself into a crouched position with his musket held at the ready as he intently scanned the area to his front. Behind him, everyone, including Flemming, did likewise. Only when he was sure they were in no immediate danger did he lean back and whisper to his superior, "When we reach the edge, deploy the men. I'll go forward. Don't come till I signal."

Thrilled at being trusted to actually do something of importance, Flemming smiled and nodded. Ian, his face set in a blank expression that betrayed no emotion, simply stared into Flemming's eyes, sending a shiver down the officer's back. Without another word, Ian stepped forward till he came to the crude rail fence that marked the end of the woods and the start of Richardson's land. Pausing, he again lowered himself into a stance from which he could either fight or flee, whichever the situation called for.

At first, he ignored Richardson's cabin, turning his attention instead to the fields and yard immediately around it. Seeing no immediate signs of activity or danger, Ian next turned his attention to the woods on either side of the opening that was the Richardson's farm and beyond the charred remains of the cabin. Slowly his eyes moved along the entire length of the forest as he desperately tried to detect anything that even remotely hinted of danger. He ignored the movement of the rest of the small detachment as it came up behind him and then peeled off to the left and right of Ian to take up positions from which they could fight. Only the last two men in the file didn't come all the way up with the others. As was their practice, they hung back, facing the direction from which they came to make sure no one followed or surprised them from that quarter.

While he could ignore Flemming as he eased his way up next to him, Ian found he could no longer ignore looking at the blackened remains of what had once been the home of a working farmer. Without taking his eyes off the sorrowful sight, Ian whispered, more to himself than to Flemming, "Can ya smell it?"

Bewildered, Flemming turned his face this way and that, sniffing as he did so. Confused, he faced Ian. "Smell what?"

Turning his head slowly, Ian stared into the young gentleman's eyes. "Death."

Though he tried not to, Flemming blinked his eyes and recoiled slightly from the battle-hardened man in whose hands he had been entrusted. Turning away, blushing slightly from embarrassment and shame, the young ensign tried desperately to sort out the cacophony of strange smells and odors that assailed his untrained nose. He was still trying to do so when Ian told him, "Stay here, and keep alert."

That a sergeant had addressed him in such a manner didn't faze Flemming. He was out of his element here, totally beyond his abilities, and he knew it. Back in Fredericksburg, he would never have given a man of Ian's standing another thought. If he had been forced to conduct business with him, Ian would never have been permitted beyond the threshold of his parents' home. But this, Flemming knew far too well, was not Fredericksburg. Here, social standing meant nothing. Men of ability, not status, ruled supreme. In time, he hoped, he could master the ways of this wild country and the hard men and women who eked out a living on the fringe of civilization. In time, he hoped, he could gain the respect and loyalty of those he was supposed to lead. But until that day came, he was at the mercy of men who had a place in this world that was no less important than his own.

●

When he was ready, Ian stood up, crossed over the rail fence, and slowly began to make his way through the fields toward the cabin. Slowly, he moved down a row of crops, now beginning to make their appearance. Though he could feel his own tension, and all but hear himself breathe in the unearthly silence that surrounded him, Ian could not help but admire the fine stands of corn that brushed against his legs as he pressed on. A man, he thought despite the potential danger that awaited him, could take great pride in fine produce such as this. It was all right here, he told himself. Everything a man needed to raise a family and build a life was right here, all around him. If only . . .

As if to remind him, Ian's nose started to twitch involuntarily. Though he knew better than to do so, he took in a deep breath, catching, for the first time, the full, unadulterated stench of burned human flesh. Pausing for a moment, Ian stood still as he choked down a passing wave of nausea. While he waited for the sensation to pass, he stared intently at the house. How tragic this all was, he thought. The odds were that poor Richardson had been no different than he. While he might not be a Scotsman, fleeing persecution for rebelling against the Crown, Richardson's travels probably matched his, with few exceptions. Perhaps, Ian thought as he started forward again, had circumstances been a tad different, it would have been he, and not poor Richardson, lying burned to a crisp in the middle of his dreams and life's labor.

These thoughts continued to linger, as did the pungent reek of death. Only after he had reached the house and made his way around the entire area to ensure that all intruders were gone did Ian call Flemming and the rest of the detachment forward. While Flemming came loping through the cornfield to Ian's side like a young pup called by his master, Ian made his way, despite his resolution, into the center of the cabin's charred remains. Sooner or later, he knew, they would need to sort out the corpses from what had once been their home and provide their mortal remains a decent Christian burial.

In his excitement, Flemming ignored the telltale signs of what awaited him. When he was still several yards from the edge of the burned hulk of the cabin, Flemming shouted to Ian, "Sergeant McPherson! What should I do with the men? Where should I . . ." It was then, when he caught sight of Ian kneeling in front of a charred corpse, that Flemming realized for the first time the horror of what had occurred there. Coming to a dead stop, the young gentleman officer stood transfixed as the color drained from his face. Even when the young man drew back, desperately covering his mouth with his hand in a futile effort to hold back the vomit that his stomach hurled forth, Ian went about the gruesome task of clearing rubble from what once had been Richardson's wife.

For the rest of the day, Ian supervised the recovery and burial of the bodies. One by one, they were removed. None of the men with him knew the Christian names of the individuals who had once lived there. And even if they had, there was little prospect of sorting out which body belonged to which name. "They died together," Ian stated flatly, hiding well his emotions. "Let us bury them together and pray they all are joined again, in heaven, for eternity."

Only when this aspect of their duties had been discharged, and the men prepared to start making their way back to the fort before nightfall, did Ian turn to comfort his officer. "It's a terrible business we're about," he consoled Flemming as he offered the young gentleman a drink from a flask he used to carry his rum in. "We seldom arrive in time to be of much use, other than seeing that the poor souls receive a decent send-off."

"Isn't there anything we can do?" Flemming protested.

For a moment, Ian thought about saying nothing, but decided against it. The youth, he knew, would soon enough come to the same conclusions as those who had stood guard on the frontiers of Virginia a long time ago. "We've been forgotten by the Crown," Ian began. "All those fine regiments of the king are up north, searching for glory and their victories in New York and Canada. We're all that's been left to do a job that's well beyond our means. Colonel Washington has too few men and too much territory to defend. Even if the gentlemen of the Burgess voted funds to raise new troops to help us in this thankless task, we still wouldn't be able to keep the Indians from coming south and killing good, God-fearing folks like these people here. It's just too much to expect."

Flemming, bewildered and confused, looked up at Ian. "Then, how will we end it?"

Ian's eyes narrowed and the grasp he held on his musket tightened as he prepared to respond. "We destroy them, before they have a chance to destroy us. We take this bloody war of theirs and visit it upon their homes, their families, their villages. Only when we have broken them, just like the English tried to break my people, will we be free to live our lives as free men, in a land we can call our own."

There was no mistaking Ian's anger, or determination. Nor could Flemming ignore the fact that there was more behind the Scotsman's anger and rage. This was more, Flemming realized, than a duty for him. His being a soldier, out here where no man with another choice would venture, was not an accident. And though he wanted to know more, both about this man and about the passions that drove him, this was neither the time nor the place to pursue either.

"We must be moving soon," Ian told his officer. "We don't want to be caught out here, in the open, if someone should decide to return."

BEING in no great rush, and tired from a long, almost sleepless night, it was near noon before Ensign Flemming and his patrol returned to Fort Loudoun. The appearance of Flemming's straggly line of men, each doubled over and moving according to his own sense of rhythm, aroused no excitement or interest from either the other members of Shaw's company or the good citizens of Winchester. They knew why these men had been dispatched the day before, and they knew by their conduct that they had failed.

The only greeting that stirred Ian McPherson from his

lonely thoughts was the voice of James McPike. From the still incomplete palisades of the fort, where he was supervising a group of fellow soldiers working on the roof of one of the buildings, McPike shouted down to Ian, "You missed the excitement, me boy. A whole new batch of recruits came in yesterday, all ripe for the picking."

Even in his sorry state of mind, Ian could not help but smile. McPike was quite fond of gambling. He had a knack for just about any game of chance and an ability to cheat without anyone ever suspecting what he was up to. Though he refused to engage his friend in even the smallest wager, Ian took great pleasure in watching him at work. "I swear, James McPike," Ian would state categorically, "someday I'll figure out how you do it."

With a grin that would do the devil himself proud, McPike would always ask the same question. "And when you do, lad, what'll you do with this newfound knowledge?"

With an equally cunning smile, Ian would reply, "Why, I'll make you a wager, of course."

There would be, however, no wagering or games till the sun was well below the western sky. While McPike turned his attention back to the group he was in charge of, Ian halted his little detachment. Flemming, with little more than a nod of his head, took his leave and headed through the gate and into the fort in search of Captain Shaw. While he was rendering his report of a rescue mission that had, in truth, been little more than a funeral detail, Ian had the task of overseeing the cleaning and inspection of the weapons of their small band of soldiers. While the unkempt appearance of the soldiers themselves was accepted as a given, neither Shaw, Ian, nor any of the other old-timers tolerated even the slightest neglect of a weapon or tool. "I don't much care," Shaw would admonish any man joining his small company of soldiers, "if you go running about naked as a jaybird, so long as your musket is clean and in good order and your hatchet has as keen an edge as the governor's very own razor." Such standards, in a company that was made up of a good number of men who had been with Shaw from the beginning, were easy to maintain.

It was mid-afternoon before Ian was putting the finishing

touches on his musket. Seated in the shade of one of the barracks buildings on a three-legged stool with his musket laying across his lap, Ian paid no attention as James McPike approached. With both hands full, McPike paused, looked about for a free stool, and kicked it with one foot until it was next to Ian's. When he was seated, he turned to Ian and offered his friend a plate of bread, some sliced meat, and a mug of rum. "I knew you'd put this off till after you had finished tinkerin' with that thing," McPike stated.

After one final swipe of the rag he had been using, Ian held up his musket, took one last look at it, then carefully stood it up next to him against the barracks building wall. "That thing, as you are so fond of calling our muskets, are what we're about, James."

McPike laughed as Ian took the plate and mug from him. "That rank the captain's given you has corrupted your brain, lad. That musket of yours is just another tool, no different than a hammer or a saw. That's all."

Though his mouth was stuffed with bread and meat, Ian countered McPike's claim. "I've yet to see a man flee in panic when faced by a hammer. And even the most vicious saw never gave me reason to be concerned."

"If I said the sky was blue, you'd tell me that it's not necessarily true, wouldn't you?" McPike countered.

"I'd do so, James McPike," Ian replied after washing down an oversized bite with rum, " 'cause that ain't always true, especially out here."

James McPike lowered his head and grunted. "Oh, lordy, here we go again."

"And what is it that you have against the west? It is beautiful country, free and open to any man who's willin' to put his back into it and sweat a little."

"Not to mention bleed, Ian, my boy. Or have you already forgotten about our dear friends and their French allies?"

With narrowing eyes and an expression that was hard and uncompromising, Ian stared at McPike. "I haven't forgotten, McPike. I'll never forget. That's why I tolerate this life. That's why I run about from burned homestead to burned homestead. Maybe, just maybe, if we keep at it, we'll catch enough of those devils and kill enough of them to convince them that we're here to stay. Just maybe."

Sorry that he had turned his friend's good mood sour, McPike tried to change the subject as quickly as possible. "Oh," he said, lightening his grave expression as quickly as possible, "there's something I forgot to tell you!"

Knowing that he had become too serious himself, Ian turned his attention to his meal of bread and boiled meat. "And what might that be?"

"A girl, Irish lass she was, from Alexandria, came up with the latest batch of recruits from Alexandria today. Henry Gowing told me she was lookin' for ya."

Startled, Ian stopped chewing and looked at McPike. "Did he mention her name? Was it O'Reilly?"

"Can't say that he did. All he could remember was her eyes. Green, he said, as green as a fresh spring leaf, he told me."

Without another word, Ian was on his feet. Pausing only long enough to hand his plate and mug back to McPike, he grabbed his musket, slung it over his shoulder, and started for the gate. Then, as an afterthought, he paused and looked back at his friend. "James," Ian called, "he didn't happen to say where she might have gone, did he?"

IGNORING the people of Winchester as they made their way to their homes in the early evening, Ian found the tavern where he had been told that he would find the girl. Despite the fact that the colonel frowned upon visits to ordinaries or inns by the garrison of Fort Loudoun, Ian paid this restriction no heed. He had no fear that even if his explanation as to why he was there didn't hold up, no one, including Colonel Washington himself, would prescribe the established punishment of fifty lashes without court-martial to him. Justice that was, on occasion, biased had its advantage.

Entering the poorly built structure, Ian paused in the doorway as his eyes adjusted to the darkness. A few of the patrons looked up at the soldier, still wearing the dirt and stench of a two-day patrol, blocking the doorway. While one or two muttered a disparaging comment to a companion, most went back to their drinking or idle gossip. From a bar that was nothing more than a couple of planks set on two large barrels, a thick-waisted, middle-aged man shouted over to Ian, "You're either in or out, boy. We don't need no sentinel to keep out the savages here."

From somewhere in the room, a slurred voice cried out, "That's 'cause we're already here."

A rousing round of laughter followed as Ian made his way through the crowd to the innkeeper. "I've been told there's a girl who came here today, seeking work?"

The innkeeper's eyes narrowed. "She's no whore, boy. I don't permit that sort of thing in my establishment and I'll pound any man into the ground who says I do."

Recoiling from the anger of the man, Ian shook his head. "Oh, no. It's nothing of that sort. You see, I, we knew each other back in Alexandria. We met there several years ago, when she was serving her indentureship as a cook's assistant."

A smile flashed across the innkeeper's face. "Well, now. Then her story is true. She can cook. That'll be a change. Last serving girl I had here didn't know the difference between a fish and a fowl."

From behind them, a man called out, "Ned, it wasn't what she did in the kitchen that concerned you, now, was it?"

After shooting a dirty glance at someone behind Ian, the innkeeper turned back to him. "She's in the back, in the cook-house, messing about with the stores and stuff. Says she needs to find where everything is."

Without waiting, Ian started to head out the door to find his way to the cookhouse when the innkeeper grabbed his arm. "Mind yourself with her, lad. She's workin' for me and I'll not tolerate any sort of foolin' about, not on my property. And if I catch her feedin' you without you payin', she'll be out on her ear, peddlin' her wares on the street."

Jerking his arm free of the man's grasp, Ian straightened

himself and glared at the middle-aged man. "Not every man who wears a uniform is scum or trash, to be kicked about and treated as if he were a dog. You'll need not worry about me, sir, so long as you keep your hands to yourself and your tongue civil."

For a moment, a hush fell over the crowded room as Ian and the innkeeper sized each other up. Only when he was sure that the fiery young soldier meant every word and had the determination and ability to back them up with action did the innkeeper lower his eyes. Seizing a dirty rag, he attacked an imaginary spot on the crude plank bar, not venturing to utter another word until Ian had left the room.

Her back was to him when he entered the small, hot cookhouse. Supposing it was the innkeeper, Megan O'Reilly started spouting off a list of things that she needed to purchase if he truly wanted her to be able to serve up a decent meal. Easing his way into the room and closing the door behind him, Ian stood there, silently watching her hips as she moved them about, bending over piles of boxes, jars, and glass flasks. Only after she didn't hear a response did she stop what she was doing, stand up, and turn to find out who had come in. When her eyes met Ian's, her confused expression melted away.

Slowly, mechanically, she wiped her hands on her apron. "At the fort they said you were gone, out on a patrol. I didn't know what to do, so I came here, into town, to see if, perhaps, I could . . ."

Slowly, her voice trailed away, then disappeared, as the two continued to stare at each other. She, nervous and unsure, waited for Ian, who was pleased, yet concerned, that this girl would think so much of him that she would follow him to this awful place, so close to danger and death. For the longest time the two did nothing but gaze into each other's eyes, neither one knowing for sure how to proceed. Finally, Ian broke the deadlock by taking a small, halting step closer to the green-eyed Irish girl. "I've thought about you often, though I never took the time to reply to your letters."

Megan smiled, taking a half-step of her own toward the

man whom she had so long ago fixed her heart upon. "I think I've always known that, Ian McPherson."

"Though I wish you would have stayed away, back in the tidewater, where it was safe," Ian replied slowly, "now that you're here, I . . ."

After having traveled so far, over roads that were little better than trails, Maggie found no difficulty making the final journey of a few feet into Ian's waiting arms. And though she had no way of knowing what the pungent, burned odor was that his uniform reeked of, she was glad she had risked all on a hunch.

Albany, New York
May, 1757

NEITHER Thomas Shields nor Katherine Van der Hoff paid any attention to the raindrops that lingered on newly sprouted leaves and fell upon them and their mounts each time a gentle breeze stirred the branches. The air, sweet with the fragrance of wildflowers and spring buds blooming, heightened the senses of the soldier, fresh from the outpost of the empire, and the heiress, too long confined by protocol and propriety.

Delayed longer than he had hoped by sloppy paperwork and the need to ensure that all was in order for the arrival of militia units at Fort William Henry and Fort Edward, Thomas wasted no time in contacting Katherine once he was back in Albany. "I can assure you, Miss Van der Hoff, if it were possible, I would have flown here to your doorstep weeks ago," he explained. "But duty is a jealous mistress that enslaves us all."

Pleased by his attentiveness and eagerness to renew his acquaintance with her, Katherine smiled and graciously accepted his excuse. "Well," she responded demurely, "if there is to be another who holds claim to your affections, I suppose duty is far better than other possibilities."

Though the weather threatened, Katherine insisted that they ride, as she had proposed at their first meeting. She wanted to be alone with her captain, safe from the prying eyes and ears of the household staff, not to mention a father who had apprehensions about the object of his daughter's attention. An accomplished rider, Katherine wanted her second meeting with Thomas to be in an environment in which he would be comfortable. Her guess that he would find the saddle far more relaxing than a quiet parlor proved right. Where he had been proper and guarded at their first meeting in April, he now spoke freely. "I can tell you, Katherine," he went on about his adventures with the rangers, "there is nothing more invigorating than having faced a foe and come away victorious. Though the trek back to where the canoes lay hidden was an arduous one, over the roughest terrain imaginable, and we were burdened with the need to carry our wounded, I felt nothing. The aches and pains that had plagued me that morning evaporated like the morning mist."

Rather than discourage his eloquent bragging, Katherine encouraged it. Smiling when appropriate, nodding her head to show that she was following his descriptions, no matter how gory and graphic they became, and letting her concern show when necessary, she permitted Thomas' ego to feed upon itself. Only once, when she lowered her head to study a field that should have been cultivated and planted by now, did he interrupt himself and ask if he was boring her. "Oh, no, dear Captain," she responded quickly. "Not at all. In fact," she told him, though she by no means meant it, "I find your story a marvelous diversion from the boring conversations my father and his associates engage in."

For the first time that afternoon, a chill passed between the two of them as Thomas drew back for a moment. That she considered his retelling of his life-and-death struggle little more than a diversion troubled him. Men had met and fought, to the death. He himself had killed and almost been killed. And though he could hardly expect a woman to understand the significance of that, he had hoped that his trials were more than simply a "marvelous diversion."

Sensing the chill, Katherine scrambled to recover. "They tell me that the beauty of Lake George, which the French had called Lake St. Sacrement before Sir William Johnson renamed it two years ago, is beyond description. Did you find that to be true?"

Pushing aside his troubled thoughts, Thomas obliged Katherine by launching into a detailed description that lasted almost until they had returned to the Van der Hoffs' stable. Only when they were within sight of the place did Thomas stop talking and fix his gaze on the mane of his own horse.

They rode in silence for a moment or two before Katherine ventured to break it. "Something's bothering you, Captain. Would I be too impertinent if I asked what it was?"

When Thomas brought his horse to a halt without warning, Katherine found herself having to bring her own mount around until their animals stood head-to-head. Only when she was halted, facing him directly, did Thomas look up into her eyes. "I am, perhaps, Miss Van der Hoff, a vain man. That, together with several other faults, have been my undoing, as you well know. Which brings me to wonder, if I may be so bold as to ask, why a woman in your position would be interested in cultivating a relationship, of some sort, with me." He looked at her, studying her eyes as he watched her weigh her response. "I have no doubt you know far more about me than I of you. I am a second son with nothing more than my name and a commission from the king. You, on the other hand, have your choice of suitors, men of power and wealth who, together with what will someday be yours, will make you an important person."

Surprisingly, Katherine smiled. "You know so little of us, don't you, my dear Captain. Yes, I have my choice, and my father is quite impatient that I should make that decision soon. But as soon as I do, no matter whom I select from the pool of eligible candidates that has been made available to me, I lose everything. I am a woman who is not comfortable with being condemned to traditional roles. Though it is unfortunate that it took my own mother's death and the melancholia that has crippled my father to bring me to this state of affairs, I cannot deny that I enjoy it."

Moving her mount until they stood side by side, Katherine looked deeply into Thomas' eyes with an intense stare that was almost unnerving. "I have had to tend to my father, over these years, as he grieved for a wife who never loved him. When my father's time comes, I will be left with both a fortune and circumstances that I have no intention of squandering away through foolishness or a poor match. Though that may sound cold, it is, God help me, the truth. And besides," she added almost as an afterthought, "I want a husband who is more than just a successful merchant."

Somehow, as he listened to Katherine, Thomas felt a stirring in his soul, like a flame being kindled. As he looked at the face of this woman, set in a firm, determined expression that radiated the passion of her words, Thomas smiled. For he saw that her passions were not unlike those that had driven him to these distant shores. In her eyes he saw himself, a person who had endeavored since before he could remember to establish a fitting place for himself in this world. And though he had always imagined that he would do so by the sword, on the field of battle, Thomas suddenly realized that there were other roads to fame, fortune, and power opening to him. "I must admit, I've given far less thought to finding a mate than you have. But were I to choose a woman, I think she would have to be something out of the ordinary, someone who was more than an ornament to be worn on one's sleeve at social affairs."

Pleased with his response, and convinced that he was sincere, a warm smile lit across Katherine's face. "We must speak again, my dear Captain, soon."

Bowing as deeply as he could in the saddle, Thomas returned Katherine's knowing smile. "I am, dear lady, your obedient servant."

CHAPTER SEVENTEEN

South of Fort Carillon,
on the north shore of
Lake St. Sacrement (Lake George)
July, 1757

ONLY WHEN he came within sight of the debarkation point did Anton pause to step out of the way of swearing, grunting militiamen as they continued to push, pull, and shove a twenty-four-pound cannon along the muddy, rutted trail. Reaching into his sleeve, the newly promoted lieutenant of artillery pulled out a handkerchief, already soaked with sweat, and wiped his face. It would take many more grueling days and nights to complete the transfer of supplies and equipment from Fort Carillon to the north shore of Lake St. Sacrement. All told, thirty-six cannons, four mortars, and munitions for them had to be hauled over four miles of a newly cut trail that barely deserved that title. In addition, the overburdened militiamen had to carry the 247 bateaux needed to transport them, the troops, all the equipmentage, and the provisions required by Montcalm's army of eight thousand for this campaign. To accomplish this feat, five hundred Canadian militiamen, without the aid of oxen or horses, worked day and night. Pleased with the progress made so far and the accomplishments of the militiamen, Anton turned to one of the newly arrived French artillery officers as he passed and pointed to the sprawling encampment and stockpiles on the lakeshore. "Quite an accomplishment, don't you think?"

The officer, a lieutenant of the Troupe de Terre who was not at all pleased at being exiled to the fringes of the empire, where mosquitoes threatened to rob a man of his blood before the red savages had a chance to do so, merely grunted. "This, my dear friend," the officer of Royal Artillery said in a tone of voice that betrayed all the disdain he could manage as he waved his hand at the encampment, "is a mere trifling affair. In Europe, a general in the field wouldn't even bother mentioning a force this size in his dispatches to the king."

"But this," Anton hastened to point out, "is not Europe."

Amused, the officer faced Anton, looked down the bridge of his nose at the young officer of provincial artillery, and smirked. Like most officers of La Marine, Anton was dressed for campaigning in the wilderness. His loose-fitting coat of light gray showed the wear and tear of pervious campaigns. Rather than wearing fine linen breeches and stockings, as prescribed by regulations, Anton's legs were protected by leather leggings, gaily decorated by the Indian who had fashioned them for him. And on his feet were a pair of well-worn moccasins, footwear far better suited for moving through the woods than the highly polished boots General Montcalm's staff and the newly arrived officers insisted on retaining. Though Anton would have been the laughingstock at any proper officers' mess in France, he was well attired to deal with the task at hand. "Ah, yes," the regular officer of artillery finally replied dryly. "So nice of you to point that out to me. I'd almost forgotten." Without another word, the well-groomed officer turned his back on Anton and made his way down to where he expected his tent would be pitched.

Though he could feel his rage building up, Anton restrained himself. The reinforcements from France that he had thought would be a blessing were instead turning into a bane, By the time his friend Jerome Pepin came up next to him, Anton was still angry. "Look at them," Anton growled as he thrust an arm in the direction of a pair of newly arrived French officers. "They complain incessantly," he ranted to Pepin, "demanding rations that would make a king blush for being so selfish. And the way they strut so! It is as if they were the Savior himself come to redeem our poor souls from the English."

Pepin, an older militia officer hardened by the land that was his home, yet as gentle and understanding as a newly ordained parish priest, listened to Anton's accusations straight-faced for as long as he could before he burst out laughing. Stunned by this reaction, Anton stopped just as he was about to launch into a new tirade and stared at the Canadian. "Why do you laugh at me so?" the young officer demanded. "Do you think these parade-ground gentlemen are worth the suffering we must endure? Or do my words amuse you?"

Reaching out with a hand rubbed raw by days of hard pulling on rough rope, the big, bearded Canadian placed his hand on Anton's shoulder and gave the Frenchman a firm, friendly shake. "Anton," the captain replied in soft, kindly words, "you must remember that not every man who sets eyes upon my country sees what we have seen. Oh, I cannot recall how many times I have heard a finely dressed officer, wandering the streets of Quebec or Montreal, murmur so that I could hear, 'This place isn't worth the expenditure of a single sous, let alone the blood of a Frenchman.'" Pepin roared as he stepped back, letting go of Anton. "You, on the other hand, have taken to this land as if you were born to it. Why, in another year," Pepin exclaimed as he waved his hand up and down while he looked Anton over, "I expect you'll be running about in a loincloth with an eagle's feather hanging from your hair."

Self-consciously, Anton's eyes shot upward as he brought his hand to his hat, touching the writing quill he kept in the stays at the rear of his tricorn. When he looked back down, the older man's face had grown serious. He was looking around at the dense, virgin forest that surrounded them, drawing in a deep breath as he did so. In the silence, Anton, too, took in a deep breath, catching all the scents and smells of the forest that had barely felt the hand of man. Then, as Pepin exhaled, he turned his face back toward Anton's. "You came here, my lad, to conquer this land, as so many others have. But," Pepin stated as he poked his index finger into Anton's chest, "it is you who has been conquered. It is in your blood now, my friend. And no man," the Canadian added as he looked out past the young officer of artillery at the quiet surface of the lake below, "can ever ask for a better fate. Not in this world, or the next."

Without another word, Pepin walked away, as if in a trance, down to the lakeshore, where his men waited for him. Anton, left alone, watched for a moment or two, then turned away from the trail and the breathtaking view of the lake and made his way into the woods. Finding a tree that was broader than his shoulders, Anton sat at its base, crossed his legs in front of him Indian-style, reached into his fringed leather haversack, and fished out his journal. Carefully, he retrieved the precious jar of ink and set it down on the ground next to him before reaching up for the writing quill he kept in the stays of his tricorn hat. As was his custom, Anton launched right into his writing, recording a stream of consciousness rather than well-measured thoughts.

It is strange to see oneself in another time and place. Has it really taken me years to see what this country is, what it means to a Europe so embroiled in petty feuds and meaningless traditions? And why cannot others see that this place offers our race a chance to start anew, an opportunity to make good all the errors that have made our homelands so stagnant, so corrupt? Pausing, Anton looked up when he heard the calling of a bird which he could not identify by name.

Perplexed, he looked down at the page before him, dipped his pen in the ink bottle, and started scratching again. *Though there is still much for me to learn, and I fear even two lifetimes will be insufficient to satisfy that need, I have come to the conclusion that my life is tied to this country, as closely as a wife ties herself to her husband on her day of marriage. Often I have written that I do not know where this journey, which I am on, is taking me. There have been moments in the past when I have been appalled by what I have witnessed. But these have been matched, time and again, by others that have left me as wide-eyed and excited as a child seeing his world for the very first time. That a place can hold such sway over a man's heart tells me that there is something more to this land than dirt, trees, and water. There is a magic, a wonderment that touches all those who are willing to see with their hearts, and not their eyes.*

Lost in his thoughts, Anton did not take note of the rustling of leaves stirred by anxious feet. Driven by a need to record his thoughts as they came to him, and lulled into a sense that these forests were his own personal sanctuary, the young Frenchman went on writing as if he were a monk transcribing holy script in a safe and secluded provincial abbey in France.

Had the intruder been the rash, impetuous young warrior he had been but a year or so before, that illusion would have been brought to a swift and ugly end. But Toolah had learned much since he had last confronted the young French officer. Patience, he had found, was often rewarded with greater satisfaction. The whites, Toolah had learned, were slow and careful when it came to confronting a foe that was well prepared and hidden in forts. It would take the French many days to move all their weapons and food to where the English waited, and even more days before they would be able to bring their overwhelming numbers to bear on the English now gathering, unsuspectingly, at Fort William Henry.

Backing away, Toolah allowed himself a self-satisfied smirk. There would be plenty of time, he told himself, to extract the vengeance that he felt he so richly deserved from the Frenchman. "It is my land, and my honor," he muttered in an unguarded gesture of anger. "So I shall pick the time."

With that, he turned his back on the lone Frenchman and returned to where his band of young warriors awaited him.

Fort Edward, on the Upper Hudson

ANY regrets Thomas Shields felt at being left behind as his regiment, the Forty-fourth Foot, sailed away to participate in the siege of Louisbourg were quickly forgotten whenever he was with Katherine Van der Hoff. While service on Brigadier General Daniel Webb's staff was routine to the point of being boring, frequent trips to Albany allowed him to continue his pursuit of Katherine Van der Hoff. "Were it not for the fact that you're finally behaving in a manner befitting an officer of the Crown," Captain Lewis Fenton commented to Thomas as he prepared to make another trip south to Albany from Fort Edward, "General Webb would be quite put out by your assignment to his staff."

Thomas ignored his friend's comments as he leafed through the stack of papers he was preparing to stuff into his dispatch pouch in preparation for his departure. "I've often heard that the power of a woman's love can reform even the most wretched creature on this good earth," Fenton continued when Thomas ignored him. "But never, till I saw you, did I believe it was possible."

For the first time, Thomas looked up at Fenton. Thomas gave his friend a sly smile and a wink. "Love has nothing to do with it. Nothing at all."

With wide eyes and a grin from ear to ear, Fenton slapped his knee. "I knew it," he exclaimed. "I knew it all along. You've had a jolly good roll in the hay with the old spinster and you've managed to win her over with your charm and sexual prowess."

Standing up as he stuffed the last of his numerous lists, requests for supplies, and receipts into the pouch, Thomas broke out into a broad smile himself. "Well, if you say so."

"What do you mean, if I say so?" Fenton responded with a quizzical look on his face. "Have you, or haven't you bagged her? I do so need to know."

"Why?" Thomas replied. "So you can win that wager you placed with that captain of the Thirty-fifth and pay off some of those debts you've been piling up?"

Offended at the question, Fenton straightened his back

and gave his vest a tug. "My financial affairs are rather personal in nature. I'd rather not discuss them in public."

"And I, my friend," Thomas shot back as he prepared to leave, "have no intention of discussing my courtship of Miss Van der Hoff, in public or otherwise."

"Oh," Fenton grinned, "so you haven't bedded the wench yet, have you?"

"Oh, step aside, you vile, base creature," Thomas demanded jokingly as he made for the doorway. "I have the king's business to tend to and little time for idle chatter."

"Is that what you tell the lady as you rush out the door while you pull on your boots?"

Laughing, Thomas waved his hand and made for his horse, waiting in the muddy parade of the small wooden fort on the Hudson. Handing his saddlebags to his batman, Thomas climbed up onto his mount, took the bags, and looked down at his man. "I'll be back in four days, perhaps five. While I'm gone, prepare my things and pack up your equipment. We're to go up to Fort William Henry for a time and see if we can't straighten out the mess Monro's quartermaster has made of things there." Then, without waiting for a response or acknowledgment, Thomas whipped his horse's neck about, made for the gate, and rode off in a gallop. He had no escort with him, though he had been advised to take one Indians, all of whom Thomas considered hostile and untrustworthy, had been lurking as far south as Fort Edward. But an escort would have been a nuisance, reducing the time he could spend with Katherine Van der Hoff.

As always while he made the fifty-mile trek to Albany, Thomas thought much of the growing affair between himself and the strong-willed daughter of the New York merchant. That her father was far from pleased with this matter was no secret. "Though your pedigree is impeccable, sir," the bitter old man told Thomas to his face one day as he waited to escort his daughter on their weekly ride, "I fear you are an opportunist."

Thomas found it amusing that this man, a provincial merchant who was incapable of showing any sign of backbone when dealing with his own daughter, would speak to him so. "As I recall," Thomas responded with his well-practiced disdain, "it was your daughter who initiated this affair. Were it not for her interest in me, I'd be back in my quarters, sitting alone and merrily drunk."

Stung by the impetuous Englishman's cutting remarks, the elder Van der Hoff's face grew red. In a rare moment of compassion, Thomas sought to ease the man's distress. "I can assure you, sir," he stated in as kindly a tone as he could manage, "my intentions in regards to your daughter are both honorable and proper."

"And, if you have your way," the old man fumed before turning to leave, "profitable."

It was this last matter that consumed much of Thomas' thinking on these long rides. While he had come to this land in search of his own fortune as much as for the pursuit of military glory, Thomas had never expected it to involve a marriage that many would consider a set down on the social ladder. Yet, the idea of becoming involved in commerce and business, while against his nature as a gentleman, was now beginning to gain a certain appeal to him. Perhaps it was Katherine's charm and beauty that made marriage to a woman of the merchant class attractive. Still, Thomas reminded himself, he was a soldier, committed to a way of life that demanded much of a gentleman such as himself.

That, of course, didn't prevent him from wondering how he could keep his pride and integrity while still enjoying the physical and monetary fruits of this union. A smile came to his face as this last thought ran its course through his mind. How wickedly divine, he mused, to be able to enjoy the comforts of Eden without fear of sanction or rejection. Perking up in the saddle, Thomas dug his spurs into the side of his mount and trotted off south, at a merry jaunt, to the woman who was waiting anxiously to become his fiancée.

On the North Shore of
Lake St. Sacrement (Lake George)

WAITING patiently in the shadows, Toolah made no move until his brother was within arm's reach. It was easy to recognize Gingego, who insisted on always wearing the faded, threadbare coat he had taken from an English soldier two years earlier. "So, brother," Toolah called out in a low, menacing voice, "you once again do as is expected of you, and not what is in your heart."

Having been raised in the shadow of an older brother who took great delight in springing at him from ambush whenever he could, Gingego hardly reacted. Instead, he stopped and turned to face his brother. Though he was as tall as Toolah, and now well accomplished in the ways of war in his own right, Gingego could not but help feel himself inferior in stature as well as position whenever he was confronted by his brother like this. Toolah knew this and, like the cat toying with its prey before the kill, took advantage of it. "How can any man," Gingego countered, "know what another carries in his heart?"

"Because," Toolah responded as he stepped closer to his brother, "the blood of our mother runs through our veins."

Forcing himself to conceal the fear that his own brother had embedded in him, Gingego stared at the face of his brother. The council fire behind Gingego played upon Toolah's face, making the black paint that surrounded his eyes and covered his forehead and the red paint that coated his jaws and cheeks seem wilder and more fearsome than usual. "Since birth, our feet have always followed different paths. If I could do so without dishonoring our mother's memory, I would have nothing to do with you."

Reaching out, Toolah took hold of the lapels of the red coat, looked at them for a moment, and then flipped them free of his fingers as if they were trash. "You dress yourselfs in the hide of your vanquished foe and display your scalps in order to prove your manhood. At times, you even make noises as if you were a man. But you do not cast a man's shadow.

You behave like a dog, a dog who serves the French when it pleases them. You bow your head and pray to their god when they ring their bell, and pick up the hatchet when their drums call for war."

Used to such taunts, Gingego said nothing. His brother, who ordinarily would have little to do with him, was after something. "If there is a purpose to this meeting, then tell me now. Otherwise, cease wagging your tongue like an empty-headed squaw and allow me to pass in peace."

Caught off guard by his brother's defiant words, Toolah blinked as he collected his thoughts and tried to frame an appropriate response. Anxious to keep the upper hand, he decided to go right to the matter. "He is here."

Now it was Gingego who was unsure how to respond. Who, he wondered as he stared into his brother's eyes, was "he"?

Satisfied that he now had the advantage again, Toolah relaxed and took on a grave, almost menacing tone. "I have sworn vengeance, and I intend to have it. I was denied a coup, justly earned, by that meddling French officer. Now he shall pay."

In an instant, Gingego knew who the mysterious "who" was. Though he himself had not been witness to the incident in which a young French ensign had stepped between his brother and a hapless survivor of the defeated Virginians some three years before, he knew the story, which had been retold many times. "The French," Gingego stated flatly, "are our allies."

"The French," Toolah countered, "are white. And you are their dog."

"It would be wrong for you to kill one of them after our chiefs have committed our people to stand by them in war," Gingego insisted.

"They are whites. They keep their promises only when it suits their needs. I will not make my heart a prisoner of their cruel and corrupt ways. I was denied what was rightfully mine to take. And if I cannot have that, then I shall have my vengeance."

Seeing no point in arguing with his brother, Gingego let

his head drop in a sign of submission. Then, lifting his chin, he stared into his brother's eyes. "Why do you tell me of this? If you want me to help you find satisfaction by assisting in this murder, then I will not."

Drawing himself upright, Toolah looked down upon his brother, haunched over in defeat. "I do not need the help of a dog."

"What is it you do need?" Gingego now pleaded.

"You must say nothing," Toolah commanded. "You were once friends with the Frenchman. Do not let that false memory snarl you into trying to help him. When the time comes, I want his death to be a surprise. I want to see fear in his eyes before I take his life."

Gingego shook his head. "Your heart is cold, brother. Cold and, I fear, sick."

"My heart belongs to me, and no other man," Toolah announced proudly. "And when I have killed the Frenchman, it will be at peace."

With a hard stare, Gingego looked into his brother's burning eyes. "You will never know peace. There will never be enough blood to extinguish the fire that burns in you."

Ignoring his brother's warning, Toolah nodded. "If that be so, then so be it." With that, he turned and stepped back into the shadows from whence he had come.

Fort William Henry, on the South Shore of Lake George

THOUGH General Webb and the other officers of the Crown tried to effect a professional air during the discussions at the war council, they could not. The disaster that had befallen Colonel John Parker's New Jerseymen just days before weighted heavily on everyone's minds. Of the 350 who had been with Parker, fewer than 100 had returned alive. With them they had brought tales of horror, massacre, harrowing escapes, and the seeds of panic. Without any solid knowledge of the enemy's strength, let alone intentions, the senior commanders charged with defending the New York frontier now gathered at Fort William Henry assumed the worse and planned accordingly.

The suggestion made by Major General John Campbell, the earl of Loudoun, to General Webb that he advance his force to the north shore of Lake George, establish an armed camp, and invest Fort Carillon was, without a doubt, no longer possible. With only five whale boats and two sloops on that lake, Webb could not possibly move his entire command, not to mention supplies and cannon, across the thirty-plus miles of water that separated him from the French-held shore. And even if it were possible to bring enough boats up from Fort Edward, lack of intelligence concerning the French might lead to a larger, more disastrous defeat.

What was clear to all present was that there was a goodly number of Indians already established south of Fort Carillon. Whether these Indians were the vanguard of a larger force or merely an oversized raiding party could not be determined from the fragments of news the survivors of Parker's force brought back. The two companies of rangers that were part of Lieutenant Colonel George Monro's garrison, commanded by Captain Israel Putnam and Captain Richard Rogers, shed little light on this matter. Though they tried, they were unable to penetrate the veil of secrecy that hid the French from Webb and Monro.

Faced with the ill-defined dangers that lay to the north, General Webb proved to be cautious and indecisive. Those decisions he did give his consent to were timid and purely defensive. The first was that Fort William Henry would be put into a state of readiness to withstand a direct French assault. That decision seemed to be the easiest.

Built in the fall of 1755 amid a lively debate, Fort William Henry was constructed along European lines on the southern shores of Lake George. From above, it resembled a distorted square with four bastions. Its walls were log-crib affairs that measured thirty-two feet at the base and tapered off to a thickness of twelve to eighteen feet. These cribs were filled with sand, making the structure rather robust and quite fireproof. With eighteen cannon mounted atop those walls and a garrison of five hundred in 1757, it could withstand all but a formal siege. Its ability to do that had been proven just that March when a strong French force of Indians, La Marine, and regulars conducted a raid on the place. Without cannon of their own, the French assault force found itself unable to induce the defenders to yield. "If they do come again," Thomas Shields pointed out to a provincial officer standing next to him as they listened to the discussions of their senior commanders, "you can rest assured they *will* bring cannon."

As to the question of how many men would be required to defend the place, there was some debate. The fort itself could not accommodate more than the five hundred souls it was built for and still make productive use of the excess. Lieutenant Colonel Monro, with more than two thousand men on hand, was faced with the decision of either sending the bulk of that force back to Fort Edward or building a fortified camp within mutually supporting range of William Henry. Faced with an unknown threat, Monro was not about to send away troops he already had in hand and might find useful. General Webb, with no better idea of what to do, was more than willing to go along with the idea of leaving the two thousand additional troops at Lake George.

As to where this fortified camp would be, several possibilities were discussed. One was to place the two-thousand-odd soldiers, mostly New York, New Jersey, and New Hampshire militia, into two armed camps. One site lay to the southeast side of the fort, on the hill where William Johnson had defeated the French regulars of General Baron de Dieskau in September 1755 with a force of New York and Massachusetts militiamen. The other was to the southwest, a location that could block French siege works from advancing against the fort from that direction. In the end, it was decided to go with only one fortified camp, built on the site of the previous battle and astride the road that led to Fort Edward. A small creek and marsh located on the west side of William

Henry was considered adequate to delay or even prevent French siege efforts from that quarter.

With the major decisions made, additional instructions were issued. These included shoveling more sand onto the roof of the magazine, raising the east bastion by the height of one log, tearing down a storehouse outside the armed camp and fort, clearing the dry ditch that surrounded the fort, and moving the troops not assigned to the fort into the fortified camp. Along with the troops went the women and children who routinely accompanied all European armies on campaign. Besides the laundresses who were authorized by law and custom to each regiment, there were a goodly number of wives, children, and other females whose sole purpose was to profit from the assembly of so many men so far from home. Even Lieutenant Colonel Monro's own daughters were accompanying him, as they had on previous campaigns in Europe.

Of all the preparations, one of the most important moves was the dispatch to the north of rangers under Captain Putnam to find out what the French were really up to. With no Indian allies at their disposal, the critical task of scouting was left up to the ranger companies that had grown out of the single company founded by Robert Rogers in 1755. Though these men were good, especially when led by Rogers himself, they could not make up for the lack of Indians. That this was a glaring fault became readily apparent when Putnam promptly returned after making it less than halfway down the lake. His report that he had sighted numerous enemy boats and troops on both shores of the lake confirmed everyone's worst fears.

The report also prompted Webb's hasty departure from William Henry and Thomas Shields' decision to stay. Though he had no command, and there would be much work for him back at Fort Edward once the militias that Webb intended to call for assembled there, Thomas knew the decisive fighting would take place here, on Lake George. If the French brought down heavy cannon and conducted a formal siege, which he himself expected, there would be even more to do that was far more suited to his temperament at William Henry. With little ceremony, Monro accepted Thomas' offer and assigned him the task of organizing the available stores of provisions and munitions that would be needed by the troops defending the fortified camp. For the first time in months, all thoughts of Katherine Van der Hoff were pushed aside as Thomas followed the one true love of his life, the pursuit of glory.

CHAPTER EIGHTEEN

On the Southeastern Shore of
Lake George
August, 1757

T HE SIGHTS, the sounds, the drill, were all quite familiar to Anton. There was the approach by water, in heavily laden bateaux, propelled by grunting oarsmen. Officers, both afloat and on shore, shouted orders to the coxswains of boats not yet beached, waving some off till others, with more valuable cargo of men or cannon, landed first. And there were, of course, the passengers, like Anton, who had little to do but wait their turn to land and add to the frenzy of activity on the crowded shore.

Yet despite the similarities of the opening moves of this campaign and those of the one on the Ohio in 1754 and Oswego the previous year, Anton could still feel his heart racing as his boat inched its way to shore. No two military operations were ever the same. The tactics applied to reduce an enemy's strong point might be written in a textbook, but the actual site where those techniques were applied were always different, especially in New France. If anything, when Marshal Vauban and his disciples preserved their experiences for the French artillerymen and engineers of Anton's generation, they never imagined that they would be carried out deep in the wilderness of North America. That was where Anton's experiences and familiarity of conditions, not to mention his ability to work effectively with the Canadian militia, became valuable.

More and more, it was the leaders and the troops drawn from France's and England's main armies who were waging the contest for North America. The massive force assembled by Montcalm to seize William Henry bore little resemblance to the motley collection of provincial Marines and Indians who first challenged the English at the forks of the Ohio little more than three years before. The appearance of these European professionals, and the introduction of traditional warfare, was changing the nature of war on this continent forever. And though raids by small, roving bands of undisciplined native warriors and colonial irregulars all along the fringes of both colonial empires were still very much a part of this war, armies more familiar to a European eye were now the crucial element of the conflict.

Yet, as in the past, terrain, seasons, and local conditions still dominated where, when, and how those operations were conducted. This campaign itself had been delayed by several weeks due to the mere fact that the Canadian grain harvest had been late this year. Not only did that keep the members of the local militias busy on their farms but it also prevented Montcalm from gathering his army till late in the season since there was nothing available to feed them. When all was finally assembled, and the army set in motion, it did so along the same lines of invasion that had shaped past wars in North America for nearly a century. In this case, it was the line of waterways and portages that led from the Saint Lawrence down the Richelieu River, into Lake Champlain, then into Lake George, the Hudson River, and eventually the Atlantic

Ocean. On a map, it seemed simple. On the ground, it was a different matter.

Even before the prow of his boat scraped the rocky bottom, Anton was up, out of his seat, and over the side, rushing to where another boat, carrying the first of the siege guns, was about to land. Wading through the water, shouting above the screams of others, Anton directed the crewmen to swing their heavy craft to where he was motioning. A flustered captain standing on the shore tried to get Anton's attention. Anton, however, ignored the officer, whose only concern was following a paper plan that had no place in this wilderness. When Anton reached the boat, he grabbed its gunwales and then began to push and shove it to where unloading the cannon could be done with far less effort than where it had been directed to land. Assisted by several gunners of the Marine, Anton beached the craft, then hopped on and began unlashing the piece.

In the midst of this, Anton felt a tap on his shoulder. "You know, Lieutenant," an angry voice protested, "you can't go about landing your boats wherever you please."

While his fingers continued to pry at a stubborn knot, Anton twisted his head about and looked over to where the captain stood, hands on his hips. "Nor can one, sir, unload a cannon in the same manner that you do sacks of flour. The planks which we use to move the piece from boat to shore are only so long. We cannot hoist this great monster up onto our backs and wade ashore with it."

Turning his head back as he felt the knot finally give way, Anton ignored the stream of threats that was being hurled at him by the unrepentant captain. "You seem to have upset that gentleman, sir," Anton's old sergeant grunted as he finished untying his knot and bent over to assist Anton.

Looking up, Anton gave the sergeant a wink. "Well, let's wait till the English guns open up on us without our ability to reply and then see how upset he becomes."

The sergeant looked up and about at the cove where the boats with the artillery were gathering. Then he glanced over in the direction of the English fort, hidden from view by a spit of land jutting out into the lake. "We'll have no need to worry about those fellows for a while. Our general has chosen our camp well."

Freeing the knot at last, Anton also looked up and about. Unlike his sergeant, who saw their separation from the English as a blessing, Anton saw it as a bane. The thick forest that came right up to the shoreline, which was beautiful from afar, gave Anton cause to grunt. "We've a lot of cutting and digging to do before we can bring these guns to bear upon the enemy. It will be days before we manage to fire our first round."

The sergeant, as always, brought a note of reality to the discussion. "Is it not better, sir, to sweat a little and dig a lot than die?"

Anton turned and looked into the face of the old veteran and replied with a smile that was oddly out of place amid the confusion and harried activities. The sergeant was one of the few men to whom he would trust his life. "As always," Anton chuckled, "the voice of reason."

"No, sir," the sergeant countered, straight-faced. "Experience and cowardliness."

"You?" Anton shot back. "A coward?"

"Yes, now and always. How else can one manage to boast of so many campaigns?" the sergeant reasoned. "Glory is a commodity reserved for officers and gentlemen. All we common soldiers have are our bodies and our mortal souls. Since I do not know where my soul will find itself upon my demise, I prefer to keep them together as long as I can. Which is why I, and the other men, follow you so closely. You have common sense. You will listen to reason. And, you are lucky."

"Luck has little to do with military affairs," Anton protested as he stood up and wiped the sweat from his brow with his overused handkerchief. "Skill, training, and courage determine the outcome of battle."

"Perhaps that is true," the sergeant agreed as he leaned forward and rested his forearms upon the barrel of the cannon between them. "But it does make a difference whether you survive them, is that not so? After all," the sergeant added with an engaging smile, "there isn't a single book that I know of that will protect a man from death if the Fates decide to toss a bullet in your direction. Only luck, sir, is the great arbiter when it comes to sorting out who lives, and who dies. Believe me, it is that simple."

Though Anton wanted to continue this discussion and exchange of views with his most loyal sergeant, there was work to be done. Anxious to get on with the task of unloading this gun, and another that was being brought into the shore as he watched, Anton nodded in agreement. "That may be true," he stated flatly as he slapped his hand on the cannon before him. "But for now, I put my trust in this gun, and its sisters, to see us through this next battle. Now, let's get on with our work and see that our friend the captain doesn't send our boats halfway back to Carillon for unloading."

With a grin and a nod, the sergeant took up the rope they had both undone, turned away from Anton, and began to shout to the others in the boat to pay out the long planks that they would need to ease the great, heavy piece of ordnance ashore.

Anton, his hands no longer needed, waded ashore. Every now and then, however, he looked back at his sergeant and wondered if all the soldiers felt that way about him. In his four years of service in New France, none of his men had ever let on that they gave him any more thought than a peasant would to a landlord. That there were bonds of loyalty, and perhaps even admiration, between him and those who followed him came as something of a revelation, one which buoyed his spirits and brought a smile to his face.

One thing was certain. There was little doubt in Anton's mind that few sergeants would ever admit to gladly following the captain on the shore directing the landing of the boats. Even as Anton came up on the shore, dripping wet from the waist down, and brushed by the harried captain, the man did little more than mumble something under his breath, huff and puff, and rush off to yell at another boat captain preparing to come in.

Fort William Henry

FROM the northwestern bastion of the fort, Thomas watched the phalanxes of French boats and canoes, stretching from the eastern shore of Lake George to the western shore, making their way to their assigned landing spots. Though the narrowness of the lake and the commanding mountains that rose precipitously from its clear blue waters made the whole invasion armada seem more impressive than it was, Thomas could see that it was more than adequate for the task at hand. In a single motion, he pulled the looking glass from his eye, collapsed it between his hands, and handed it to the drummer boy behind him. The lad, a boy of fourteen, was now serving as his batman after his regular man was stricken with the pox. "Well, boy," the normally quiet captain of grenadiers mused, "we've certainly got our work cut out for us, don't we?"

With the nervousness of a young boy facing his first battle, the drummer boy swallowed and nodded as he looked past his master at the assembled host before them. "Yes, sir. I imagine we do. But," he added quickly as he forced a smile, "I'm sure we'll show 'em, won't we?"

Turning his head, Thomas looked down at the boy whose eyes were still transfixed on the spectacle before them. Thomas couldn't tell if the boy's comment had been a statement or a question. Not that it mattered. What he thought didn't matter. All that mattered was that he, and the others of Monro's command, did as they were told and stayed with the colors. Not that the latter would be hard. Looking back around to the west, over the fort's vegetable garden, and then to the southwest, Thomas could already catch glimpses of bodies of French troops and savages making their way through the woods toward the road that connected Fort William Henry with Fort Edward to the south.

"They'll be cutting the road," Thomas stated blandly as he nodded toward the south, "and, no doubt, they'll soon be testing the strength of our fortified camp."

"Will we be staying here, sir, in the fort, or over at the camp?" the drummer boy asked with a note of concern he could not hide.

"The camp, I think," Thomas responded as he looked about the parapets and bastions of the fort, overcrowded with anxious men moving guns and preparing for the opening of the siege. "There is precious little room for us in this fort, and even less work. The fight here belongs to the gunners, theirs and ours, as we try to keep the Frenchies from pushing their works forward while they endeavor to bring their batteries within range and open a breach in these walls. The real challenge," he stated with a note of excitement in his voice, "will be in the camp with the provincials. We'll have a devil of a time keeping them together and at task. They're the most miserable excuse for soldiers that I've ever laid my eyes on."

"Oh, I don't know about that, sir," the drummer boy piped up without being asked. "I hear tell they can give a fair account of themselves, when they have a mind to."

Surprised that the boy didn't know that his statements were not meant to be answered by him, a lowly drummer on his first campaign, Thomas looked down at the lad as the boy watched the coming and goings of the people about him. The lad was a true innocent, still quite naïve to the ways of the world, let alone military etiquette. Under different circumstances, Thomas would have chastised an enlisted man for talking back to him in such a familiar, unmilitary manner. But there was something about the boy, something refreshing, that not only held Thomas in check but brought a smile to his face. "What's your name, lad?" Thomas asked.

With a grin as broad as his freckled face could bear, and oddly out of place with the oversized military hat that kept sinking down over his brow, the boy turned and looked up at Thomas. "Jones, sir. Perry Jones."

"You're Welsh, aren't you?"

The boy shrugged his shoulders, barely moving the ornate musician's coat that hung loosely about his skinny frame. "I don't rightly know, sir. I never knew my mother or father. And no one ever came forth to claim me, 'cept for the recruiting sergeant offered me a shillin' and a chance to escape the orphanage."

"An orphanage," Thomas mused as he looked up and about at the crude fort being made ready for battle. "Right about now," Thomas replied with a smile, "I'll bet you're wishing you were back there, safe and snug in that orphanage."

With a look of horror that erased all traces of the smile that had brightened his face, the drummer boy all but shouted, "Oh, no, sir. Not in the least, sir. Here is where I want to be. Here, with soldiers such as yourself, with a man-sized job to do."

Surprised and pleased, Thomas' smile grew. Placing his hand on the boy's shoulder, Thomas gave it a squeeze. "Well said, lad. Now, let's get on with that work." With that, the pair made their way though the masses, side by side.

Whatever joy Thomas felt about being part of the coming fight was soon tempered by the sights, sounds, and smells that greeted him and Drummer Jones once they reached the fortified camp. They were little better than those they had left behind in the overcrowded fort. The only saving grace of the newly constructed camp was that it was, in fact, new. The effect of crowding nearly two thousand soldiers and camp followers into a small, confined area had not yet permeated that place. It would not be long, however, before the stench generated from cook fires, waste, and unwashed bodies rivaled, or even exceeded, that of the fort.

"Provincials," Thomas muttered as he made his way along the crowded streets to where Colonel Monro had established his headquarters. Colonial soldiers not on duty lounged about at the entrance of their small tents in all states of undress and posture. None made any effort to acknowledge or salute Thomas. Those who bothered to return Thomas' haughty stare did so with bland looks or expressions that spoke of the contempt they held for him, an English officer.

"They're not really so bad," young Jones piped in, assuming Thomas' remark had been directed toward him. "I've met some of 'em. They seem to be a decent and God-fearing sort. Most, especially those from Massachusetts, are far less profane than our men."

Undisturbed by Jones' insolence this time, Thomas snapped back, taking no pains to keep his remarks from reaching the ears of the very soldiers he was speaking of. "To a man, they are dirty, overbearing, and quite ignorant. The only creatures on this earth more ignorant of military affairs, proper discipline, and common hygiene are the officers who pretend to be their leaders."

"Yet, sir, I hear say they fight well," Jones insisted, "when it really matters. Why, it was here," he stated as he opened his arms and gestured about the encampment, "just two years ago, the colonials under William Johnson beat the best the French had."

Thomas stopped in his tracks, turned, and faced Jones. For the first time since they had started their disjointed discussion, Jones looked up and saw the anger in Thomas' eyes. "Boy," Thomas thundered, thrusting a finger at the little drummer's face, "don't you ever forget who, and what, you are. You're as ignorant as to what war is about as these malcontents. Till you've felt the heat of battle, and seen the cruelties that one man can visit upon his fellow human being in war, don't even imagine that you've a right to lecture me on the subject."

The effect of Thomas' sudden outburst was shattering. Though he tried hard not to, Jones took two short steps back, away from the man who towered over him and shook an angry, threatening finger in his face. Of the countless offenses in the English army for which a soldier could be punished, disrespect of an officer was perhaps the most grievous. Even as he continued to stare up at Thomas, wide-eyed, the image of a cat-o'-nine-tails, its long leather tentacles studded with razor-sharp lead tips shredding the back of a soldier under punishment, flashed before the lad's eyes. Unable to control himself, Jones began to shake in fear.

Ordinarily, Thomas would have found the effect he had on the boy amusing. It was good, he had been told, to keep one's soldiers in fear of their officers. "Fear of what will happen to them if they fail in their duty," he had often been told, "is far more compelling than fear of death. It keeps them to the task long after courage and loyalty have faded." Yet, strangely, Thomas felt no great satisfaction in having evoked such a response from Jones. On the contrary, despite years of conditioning and hardening, Thomas felt upset that he had scared the lad. Before his trained, disciplined mind was able to exercise any restraint, Thomas dropped the hand he had been shaking in the boy's face to his side. Lowering his eyes to the ground, as he had so many times before when called to task by his domineering father, Thomas bowed slightly. He paused, then looked down into the astonished eyes of the drummer boy.

With little more than a shake of his head, as if he were clearing away a hazy thought, Thomas finally got a grip on himself. Pulling himself together, he stood erect, turned about on his heel, and marched away. Behind him, Perry Jones, still befuddled by this totally unprecedented incident, ran to catch up to the rather extraordinary officer he had been assigned to serve.

In the French Siege Lines
Before Fort William Henry

WITHIN a day, the camps of the French regulars had been established, along with the preliminary reconnaissance and surveys for the opening moves of the siege. Now came the digging. Unlike open field battles between two mobile armies, where soldiers stood tall and erect, with flags flying and officers trooping six paces in front of their regiments to lead them forward, siege operations were characterized by the digging of trenches and the erection of earthworks. Much of this was done under the cover of darkness, not to mention the guns of the enemy and the constant threat of sortie by the garrison under siege. Here, it was the precision of the engineer and the accuracy of the gunner, not the bravado of the cavalrymen or the steadiness of the infantry, that would determine the outcome of the battle.

Work started quickly for the militia. As was the practice,

they were drafted to perform the manual labor. Under the direction of the Sieur de Bourlamaque, Pepin and his men first threw up a trench to protect the main French camp and from which an approach trench dug at an angle to the English fort could be opened. In all, some eight hundred men, protected by as many as seven companies of light infantry and three companies of grenadiers, worked day and night. The work was made difficult by the large number of tree stumps encountered by the militiamen and the efforts by the English gunners to disrupt, or stop, their progress. "It is a very difficult thing, I tell you," Pepin grunted as he came across Anton and his gunners after a long night of digging, "to keep pushing ahead while someone with a very large cannon is trying to push you back."

To this, Anton simply smiled. "Once we have these in place," he stated as he patted the eighteen-pounder his arm was casually resting on, "it will be the English who will be uncomfortable."

"Tell me, my friend," Pepin asked as his face suddenly turned serious, "is it true that our general offered the English an opportunity to surrender this fort?"

"Yes," Anton responded, nodding his head slowly. "That is correct. He informed the English commander that humanitarian considerations compelled him to do so. His note, so I am told, made it quite clear that he was providing him an opportunity to leave while we still had control of our Indian friends."

This last part caused Pepin to chuckle. "Do you truly believe," he asked with a grin, "that a gentleman of his character would unleash our savages on the English?"

Anton shrugged. "We may be following the teachings of the great Marshal Vauban as far as the conduct of our engineering is concerned. But even I, accused by many of being a dreamer, do not believe that all these Indians, who have come so far to taste the blood of the English, will be satisfied to go back with little or nothing to show. Already they are chafing at what they consider our slow and ponderous progress." With a grim expression, Anton shook his head. "No, my friend. There will be blood, and much of it. First, we will spill what the English are willing to expend in the defense of their honor. Then," he added as he looked beyond Pepin at a group of Indians making their way toward the fort, "they will take their fill."

For a few moments, Pepin and Anton watched the parade of wildly painted and decorated Indians troop by. They were a far cry from the well-ordered ranks of the grenadiers encamped not far from the earthworks. Yet, even in their variety, Anton was beginning to see a sameness that was slowly leading him to feel indifferent toward them. Lost in his deep thoughts, Anton didn't notice an exhausted Pepin as he moved on to join his men in a much deserved meal and sleep.

That night, like so many in the past, Anton could not sleep. It was his troubled thoughts that robbed him of his sleep, not the sound of cannon reverberating off the waters of the narrow lake or the sound echoing down the narrow gap between the mountains. Turning, as he often did, to the solace of his journal, Anton recorded his thoughts and feelings, even though he found they were becoming uncomfortable. *We have come to this land,* he wrote slowly, hesitantly, *and changed it. We are leaving our mark upon this vast continent, though I do not believe it is for the good.*

Sitting upright, Anton looked down at the passage he just wrote, then out through the open flap of his tent. In the distance, just beyond the trees, he could see the flashes of English cannon as they hurled shot and shell at the Canadian militiamen burrowing their way closer to William Henry. If he tried hard, the flashes could, on occasion, remind him of lightning. But such fantasies were hard to hold on to. He had by now seen far too much of war, war that was as cruel and as brutal as it comes, to hang on to his naïve illusions. For, like the young leaves of spring, all cherished dreams wither and die when touched by the cold, harsh winds of war.

Looking down at his journal again, Anton read the words he'd written. It bothered him that he spent more and more time dwelling on such dark, foreboding thoughts. Gone, he realized as he absentmindedly flipped though the filled pages of his journal, were the bright, lively narratives that spoke of newly discovered wonders and sights that defied description.

Lost in the grind of a war that now permeated every fiber of his soul, in the same way that it consumed the energies of all of Europe, were the reflections of a young man let loose in a world filled with wonder and beauty.

Leaning forward once more, Anton took up his pen and began to write again. *I fear we have failed to make good use of this new land of ours. I fear we have brought over to this continent, hidden under the wail of our culture and civilization, the same ills and sickness that have crushed the very spirit of humanity and decency in Europe.*

Tired, in body and soul alike, Anton looked down at his words again, then slammed the journal shut with a snap without giving the newly penned lines a chance to dry. Standing, he looked once more out into the sleepless night, and wondered where this would all end. What did God, he asked himself, have in store for them?

Unwilling to allow his overactive imagination an opportunity to answer that question, Anton turned and threw himself onto his bed roll. As he had on so many nights, he buried his face in his pillow in an effort to seek solace in a sleep that would not come.

TOOLAH, together with those who had chosen to follow him rather than their appointed tribal war chiefs, made his way toward the entrenched English camp. Like many of the more passionate members of the Indian contingents, he refused to sit in camp while the French dug in the dirt like women. Nor would he waste his time wandering through the woods between the two English forts as the French wanted them to do in the hope that they would catch a messenger or two. Toolah had agreed to follow the French for one purpose, and one purpose only. And that was to fight. If the French chose not to open the fight with the English, then he would strike off on his own, as many others did, and do so for them.

Having no desire to face the big English guns hidden behind the thick walls of the fort, Toolah led his small following around, through the woods, toward the entrenched camp. Though the English still had cannon there, they were far fewer in number and much smaller. For him and those of like mind, the approach march to the entrenched camp was easy and quick. The distance was so great, they didn't even need to seek the cover of the woods. Moving forward to within range of the English, however, was more difficult. The English maintained a sharp vigilance, day and night, to keep from being surprised. Torches lit at regular intervals allowed the enemy stationed along the barricade of stones and logs to see well into the cleared area before the fortifications.

But the light from those same torches, Toolah found, also fell upon the English themselves. If he could manage to crawl within range of the wall, he would have no difficulty killing one or two of the more careless sentinels.

Instructing his anxious followers to wait until he was well on his way, Toolah lowered himself slowly onto the ground, cradled his musket in his arms, and began to wiggle forward like a snake. Each and every move was made with great deliberateness, and only after Toolah had ensured that there would be a place for him to hide along the way. Frequently as he slithered forward, he would look toward the stone and log wall, trying hard to catch a glimpse of a foe's musket being extended over the barricade or the sudden appearance of a watch face. Once or twice, Toolah caught the edge of a shadow moving along the wall. Instinctively, he froze, listened, and watched. Not until he was sure that he was not in danger did he move again. This was not the time or place to be rash or impetuous. All too often, death and scorn were the only rewards for reckless courage. So Toolah continued to pick his next spot carefully, with an eye for protection as well as for a place he could fire from.

When he finally had ventured close enough to where he could be sure his shots would be effective, Toolah stopped, settled into a comfortable position, and waited. As with his approach, he was in no great hurry to fire. After all, there was always the possibility that he had been spotted by an alert foe who was just as skillful and patient as he, and was, at this very moment, waiting for Toolah to expose himself to the perfect shot. But as the minutes dragged by with the same slow tediousness that had characterized Toolah's laborious approach and still nothing happened, he began to seek his mark. Now it was his turn to look for someone who was foolish enough to expose himself.

He didn't have long to wait. While he watched, another intrepid brave, somewhere off to his left, fired on the English fortifications. Whether he hit anything didn't matter to Toolah. What mattered was that the shot brought a curious head out from of the shadows for a brief moment, where Toolah could see it. Though he had barely caught a glimpse, it had been exposed long enough for Toolah to mark the spot and bring his musket to bear. Like every action up to this point, he slowly eased the hammer of his piece back, into the full cocked position, before wrapping his hand around the small of the stock. While he sighted down the long barrel at the spot, Toolah snaked his finger around the cold steel trigger. Then, when all was set, he waited, hoping that the Englishman who had appeared was too lazy to change his location.

Like so much in battle, long hours of boring, tedious preparation are followed by hurried seconds filled with sudden, frenzied action. A dark form appeared within an easy stones' throw from where Toolah lay, and right where the end of his barrel was pointed. Toolah had guessed right, and needed only to make a minor correction before he squeezed the trigger and fired.

In an instant, the vision of the shadow before him disappeared in a cloud of smoke and flame as the powder in the pan of his musket ignited. Holding his weapon steady, Toolah waited for the kick in his shoulder that would come when the burning priming powder set off the charge of powder in the barrel. Even before the smoke cleared, the one-ounce ball rattled down the length of the musket's barrel and closed the twenty-five-yard gap that lay between Toolah and the shadow he had fired on.

Once he felt the recoil of his musket subside, telling him

the shot was away, Toolah dropped behind the stump he had been using for cover and flattened out on the ground. It was pointless to stay exposed. Even if he had hit his target, the smoke from his own firing, combined with the darkness and the concealment provided by the logs and stones, would deny him a clear view of the shot's effects. Fortune, however, favored Toolah that night. No sooner had he finished curling up into a ball in an effort to escape observation and return fire than he heard a scream. Voices, a scampering of feet, and shouts were followed in close order by a flurry of wild and unaimed shots. All of this was accompanied by incessant screaming and shouts not far from the spot he had fired at.

Though Toolah could never be sure that he had, in fact, hit anyone, it didn't matter. He was doing something, something worthy of a warrior and distressing to his enemy. In the morning, he would go back to camp, where those too lazy to stir themselves to act as men should would be sitting around fires, telling stories that had grown stale, just as they had been when Toolah had left. He and his faithful companions would have new stories to tell. He, a warrior worthy of that title, would be the center of attention once more. That alone, Toolah thought, would make all this worthwhile.

CHAPTER NINETEEN

In the French Siege Lines
Before Fort William Henry
August, 1757

THE OPENING of the third day of siege was heralded by two howitzer shells and a single cannonball hurled from William Henry at the French works that were growing nearer with each passing day. The English gunners showed no haste as they went about their labors, swabbing out the hot barrels before loading the next round. Their shots had been random, rather than a single, thunderous volley.

The response from the French works that morning, however, was quite different. Unlike previous challenges to the French efforts, this one was met with an immediate and overwhelming response. Standing between the two guns that he was charged with, Anton watched the battery commander, anxiously awaiting the signal to fire. At each of the two cannon, the gun captains watched Anton with equal attentiveness. On the command of the battery commander, the guns began to fire, in sequence, starting from one end and working their way down the line at a slow, steady cadence to where Anton's two were. When the battery commander gave him the nod, Anton turned to face the gun captain of the first cannon and raised his arm. As he brought his arm down, he shouted "FIRE" for all he was worth, just as the other officers of artillery had. The gun captain, in turn, repeated the order to the gunner. With a few smooth motions, the gunner brought the linstock, with the slow-burning match attached to the end, down to the gun's touch hole, and lightly dipped the glowing match to the small pile of priming powder. When it caught, the gunner raised the linstock, took one step back, and, like the rest of the crew, turned his attention to the section of wall their gun had been aimed at.

In quick order, the burning primer reached the main charge, igniting it and sending the eighteen-pound solid shot careening down the long barrel of the gun. Anton had found that if he looked close enough, he could catch, on occasion, a glimpse of the shot while it was in flight. This morning, though he tried, he failed to do so. But there was no mistaking where it went, or its effects. Not more than a second after being hurled at the English works, a great shower of splinters and sparks, followed by a small plume of sand and white smoke, was thrown up by the impact of their first round. This was quickly followed by the firing of Anton's other gun. Even before the debris of the second round's impact had finished fluttering back to earth, a great, callused hand slapped Anton's shoulder. "My friend," Pepin roared, "with those two shots, you have made the work of my men these past weeks all worthwhile."

Recoiling from the impact of the large man's celebratory beating, Anton turned and gave Pepin a hesitant smile. Then, without a word to his friend, and with all traces of his fleeting smile gone, Anton went about the task of directing his gunner's next shot. They had hit too high, almost near the top of the English works. A few inches more and the nonexploding solid shots would have flown harmlessly over the fort. It was the task of his guns, and the other heavy cannon, to literally batter their way through the thick walls of log and sand and open a breach. Once that was done, the grenadiers and infantry, lounging about in their camps, would be ordered forward to storm through the breach and seize the fort by force of arms.

Of course, no one expected that this step would be necessary. The English commander, as well versed in the art of siege warfare as any of the French officers, would, once his walls were breached, ask for terms if they had not already been offered before that point by Montcalm. "This," Pepin would shout, throwing his hands in the air, every time Anton tried to explain it all to him, "is where I find the logic behind your way of making war lacking." With eyes enflamed with passion, Pepin would lean forward until he was inches from Anton's face. Then, inevitably, he'd bring his index finger up, jabbing it into the space between them. "This, lad, is the time to strike, to bring them to their knees. Break them! Break them till they holler for mercy. Then," he'd add with a twinkle in his eyes, "let our savage friends have their way with them. There is no doubt, sir, if your General Montcalm could bring himself to fight this war to its fitting conclusion, it would be the last we poor Canadians would see of the English."

Anton could do little more than shake his head. "My friend," he would mutter, "that simply is not the way things are done."

"In Europe, perhaps," Pepin would thunder.

"We are a civilized race and a Christian nation," Anton would reply, with all the conviction of a well-educated officer. "It simply would not do to leave our fellow Christians open to having their heads bashed in by our Indians."

"Oh, I see," Pepin would roar. "It is far better to smash your brother Christians' skulls with a bloody big ball of iron at five hundred yards. All this killing and maiming is acceptable, provided it's done scientifically and in accord with your holy rules of war."

It was a frequent discussion that Anton allowed himself to be drawn into, one that was never resolved one way or the other. Both men, raised under a common flag but with far different views of the world, could not be convinced that the other's argument had validity or merit. For despite being in New France for close to five years, Anton was still very much a product of his culture and his way of life, just as Pepin, raised from birth in the hard realities of French Canada, saw life through the prism of his past.

Such philosophical discussions as these, however, were reserved for the mess or around the fires at night, when there was little to do. At this particular moment, it was Anton, the officer of artillery, who moved about the muddy gun platform, checking and correcting the aim of his gun captains. Amid the thunderous reports of the other guns, few words were exchanged, for few were needed. The drill for loading, rolling the gun back into position, and aiming it were well ingrained in each of the gun crews. Each move was swift, yet unhastened. Quick, without being frantic. Gunnery, after all, was a science, perhaps the purest science of all the arts of war.

Yet, it was not totally devoid of human feelings or emotions. Even as Anton prepared to unleash another salvo from his guns, a cheer went up from the gunners gathered around him and all those from the camps who had come out to watch the spectacle. Looking up to see what had evoked the wild shouting and hollering, Anton caught a glimpse of the fort's flag, still attached to a section of pole severed by a stray shot, fluttering its way to the ground. "A fine shot!" Pepin roared with great delight.

Anton, of course, did not agree. The round had missed the wall, where it should have been aimed at. It was, from a technical standpoint, a wasted shot. But looking up and down the length of the battery, now shrouded in dirty white smoke, Anton could see that this symbolic blow brought much cheer to his men and the crews of the other guns. Morale, a commodity that defied all efforts to measure it, was just as important to success on the battlefield as a well-aimed gun. So Anton, the officer of artillery, allowed himself to accept that this shot was, after all, not a waste.

Within moments of the first incident concerning the fort's flag, another followed, one that was just as symbolic, though far more sobering. In clear view of both defenders and attackers, an English soldier climbed up the narrow pole, flag draped over his shoulder, with the clear intention of restoring his national colors to their rightful place. This act of courage, however, was quickly rewarded by death as a second cannonball, as poorly aimed, yet guided as if by the hand of fate itself, took off the Englishman's head in the twinkling of an eye.

Even before the body, with the bloodied Union Jack fluttering down behind it, disappeared below the level of the fort's parapet, Pepin poked Anton in the rib. "Civilized warfare, eh?"

Anton did not reply. He didn't even acknowledge his friend's snide remark. Instead, he took his position, brought his gun crews to readiness for firing, and carried on with the deadly work at hand.

Within the Fortified Camp, near Fort William Henry

THOUGH the fate of those in the fortified camp was inevitably tied to that of the fort, there was little they could do to assist them in their struggle or to alleviate their suffering. The garrison of the fortified camp had its own battle for survival to contend with. Constant sniping, much of it at close range, while not particularly threatening, was sufficiently irritating to warrant occasional sorties whose aim was to clear away their foe and discourage boldness. Besides providing a brief respite to those charged with patrolling the long walls of stone and logs, an occasional sallying of a company or two of regulars and provincials kept alive the hope that all was not lost. "A little nip," Thomas told Perry Jones as if he were instructing a young ensign, "will keep the French at arm's distance and buoy the spirit of our troops."

Always free with his comments, Jones shook his head as he watched the assembling of the troops Thomas had been charged to lead. "Well, sir, I can tell you for sure, I hope someone is appreciative of what we're about to do."

A smile lit across Thomas' face as he looked down at the little drummer by his side. Even in his tall, fur-trimmed grenadier's hat, the lad didn't stand any higher than Thomas' chest. Yet, this young, frail boy who was not yet old enough to shave brought a joy to Thomas' heart that he hadn't felt in years. The emotions Katherine Van der Hoff evoked in him paled in comparison. Though he wished he could eventually learn to love that woman with something akin to the affection that others he knew held for their spouses, passion somehow did not seem to be part of the equation when it came to the two of them. At times, they approached their courtship more as a business partnership than as a union between two lovers. For despite the fact that Katherine had the face of an angel, the eyes of Venus, and the figure of a goddess, her mind worked with a cold, calculating, machinelike precision.

Perry Jones, on the other hand, puny in stature and brassy in manner, brought Thomas a simple and pure joy, even here, in the midst of the adversity they faced. Perhaps it was the nature of the crisis at hand that heightened his response to Jones' free-spirited comments. Thomas had always been an easy mark when it came to a spirited horse, or lively companions who strayed just to this side of decency. Whether it was that Thomas depended on the liveliness and spirits of others to bring out the best in him or it was just that his dour background drove him to seek people unlike those he grew up with was not important. What was important was that Drummer Jones was drawn to him in a relationship that was more akin to that of father and son than that of drummer and commanding officer.

"Now, remember," Thomas stated matter-of-factly as he looked over the ranks of men awaiting his orders, "you're to stay at my side at all times, lad. When the firing starts in earnest, it will be your drum, and not my voice, that will be heard and obeyed."

"Yes, sir," Drummer Jones acknowledged, swallowing hard, though his mouth was quite dry.

"We will follow the detachment of the Thirty-fifth," Thomas continued, "which will go through the sally port first. Behind us will come the two companies of provincials. The regulars of the Thirty-fifth will provide the core upon which we will anchor our line. Only when we're set will we go forward."

"But won't all this maneuvering about scare off the Indians before we have a chance to close on them?" the boy asked as he continued to fidget nervously.

Again, Thomas smiled. "Our aim is to do exactly that. Whether we do so with or without a fight is really unimportant."

"And what, sir, if I may ask, do we do if the French send a large force after us while we're out there, alone?"

"Then," Thomas smirked, "it will be our turn to run like hell. Now," he commanded in a tone of voice that was all business, "beat the assembly and let's get on with it."

With all the enthusiasm that he could muster, Drummer Jones tapped out the notes of assembly, bringing all the officers and soldiers to attention. Those who were around Thomas' small command tending other chores or minding their personal business hardly gave those selected to sally out a second thought. This was, after all, a military camp, and these were soldiers doing what soldiers were paid to do.

With the same sharp, clear commands he had used when drilling members of the Coldstream Guards in Hyde Park in London, Thomas put his command in motion and marched it to the point of the works through which they would sally. The men at the sally port, already warned of the plan, opened the crude gate and stepped aside. When Jones saw the barren space between the camp's works and the woods where the French camp lay framed by the open gate, his eyes grew wide. He had to struggle with his natural urge to slow his pace and hang back. Thomas felt this conflict in the boy, marching so close to his side that their sleeves occasionally brushed. "Steady, boy," Thomas whispered. "Stay with me and you'll be all right."

Though he could feel his stomach churning, Jones kept his pace and maintained his drumming without missing a beat. "Aye, sir. I will," was all he could manage to say.

With the lead detachment of the Thirty-fifth Foot through the works and he and Jones coming up even with them, Thomas turned his full attention to the provincials behind him. "Sir," Thomas shouted to the captain in command of the unit behind him. "You may bring your men up into line now." To emphasize his command, Thomas raised his sword arm and pointed to the right of the detachment of regulars.

Though they did not do so with the same precision and smartness that the severely drilled soldiers of the Thirty-fifth performed all their movements, the provincials nonetheless came up quickly and aligned themselves with their English counterparts. With the sound of musket fire opening up to their front, Thomas repeated his order to the commander of the second provincial company, this time pointing to the Thirty-fifth's left. By the time this company was in place, the entire command had moved well into the dead zone that lay before the entrenched camp.

This bold movement hadn't been executed without cost. Steadily, like a gathering rainstorm, the tempo of enemy fire increased with each step Thomas' command took. Jones, intent on his drumming, was shocked to see the first red-coated body, still writhing in its final agony. Thomas, who had to step over the stricken soldier, anticipated Jones' distress. "Steady, boy. He's done his duty. Now keep to yours."

This time, Jones did not respond. For a moment, he closed his eyes and tried hard to blot the sight from his mind. But even as he did so, he continued to maintain the rhythm of his drumming and the pace that stretched his short legs to their maximum. Above the growing cadence of fire directed at their ranks from Indians grudgingly giving ground, Jones heard Thomas' voice, stern and clear. "Straighten up now, lad, and pay attention."

Then, with a loud and distinct parade-ground tone, Thomas began to issue orders. "TAKE CARE TO HALT," he bellowed. "HALT!" Though the response varied, with the regulars coming to an immediate stop and the provincials drifting forward a pace or two, the command was obeyed promptly. With that accomplished, Thomas waited while the lines of the companies were dressed by the company officers.

Perry Jones, recovering from his momentary bout with panic, opened his eyes and looked around.

Before him he could see the red backs of the soldiers of the Thirty-fifth, arranged three ranks deep, standing firm and motionless. Even when one of their number was thrown backward, hit square in the chest by an enemy ball, the soldiers to either side did little more than close the gap and resume their silent, motionless vigil. Within the companies on the Thirty-fifth's flanks, the provincial officers adjusted their alignment while the men in those ranks nervously fidgeted with their weapons, waiting to return the grueling fire. This observation brought Jones' own nervousness to his attention. Sheepishly, he forced himself to stand still, even while looking up at Thomas, who was standing motionless beside him. Only his eyes, and an occasional turning of his head, could be detected as the captain of grenadiers eyed the situation before them.

"All right now, lad," Thomas stated calmly as he looked over and down at Jones. "It's time to give them their due."

The calmness that Thomas displayed, to include a slight smile and a wink, worked wonders on Jones. Puffing out his chest in pride at having such a marvelous commander to follow, Drummer Jones returned Thomas' smile. "Ready, sir."

"TAKE CARE," Thomas ordered, "TO FIRE BY PLATOON. FIRE."

With each command, Jones tapped out the appropriate tune. When the last note of Thomas' final order was sounded, Jones let his drumsticks come to rest on the drumhead of his instrument. From his spot at Thomas' side, he watched in awe as the line of musketeers, starting with the first platoon on the right, opened the rolling volley fire that made English infantry world renowned. Though he had seen this drill practiced many times by the companies in his regiment until it was second nature to all, this was the first time he was witnessing it being directed at a living foe. That fact heightened the effect of the experience. Yes, Jones thought to himself as he caught the first whiffs of gunpowder. Now it's *our* turn to give the French what for.

Though his attention was focused on the manner in which his subordinate commanders were executing his orders, Thomas could not help himself from sneaking a glance, every now and then, down at young Jones. Each time he did so, Thomas imagined that he caught the small glimmer of excitement, the same sense of being fully alive, that he himself felt every time he entered combat. This thought, and the blessing that had brought this fine young lad to his side, evoked a twinge of joy in Thomas' heart.

With an understanding of his foe's way of war, Toolah had little to fear from the volleys unleashed by the dense ranks before him. It was all a matter of timing. One simply had to know enough English, and be aware of which group was pointing in one's direction, in order to duck at the appropriate time. Of course, that did not mean that the efforts by the English were for naught. There were those around him who had not yet learned the ways of their enemy, or simply did not have the nerve to lay and wait till the storm of fire had swept over them before raising their heads from cover. From his comfortable hiding place, Toolah could see a few of his fellow braves, rattled by the appearance of the English soldiers and their firing, stand and bolt to the rear. It was these foolish souls who felt the wrath of the English muskets. Struck down in their backs like dogs, Toolah didn't bother to watch as they thrashed in their death throes. There was too much to do, such as preparing his own musket for firing once the enemy's fire had swept by him.

Knowing when that happened was easy. One moment there was a shouted order, then the next, an ugly buzz, like a swarm of angry bees, passed overhead. Taking advantage of the momentary break in his foe's mechanical firing, Toolah popped his head and shoulders up and around the tree stump he was using for cover that day and took aim. The dense mass of enemy made aiming quite easy. All he needed to do was point at the line of knees before him and pull the trigger. As he had the night before, he didn't wait to see what effect his return fire had. There would be other occasions, he knew, when he would be able to stand and gloat above a vanquished foe. Today, he would content himself with merely holding his ground for as long as was practical, and making life difficult for the English.

From the fortified camp, Thomas heard the three drums tapping out the prearranged signal that the water party his sortie was covering had made it to the stream, fetched the water needed by the garrison, and returned. Now it was time for his own command to retrace their steps. Without any great haste, Thomas gave the orders for one, then the other, company of provincials to disengage, move back from the firing line, and return to the fort. The detachment of the Thirty-fifth, having taken half a dozen or so casualties, stood their ground and covered the withdrawal. When they did receive the order to pull back, they did so with their front to the enemy, moving backward slowly and defiantly, pausing every few yards to fire a volley as a warning to any savage foolish enough to follow. Only when their backs were literally up against the wall of the fortified camp did the officer in charge of the detachment of regulars give his men the order to about-face and file back into the protective enclosure.

In doing so, they passed Thomas and Drummer Jones, who stood outside the log and stone barricade until the last of the small command had passed them by. Even then, Thomas made a show of it, calmly replacing his sword in his sheath and turning his back, in total disregard of the danger that still lay behind him, and slowly reentering the fortified camp with a gait no more hurried than if he were returning from a stroll in the garden. A few who were watching were impressed by this show of bravado.

Among those few were Drummer Jones. To him, Thomas epitomized all that an officer should be. For him, Thomas had become a god who could do no wrong.

Fort William Henry
August, 1757

IF the outcomes of battles were determined solely by the courage and determination displayed by one side or the other, the English would have stood a good chance of prevailing over the French on the shores of Lake George that August. But all too often, numbers and the cold hard truths of mechanical warfare turn aside the best the men have to offer. With the same inevitability that a mathematical formula grinds toward a predetermined solution, the French guns battered the English garrison to the brink of destruction. By the fourth day of the siege, when the heavy guns finally opened a breach, all hopes of being saved by General Webb, who still sat idle at Fort Edward, were gone.

Early on the morning of August 9, six days after the French had invested William Henry and three days since their batteries had first fired on the fort, the English leadership gathered to discuss capitulation. Like the other officers in attendance, Thomas knew full well that there was little point in carrying on a futile defense. All but a few of the smaller cannon in the fort were out of action, as much from bursting during firing as from enemy action. For those that remained, there was precious little ammunition. Smallpox was ravaging both the fort's garrison and now the troops of the fortified camp. Both sets of soldiers suffered from fatigue, brought on by the almost constant bombardment by the French or the sniping of their Indian allies. And to add woe to misery, Montcalm's own aide-de-camp delivered a letter, dated some days before and intercepted by the French from Webb at Fort Edward, that made it clear that Webb had no intention of relieving William Henry. With a third French battery now open and firing on the fort little more than three hundred yards away and a breach about to be stormed, Lieutenant Colonel Monro knew he had no alternative but to surrender.

With Drummer Jones at his side, Thomas Shields watched the flag of truce as it was raised over the fort's battered parapets, announcing the garrison's desire to parley. "That is one duty," Thomas muttered, as much to himself as to young Jones, "that I am glad to have avoided."

"I find it odd, sir," Jones responded as the two stood there, "that of all the officers available, Captain Faesch, a Swiss of the Royal Americans, would be the man selected to parley with the French commander."

Thomas chuckled halfheartedly, looked down at Jones, and began to walk slowly along the parapet of the fort. It wasn't that he had anywhere to go, or something important to do. Until the terms of the surrender were known, no one had much of anything to do but wait. Still, Thomas could not simply stand about and do nothing. Even aimless wandering was far more preferable to sitting, wondering, and worrying.

"If I may, sir. Why did you laugh just then?" Jones asked as he labored to keep pace with Thomas' long strides.

Sensing the hurt feelings in Jones' voice, Thomas slowed his pace some and tried to explain. "Captain Faesch, Perry, served in the French army. That makes him quite familiar with the French mentality and niceties, not to mention a language that my own tongue has great difficulty wrapping itself around."

The last part made Jones laugh. This brought a smile to Thomas, who found it pleasing to have gotten such a response from the boy. "I'm quite serious, you know. Have you ever tried to pronounce some of those words of theirs? I mean, how on earth can anyone make sense of a language and a people who somehow make the letters O-U-I come out to sound like *we*?"

Again, Jones laughed, causing some of the soldiers lying about, waiting to find out what their fates would be, to look up at the odd pair with questioning stares. Thomas, enjoying himself, ignored them. "I'm sorry, but, try as they might," Thomas continued, "the best tutors in the Kingdom couldn't train my undisciplined tongue to embrace the language of love."

"I can understand that, sir," Jones beamed. "A sergeant tried to teach me my letters. He gave up, though. Said I was too dense to learn anything of value. Even my drummin' isn't what it should be. That's why they gave me to you. Said I was worthless to 'em."

This caused Thomas to frown. Stopping, he turned to face the boy, placing his hands upon the bony shoulders that were engulfed in a coat two sizes too large. "Drummer Jones," Thomas announced firmly, yet with affection shining though his every word, "don't let anyone, man or woman, ever again tell you that you're worthless or stupid." Though the boy looked up with confusion on his face, Thomas continued. "We will show those naysayers, you and I, that they were wrong. When we're out of this, you'll learn your letters, properly this time. Now," Thomas added as he looked up at the quiet, sullen faces of people unsure of their future, "all we need to do is keep our wits about us over the next few days and muddle our way through this mess."

Fort William Henry

THE choices that Toolah now faced were difficult ones for him. He could take advantage of the marvelous opportunities that the English surrender presented to him by collecting scalps and hence enhancing his own personal stature within the tribe. Or he could turn his back on the rich spoils that now lay within arm's reach and fulfill his personal vendetta with the Frenchman. Even as he watched the English soldiers march from the fort, under arms and with flags flying, he was unsure of what he would do.

Toolah was still wavering when the last of the English soldiers left the fort. For a moment more, he tottered on the edge of indecision. Then, when several other braves who had been waiting anxiously off to one side rushed forward through the open gates of the now undefended fort to seize what plunder they could, Toolah abandoned his struggle and joined in the rush. Hadn't he, he reasoned as he shoved his way through the throng, earned the right to take that which he had been promised? Hadn't he held his passions in check long enough? And hadn't his actions these past few days been equal, or superior, to many of his fellow warriors whom he now pushed aside with total disregard? Unlike those who listened to the Frenchmen, who lied to them incessantly, Toolah was determined to do as he saw fit, and at the moment, joining in on the sacking of the English fort was what he chose to do.

In short order the rampaging mob of excited Indians found the abandoned store of rum. With tomahawks and musket butts they smashed in the ends of the kegs and began scooping up the wonderful liquid in anything that was handy, to include their own cupped hands. Toolah, coming across a fellow warrior who was trying to monopolize one of the barrels of rum, lifted his foot, kicked the selfish brave in the small of his back, and then used the butt of his musket to push the man, bent over in pain and wailing, out of the way. Hovering over the barrel like an anxious predator protecting a fresh kill, Toolah warned off all possible competitors with a look that told them he would brook no dispute over what he had rightfully taken. Even those who failed to recognize him shied away from the sharp-eyed warrior with his weapons held at the ready. Only when he felt it was safe to do so did Toolah scoop up handful after handful of rum and all but throw it into his open mouth, spreading the sweet, sticky liquor all over his face and bare chest.

After spending several minutes standing over the barrel, drinking as quickly as his hands could carry the rum to his mouth, Toolah began to feel warm and energized. When he was satisfied that he had had his fill, the warrior turned his back and began to walk away from his prize. First, however, he knocked over the open keg, spilling the contents all over the ground and sending half a dozen impatient braves scrambling to lap up whatever they could before the rum was absorbed into the ground.

Feeling even bolder and more assured of his superiority than usual, Toolah made his way into one of the dark casements from which the screams and cries of men could be heard. His progress was slowed, in part by the dizziness that was beginning to overcome him, and in part by the steady stream of delighted Indians running out, holding aloft trophies they had collected from the Englishmen they had found within. Never having any patience with a man who assumed that he could jostle and bump him whenever he pleased, Toolah stopped every so often and whacked, or attempted to whack, any offender he could reach. But there was simply not enough time to respond to all. Besides, Toolah found that several of his swings were missing their intended mark by a wide margin. Worried that he would not reach the English before all scalps had been taken, Toolah forgot his quest for vengeance for the moment and continued into the center of the room under the casement.

Once there, he was greeted by a sight that resembled a scene from hell. The room, dimly lit by candles and lanterns with sooty glass panes, was filled with English soldiers who had been too injured, wounded, or sick to march out with the rest of the garrison. Hovering and moving about them, sometimes even standing on them, was an equal number of Indians, some hacking away at a hapless victim's scalp even while the poor soul was screaming and flailing about in protest. None of this put Toolah off. On the contrary, already fired by his desire to extract some worthy prizes, and even more frenzied by the alcohol he had just consumed, Toolah flashed a wide, evil smile, let loose a vicious scream, and threw himself upon a man with only a stump where his left arm had been.

There wasn't much of a fight. The man, already severely weakened from all the blood he had lost, first to his wound, then to the amputation of his arm, melted away upon Toolah's approach. Sliding down between two beds now filled with the corpses of fellow soldiers, the wounded Englishman managed only to raise his one good hand before Toolah smashed the man's face with the butt of his musket. This ended all resistance and allowed Toolah to sling his musket over his shoulder, pull his tomahawk from his belt, and begin hacking away at the man's neck with great enthusiasm. Between the effects of the rum, the darkness of the room, and the crowded conditions that led to brave and foe alike bumping into each other, Toolah made a mess of the decapitation. Still, he managed to get the job done. When he was sure the head was about to come off, he grabbed a good, solid handful of hair, pulled the now nearly severed head upright, and gave the few strands still connecting body to head one more whack. As expected, the last powerful swing did the job and left Toolah holding the slightly battered and very bloody head.

Turning, he hoisted the trophy above his head, gave a yell, and began to run out the entrance, still crowded with more braves rushing in in an effort to claim their prizes. In the open courtyard, filled with cheering, screeching, and delighted Indians, Toolah and his prize were greeted with shrieks of joy and excitement. Only a priest, flustered and agitated that his exertions to show mercy to the sick and wounded foe were useless, gazed upon Toolah with disgust. For a moment, Toolah stood there, holding the dead Englishman's head above his. From bits of muscle and veins dangling from the severed head, blood dripped onto Toolah, mixing freely with the rum he had splashed upon himself, Toolah's own sweat, and the smeared war paint he wore. Seeing there was no use in trying to do anything with Toolah, the priest dropped his head, muttered something, and went in search of a soul he could save. This left Toolah free to run through the dense crowd and out the gate, screaming like a child with a great prize.

WITH the fort stripped of all worthwhile plunder, the Indians turned their attention to the fortified camp, where the English were now huddled together, waiting to be escorted south to Fort Edward, as per the terms of the agreement of capitulation. Under those terms, the regulars and provincials were to be paroled for eighteen months, during which time they could not take up arms against the French. For this, the English were to return all Frenchmen captured in the war to date, within three months. By European standards all of this was rather common, and Montcalm no doubt expected that all provisions would be executed as agreed.

But this was not Europe, as Anton had come to realize. The Indians, a third party, who were every bit as much players in the affairs of the continent, had their own ideas of what was just and acceptable. That the women and children accompanying the various units were not addressed by the instrument of surrender left them in a very vulnerable position, which none of the victorious Indians could ignore.

Even before the last of the plunder worth taking was being hauled from the abandoned shell of William Henry, the Indians began to make their way to, and into, the fortified camp. The Englishmen there, regular and provincial, soldier and civilian, drew back as much as they could from the wild savages as they wandered about the camp. The Indians, many now drunk from the rum they had consumed, went about poking their heads into every tent they came across, running their fingers through the hair of terrified women whom they soon expected to seize and rummaging through the personal effects of officers and soldiers alike while the owners of those items held back and watched in horror.

Having come up to William Henry with a view of staying only a few days, Thomas Shields had few personal possessions with him. Only one thing within the fortified camp mattered to the second son of a minor English nobleman that day. "Perry," Thomas kept telling Drummer Jones as he clutched the boy tightly, "stay with me, lad. Whatever happens, don't go wandering off on your own, for any reason. Do you understand?"

Thomas' repeated warnings were quite unnecessary. Hanging on to the tall officer in a most unmilitary fashion, young Jones kept to Thomas' side. At times, he even swallowed his pride as he slithered behind Thomas' back whenever an Indian seemed to take notice of him and threaten to approach. Thomas did his best to shield the boy, with both his own body and a defiant stance. For the most part this worked, for Thomas had been allowed to retain his sword. He made great show of wrapping his hand around the hilt of the weapon when he felt a show of force was necessary. In most cases, this was all that was needed to keep the curious at bay. But not every Indian was cowed by so simple a challenge.

When Toolah spotted the boy, hanging on the English officer like a possum's baby, he knew what he wanted. To bring home a young captive, a boy that his childless wife could raise as their own, would be a fitting reward for the risks he had taken these past few days. Taking a deep drink from the jug he had taken from another warrior who was foolish enough to give it up without a struggle, Toolah decided not to wait until the next day to take what was rightfully his. Though his vision was somewhat blurred, and the dizziness in his head made him stagger about in uneven, faltering steps, Toolah made his way over to the oddly matched pair.

Concentrating all his attention on a particularly vicious-looking character who stood some distance off glaring at Thomas, the captain of grenadiers didn't take notice of Toolah's approach. It wasn't until that warrior had come within arm's reach and had managed to seize one of Perry Jones' arms that Thomas became aware of the new danger. The lad, already frightened beyond belief by stories he had heard from colonials before the battle, stories now made real by the events unfolding all about him, kept his head buried in the small of Thomas' back. With his eyes clamped shut, he was unable to detect Toolah's approach until that brave already had a firm grasp on his arm.

With a yank, Toolah jerked the boy away from the English officer. The lad, shocked by the jerk, let out a scream. This caused the officer to wheel about on one foot, drawing his sword as he did so. The swiftness of the Englishman's response, and the sight of naked steel flashing within inches of his eyes, caused Toolah to rock back on his heels. Already made unsteady by the huge amounts of rum he had consumed, and with both hands full, Toolah was unable to keep his balance. Inevitably, Toolah tumbled over, letting go of both the boy and his jug of rum in the process. Hitting the ground with a great thud, Toolah felt his breath knocked from him, leaving him flat on his back and totally defenseless.

Thomas, enraged by his momentary lapse in his efforts to protect the boy he had grown so fond of, was not content with simply warding off the attack. Taking a quick step forward, he lay the tip of his sword against the exposed neck of the offending savage. Only at the last moment did Thomas catch himself and stop his arm from thrusting his sword forward. It would have taken only a tiny bit of effort, one, maybe two inches of a downward thrust, to end that animal's life. But Thomas checked himself. It would have been suicidal to spill an Indian's blood here, in the presence of so many, for any reason. Caution and vigilance in so precarious a spot were what was needed to see them through this. He knew this and withdrew his blade. But not before leaning forward just a little, so that the point of his sword left a tiny nick as a warning to the drunken Indian.

Embarrassed almost as much as he was angered by his clumsy performance, Toolah lay on the ground for a moment and looked up into the eyes of the Englishman. Like Thomas, he realized that this was not the time to challenge the white officer who had managed to make him look inept and foolish. Collecting his thoughts as he struggled to regain his breath, Toolah resolved that he would have the last say in this matter. He would come back in the morning, when the English were on the move, and both extract his revenge and collect the boy. Gathering himself up slowly, awkwardly, Toolah brushed himself off, collected his jug, and stood as tall and erect as he could. Then, in an act of defiance, he advanced upon Thomas until their faces were but inches apart. With a steady, hateful glare, Toolah stared into the Englishman's eyes.

Thomas, still holding himself back, stood his ground. Despite the disgusting odor of the savage, and his breath that reeked of rum, Thomas met Toolah's gaze and returned it. Even after the Indian turned away from him and began to make his way along the line of tents in search of other plunder, Thomas stood at the ready, with sword in one hand and his other wrapped tightly about Drummer Jones. "You stay close to me," Thomas warned again with a note of desperation in his voice. "Do you hear, boy? *Stay with me.*"

Badly shaken and frightened beyond belief by the experience, Jones found he could not utter a single word, not even a noise, in response. The best he could manage was a slight nodding of his head. But this was enough. Thomas felt the small boy's head, burrowed against his side, and felt reassured. Squeezing the boy tightly against his side, Thomas kept an eye on the Indian until he had disappeared from sight.

The French Camp,
Before Fort William Henry

ENJOYING a well-deserved sleep, it took Anton several moments to notice the shouts of excited voices as they rippled their way throughout the camp. As this was the first full night's rest he had been able to enjoy since the beginning of the siege, it was not surprising that he became angry when the shouts, growing louder and nearer, continued. At first he couldn't make out what was being said or even imagine what could possibly be causing such agitation. Then, slowly, like a forgotten pain making its way from an obscure corner of the body to his consciousness, Anton realized what the commotion was about. The butchering of the English that he had so casually predicted had begun.

Still, Anton did little at first. Only slowly did he open his eyes and stare blankly at the canvas stretched out over his head. It would be dawn soon, he guessed by the faint light that glowed through the white canvas of the tent. Except for the harried shouts and calls for assistance, the only other sound that Anton could hear was the irregular snoring of one of his tent mates. Turning his head, he looked over at the lifeless forms of the other two officers of artillery he shared the tent with and watched them for a moment. Neither of them seemed to be disturbed by the hollering just outside or the thought that a few hundred yards away their erstwhile allies were falling upon a helpless foe that now depended upon them for protection.

Perhaps, Anton told himself, he could shut his eyes, force his mind to block out the cries of alarm, and manage to drift away back into the blissful emptiness and refuge of sleep. After all, he reminded himself, what was happening to the English was unavoidable. Any fool who had spent even the slightest bit of effort to learn the ways of this land knew that you simply did not gather so many of its native people, arm them to the teeth, lead them to war, and then, when the enemy was defeated, deprive them of what they considered their just reward. Only a naïve fool, he mumbled to himself, could delude himself into thinking that he could impose a European code of ethics upon a race of people who were just as proud of their way of life as any European was of his.

Sleep, however, did not return. Nor did any of his efforts to shut out the thoughts that a massacre was unfolding outside succeed. Slowly, Anton began to stir as he found himself becoming just as agitated as the frantic voices outside were. Finally, when he could pretend no more, Anton sat up, shook his head, and surrendered to the fact that he was still, as he probably would always be, a fool when it came to matters of right and wrong, ethics, and dreaming that he could do something to make things better.

In the Camp of the Caughnawaga near Fort William Henry

As the sun had managed to make its appearance over the steep mountains that cradled Lake George in their lap, it fell upon Toolah, still lying where he had fallen the night before in a drunken stupor. Cold, aching, and befuddled, Toolah was unable to comprehend what the shouts and screams of glee were all about. Nor did he care. His head was pounding unlike anything he had ever experienced, confusing his random thoughts. Only when he felt a sharp kick on the sole of his foot did he try to focus his eyes in an effort to see what manner of man was foolish enough to strike him so.

"You are being missed by that pack of wolves who follow you," Toolah's brother sneered. "But they do not need you, not today."

Slowly, the blurry image of Gingego, towering over him in his faded, ragged red coat, came into focus. "I have no need of your childish riddles, brother," Toolah grunted. "Go and amuse your French masters."

"It is the English," Gingego stated with pride, "that I have been entertaining, making them pay while you lie about like a sick dog. Look up, brother, and see what they have to offer for those who were willing to wait."

Confused as ever, Toolah slowly raised himself up on one arm and squinted in an effort to bring into focus the object Gingego was waving before his face. In an instant, the sight of a freshly collected scalp, blood still clinging to bits of skin and hair at the edges, animated Toolah. "The English? You have already attacked the English?"

Gingego withdrew the scalp from before Toolah's face, stood upright, and smiled. "The dogs tried to slip away, under French guard, before we had a chance to take that which we were promised. But many of us were wise to this trick, and we were ready. And our patience has been rewarded. Look, brother," Gingego shouted as he pointed behind him.

The sight of a wretched white woman standing behind the red-coated brave with head hung low, hands tightly bound, and a rope about her neck reminded Toolah of the boy he had selected to be his. Ignoring his disorientation and the soreness of his limbs, Toolah jumped to his feet, fetched the tomahawk from his belt, and rushed past his brother. Were it not for the embarrassment of being left behind like this, and missing the chance to collect the trophies that would make this raid worthwhile, Toolah would have struck his brother. But there was no time for this. Even as he started running, he could hear the cries of other braves rushing from their camps to join the excitement. So Toolah was forced to ignore his brother's mocking laughter.

On the Road to Fort Edward

THE movement of the English and provincials, together with women, children, and camp followers, never did manage to get under way. The regulars of the Thirty-fifth Foot and Royal Artillery contingents had barely managed to make their way out of the fortified camp and close up on the French escort before the ever-watchful Indians swarmed over them looking for plunder, captives, and rum. Within short order, the possessions of officer and soldier were taken or given away in the hope of appeasing the Indians. This gesture, however, did little to placate the now excited natives. If anything, it encouraged them. Soon, as more and more Indians swarmed forth from their camps to claim their rightful share, all semblance of order dissolved and a proper massacre began.

Thomas Shields found himself in the middle of all this. He, together with a number of soldiers from the Royal American regiment, had been assigned to assist in bringing up the rear of the detachment of the Royal Artillery. Had all gone as hoped, there would have been no problems. But the ensuing confusion and panic left Thomas torn, for the first time, between his duties and his ardent desire to protect Drummer Jones. It was obvious to all that the safest place to be was at the front of the column, right behind the contingent of French Canadians assigned the task of escorting the English south to Fort Edward. As more and more Indians made their way down the column, Thomas found it increasingly impossible to maintain order within his ranks. Nothing seemed to work, because nothing satisfied the savages who came forward, individually or in small knots, pulling and ripping away whatever struck their fancy. When there were no more packs or personal possessions, the Indians began to take the very clothes off the soldiers' backs and drag away women, children, and even the black soldiers who had stood and fought as equals in the provincial units.

For Thomas, this entire experience, coming after a sleepless night that had capped an exhausting six-day siege, was unnerving. Never before had he been faced with a conflict that pitted personal needs against his professional duties as an officer of the king. Never had he found himself in such mortal danger, with no way of striking back or even defending himself. And never had he found something more valuable to fight for, to protect, than the seemingly insignificant life of a drummer boy who had managed to touch a place in his heart as no other mortal had ever done before.

Still, Thomas was a professional soldier, an officer holding the king's commission and trust. He had his duties and he was determined to carry them through, despite the desperate odds, personal considerations be damned. "Close up and face out!" he shouted as Indians forced their way into their ranks, grabbing, tearing, shoving. "CLOSE UP!"

Few, however, heard him. With no ammunition, and their muskets slung upside down in a sign of submission, the terrified soldiers gave way to their fears and cowered where they stood. Shoving Drummer Perry Jones under the carriage of the lone cannon that the French had permitted the English to carry away, Thomas leaned over and ordered the boy to stay there, hidden, till he returned. "For God sakes," Thomas whispered as gently as he could while still making himself heard over the growing cacophony, "whatever happens, stay here and keep hidden." Though it broke his heart to do so, Thomas turned his back on Jones and made his way through the press of soldiers and savages, vainly trying to restore order and control.

By the time he reached the fortified camp, Toolah had managed to regain full use of his senses. Though his head still ached, he was ready when an excited warrior let out a war whoop, the universal signal for attack. Together with Sauk,

Fox, Iowa, Miami, Potawatomi, Ottawa, Abenaki, Algonquin, Nipissing, Iroquois, and fellow Caughnawagas, Toolah fell on the column of refugees already dissolving into a formless mass.

Defenseless and abandoned by their French guards, each individual reacted differently. Those who resisted were overwhelmed, struck down, and scalped in quick order. Others, frozen in abject terror, were grabbed, bound, and hauled away quickly, before the French had a chance to rouse their moral indignation and intervene. Most of the Englishmen stood where they had been lined up waiting to march south, bunched together like frightened cattle in the midst of a summer storm and left to grovel for mercy in a place where that word was unknown. Many turned and fled, either toward the presumed safety of the nearest French soldier or to the woods, where they hoped to hide or, God willing, escape.

With so many opportunities to collect an easy scalp or seize a captive who would bring him ransom money from the French, Toolah found it hard to continue his search for the young boy he had attempted to seize the day before. He had hoped that the brightly colored and ornate coat the boy had been wearing would make him an easy mark. But too many of the English had been stripped of clothing to depend on that. Slowed by the necessity to examine each gaggle of huddled whites, as well as the faces of those already taken captive and being hauled off, it took some time before Toolah managed to find Drummer Jones. When he finally did spot the frightened boy, partially hidden beneath a cannon abandoned by its crew and left stranded with no horses to pull it, Toolah let out a scream and ran for all he was worth to claim his prize.

As if alerted by a sixth sense to the danger, Thomas turned just as Toolah reached the abandoned gun where Jones was hiding. Thomas' screams of anger, rage, and warning were drowned out by the howls and shrill shrieks of both the hapless victims and their animated assailants surrounding him. With almost superhuman efforts, Thomas began to push, shove, and claw his way through the press of bodies as he raced to save the boy he had grown to love.

With his every thought and effort focused on that one object, Thomas saw nothing else, not even the butt of another Indian's musket as it came smashing into the side of his head.

The sight of the wild melee in and around the fortified camp was even more appalling than Anton had imagined. There was no sense or reason to the wild scene before him. No center, or even discernible fringes. Just one gigantic frenzy of killing, scalping, and wanton violence as far as he could see. For a moment, Anton paused, unsure of what to do, where to go, and how to stop the slaughter, if, indeed, it could be stopped.

Then his eyes fell upon one small drama being played out. Not far from the lone cannon near the front of the now dissolved column he spotted an Indian kneeling over the prostrate body of an English officer. With knife drawn, the Indian was preparing to take the man's scalp. Angered by the symbolic savagery of the act, Anton roused his anger and took off, as fast as his legs could carry him. With the same single-mindedness that had possessed Thomas moments before, Anton ignored everything and everyone around him, including an Indian struggling to carry away a small drummer boy who squirmed and thrashed his arms about for all he was worth.

Toolah, however, was not as absorbed by his efforts to haul away his captive. Hit in the shoulder by a French officer racing by him, Toolah looked up and saw that it was Anton. Surprised and bewildered, Toolah stopped and watched Anton as he closed quickly upon a fellow brave who was engrossed in his own hunt for trophies. Suddenly Toolah found himself faced with a real problem. He could, he realized, give up the boy and instead satisfy his quest for personal vengeance against this naïve and bothersome Frenchman. Unable to think clearly, with a throbbing pain racking his head, Toolah paused and watched while he weighted the relative value of these two mutually exclusive pursuits.

Even as he ran, Anton watched in horror as the savage slid his razor-sharp knife across the top of the English officer's forehead, opening a bloody furrow in its wake. With one final effort, the excited French officer of artillery managed to reach the hapless victim just as the Indian withdrew the knife and prepared to strip the hair and skin of the Englishman's head away from the skull.

"BASTARD!" Anton screamed as he lifted his boot as high as he could and brought it down with all his might against the side of the Indian's head. "BASTARD!" he repeated as he reached over and grabbed the shoulders of the English officer, now free as his assailant recoiled from Anton's blow.

Rolling over onto his side, then gaining his feet, the Indian turned and faced Anton. His anger was matched by Anton's, just as his knife, held closely at his side, was matched by Anton's drawn sword. Though he had no idea if the Indian understood French, Anton warned the man to back away and leave them alone. To emphasize his point, Anton tilted the blade of his sword up an inch or two until it was aligned with the Indian's throat. "Back," he shouted, "or die where you stand."

With the joyful screams of fellow Indians celebrating their small victories or cheaply won prizes surrounding him, the Indian confronting Anton decided that the effort to collect the scalp he had begun to take was not worth the risk. Standing upright, the brave gave Anton one more scathing glaze, then turned his back on him and walked away.

Only when he was sure that they were, relatively speaking, safe did Anton let his guard down. Dropping to his knees, Anton looked into the half-opened eyes of the English officer he had saved and asked in French, "Are you all right?"

Struggling to sort out thoughts muddled by the unexpected blow and the sensation of warm blood running down his forehead into his blurred eyes, Thomas heard the French words, but made no sense of them. "The boy," he mumbled as he began to struggle to regain his feet. "Must find the boy. You must help me."

Believing the Englishman still was in fear for his life, Anton tried to calm his charge. "It is all right, monsieur. I will make sure no harm comes to you. Stay down," he ordered Thomas in French as he tried to push the English officer back onto the ground. "All will be well. Just stay down."

Thomas, however, could not be stopped. Anton's soothing words, spoken in clear, concise French, and his reassuring hands on his shoulders could not stop Thomas from pressing on with the rescue he had been attempting to make when he was stricken. "The boy!" he continued to mutter in English. "Stop the bastard. You must help."

With great reluctance, Anton stood up and did his best to help Thomas to his feet. The English officer, however, could not stand on his own. Bewildered and dizzy, he wavered before falling heavily against Anton, almost knocking to the ground the Frenchman whom he towered over. Pausing only long enough to let the spinning in his head pass and wipe away some of the blood that was blinding him, Thomas began to look about the surreal scene of chaos and pandemonium in search of his charge. As if guided by an unseen hand, Thomas' eyes turned to where Toolah, with Jones' thin neck wedged in the crook of his arm, stood watching him. "There," Thomas shouted in English, raising a shaky arm and pointing to the Indian and his captive. "We must save him," he ordered Anton.

Only slowly did Anton begin to understand what the Englishman was ranting and raving about. Following Thomas' outstretched arm to the tip of the finger, Anton looked out to see what the man was pointing at. It was the boy he saw first, the very same one he had passed when he had run to this spot to save the Englishman. It was another second or two before he bothered to look up into the eyes of the savage who was holding the boy so tightly that the lad was turning blue. But when he did, he understood everything. The burning, hateful eyes of Toolah returned Anton's gaze. Only Thomas' clumsy efforts to lurch forward to rescue the boy broke the icy trance that fell between the two old foes.

"Yes," Anton responded resolutely in French as he pulled Thomas' arm over his shoulder with one hand and wrapped his other arm around Thomas' waist for support. "We must end this, now."

The approach of the two white officers, arm in arm, brought Toolah's crisis to a head. He now had little time in which to decide which of his two promises he would fulfill. To settle his personal affair with Anton would mean the loss of his captive, a boy who would make any man a fine son. Yet, if he turned his back on Anton and failed to settle matters with him now, the memory of his embarrassing confrontation would haunt him for another long, cruel winter. Like a deer transfixed by a hunter closing on him, Toolah stood there with the boy in his arms and his gaze fixed on his approaching foes.

Then, like a bolt of lightning, a solution that would allow him a victory of sorts over both white officers flashed though Toolah's mind. With great deliberateness, he eased his grasp about the boy's neck. With one hand, he gathered a fistful of the boy's hair and slowly began to pull it upward until the boy had to stand on his toes. With the other hand, Toolah reached down and drew his knife, bringing the sharp weapon up to the boy's neck.

The sight of the morning sun flashing off Toolah's knife raised a scream of horror from both men. Each in his native tongue shouted out pleas in a vain effort to dissuade Toolah from harming the lad, even as the two lurched forward in one final, desperate effort to reach Drummer Jones.

But they were too far away, and Toolah was committed. With an intense stare, he locked eyes with Anton. A smile as evil as any Anton could imagine began to light Toolah's face, even as the Caughnawaga warrior pressed the razor-sharp blade of his knife against the soft skin under Jones' left ear. With ever-increasing pressure, Toolah pushed the edge of the blade into the boy's throat and slowly, methodically, brought it around under Jones' chin and then up, until it almost touched the right ear.

Defeated, sickened, and unable to carry on, Anton dropped to his knees even as his eyes turned to the sky and he yelled "No!" over and over and over. Thomas, equally crushed, let go of his grasp on Anton and fell, with a crash, to the ground. His eyes remained firmly fixed upon those of young Drummer Perry Jones, eyes that were filled with terror. That look of betrayal cut Thomas deeper than any bullet or bayonet could ever hope to. Unable to endure it, Thomas buried his head, still bleeding from the wound that ran along the edge of his hairline, in his hands while blood and tears flowed and mixed freely as they fell to the ground before him.

When he felt the boy in his hand go limp, and the dead weight of the small body pull against the handful of hair he held, Toolah let go. After giving Anton one more triumphant look, the Indian warrior turned and walked majestically off the field, knowing full well he had left a scar both soldiers would carry to their graves.

PART FIVE

Hollow Victories

CHAPTER TWENTY

Winchester, Virginia
October, 1757

WITH THE COMING of fall, the heat in the small cookhouse where Megan O'Reilly spent most of her time was becoming bearable. In another month it would be downright cozy. Yet that, too, that had its downside. Her frequent trips back and forth to the tavern hauling meals and fresh breads would no longer offer her the relief that they had during the summer. Still, she imagined that the coming of winter would reduce the number of trips she had made during the previous seasons, especially when the militias were called to Winchester during emergencies. Whenever that happened, the entire town, and especially the taverns, were flooded with bands of ravenous men with little to do.

Of course, the coming of winter did not mean that Megan

would be idle. Keeping herself gainfully employed was one thing she had no problem with. Whenever she wasn't cooking for the inn where she lived and worked, Megan found other ways of earning income. Some were related to the inn. Others, which she had managed to arrange on her own, mostly involved doing chores for the soldiers of the Virginia Regiment stationed at Fort Loudoun.

It had all started very innocently when Ian McPherson and Megan were sitting under a tree near the fort's garden on a Sunday afternoon, passing a quiet day together, free of work and duty. Ian, never handy with needle and thread, was attempting to mend a hole in a pair of his breeches. For the longest time Megan sat and watched in silence, amused by his fumbling efforts to make the simple repair. Noticing that she was watching his every move only added to Ian's lack of coordination as he clumsily wielded the needle and thread. Eventually, after watching Ian impale himself with his needle once too often, Megan abandoned her self-imposed restraints and laughed out loud. Angered by the fact that he had managed to make a complete ass of himself in front of the woman he loved, as well as at stabbing himself, Ian became totally flustered, throwing the breeches on the ground. "To the devil with you," he shouted at them, as if they had feelings. "If the captain wants me to have breeches without holes in 'em, he'll supply me with new ones."

Knowing full well that the colony of Virginia was not about to replace a pair of breeches at a time when they couldn't even pay the soldiers they had raised, Megan picked up the trousers. Taking the needle and the tangled ball of thread from Ian, who was now too busy mumbling to himself to care, she offered to mend them for him. She spent half the night sitting before the dying embers of the cook fire, straining her eyes in an effort to patch and mend Ian's tattered clothing till they looked almost as good as new.

It was the loving care she had put into every stitch that was her undoing. Impressed with the quality of workmanship Megan had displayed in the restoration of his favorite sergeant's uniform, Ian's captain, John Shaw, asked if Ian could inquire if she would be willing to make some badly needed repairs on his clothing. Unable to say no to anything Ian asked of her, and anxious to build up her nest egg for the day when they would be married and need money to start a proper household, Megan took on the new work. After that, Megan was never wanting for work.

This situation was not without its pitfalls. "The minute you forget who's payin' ya the most, not to mention puttin' a roof over your head," the loud and obnoxious tavern owner bellowed every time he caught her with needle and thread in her hands, "is the last day you'll work for me, girlie." And though she had no fear of the lout, for he was a cowardly bully who was thoroughly intimidated by Ian, Megan kept all things in balance and made sure he had no cause for complaint when it came to her work.

With her attention focused on the bread she was making, Megan hummed an old song she had carried away from Ireland with her. She was careful to make just what was needed, wasting nothing. Some would be used that day, with the noon meal. Later, in the evening, those locals who frequented the tavern would wander in to gossip, drink, and consume more of her bread. The rest would go in the morning, consumed by those travelers who were foolish enough to curl up in a corner on the dirt floor of the public room or on one of the unwashed tables wrapped in threadbare blankets the owner supplied for a fee. "I've never seen the likes of such conditions," Megan told Ian time and time again. "A person would have to be mighty desperate to stay in a filthy, rat-infested hole such as this for the fee he charges." Then, as if there were a glimmer of a dream trying to make its way out, she'd inevitably add her own view of how things should be. "Imagine," she would speculate, "what could be done with this place if someone with a wee bit of ambition had a hand in running it. With a bit of ox blood mixed in with the dirt, the floors of this inn could be pounded down till they were as smooth and firm as marble. That'd make keepin' this pigsty clean easy. And some proper furniture, instead of planks set on barrels, fashioned by a man who knew how to use tools, would make this place respectable, inviting."

Ian, now a sergeant with more than three years' service

in the First Virginia Regiment, knew where Megan's thoughts were going. Still harboring his own dreams of returning to Scotland, and having no desire to say anything that would encourage Megan's plans, Ian cut her short. "I'm a soldier, Megan," he told her whenever that gleam would light her eyes and she'd speak of redoing a place she didn't even own. "Even if someone was willing to pay handsomely, I've not the time nor the desire to throw my efforts into a place I have no wish to be associated with. Besides," he'd add in all sincerity, "I truly don't see what you find so distasteful and unpleasant about what the innkeeper offers. The barracks of the fort are little better. And I've spent too many a night with little more than a blanket to shield me from rain, snow, and whatever nature picked to throw at us to scoff at any room that was dry and warm. I'm sure," Ian would respond innocently, "he does his best."

"The man's a lout," Megan would screech, half in anger, half in surprise that Ian would defend the man. "He beats his wife, drinks as much as he serves his customers, and deals in goods stolen from your very own regiment."

To this Ian would laugh, an action that would serve only to further infuriate the fiery Irish woman. "My dear lady," he'd roar, "half the people of this fair town steal us blind in one manner or another and sell what they get to the other half. Why do you think Colonel Washington forbids us from frequenting these places?"

"Well," Megan would huff, still upset at the fact that Ian had laughed at her, "your colonel's order doesn't seem to stop you from running down here every chance you can, now, does it?"

With as serious a look on his face as he could muster, Ian would explain, "Ah, well, I've an important position, and company business compels me to come this way . . ."

"Compels?" Megan would yell before he even finished. "Well, now, such fine words you've managed to learn. Next you'll be lording over me like a landowner."

By this time, well clear of the subject he wanted to avoid, and unable to hold himself back, Ian would drop the lively banter and end it by embracing his love and smothering her with kisses that always cooled her fiery Irish temper. Though she would never admit it, she was fond of those moments, moments that were so innocent, and so promising. Totally unaware of Ian's dedication to fight for the freedom of a land that was no longer his, Megan continued to dream her dreams. She yearned for the day when the two of them would share all their days like that in this strange and savage wilderness.

Megan was all dreamy-eyed and enthralled by the memory of one such moment as she kneaded the bread dough to the tune of a lively song. She failed to feel the cool breeze upon her back when the door to the cookhouse was slowly opened. Her humming of an old Celtic melody covered the hesitant footfalls behind her. It wasn't until the reek of rum overpowered the scent of vanilla and rising bread dough that Megan knew she was no longer alone. By then, all she had time to do was tense up to defend herself.

Even as he reached around in an effort to grab Megan's bosoms, the innkeeper was leaning over her. "You've been a good little lass to your soldier," he whispered in her ear. "Now it's time to share your treats with me."

Angered at being so careless as to leave the door unlatched as much as she was by being mauled by the filthy drunk who ran the tavern, Megan managed to bring her arms up before her and keep her employer from sinking his pudgy little fingers into her breasts. "You pig!" she screamed even as she began to push her pinned arms out in an effort to break free. "I'll, I'll . . ."

"You'll what, you little slut?" the innkeeper replied, half menacing, half mocking.

Straining, Megan didn't respond at first. Only when she relaxed a moment or two to catch her breath before redoubling her efforts to free herself did she hiss out her warning. "I'll cripple you, you filthy little worm. Now, let me go this . . ."

Feeling Megan's momentary slackening of resistance, the innkeeper eased his grip in preparation to spin her about to face him. But he took too long, for Megan pushed her arms out with a renewed burst of energy just as he was least expecting it. The timing, purely accidental, was perfect. Surprised by her sudden move, the innkeeper's arms flew apart wide enough for Megan to duck down and slip out from the tight spot she had been wedged in between her employer and the heavy table she had been laboring over. Caught off guard, the innkeeper fell forward, trying hard to regain his balance as he did so. Failing, he sprawled across the table, doubled over, and sent everything before him flying this way and that.

Positive that her escape was but momentary, Megan grabbed for a heavy wooden bowl that still contained a ball of dough, hoisted it above her head, and began to back away toward the door. She ignored the plop as the dough fell from the upturned bowl and hit the floor, for the innkeeper, furious and embarrassed, had managed to recover from his humiliation, turn, and face the young woman. "You little bitch," he growled. "How dare you treat me like that," he continued as he took a step toward Megan. "This ain't no nunnery, little girl, and I'll have my due for all the kindness I've shown you."

Despite her precarious predicament, Megan managed to laugh, even as she continued to inch her way to the door. "Kindness? I'll give you kindness." With that, before either knew what happened, Megan brought the solid wooden bowl about in an arc and smashed it into the side of the innkeeper's head. The bowl, being of solid wooden construction, didn't give a bit. But the innkeeper's head did. With a sickening look on his face as his eyes rolled up into his head, the man staggered, stopped, wavered this way, then that way, and finally toppled over, face first. Forgetting what he had threatened her with, all Megan could think of was what she had just done. Frightened, she didn't wait to see if she had really killed the man. Instead, she turned, flung open the door, and fled.

GRIM-FACED, Ian McPherson marched out of the barracks that housed Shaw's company and headed over to his commander, who was standing expectantly in the center of the parade ground. Even before Ian reached him, Shaw glumly called out, "Well?"

Ian stopped, forgot to salute, and looked down at a scrap of paper he was holding. He had no need to read the complete listing Ensign Flemming had made. Ian knew what Shaw was most concerned about and reported appropriately. "He's taken his musket," he stated frankly, "but," he added as he looked up in Shaw's eyes, "he left his bayonet and scabbard."

Shaw chuckled. "Can't say that I blame him. They make miserable candle holders."

Ian shared his commander's effort to lighten the mood and joined in the laughter. "Aye, sir, that they do."

"Well, now, Sergeant McPherson," Shaw asked as a smile brightened his face despite the insult that this most recent desertion left against his name, "what else belonging to the Royal governor did our reluctant volunteer make off with when he decided to up and leave this fine band of brothers?"

Letting his hand that held the list drop to his side, Ian repeated the litany of items in the sequence he felt was most important and not in alphabetical order, as Ensign Flemming had so painstakingly arranged them. "He took the cartridge box, of course, as well as his blanket and one belonging to another new fellow, the one named Supple."

"Didn't Supple notice the chill when his blanket was filched?" Shaw asked.

Ian shrugged. "It seems, sir, Supple is not used to living inside. The man claims he had no need of his blanket last night."

Shaw laughed again. "Well, I hope he doesn't suddenly develop a taste for the finer things in life, like warmth, before we can replace his blanket."

"Oh, I don't think that'll be much of a problem," Ian replied without hesitation.

"Well," Shaw asked incredulously, "how so?"

"The chaplain has told us, as you know, sir, time and again, that some benefit comes from even the most terrible events. Well, it seems a poor lad from the other company laid up in the hospital has left us for the hereafter, this very night.

Seeing as he wouldn't be needing his blanket any longer since the chaplain himself admits the boy's soul is headed where the fires burn hot, I arranged for a trade."

Showing sufficient righteous indignation befitting his position of an officer, Shaw looked at Ian though narrowed eyes. "Oh? And what did you trade for?"

Ian looked down on the ground before he answered, shuffled his foot, and then looked up and winked at Shaw. "Three days' double rum ration to the hospital steward."

Placing his hands on his hips, Shaw stepped back. "And who are the poor unfortunates who'll lose their rations. Not Supple, I hope."

"Oh, no, sir," Ian responded quickly. "Course not. It was ours I bargained away."

"You what?" Shaw demanded.

"Well, sir, you're always tellin' me that it's our duty to care for the men. Well, I saw this was a good time to do just that."

Shaw had brought his index finger up in front of Ian's face and was about to launch into a lecture on the perils of being too overzealous in one's duty when a commotion at the front gate interrupted his thoughts. Turning to see what the cause of the ruckus was, both he and Ian were surprised to see Megan, without a shawl, trying to push her way past the sentry to where the pair stood.

"Ian!" she yelled desperately as she made her way into the fort. She was breathless, hardly able to talk above a whisper, when she reached the two men. Clasping Ian's arm with a death grip, she pulled herself up to his face. "Ian!" she gasped between breaths. "I've killed the bastard. May the saints in heaven forgive me, I've killed the lout."

It took some doing, but between Ian and Shaw, the two men managed to calm Megan to where she was able to tell them the whole story in the privacy of Shaw's small room. "I didn't mean to kill 'im," she kept telling the two men as Shaw tilted a mug of rum to her lips while Ian, sitting on the floor at Megan's feet, held her shaking hand. "All I wanted to do was knock some sense into 'im. I will admit to that. But kill 'im, oh, lordy, I didn't . . ." With that, she lapsed into another bout of crying.

"Megan, darling," Ian whispered, patting her hand. "You've gotta pull yourself together. We've got to go over there, explain everything, and tell the constable what happened."

Lifting her head up, Megan looked at Ian with her red, puffy eyes, brimming with tears. She tried to smile, but couldn't. "They won't believe me. He's one of them, a citizen of the town. No one will believe my story. Everyone will think I started the trouble, that I encouraged him. I have no one to tell 'im it just isn't so." This statement, like others before it, was followed by a few sobs and an effort by Megan to bury her head on Ian's shoulder.

Getting up off the one knee he had been on, Shaw placed his hand firmly on Megan's shoulder. "Come along, girl," he stated in a stern, almost fatherly tone. "We'll all go down together. I'll vouch for ye. Between the three of us, we'll make them believe."

Though they had left the fort with great confidence, by the time they reached the tavern, much of that élan had eroded. With Ian and Shaw leading, and Megan following in their wake, head bowed and watching their feet, the trio entered the tavern, empty except for the innkeeper's wife, the constable, the undertaker, and the innkeeper's young daughters. Like soldiers trooping into battle, Ian and Shaw stormed into the dark room. Everyone turned and looked to see who these men were, and why they had come at such a time. The constable, never having any use for the soldiers at the fort, stood up from the seat where he had been consoling the widow. "The tavern is closed," he announced gruffly. "Go find another place . . ."

"Megan!" the sobbing innkeeper's wife shouted when she saw the young woman lurking in the shadow of the two soldiers. "Praise the lord, girl, you've come back."

Before anyone could move, the innkeeper's wife was on her feet, across the floor, and embracing a very confused and embarrassed Megan. "Oh, dear girl," the woman wailed as she rocked Megan to and fro. "It must have been terrible for you, finding my husband dead, on the floor like that." Then, pulling away until she held Megan's arms in her hands, the woman looked into Megan's wide eyes. "We were all afraid that you had lost your wits and fled into the woods or something. I was so worried for you, girl."

While all this was going on between Megan and the innkeeper's wife, Ian and Shaw looked over at each other. Neither man said a word, but both knew what the other was thinking. With a nod, Shaw signaled he would take the lead. "Ah, well, ma'am," he said haltingly as he interposed himself between Megan and the innkeeper's wife. As Shaw kept everyone's attention, Ian came up behind Megan, took her by the hand, and led her off to one corner. "The girl," Shaw went on to explain, "was quite shaken, as you can imagine. Well, she did take off. Ran right to the fort, she did, to tell her fiancé about your dear husband's untimely death."

Confused, Megan looked at Ian, who was watching the entire affair with a cold, detached stare, and then back at Shaw. "But . . ." she started to venture, until she felt the firm, hard grip of Ian's hands tightening about her arms. Stunned, she turned her head and looked into Ian's eyes, which failed to betray any emotion. His only response was a slight shake of the head, a motion he hoped no one else saw.

"Well," Shaw continued, raising his voice in an effort to cover the noise of the commotion that he heard going on between Megan and Ian behind him, "we rushed right down here to see what assistance we might render, seeing how our dear Megan worked here. We feel close to this town and the kindly gentleman who she worked for . . ."

"My husband, sir," the woman suddenly interrupted, "was no gentleman." Her words, as cold and uncompromising as her expression, caught Shaw off guard. "The words I would choose to describe him are not ones a true Christian woman would repeat, not in public. My only regret over this entire affair is that this poor girl is the one who found the lout."

Stepping back into the center of the room, the newly widowed woman pulled her shawl tightly about her and held it close to her bosom with both hands. "I knew someday his drinking would get the better of him," she stated slowly, deliberately. "That he'd come across someone who was unwilling to put up with his guff and give him his just reward was only a matter of time."

With those words, she stopped, turned, and gave Megan a cold, hard stare. Then she turned her head slightly and did the same to Shaw. Though he couldn't be sure of what, exactly, she was trying to convey to him, Shaw took it to mean that even if she did suspect Megan had a hand in her husband's death, she held no ill will against the girl.

As if she were satisfied that her meaning was understood, the innkeeper's wife looked down at the floor, thought for a moment, and continued, pacing about the room slowly as she did so. "Now I'm on my own, with two small children and a tavern I couldn't manage on my own if I tried. Though he was not the most Christian soul on this earth, he did see to our welfare, as far as food and shelter was concerned." Pausing behind a high-backed chair, the innkeeper's widow let go of her shawl and reached out to the side of the chair with both hands. After grabbing it firmly, she tilted her head slightly and gave Shaw a curious, sideward glance.

For a moment, Shaw hesitated, looking first at Megan, who stood staring at the widow, bewildered, then at Ian, who returned his intent stare. Finally, Shaw looked back at the widow. "Well, dear lady," he stated as he crossed the room and laid both of his hands on her shoulders as if to comfort her. "As I see it, you're not alone. Megan, a fine, God-fearing woman who's not afraid of an honest day's work, is here to help you in your time of need. Together with the man who will soon be her husband, a good soldier who'll keep an eye out for both of you, I'm sure you'll do just fine."

Turning, the widow looked up into Shaw's eyes. Reaching out with both hands, she took Shaw's right hand, lifted it to her cheek, and laid her face against the back of it for a moment. "Oh, bless you, sir," she said with words that sounded sincere, but somehow lacked true emotion. With a smile, she looked over at Megan. "Dear child, will you become my partner? Will you help me keep this humble tavern?"

Before Megan could utter a sound, Ian squeezed her arms till she all but cried out in pain, then replied for her. "Madam," he stated stiffly, "she'll be honored to continue to render your family whatever service she can."

With that, the innkeeper's widow faced Shaw. Taking his hand in hers, she looked deeply into his eyes. Shaw returned the stare, as if agreeing to a secret pact, and nodded.

THE couple sat in the quiet cookhouse for hours. Neither spoke as both were lost in thoughts they kept to themselves. Ian, enjoying an evening away from the barracks, was squatting on a three-legged stool before the fire in the tall, open hearth. With stick in hand, he stirred and poked at the burning embers. Every now and then he would corral a half-consumed log as it tumbled, fell, and threatened to flee the conflagration of those below it as they burned through and broke in half. His thoughts were unfocused and meandering. One moment, his memories were of his boyhood in the Highlands of Scotland, where he spent many a day doing just what he was doing. Then, in the twinkling of an eye, they led him to wonder halfheartedly what his life would be like after he was finished with the regiment and he could pursue his dream of returning to his beloved Scotland.

Ian had never given the idea of living with Megan on an isolated farmstead, like those he came across in pursuit of French and Indian raiders, much thought. It was a hard life. He could see it in the eyes of the farmers and their families. It demanded their every waking hour, their every ounce of energy. They were constantly at the mercy of the weather, the seasons, and, when the mood took them, Indians who traveled many miles to destroy all they came across in an orgy of blood and fire. It was a hard and demanding life, one whose only reward, it seemed to Ian, was an early grave.

Across the room, while Ian's nimble mind swung from memories that were warm and cherished to thoughts that were as dark and foreboding as the night sky outside, Megan sat in the corner. She had retreated there, curling up into a ball as she had done when she was but a child and wished to make herself as small and inconspicuous as she could. For her, the flickering flames bathing the room in reddish tones were far from being soft, warm, and comforting. Rather, they were harsh and sinister, like the terrible deed she had been party to that day. With her eyes fixed and unflinching, she stared at the spot where the innkeeper's body had lain until Ian and Shaw had removed it. Megan wondered how she would ever bring herself to accept what she had done in that one moment of passion that now haunted her every thought.

It had been her fault, she told herself over and over. All of it. Ian had been right, she realized now. She had been a fool to come out here, following him like a common camp follower. It had been an even bigger mistake to accept the offer of a job in this tavern. Only now was she beginning to understand why Ian had repeatedly warned her that decent Christian women didn't work in such places. How foolish she had been, she kept telling herself over and over again. Foolish and inattentive to the ever-present evils that lurked about, waiting to snare careless, innocent, and foolish girls such as herself.

Without preamble, Megan spoke, as if to herself. "Perhaps I should go back."

Caught in the midst of a thought, it took Ian a moment or two to realize that Megan was still in the room, and that she was speaking. With a shake of his head, he turned and squinted at the darkness behind him until he caught sight of Megan lost in the deep shadows of the room. "Go back? Back where?" he asked innocently.

There was a pause, for Megan hadn't really thought that far ahead. "I don't know," she finally whispered. "Somewhere. Anywhere. Just go."

"Don't be daft, girl," Ian replied without thought. "You've nowhere to go. No one ever goes back to Ireland or England. Least not anyone such as we."

In a flash, the sudden contradiction between what he had just said and the driving force that gave his life meaning was obvious to Ian. Had he really meant what he had just said? Ian wondered. Was his own voice a voice of reason and his dreams those of a foolish patriot who still believed in a cause long ago lost and all but forgotten by the world?

Whether it was the tone of his voice or the harsh reality of her plight, Megan began to whimper, though she tried hard to hide it. "Oh, Ian, I'm so scared."

Knocked back to reality by Megan's words, Ian realized that his words had been cold and unfeeling. Standing up, he crossed the room to where Megan huddled. For a moment he stood over her, towering above the young Irish woman and reminding her of her father, tall, dark, and menacing. Unaware that she was doing so, she recoiled as far back into the corner as she could. Ian, sensing her unease, dropped to both knees as quickly as he could until their eyes were even and took both of her hands in his. "Dear girl," he pleaded, "I didn't mean to be so uncaring. Nor did I wish to frighten you so. I love you. I love you like I've loved no other. You must believe me."

Still unsure of herself, Megan held herself and her emotions in check. "But I've killed a man, Ian. There's blood on these hands," she said as she pulled her hands from his embrace and held them before her eyes, "The blood of an innocent man."

Unmoved by her claim, Ian took Megan's hands in his again and pulled them toward him. "Dear, sweet girl, I know what you've done, just as you know what I've done. A week doesn't go by without my rememberin' once or twice where I've been, and what I've had to do as a soldier. Do you think there is any difference in the eyes of God between taking the life of a man standin' fifty paces away and one who's right there, on top of you?"

He paused, hoping that his words would take root. "Megan, darling," he continued, "I was fourteen when I killed my first man. Fourteen! To this day," he stated solemnly, closing his eyes for a moment, "I can still see his eyes, eyes that told me he was just as frightened and scared as I was. Sometimes at night I see them staring at me as their owner's blood ran down the blade of my broadsword."

When he opened his eyes, Megan could see that they were moist, tearful. "Not every savage has red skin," he told her. "And not every animal lives in the forest. You did what you had to do, and for that you owe no one an apology. I only thank God that you're still here, alive and healthy, and able to share whatever time He sees fit to give us together."

Unable to resist Ian's logic, and badly in need of comforting, Megan lurched forward and wrapped her arms around Ian's neck as streams of tears, so long held back, burst forth. No more words were exchanged that night. No sounds other than an occasional sob were heard above the cracking of the dying fire in the hearth. Only dawn and the appearance of a sunbeam in the morning, falling upon the pair of young lovers huddled in the corner, broke their long embrace.

Albany, New York
November, 1757

LONG after the commander of the New York Frontier was convinced that the danger from the north had passed and had left Fort Edward, Thomas lingered. His reluctance wasn't due to the dark scar that neatly followed the trace of his hairline. He'd already managed to find a way of arranging his hair to cover that. Nor were his duties so pressing that there had not been ample opportunities for him to escape, for a few days, from the overcrowded chaos and stench of England's northernmost bastion in the colony of New York.

Everyone else, save Thomas, had seized any opportunity to escape the boredom of waiting for an attack that would never come. "Old Montcalm," Captain Lewis Fenton was fond of reminding everyone, "has thrown away his last good chance to roll us up like a ball of string and end this war with a French victory. Why," he would boast to his fellow officers almost nightly at the officers' mess, "if the old Frenchy had just pushed down that road another fourteen miles and knocked on the door of this fort, it would have been his for the asking." Others, who disagreed, took great pains to remind Fenton that Montcalm had neither the support of his Indian allies after the Fort William Henry massacre nor the necessary draft animals to haul his heavy ordnance overland to Fort Edward. Fenton, unconcerned with issues he termed trivial, persisted. "He threw it away, once and for all, I tell you. Now," he declared triumphantly, "when the spring comes, it'll be our turn to go north, though I can say I don't exactly fancy the trip."

Thomas barely managed to endure Fenton's frequent commentary on a campaign that had scarred him so deeply, both physically and mentally. Only the deep, almost crippling melancholy that gripped him kept Thomas from lashing out at a man whom he had once considered to be a funny fellow. For his part, Fenton, as well as the others of Webb's staff, left Thomas alone. In one sense, the savage's aborted attempt to scalp Thomas was a blessing. It gave him a ready excuse to remain apart from the others, free to wallow in his unending self-pity and brooding. He had no need to explain that the darkness that encased his heart in perpetual gloom and mourning was due to the death of a wisp of a drummer boy who could neither read nor write.

The memory of Drummer Perry Jones put Thomas at odds with his feelings concerning Katherine Van der Hoff, though she didn't know it. Thomas had always been a self-sufficient man, taught from earliest childhood that his world and fortunes would be whatever he could manage to secure on his own. He had never imagined, in all his travels, that passions and emotions could hold such sway over a human being. Love had always been an abstract concept, a silly notion that only poets and fools indulged in. It had never, as best as Thomas could remember, visited him. That he would discover such feelings for a boy he had known less than two weeks was mind-boggling. Though it was pure, innocent love, like that which a father holds for his own sons, the intensity with which it had burned him was no less searing than that which poets and playwrights spoke of in their many tales of love and romance.

It was this last point that soon came to dominate Thomas' thoughts as he found that he could no longer delay dealing with Katherine Van der Hoff again. It was clear, now as it had been from the beginning, that a woman such as Katherine had no place in her heart for love as Thomas now understood it. It would be, he reasoned with the same cold calculation that he used to measure military matters, a waste of time to try to educate her to the joys of such a love. And it was a most foolish notion, one that Thomas dismissed out of hand, to imagine that he could trick a woman such as Katherine into falling in love with him in a manner that would be mutually satisfying and enjoyable. No, Thomas concluded after weighing all possible options and alternatives. Whatever sort of relationship he established with Katherine Van der Hoff, if indeed he could still bring himself to do so, would have to be one that was strictly of convenience.

With those thoughts in mind, Thomas led his horse south, trailing behind the small escort. Somewhere in the fifty miles that lay between Fort Edward and Albany, a thought came to Thomas that promised to make his arrangement with Katherine Van der Hoff worthwhile and, perhaps, fulfilling. As his horse pushed on against the cold fall wind, tearing the last of the gold and brown leaves from the branches that hung overhead, Thomas mulled over again and again his feelings on his pending union with the merchant's daughter. By the time he had reached Albany, all his thoughts were in order. For the first time in months, he prepared to meet the woman he was destined to marry and satisfy his quest for fortune. That she would be able to satisfy his other needs remained to be seen.

The feeling of warmth that had greeted Thomas the first time he had stepped foot in the Van der Hoffs' Albany home was still there. It took but a minute for Thomas to push aside the sense of uneasiness he felt at being in a private residence after months of living in crowded military barracks, tents, and an occasional night curled up on the ground with nothing more than a bear skin and a blanket. The announcement by a slight serving girl that her mistress was ready to receive Thomas scattered these thoughts. Pausing only long enough to give his vest a slight tug and glance quickly in a mirror to ensure that his hairline was well concealed, Thomas followed the girl along the now familiar hall to where Miss Katherine Van der Hoff would be waiting.

Even as he approached the room where Katherine was waiting, Thomas was still unsure of how he would react. Though it had been only four months since he had last visited this house, much had changed within him. The fire and the passion of a military life, so badly bruised after Braddock's unfortunate adventure in the forests of western Pennsylvania, had been shattered, perhaps for good, by the recent experience at William Henry. Unlike the aftermath of the Braddock disaster, however, Thomas had a new aspiration to replace the quest for martial fame and glory that had so far eluded him. This time, there was no need to resort to liquor or brooding. This time, he had a goal that he could latch on to. The question running through Thomas' mind as he entered the room where Katherine sat, adorned in rich, dark green satins trimmed in fine Spanish lace, was what price this woman would demand of him, provided, of course, she agreed to the idea.

From her seat, Katherine, despite her efforts not to do so, looked up at Thomas' forehead. She had been forewarned of the wound he had received while tarrying about at Fort William Henry with the army. She was greatly concerned, since everyone who mattered knew of the incident, which left Katherine in an awkward position. Fortunately, Thomas' self-imposed exile had spared her the need to play the role of dutiful nurse and minister to the needs of the stricken warrior. With that concern aside, there was still the matter of the scar. While nothing changed Thomas' status and her ideas on his role in an arrangement, Katherine did harbor concerns that an obnoxious scar would make Thomas an oddity and an embarrassment. Though she had never planned to do more than what was called for concerning social engagements and such after her marriage to Thomas, the last thing she wanted was to be saddled with a husband whom everyone gossiped about and stared at for all the wrong reasons.

It took only a moment to erase all such fears and apprehensions. Rather than wear his hair pulled straight back and taut, as he had in the past, Thomas had managed to arrange it so that a decent tuft of hair hung down over the upper part of his forehead in a most striking and masculine way, concealing whatever damage the red savages had done to him. Freed of this worry, Katherine was able to flash her well-practiced smile and, with a graceful sweep of her right hand, direct Thomas to sit. "You can't imagine, sir," Katherine stated sweetly, "how concerned I have been over your wounds. Though I admire your sense of duty and desire to stay at your post in the service of your king, I was most distressed by your long absence."

Caught up in his own thoughts, and very self-conscious of his appearance, Thomas missed Katherine's reference to George II as "your king." Instead, he responded to her overture by raising his hand to his forehead and waving it about cautiously in the air a few inches from it. "Madam," he replied stiffly, and in earnest, "I consider myself most fortunate to have my hair, not to mention a head to store it upon."

Thinking this a light and gay repartee to her show of deep concern, Katherine allowed herself to laugh for a moment over Thomas's effort to be witty and charming.

Though he was holding his responses and emotions tightly in check, Thomas couldn't help but flinch and noticeably recoil at Katherine's reaction. Ever mindful of all that occurred and was said around her, Katherine took note of Thomas' response and amended her behavior quickly and flawlessly. Reaching out, she placed her soft white hand upon the rough hand he was clutching his leg with. "I was worried about you, Thomas."

Clearing his throat with a nervous cough he covered with his free hand, he looked down at her hand, then up into her eyes. "Yes, madam, I am sure," he said with a lack of concern matched only by Katherine's absence of sincerity.

Pulling her hand away as soon as it was proper to do so,

Katherine turned her full attention to pouring the tea that had been set out before her prior to Thomas' entry. "I am so glad, Thomas, that the dreadful affair to the north, as costly as it was to both this colony and your country, is over."

Unsure exactly what she meant, but assuming that it was only the campaign for William Henry and not the war or Amherst's aborted seizure of Louisbourg, Thomas searched for a suitable reply. "Ah, well, we were fortunate in that the marquis did not have the wherewithall to press his advantage. Otherwise, we'd all need to learn French, a most dreadful language for me."

Better prepared this time, Katherine glanced up to see if she could tell if this last comment had been meant as a joke. Unsure, she satisfied herself with a simple smile. "Well, sir, I have all the confidence that the Crown's forces will bring this war to an acceptable conclusion, and soon." Thomas, busy accepting the small, delicate cup of tea from Katherine while his mind worked on framing a serious, yet acceptable, response, wasn't permitted the opportunity to deliver that reply before Katherine continued her thought. "That, dear Thomas, and a final settling of an arrangement between us would be, to me, a perfect way to end this sad year."

Freed from the burden of having to tiptoe about in a discussion on politics and warfare that he was not at all interested in engaging in with her, Thomas launched into the matter that had been weighing heavily on his mind. "Ah, yes. Those would be very, very laudable achievements, my dear lady. Unfortunately, we two can influence only one of them. And it is in pursuit of that matter which I have called upon you today."

Happy that the preliminaries were at an end, Katherine leaned back in her seat, took a sip of her tea, and pretended to relax while she listened to what Thomas had to say.

"Needless to say, Katherine, I have given the matter concerning our union much thought." Having mulled over what he would say for days, Thomas was determined to forge ahead, even if it came out somewhat less than romantic. Looking down so as not to be distracted or befuddled by Katherine's large, brown, piercing eyes, Thomas continued. "I find our marriage just as appealing now as it was when we first discussed it." Though this was, in fact, a lie, Thomas knew it didn't make any difference. There would be many more lies to follow, so starting out with a small one was of little consequence. "Other thoughts, since that time, have, quite naturally, wound their way though my mind."

Rather than the complete and unconditional acceptance of her proposal that she had anticipated, Katherine was unprepared for Thomas' setting of conditions. Visibly caught off guard, she set her teacup down and clasped her hands tightly in her lap. "Why, yes, of course," Katherine stated sharply, momentarily interrupting Thomas' thoughts. "I rather expected things would not be as idyllic and easy as we first thought, when the idea of marriage was fresh. These things are never quite as easy as one imagines in the beginning, are they?"

Looking up, Thomas could see that Katherine was on edge. Taking her last comment as an admission that she was willing to accept some terms and conditions, Thomas went on, maintaining his gaze in Katherine's eyes in an effort to gauge her true reaction. "Katherine, I've had nothing, until now, but the army. I have loved it, served it, and given my all to it since I was old enough to take to the field. It has, until recently, meant everything to me. But within these past few months, I have come to learn that there is something even more important to me, something that makes any reward or honor the army could ever hope to confer on a man such as me trivial."

Pausing, Thomas waited to see if Katherine would respond to his soliloquy. Katherine, however, did not move. She neither spoke nor changed her expression. Instead, she sat there still, gripping her hands, waiting, almost breathlessly, for Thomas to state what he would demand of her.

"Katherine," he stated in a tone that was driven by the feelings that lay in his heart, "I want a son."

For a moment there was silence, as Katherine absorbed this idea and waited, expectantly, for more. When nothing else followed but the continuous, hard gaze of the man she had selected for marriage, Katherine blinked, drew in a deep breath, and ran the idea quickly through her well-ordered brain. That she would have to endure certain wifely duties was, and had always been, a given. Both her station in life and the society she cherished above all else demanded as much. Yet she had never, in all her nicely balanced calculations, addressed this particular aspect of the proposition in such harsh, uncompromising terms. Looking again at Thomas' forehead in an effort to detect any hint of his scar, Katherine quickly considered his demand. Satisfied that both his physical appearance and his request were reasonable and acceptable, Katherine looked into his eyes and gave him a slight smile that conveyed no warmth. Nothing, in truth, had changed from when she had first set her sights upon him. Her assumption that he, a dedicated professional soldier, busy with tending to the king's business, would leave her to manage her father's when it came time for her to inherit it hadn't been changed by his new demand. "Why, yes, Thomas," she finally replied. "It is only natural that we cement our bond with heirs that will carry on both our family names and fortunes."

That she intended to dominate how those children would be raised was, in her mind, no more a question than who would control the immense fortune that she expected to inherit. There would be sufficient time, after the marriage, to discuss such details.

Thomas, more than satisfied with Katherine's response, relaxed for the first time. Even as he was reaching out to pry one of her hands free from her lap, the image of Drummer Perry Jones, his smiling, freckled face all but lost under the oversized hat he wore, flashed though his memory. Bending over, he kissed the soft, cold white hand he held. "Thank you," he stated in relief. "Thank you, my dear Katherine."

CHAPTER TWENTY-ONE

Quebec, Canada
January, 1758

T HE MAIN COURSE of the meal had yet to be served, and already Anton was sorry that he had consented to attend the formal dinner in lieu of his commander. Within minutes of his arrival at the residence of the intendant, it was quite obvious to Anton why Captain Gerrad had found his duties so pressing. Cards, it seemed, despite the prohibition against gambling, was the focus of the evening. "Your captain's luck, Lieutenant," one of the ladies informed Anton when it was found out that he was sent as a supernumerary, "has managed to burrow deep into Monsieur Bigot's pocket. He is quite anxious to reclaim his money. So, do not be upset if you are ignored."

Thus, rather than being a relaxing and enjoyable evening away from the tedium of his cramped quarters, as he had hoped, Anton found himself trying hard to remain inconspicuous. If it weren't for the promise of enjoying fine foods and delicacies that could not be found anywhere else in New France, Anton would have excused himself and fled into the bitter cold of the long, harsh Canadian night. But good food was hard to come by in a city where horse meat was being issued to the troops as well as the civilians. So the young officer of artillery swallowed his pride. With the same practiced skill that he had found necessary when dealing with regular officers who had been sent from France to save this colony, Anton passed his time by watching the comings and goings of those belonging to New France's ruling elite.

It wasn't long before Anton was able to see the people around him as little more than the cast of a play with a poor plot. In one room, those gentlemen and officers who had both the courage and the funds to do so played cards. Clustered around them stood a group of spectators made up of men who lacked one or the other and women who were anxious to see who would walk away with the most and have, if they were lucky, an opportunity to bestow their favors upon them. It was easy to tell who the winners were by the number of people gathered behind their chairs as well as by the posture of the players themselves. Anton had seen men face death in battle with far calmer expressions than those worn by gentlemen who were having a run of misfortune. Hunched over, they would stare at the handful of cards that foretold their financial ruin and disgrace. Were it not for the fact that many of these men were involved in the buying and selling of goods and food upon which the majority of the colony depended, the whole scene would have been comical. But Anton could not ignore the fact that money lost here, in this room, would be made good by the practice of charging astronomical prices for food, supplied by the Crown, to the hapless habitants of a colony that was forever teetering on the brink of starvation. Profits of 40 and 50 percent, most of which was gambled away right here, in the very room Anton was standing in, were not unheard of. Tiring of this pastime, Anton made his way into the ballroom, where others, equally bored with the serious business of wagering, were gathered.

Though the atmosphere there was not nearly as intense as it was in the room where card playing would go on until the following dawn, the pursuits of the guests populating the other rooms were little better. In small clutches or pairs, they stood about, drinking whatever was offered them and gossiping about one thing or another. Some, by the glimpses they slyly tried to catch of him as he went by, were, no doubt, discussing him. After a while, Anton caught himself glancing in any mirror he passed, looking to see if he were breaking out with the pox or bearing the mark of Cain upon his forehead. How quickly, he realized, one became paranoid when surrounded by paranoid people.

In an effort to escape the lot of them, Anton made his way into the hall, where he found a chair off to one corner next to a small table with a book sitting on it. Taking a seat, he lifted the book, held it in front of his face, and absentmindedly began to thumb through the pages. Unfortunately for Anton, it was so dull that after spending less than five minutes glancing over the flowery words that filled it, he still had no idea what it was about. But that was of little consequence, for by then his attention had been captured by another, more enjoyable diversion. The appearance of a girl, busily moving from the rear of the house toward the dining room, where the table was being prepared for the long-awaited feast, caught his attention.

While other servants had passed among the guests all night without Anton taking any notice of them, this girl was different. At first Anton thought that it was the slight limp, caused by her favoring of her left leg, that set her apart from the others. Quickly, however, he dismissed this, for the limp was noticeable, he noted, only if one watched her take several steps. In a palace where there were many servants, all attired in the same austere costume, he never would have taken enough time to observe that minor deficiency if something else hadn't made an impression upon him.

Maintaining the pretense that he was reading the book he held, Anton looked over the top edge of the printed gibberish and began to observe this girl's every move, studying each and every feature and line he could manage to see. She was of slight build, almost a wisp of a girl. And though her skin was as pale as fine porcelain, it was unlike the pasty or sickly color favored by the well-to-do female guests who ignored her. The one feature that seemed to set her apart was her flaming red hair. Framed by this and the crisp white cap she wore on the back of her head, her face appeared to be most angelic and, despite the heavy trays of food she carried, quite serene.

Absorbed by his clandestine observation of the serving girl with flaming hair, Anton lost track of time as his imagination began to run wild. She was, he guessed at first, a Norman, or perhaps a Breton, sent to New France from the stormy, wind-swept coast of that rugged province to serve the needs of this outpost's petty nobility. Or maybe, he ventured, she was the daughter of a voyager, left here in Quebec while her father roamed the vast wilderness in search of beaver pelts. Perhaps her past was far less adventurous than that. Instead, Anton imagined, she was the offspring of a local merchant who, oppressed by outrageous prices for all goods imported from France, had been forced to send his only child to labor for the very people who were squeezing the lifeblood from the people they were supposed to be serving. So intrigued by the many wonderful possibilities this girl's past conjured up in his mind, Anton found the call to dinner unwelcomed.

Still, once he was seated, Anton discovered that the meal placed before him was an adequate compensation for the interruption. Seated between a rather healthy woman who had difficulty maintaining her bulk on the small chair she was seated upon and another woman of great beauty but no intelligence, Anton devoted his full attention to the food set before him. Made from peas as rare in New France as hard currency, the pea soup, prepared with hearty portions of onion and salt pork, was worth the agony he had endured waiting for the meal. It took all of Anton's effort to remember that he was seated among gentry, where table manners acceptable in camp and barracks were not appreciated. Though he had no doubt that his presence would never again grace this table, he was still an officer of the king, and therefore a gentleman. And while others slurped their soup with the most vulgar noises, he would conduct himself as his rank and station dictated.

It was only when he had finished, and the empty bowls were being removed from the table by servants passing silently behind them, that he was jarred back to his previous thoughts of the girl. When a thin arm, pale and dotted with clusters of freckles, appeared before him, snatching the bowl he had cleared of all traces of soup, Anton could not keep from twisting his head about and looking into the face of the girl. For her part, though, she tried with all her might to maintain her composure and keep her gaze down, as her position required. When she felt Anton's eyes upon her, the serving girl turned her head, ever so slightly, looked into Anton's eyes, and smiled.

That single smile was, for Anton, his undoing. It had been so unexpected, so innocent. Yet, he told himself as he absent-mindedly muddled his way through the rest of the meal, it was meant to be. Fate, the strange force that holds sway over the affairs of so many men, had led him here. It had permitted him to set eyes upon a girl who, in his heart, he knew was meant to be his. As the soup gave way to fish stew, to be replaced by generous portions of roasted rabbit, and, in turn, followed by apple tarts, Anton felt himself forced to consume his food hurriedly in the vain hope that he would be afforded the opportunity to see his red-haired serving girl sooner.

Across the table sat a minor functionary of the governor. He had been watching Anton throughout the meal. Even now, as the last of the empty plates were being removed, and Anton continued to stare at the redheaded girl as if she were the only other person in the room, the man kept an eye on Anton. When their host decided it was time for him to return to his cards, he stood, signifying that the meal was over. Those who had been playing before the meal scrambled to the card room to pick up where they had left off. Others, with wife or mistress in hand, made for the ballroom. The remainder, mostly women whose spouses were consumed by their need to win, no matter how long it took, gathered about with friends and confidantes to exchange whatever new news or gossip had come to them during the meal. Within minutes, all that remained in the dining room was a table crowded with empty plates, drained wineglasses, and Anton. He sat there for several minutes, staring at the door, as he waited for the red-haired serving girl to reappear. Only after waiting what seemed to be an eternity did Anton rise out his seat and retreat back to his corner, where the dull book sat, patiently awaiting his return.

Within minutes of resuming his former posture, the gentleman who had been seated across from him during the meal slowly promenaded down the hall to where Anton sat. Without so much as a preamble, the government functionary looked down at Anton and gave him a sly smile. "She is a handsome woman, Lieutenant Chevalier, but not a suitable match for an officer with a future."

Looking up at the fellow who sported a belly that had spent too many hours at the dinner table, Anton closed his book and laid it in his lap. "Oh, well," Anton stumbled as he searched for some way to escape being labeled wrongly. "I was simply admiring her beauty. Nothing more."

The governor's man now laughed. "Please, sir. Do not mistake me for a fool. I saw that look in your eye every time she entered the room. For that matter, everyone else did, too. It is, after all, a pleasure to see a woman who is not trying to copy what she believes is the latest style in Versailles."

Not sure where this man was going with this conversation, Anton placed the book back on the table and stood up. "I do admit that she was difficult to ignore, and that I perhaps paid too much attention to her. But that is all. She's little more than a passing thought."

"Ah, yes, well, I am sure she was," the government official replied as he stepped back and bowed his head slightly. "I am sorry that I mistook your attention for the girl. Is there any way in which I could make good my presumptuous innuendo?"

Without hesitation, almost without thinking, Anton blurted a request. "Well, since you are a gentleman, and appear to be a man who commands vast knowledge, perhaps you could help me with one small matter. You wouldn't happen to know," Anton asked without hesitation, "where that young lady resides, would you?"

THE bitter cold winter wind, slicing its way along the tight, narrow streets of Quebec, hit Anton square on as he rounded the corner. For a moment, he was rocked back by a wall of frigid air that took his breath away. Yielding to the wind, Anton retreated back behind the corner, where he leaned against the cold stone building that was now serving him as a wind break. While he struggled to regain his breath, Anton pulled his scarf up over his mouth and nose a little higher. Then, with one hand planted squarely on top of his hat to keep from losing it and the other holding up the thick wool scarf, Anton gave his advance on the convent another try.

His progress was slow, not only due to the wind but also to the icy snow on the street that had been packed down by many a passing foot, hoof, and sled runner. He thought about going into the fresh, untrampled snow, and thus avoiding all the hazards of the ice. But to do so meant that he would have to beat down his own trail through drifts that were higher than the tops of his boots. This would have left every stitch of his clothing wet, which would have made him quite vulnerable to any number of illnesses that plague soldiers cooped up in winter quarters. After giving the matter a few seconds' thought, Anton opted to stay on the road, since there was only a slight chance that he would slip and fall while there was little doubt that tromping through snow would leave him soaked to the bone.

When he finally reached the door of the convent, Anton paused a moment while he tried to decide which hand to use to grasp the heavy metal ring that served as a door knocker. It was a plain piece of iron, with no effort made to adorn it or the striking plate. Like the door itself, it was massive, functional, and rather ordinary. Letting go of his scarf, Anton reached up, pried the ring free, for it had frozen to the door, and rapped it twice. Satisfied that someone had to have heard his summons, Anton let go and placed his hand over his scarf again.

But no one came to the door, not at first. Worried that perhaps his first effort had not been heard, Anton tried again. This time, the door opened slightly, even before he could return his hand to its task of securing his scarf over his mouth. Through the crack, Anton caught sight of an eye staring at him. "Monsieur," a harsh feminine voice called out. "What brings you here on a day such as this?"

Shivering, and not quite sure what to say under these circumstances, Anton stuttered, as much from his unusual request as from the cold, "To see a girl I was told lived here."

The eye narrowed till it was little more than an angry slit. "Monsieur, this is a convent, not a brothel."

Then, without a word, the door started to close. Instinctively, Anton thrust the toe of his boot into the narrowing gap in an effort to keep the door open. "It's not at all like that, madam," Anton pleaded as the door slammed against his boot and sent a wave of pain up his leg. "I would like to be introduced to this girl and court her properly, as prescribed by the mother church. Please let me in. My intentions are honorable."

Though he hated the manner in which he had been forced to blurt his intentions, his words had the desired effect. The pressure on his toe let up as the door opened a bit wider. "Wait here," the voice commanded before the door was firmly slammed shut once Anton's foot had been removed. For several minutes he stood there, long enough to realize that he was behaving like a fool. Within minutes he found himself wondering if, perhaps, it would be best if he gave up his efforts and left for a warm place where he could salvage whatever pride he had left and thaw out.

Just as quickly as this resolve had been finalized, and he was preparing to put it into action, the door that had been bolted shut to him swung open. Before him stood a nun, nearly as tall as he. Another nun, perhaps the one who had answered the door, was peeking around the corner of it. "Monsieur," the tall, stone-faced nun announced with a deep, resonant voice, "you may enter."

Slightly intimidated by this woman's stature and manner, Anton crossed the threshold of the convent, removed his hat, and gave the guardian of the door a nod. "Thank you, Sister, for letting me . . ."

"I am the mother superior of this convent, charged with protecting my flock and the sacred word of our Lord," she pronounced.

Though he had had no way of knowing he had offended her, Anton acknowledged his error by giving the woman a deep bow while sweeping his hat across his chest. "My humble apologies, Mother Superior, for disturbing you." After waiting for her to accept his apology for a minute or more, Anton cocked his head and looked up at the nun who had neither moved nor changed her expression. He quickly realized that if he allowed her to do so, she would keep him in his awkward position forever. Unsure of what church protocol was in such matters, Anton stood upright, pulled himself and whatever dignity he had left together, and stated his business. "Yesterday evening there was a dinner held at Monsieur Bigot's palace. One of the serving girls, a redheaded woman, who was present at that affair, I was informed, lived here under your protection. I was, how can you say, quite taken by her charm and manner. Therefore, I have come here in the hope of securing an introduction."

The mother superior, having eyed Anton from head to toe while he was fumbling about with his introduction, hesitated while she considered the matter. "On your word as a gentleman, and an officer of the king, are your intentions honorable and pure?" she finally asked.

"Yes, Mother Superior, quite honorable."

Again there was a long pause as the Mother Superior considered the matter further. Finally, she turned to the door-keeper, who had been hovering in the shadows. "Sister Angela, go bring Sarah here."

Not quite sure what to expect next, Anton removed his cape, now soaked from the snow that had been driven into it during his trek to the convent. Unused to dealing with the stern and independent nuns, Anton held his cape over his arm a moment before realizing that the mother superior had no intention of offering to take it for him. Sheepishly, for he realized she knew what he had been thinking, Anton walked over to a stool near the fire and draped his cloak over it, hoping that he wasn't violating some sort of taboo.

Sister Angela returned while Anton was tending to his cloak. Standing upright, he turned and found himself face-to-face with the red-haired girl. "I am afraid," the mother superior stated as Anton gazed at the girl, "I do not know your name."

"Lieutenant Anton Louis Chevalier," Anton replied without taking his eyes off the girl.

"This is Sarah Carter," the mother superior announced. "She is a resident of the colony of Massachusetts, currently waiting for someone to arrange a ransom for her."

This time, Anton did turn and look at the mother superior, who now wore a self-satisfied expression on her face. When he looked back at the girl, Anton saw the same sad smile she had given him before, at the meal. With a little curtsy, she welcomed him. "Monsieur," she stated in a soft, almost breathless voice, "I am honored that you remembered me and took time to inquire after my health."

Though her accent was quite pronounced, Sarah's French was far better than Anton's stilted English. He therefore replied in his native tongue. "Ah, well, I was hoping that, perhaps . . ." he started as he nervously glanced first at Sister Angela, who stood behind Sarah, then at the mother superior.

"You may visit with the lieutenant," the mother superior stated firmly to Sarah, "until afternoon prayers. Sister Angela will remain with you and serve as chaperone."

With a curtsy, Sarah thanked the mother superior as she withdrew. Then, turning to Anton, she offered him a seat on one of the few chairs in the room. While he seated himself, Sister Angela withdrew to a seat across the room from which she could watch the two, as well as hear every word. Not until both Anton and Sister Angela were seated did Sarah limp over to the last chair in the otherwise barren room and take her own seat.

"I must admit," Anton started, the nervousness in his voice showing with every word, "I did not know quite what to expect. I only knew that I could not let this matter drop without at least knowing your name and meeting you."

Innocently, Sarah tilted her head. "What matter, monsieur, would that be?"

Anton was unsure whether she was being coy and simply playing with him or if she truly did not understand his motivation as well as the mother superior seemed to. For a moment, he tried to find a clever way of phrasing his response, but found that he could not do so. The pale blue eyes of the girl, staring intently at his while they awaited an answer, were quite disarming. "I do not know exactly how to put this, so forgive me if I seem like a clumsy oaf as I stumble about in search of the right words."

"Oh, please, monsieur, do not be afraid if you cannot find the right word," Sarah replied. "I know what it is like to be unable to find words to express myself, especially with my miserable French."

"Mademoiselle," Anton ventured, "there is no need for you to apologize for your French. It is quite clear and distinct. I only wish that my English were half as good."

Sarah's laugh was hesitant, almost restrained. "You flatter me," Sarah replied.

Looking across the room, Anton took note of Sister Angela, who made sure that he remembered that she was there and could hear everything by showing him a stern expression. Trying his best to ignore the nun, Anton returned his full attention to Sarah. "Tell me, if you would, how a girl from an English colony found her way to a nunnery in New France."

With a voice that never wavered, Sarah related her story to Anton with words that were as clear and concise as her limited command of French allowed. She told of the farm she and her husband had established in the Berkshire Mountains of Massachusetts, not far from the boundary of New York. She told him of the small family they had started, a boy of three and a newborn girl. Then, without changing her tone or expression, she recounted for Anton how the Indians had come, without warning, late in the fall of 1756. A raiding party, led by a Canadian voyager, descended upon their small farm while they were all out gathering the last of their corn. There had been no time to run for the house to fetch weapons foolishly left behind. Nor had there been time to hide the children. "Within minutes," Sarah told Anton with a sigh, "they were upon us."

With his face covered in an expressionless mask, Anton listened as Sarah told of the murderous march that took them to Canada. "At first, the Indians didn't feed us, not even the children, though they cried so for food. I had all I could do to keep them quiet, lest our captors became angry and punished us. It wasn't until we started to fall behind that they shared what little food they had for themselves with us. I suspect that this had been taken from another white farm they had attacked before ours, for three of the braves carried scalps that were but a few days old." Then, casting her eyes on the ground, Sarah digressed for a moment. "Often during that horrible experience, I looked at those scalps, especially the long one that could only belong to a woman. I asked the Lord, time and time again, why they had to pick our farm second, and not first, for I came to envy the woman whom they had slain." Then she lifted her gaze to Anton. "You see, monsieur, had they come to our humble farm first, it would have been my scalp hanging from the Indian's belt. My suffering, the horrible suffering my innocent children were enduring, would have been over."

As if Anton's wishes had deemed it to ring, the bell for afternoon prayers sounded. Shaken from her trance, Sarah stood up and pulled away from Anton. "Forgive me, monsieur. Sometimes I forget myself. I hope that your visit was not a disappointment." Then, without waiting for a response, Sarah turned and fled through the door that Sister Angela had opened when she had brought her in to meet Anton.

With no trace of an expression, Sister Angela rose and went to the door that led to the street. "Monsieur, it is time for you to leave."

Slowly, Anton gathered up his cloak and hat as he made his way to the door. When he was there, next to Sister Angela, he paused. "What of her husband and children? Where are they?"

Sister Angela shrugged. "We do not know. Perhaps they are still with the tribe that captured them, adopted by a savage who had lost a loved one in your wars. Perhaps they never survived the running of the gauntlet, an experience which left Sarah crippled. Or perhaps they are at peace and with God. Who knows?" Then, unable to resist making a comment on the manner in which the captives were treated, the nun added, "Sarah is a victim of a barbaric custom that humans are dealt with as if they were nothing more than cattle, to be bartered, purchased, or traded. War or no war, human beings deserve to be treated better."

Then, without another word, Sister Angela shoved Anton out into the bitter, howling wind using the door. Strangely, the coldness that bit his exposed skin did not in any way compare to the sting that he felt in his heart as he pondered his short visit with Sarah.

CHAPTER TWENTY-TWO

The Shenandoah Valley, Virginia
April, 1758

I N THIS, the beginning of the fifth year of war for Virginia, the coming of spring had become a dreaded event. For the settlers who hung on to the western fringe of that colony's frontier in the face of danger, it was both a time to plant and a time to prepare for the beginning of another season of death. Already word had spread down the valley to Winchester that a French-led war party had wiped out an entire community of mote than fifty souls near Woodstock, Virginia. Those who were not killed outright at Mills Creek were carried away to be tortured or adopted by the Indians as they saw fit. Even those farmers who lived within easy reach of Winchester itself were not immune to the dangers that seemed to lurk on the very edge of every farm clearing and wood lot. Alarms, real and imagined, caused the troops of the Virginia Regiment to scurry hither and yon in pursuit of imagined phantoms or war parties that had long since moved on.

With as much knowledge of the area as any white, Ian McPherson found himself increasingly leading more and more of these desperate forays in pursuit of a foe who was seldom seen but often felt. On this April day, the crisp, fresh scent of newly bloomed flowers and lush green grass was tinted by the reek of torched homesteads and the pungent odor of burned flesh. The attacks around Winchester, in comparison to those that ravaged the upper valley, were trivial and infrequent. But to the hapless farmer who caught the brunt of these trifling raids, they were just as deadly.

With a detachment of a dozen members of the regiment and a handful of locals bent on reaping whatever vengeance they could, Ian made his way to the site of a homestead just west of town. Word that a party of Indians was sighted in the area was enough to cause the commander of Fort Loudoun to shake out a patrol in the hope that it would catch the enemy before they struck or, failing that, dissuade them from lingering in the area. This had been the sole military strategy of the Virginia Regiment since the late days of 1755, and with each passing year it proved time and again to be a bankrupt one. "Always too little, too late," the farmers visiting Winchester bitterly complained whenever they spotted a member of the Virginia Regiment. "The Frenchies and savages know where all your forts are and what you're up to before you do. They avoid ya like the plague and strike where you're not. All the money and effort spent on your fine forts, fancy uniforms, and pay is a waste."

To these comments Ian had no response, for the allegations were true. In the years of 1756 and 1757, he could not think of a single instance when any of the forays he went on prevented a raid or arrived in time to save a hapless victim. It was an exercise in futility, and everyone involved knew it.

Still, Ian told himself over and over that they were doing something meaningful and good. That thought, and the promise of land after the war, were the only things that allowed him to endure the squalid conditions of garrison life and the abuses freely heaped upon them by the residents of Winchester who slept peaceably under the shadow of Fort Loudoun.

Such concerns were far from Ian's mind at the moment. It did not pay to let one's mind wander too far from the task at hand when on a scout. More than once the Indians had intentionally torched a farm in the hope of luring a patrol of soldiers into an ambush. And more than once, members of the Virginia Regiment obliged them. Ian, now a well-seasoned veteran, had no intention of allowing that to happen to himself or his men. Depending more on his senses than on what he saw, Ian knew when to slack off and move along at a good pace, and when to proceed with caution. Whether it was the rustling of a bush or the unnatural stillness that caused the hairs on the back of Ian's neck to rise did not matter. He came back with every man he took out and, while he seldom did any good, he took pride in the fact that he caused no harm to his own.

Instinctively, he knew danger was at hand. With all the caution of a cat creeping up on its prey, Ian slowed his pace, making his way forward slowly, carefully. Behind him, the soldiers in his detachment noted Ian's increased vigilance and took care to ready themselves for whatever might happen. The civilians, serving their mandatory militia time, didn't quite understand why the soldiers suddenly changed their attitude and postures, but followed suit and took up a keener watch.

Then, off to his right, a movement caught his eye. In a single swift motion, Ian twisted his entire body about, brought his musket up to the ready, and prepared to fire. But he didn't fire. At the last moment, as his finger began to apply pressure to the trigger, he checked himself. Something inside him told him to hold, and hold he did. Though he kept his piece tucked up tightly into his shoulder, he eased his cheek off the stock and looked down the long barrel of his musket at what he had been ready to fire at.

The form moving toward him appeared to be more an apparition than a human. It was pale white, half the size of a normal human, and advancing with an unwavering deliberateness that ignored all obstacles. James McPike, who had come up on Ian's shoulder and had been ready to back up Ian after he had fired his shot and was reloading, lowered his musket. "What in blue thunder?"

With nervous tension that had found no relief, causing him to shake, Ian also lowered his piece. "It's a child. A white child."

For a moment, the two fully dressed men, armed to the teeth and ready to kill, watched as the naked child continued to stagger toward them. At first Ian thought that the child hadn't seen them, that it was in such a stupor, it would continue to go on walking, right through the file of men now gawking at it. But it stopped, not more than an arm's length from them. For a long, awkward moment, the boy, perhaps four or five by Ian's reckoning, stood before the men, gazing at each of their faces in turn. The bewildered, unblinking expression the child wore did not change the entire time. Ian studied the child, noting the innumerable cuts, bruises, burn marks, and gashes that covered the boy's filthy body.

From down the file, a man moaned. "Dear God, what have they done to him?"

That comment snapped the spell that had fallen over Ian. Handing his musket to McPike, he carefully moved toward the boy, fearful that any sudden move might cause him to flee. But the boy just stood there, watching Ian as he knelt down before him and slowly reached out and gently grasped him by the shoulders. "You're gonna be all right, now. You hear?"

No acknowledgment to Ian's gentle words was returned. The boy simply stood there, between Ian's callused hands, like a stone statue, staring at him with brown eyes that were as vacant as a bottomless pit. Calling over to McPike to give him a hand, Ian quietly ordered the rest of his patrol to circle about and keep their eyes opened. Already the fear that he and the rest of the men had spent far too long looking at the boy and not keeping an eye open for further dangers was gnawing at him. "Jimmy," he told McPike as he unrolled his blanket and wrapped it about the boy, "I'm leavin' you and the new man here to watch over the boy. There may be others. Or the savages might be huntin' their little lost trophy. I'm going to circle about the area with the rest of the boys, just to make sure."

They spent about half an hour cautiously circling the spot

where James McPike, a new member of the regiment, and the boy huddled. And while Ian wanted to make sure they didn't miss any other strays who might be wandering about the woods aimlessly, he also needed to consider the safety of his patrol. While it was true that if the boy had been bait, the Indians would have already jumped them, it was equally true that the savages might come back in search of their missing captive. With the afternoon quickly waning, and having no desire to run into a band of Indians at night, Ian called off the search and led his patrol back to Winchester along a different route. As McPike explained to the new soldier, "We get to see twice the ground and keep any unfriendly sorts who might be waitin' along our outbound trail waitin'."

The chill of early evening was descending upon the weary men as they staggered into town. Ian, with the boy securely wrapped in his blanket, carried the lad straight to the tavern where his wife, Megan, worked. "Go back to the fort and report to Captain Shaw," he told McPike. "He'll understand." With that, the Scotsman parted company with the other men and made his way to the warm, brightly lit cookhouse where he knew he'd find Megan waiting for his return.

Megan's relief at seeing her husband again quickly turned into concern as soon as she laid eyes on the bundle that Ian held. She'd been ready to tongue-lash him for kicking the door open like a common drunken lout till her eyes fell upon the listless face of the boy. "Oh, dear God in heaven," she exclaimed as she snatched the huddled bundle from Ian's arm. "Go fetch Ann," she ordered Ian, "and tell her I need her here right quick." Without another word, she slammed the door shut with a bump of her hip, told Ian to sit over in the corner as if he were a child, and set about caring for the boy. The owner of the inn, Ann Charter, was equally swift in her response to the emergency, shouting to all the patrons seated about the crude tables in the common room to fend for themselves and leaving her oldest to make sure none of them cheated her. Rushing to Megan's side, she joined her in an effort to rehabilitate the boy while Ian waited patiently off to one side.

"Dear Lord in heaven," Megan repeated every time she

came across a deep cut that needed her attention, "what have those bloody savages done to you?"

Ann would reply with a soft "Oh, lordy" or a simple "Dear, dear." The boy, standing perfectly still, with the same wide-eyed expression he had worn since his discovery, made no sounds and did nothing to hinder their work. All he did was stare at the fire in the hearth with vacant and unblinking eyes. Even when Captain Shaw and the adjutant came tumbling into the room, now threatened with overcrowding, the boy didn't blink or turn to see who had joined them. He simply continued to stare at the fire as if it were the only thing in the world.

Rushing over to Ian's side, for he was far too wise a man to interfere with the work of the women, Shaw began to ask Ian if anything had changed from what McPike had reported. Ian shook his head slowly. "Not a word. 'Twas like they had cut the lad's tongue out of his own mouth."

At that, Megan stopped what she was doing, took her hand, and squeezed the boy's cheeks, forcing him to open his mouth. When the tip of a bright pink tongue protruded, she looked up at the ceiling, uttered a silent prayer, and went back to tending to the numerous cuts that covered the boy from head to toe.

"He's not said a word. And there wasn't a stitch of clothing on him with which we could identify the poor wretch," Ian continued.

"Patrick is not a poor wretch," Megan snapped as she continued to dab a cut with a clean cloth soaked in warm, soapy water.

Both Ian and Shaw shook their heads and stared at Megan. "Patrick?" Ian called out in astonishment. "How did you find out that the lad's name is Patrick?"

Megan didn't bother to look their way as she explained. "I figure the boy's not unlike our dear Saint Patrick, sent to clear the snakes from the Emerald Isle itself with only the Lord to watch over him."

"Megan," Ian protested, "the lad's a name of his own. You can't go about renaming the boy simply because you fancy doing so."

Now Megan turned and looked Ian square in the eyes.

"Oh, for sure, Mister Sergeant. And what, pray tell, would that name be?"

Recoiling from her attack, Ian shrugged. "Well, I don't know. No one here does."

With a smile that sealed her victory, Megan returned to her work. "Well, now, seein' as no one else has any better ideas, you'll just have to be my Patrick."

Then, for the first time, the boy responded to Megan's voice. Pulling his wide, vacant eyes away from the flames, he looked into Megan's warm eyes. The only sign that there had been any connection between him and Ian's wife was the hint of a tear, slowly forming in the corner of one eye, that welled up but refused to fall.

When it became apparent that the boy was unable to provide any useful information, the adjutant left. Odds were, Ian thought, this incident wouldn't earn more than a single line entry in the daily report of the regiment, if that. It wasn't that the event wasn't important to the boy or those involved, or that the regiment viewed the suffering of the people they were charged with defending as trivial. Rather, the hard fact was that such occurrences had simply become too common to labor over. Even Ian and Shaw did not tarry long in the cookhouse of the tavern. Not only did Megan and Ann make sure they felt that they were little more than supernumeraries now that they had the boy in hand but there were other matters that needed to be discussed and tended to.

For several minutes, the two men walked back to the fort in the silent darkness that had descended upon the small frontier community. Few people stirred outside their homes, tightly secured against the ever-present dangers of a wilderness that surrounded them like a besieging army. Shaw spoke first, doing so in his usual, familiar tone of voice. "Colonel Washington has come back from Williamsburg with much news, Ian."

Sensing that the news of which Shaw was speaking was going to entail a new campaign of some sort, Ian readied himself. "Aye. I expected as much. He had that look about him, all business and excitement. Not at all like the last few years."

"Yes, Ian, it's been a miserable two years out here. It's hard to soldier, you know, when the very people who send you out to meet the foe can't even manage to find the funds to buy an entire company a pot to cook their rations in. You know," he said with a hint of awe in his voice, "what has surprised me these past two years is not how many of our men have deserted. No, it's how many have stayed, despite the illness, the deprivations, the want of blankets, the poor rations, and the long periods without a single shilling for pay. Oh, Lord, if I had a single pence for every time I wished I was back on my farm instead of standing here, tending this miserable post, I'd be a wealthy man."

Knowing that his captain was slowly working his way toward something, and impatient to find out what he had on his mind, Ian slowed his pace. "What fine designs, Captain, do the gentlemen in Williamsburg have in mind for us now?"

"Oh, it's not just the governor and the Burgesses that have a hand in this one," Shaw responded. "No, William Pitt himself, the prime minister in far-off London, is the grand architect of this year's campaigns."

It was more the manner in which Shaw spoke his words than the words themselves that caused Ian's stomach to knot up. Knowing full well that Shaw was about to tell him of these plans, Ian didn't bother to ask.

"It seems His Majesty's forces, ably assisted by we humble provincials, will move against the French from several different directions. There will, of course, be another try against the bloody big French fortress at Louisbourg. That'll include the New Englanders and the Royal Navy. And in New York, the commander in chief himself will take on the French on Lake Champlain, reducing their forts there."

"And we're to march to the Ohio," Ian interrupted, "again."

"Yes," Shaw responded bluntly. For several minutes, the two men walked along without talking. Then Shaw continued. "The commander of this expedition will be a Scotsman, a brigadier general by the name of Forbes."

Though Shaw couldn't see his expression, he knew the name Forbes stung Ian, for his pace faltered at the mentioning of it. Recovering, Ian quickened his pace to catch up.

"He's a traitor, you know," Ian growled. "He turned on his own kind during the '45."

"He's the commander of the Southern District, and the man who'll lead the campaign against the French at Duquesne," Shaw countered.

"And I suppose we're to be part of this grand design," Ian bitterly remarked.

"Yes, of course. We," Shaw explained, "and the Second Virginia Regiment are to join Forbes, a regiment of Highlanders, a battalion of the Royal Americans, regiments from Pennsylvania and Maryland. We're all to march on the Ohio this summer."

"Highlanders, you say?" Ian thundered as he stopped in the middle of the road and stared at Shaw. "Scotsmen? I'll wager you there isn't a man among them who stood by their rightful king when it really mattered. I know of no self-respecting Scot who'd wear the bloody red coat of German George."

Shaw let Ian run off with his anger for a moment before he responded. "Ian, that was another time, and another place."

"Not to me," Ian shot back. "You cannot ask me to forget what those bastards did to my country. You cannot expect me to march side by side with such scum and like it."

"I'm not asking you to go," Shaw announced. "That's why I'm telling you all this."

Shaw's statement had the desired effect. Ian stopped his ranting and stood there for a moment in the darkness, thinking of what Shaw had just said. Finally subdued, he asked, rather sheepishly, "If I don't go, what'll you have me do?"

"We'll need to leave some men behind, a few, to continue to tend to matters here," Shaw explained. "I planned on leaving you."

Again there was a pause. Then Ian marched up until he was face-to-face with Shaw. "You'll do nothin' of the kind, Captain Shaw. I've been with you this long, and marched on that damnable place twice. Though the very thought of marching side by side with Forbes and his Scottish mercenaries is distasteful, I'll not be left behind."

Shaw smiled as he reached out and grasped Ian's arm. "I expected as much. Now," he said with a change in tone, "we'll have much to do between now and then. Colonel Washington, I am told, will be followed by a wave of new recruits. We'll need to whip them into some sort of shape before we march, won't we?"

Ian sighed. "I hope this batch is better than the last, seein' where we're goin'."

Albany, New York
April, 1758

THE coming of spring brought few comforts to Katherine Shields. Instead of a time of great activity and numerous trips to New York City and around her father's many holdings, Katherine had only solitude and internment to look forward to. That and the morning sickness. With a moan, she bent over and emptied the contents of her stomach into her chamber pot for the second time in as many hours. Morning sickness followed by an ever-expanding waistline that would never be the same again angered her as she had never been angered before. The only ray of brightness in the whole matter, she told herself as she wiped away specks of vomit that dotted her white chin, was that she'd be rid of Thomas and his friends soon.

Even as she anticipated her coming redemption, the sound of her husband's heavy boots advancing down the hall to her room could be heard. It didn't seem to matter whether he was at home or on the parade ground. Thomas always moved about with the same, steady, confident cadence. He was not at all like her father, easily swayed to meet her expectations and desires. And though he had been quite sincere in keeping his promise to her that he would do nothing to interfere with her conduct of her father's business, he was equally insistent that she fulfill his expectations of delivering to him a son.

Katherine, of course, had expected that she would have the convenience of picking the time when she would be required to live up to that part of their deal. Unfortunately, she had sadly underestimated the single-mindedness of Thomas' desire to have a son as well as the sexual prowess of a soldier confined to winter quarters with little to occupy his time or imagination. "Katherine," he reminded her whenever she protested, "you are the wife of an officer of the Crown and a member of the commanding general's personal household. You're not dealing with provincial merchants and Dutch shopkeepers any longer. There are obligations which neither I nor you can ignore. If you intend to take advantage of the world your marriage has opened to you, then you must make the effort and play the game the way it is played there."

For his part, Thomas did serve as a connection to the circles and contacts that Katherine had hoped for, and more. As an assistant to the quartermaster for the New York Frontier, Thomas knew the needs of the army as well as having a hand in directing where purchasing agents went to fill them. "It's well known, my dear," he told Katherine with great confidence and in a condescending tone that always managed to grate on her nerves, "that while serving His Majesty, King George, is an honor, the king is in no position to provide properly for his loyal servants. So everyone winks a bit at those who can take care of themselves. After all, a little bit here and a little bit there isn't missed by anyone when you consider the overall size and wealth of our empire."

Yet, even as the scope of her father's business grew, the price she had to pay was far beyond anything she had anticipated. From being the center of attention at any social affair which she chose to attend, she was now regarded simply as another wife. Some of her detractors even began to refer to her as "the camp follower." Thomas, for his part, did nothing to discourage such talk. Katherine suspected that he reveled in seeing her humbled. The idea that he didn't even notice her discomfort never entered her mind. To Thomas, this marriage, even if it were arranged more like a business merger than a union between a man and a woman, was like any other marriage he had ever observed. As he liked to brag to his fellow officers, "Though she's not near as lively as a common whore, I can walk away in the knowledge that my moment of joy won't bite me the next day."

The soft rapping of Thomas' knuckles on the door of her bedroom was the only subtle part of their lovemaking. "Katherine," Thomas announced in what he assumed was a romantic tone, "I'll need to be leaving soon. I was hoping that, perhaps, before I depart, we could enjoy each other's company. It will be sometime, I fear . . ."

Having no intention of letting him finish his fumbling advance, let alone touch her, Katherine jammed her finger down her throat as far as she could manage.

On the other side of the door, the horrid noise of his wife heaving forth the contents of her stomach was more than enough to convince Thomas that there would be no farewell bliss for him. With a shrug, he turned and walked away from Katherine's room. At least, he thought as he made his way down the steps, there would be a son for him when he returned from this year's campaign. That, he told himself as a gleam came into his eye, would be a marvelous way to cap the glorious victory that all expected to find on the shores of Lake Champlain.

Quebec, Canada
June, 1758

As was their custom, Anton met with Sarah in the small garden of the convent at the appointed time. Sarah, ever mindful of the eyes of one or more nuns upon her, would greet Anton with a proper curtsy and a pleasant welcome in French. Anton, appropriately chivalrous and correct, would bow at the waist and present Sarah with a small gift of sweets or a nosegay of flowers. For Anton, this was not at all unusual. The rules governing the interactions between males and females had been drilled into his head with the same care that the mathematics governing the ballistics of a cannonball had been. And even though he was the bastard son of a noble, he never forgot that his personal conduct was a reflection on his father and his class.

Sarah, never having been courted in such a manner, was awed by the Frenchman's attention and his charm. The two could not have been more different. Though their ages were within a year of each other's, Sarah's life up to that time had left her far more mature, in worldly matters, than Anton.

"What, dear Lieutenant, shall we discuss today?" Sarah asked in English, as Anton had asked her on many occasions.

At first, she thought his delay in responding was due to his slowness in translating her words into French. But she quickly saw that his expression was not unlike that of a love-struck girl of fourteen. While she took a seat under a tree, Anton remained standing and speechless as he gazed down upon the pale white skin of Sarah's serene face.

Sarah's half-smile, highlighted by sunlight that poked through the fresh, tender leaves of the tree she sat under, reminded Anton of the ageless beauty that so many artists in France worked a lifetime to capture. The sparkling white ruffled cap, set back on her head, seemed like a halo. Only when he saw her cheeks glow red, like two hot coals in a fire fanned by a burst of air, did he realize that he was causing her embarrassment.

As quickly as the moment had come, it passed, with both of the young people averting their eyes, each in a different direction. Nervously, Anton looked over at the nun who sat in an obscure corner of the garden, tending to her sewing and apparently paying no heed to the couple she was tasked to mind. Anton's thoughts were pulled back to Sarah when he felt the gentle touch of her hand upon his.

"Lieutenant, please," she murmured. "Sit here beside me."

Unable to refuse, Anton took a seat on the crude wooden bench Sarah was seated upon. Changing to French so that the meaning of what she was about to say could not be mistaken, Sarah began to whisper. "I have tried to find the fine words that would make what I am about to ask sound more proper. But I am, as you know, of humble origins. Until you taught me, I could not even write my own name."

"Sarah," Anton hastily interrupted as he drew nearer to her, almost touching his arm against hers, "please do not let words stand between us."

Surprisingly, Sarah drew away, confusing Anton. "Please, monsieur, do not make this any more difficult than it already is."

Easing away from the woman, Anton nodded. "As you wish, madam."

"Anton," Sarah started again, this time as she leaned toward him, "I am a married woman. At least, I think I am still married. God willing, both my husband and my babies are still alive somewhere, in the hands of a caring Indian who has taken them to her heart as if they were her own or given up to the French, like me, to be ransomed." The words, spoken softly, betrayed little emotion. It was as if she had cried all the tears she could over the family she had been separated from and had no more to spare for them. "Perhaps I will be reunited with them all again when we are finally exchanged. Perhaps not. Only God in heaven knows that for sure, and He has seen fit not to share that knowledge with me, though I pray every morning and night that He would."

"I am sure, madam, that He is looking out after your loved ones, whether they are in this world or the next," Anton added.

Sarah gave Anton a shy smile, then looked down at the ground between her feet. "Please, monsieur, do not think you are obligated to honor my request if in any way you do not think it proper or correct."

"Sarah," Anton offered in haste, "there is no request that I can refuse you."

Looking up into his eyes, eyes that were waiting patiently for her request, Sarah paused, looked down once more, then fixed them with a steady, unflinching gaze. "Anton, I want a child."

Though he tried to maintain his calm, Anton blinked and pulled away. Sensing his surprise, and taking it as revulsion, Sarah looked away and stood up. "I am sorry, monsieur," she blurted as she started to walk away. "It was wrong of me to . . ."

The soft touch of Anton's hand on her arm, and the gentle tug that arrested her flight, caused Sarah to look back at the young lieutenant of artillery. "Please," he pleaded, "sit down. Talk to me."

Unable to resist, and too committed to turn back now, Sarah willingly complied. "This is hard for me, monsieur," she started, not daring to look into his eyes. "If my husband is alive, I will be committing a mortal sin."

"But this is war, madam," Anton countered. "And a most brutal and difficult war. I know, I have seen it."

Looking up, Sarah gave Anton a strange look as she realized, for the first time since they had met, that it was a Frenchman, not unlike the very man she sat next to, who had led the Indian raid that had torn her from her family. But just as quickly as that thought darkened her mind, it passed until, once again, she saw the sweet, caring man she had come to love.

"Perhaps it is wrong for us to place so much faith in God's willingness to forgive our transgressions," Sarah offered in response to Anton's statement. "Perhaps it is because we demand so much of Him that He brings such pestilence and woe that we both have witnessed down upon us."

At first, Anton didn't respond. Instead, he turned his gaze in the direction of the nun, sitting in her obscure corner of the convent's garden, sewing away. "Look at her," Anton commanded. "She does all that is humanly possible to ensure that she remains in God's good graces. If any of us are to be accepted into His arms when we die, it will be her. But," he countered as he turned and looked into Sarah's eyes, "she will never have known life as we have, will she?"

Shyly, Sarah shook her head. "No, monsieur, she will not."

"We are placed here with the passions, emotions, and

desires that He gave us. To me, the greater sin would be to refuse to use those gifts which each of us has within us."

Slowly, a smile began to creep across Sarah's face and she took Anton's hand in hers. "My child was special to me. I truly think I did love my husband, though he never said he loved me. But my baby, she was special. I could look into her eyes, and see so much love, so much joy in those tiny little eyes of hers. And the thought that I gave her those eyes, and somehow, giving all my love, well, it made me feel special, too."

Sarah paused, letting her chin drop as she struggled to hold back a tear, the first Anton had seen her shed. With the lightest of touches, he brought his hand up to her chin, and raised it again until her eyes met his. "I cannot speak with any authority when it comes to the love that a mother holds for her child. Alas, I am a man. But as a man, I can tell you of what it feels like to love a woman. And Sarah Carter, I love you, with all my heart."

It was only with the greatest restraint that Sarah kept herself from falling into Anton's arms, arms that would have gladly accepted her regardless of all the penitence he would have had to pay for doing so. After catching her breath, Sarah asked, as if to reassure herself that she fully understood Anton's commitment, "Then, monsieur, you will help me bear another baby?"

Slowly lifting her hand without ever taking his eyes away from hers, Anton brought her pale fingers to his lips and planted a soft kiss upon them. "*Oui*, madam. I am yours. Now and forever."

CHAPTER TWENTY-THREE

On the Southern Shore of
Lake George, New York
July, 1758

TO THOSE who had been there the year before, the sight of Major General Abercromby's vast fortified camp was unbelievable. Where barely more than 2,200 troops had struggled unsuccessfully to beat back 8,000 French and Indians, an English army numbering more than 13,000 now assembled for the drive north into the heart of New France. While the numbers alone were impressive, what really struck Thomas was the quality of the troops that formed the core of the army. Where Monro had had to make due with but five companies of the Thirty-fifth Regiment of Foot the previous year, Abercromby had four regiments of regulars, to include Thomas' own 44th Foot, as well as Brigadier General Thomas Gage's newly raised regiment of light infantry. "It will be a blessing,"

Lewis Fenton crowed as he watched the soldiers of Gage's specially recruited regiment prepare to embark for the thirty-mile trip up Lake George, "to have reliable scouts with the army."

Thomas, standing next to Fenton, said nothing. Unlike many of his peers gathered in the midst of a monumental collection of men, equipment, guns, boats, and mountains of supplies, he had confidence in Rogers' companies of rangers. Though they were an unruly lot, always rowdy and at times insubordinate, they knew these woods, their foe, and the art of warfare as it was waged in the forests of America. He was not at all sure that a smartly uniformed unit led by provincial officers under English tutelage would be as good, but only Sir William Johnson and his band of Mohawks were held in lower regard.

Still, Thomas held his opinion to himself. A professional officer, trained in the classical art of war, he felt quite at home as part of a European-raised and -trained army. And while it was true that the provincial regiments from Massachusetts, New Hampshire, Connecticut, New York, Rhode Island, and New Jersey made up the bulk of the army, few had any doubts that it would be the regulars who would bear the brunt of the serious fighting and make the difference in the upcoming battle. "We only need to march this army to the gates of Fort Carillon, and the place will be ours," Fenton announced, not knowing how similar that prediction was to one Thomas himself had made in 1755 when he embarked on another march against a different French fort.

There was, however, little time for Thomas to reflect upon past failures. He had all he could do to cope with the vast problems of moving the current campaign forward. His familiarity with the area of operations and his dealings with provincial officers were, in and of themselves, sufficient justification for his commander to turn down his request to rejoin his regiment as a line officer. "To hell with the grenadier company," he shouted in frustration as he tried to persuade his superiors that he deserved to be sent back to the Forty-fourth. "I don't much care what company I am given. All I want is an opportunity to do what I was trained for." But all his pleas and protests fell on deaf ears. He was retained on the staff of the quartermaster general due to his excellent abilities in solving problems and handling matters concerning supplies and their movement.

Serving on the staff was not all bad. At least there he had the opportunity to observe, firsthand, a man who had quickly earned the respect and affection of the entire army. The introduction of Viscount Lord Howe, a thirty-four-year-old brigadier who was much favored by the prime minister, William Pitt, was as masterful as Pitt's plan for the summer's campaign in the Americas. Unlike previous senior English officers who had come to America and done their best to impose European methods upon this savage land, Howe had taken the time to study the problem. Unlike Thomas, he had gone out with the rangers voluntarily and studied their methods. As a result, he forced many common-sense reforms upon English regulars and provincial units gathering for the new campaign. No detail was too small. Everything from shortening the coattails of the soldiers' uniforms to eliminating laundresses and camp followers was adopted. Officers used to large personal retainers were reduced to one blanket and a bearskin for a bed roll, and a knapsack in which they had to carry the same thirty days' rations that the commonest provincial private packed. The bright silver barrels of muskets were browned, long hair was cut short, and leggings were issued to make fighting in the forest easier. When all was said and done, Thomas could see that the army was trimmer and better prepared for combat here, in the wilderness, than he had ever imagined possible. Of course, not all shared his enthusiasm. "We look absolutely disgraceful," Fenton fumed day after day as he lost the struggle to keep up appearances. "Given time," Fenton wagered, "he'll have us paint our faces and teach us to take scalps."

Though Thomas did miss many of the advantages being an officer usually afforded, he was far too busy to commiserate with his fellow officers who had little else to do but drill their troops and engage in idle gossip. Thomas threw himself into his duties, day and night. This included, as always, dealing with civilian contractors and arguing with backwoods teamsters who were all out to make as much as they could while exposing themselves to the least risk. Despite the fact that he was now married to the daughter of a very wealthy merchant, and was beginning to understand their ways, he found their attitudes difficult to reconcile when the king's duty was involved. "Rascals," Thomas declared every evening when he returned to the tent he shared with Fenton. "They are all conniving, scheming, penny-pinching rascals who don't give a hoot who wins or loses this war, just who offers the highest bid."

Fenton, never subtle in his manner or comments when talking to Thomas, raised an eyebrow as he watched his companion pace back and forth, fuming and muttering. "Well, if what I hear is true," he quipped, "your father-in-law is doing quite well due to this little party General Abercromby is throwing for the French."

Stung by the accusation, one that he had heard muttered by others before, Thomas stopped his pacing and faced Fenton. "Are you accusing me of taking advantage of my office? That I'm an opportunist?" he thundered.

Fenton smirked, knowing full well that Thomas' reaction was more for show than out of anger. "Oh, please, my dear Thomas. Don't imagine for a moment that every officer in this army doesn't know who you are married to, and who is not only supplying a sizable part of the provisions for this army but the wagons and horses used to haul it up here from Fort Edward." Fenton paused, looked down, then shrugged. "And to tell you the truth, with few exceptions, you're envied. After all," he continued as he looked up at Thomas with a sad expression, "when all is said and done and this campaign is over, most of us will have little or nothing to show for all our efforts. You, on the other hand, my dear, offended friend, will have a fine wife, a family, and a future to enjoy. The rest of us poor sods will have nothing but the army, condemned to living on half-pay, when peace comes. So, you see," Fenton summarized, "I wouldn't worry what others think. In the end, it will be you, sitting before your fireplace, smoking a great pipe, who will have the last laugh."

Thomas, unmoved by Fenton's justification, stood before his friend. "Is that what you believe? Do you think, for one moment, I would place personal gain above my duty to king and country?"

Fenton's silence was more than Thomas could stand. Angered by his own stupidity for thinking that he could advance his own personal future while maintaining an unblemished record as an officer, Thomas stormed out of the tent. For hours, he wandered through the camps of an army poised to move north and claim a victory that all believed was theirs for the taking.

The French Encampments around Fort Carillon July, 1758

THOMAS was not the only officer unable to sleep that night. Since his departure from Quebec, Anton found his thoughts turning again and again to the woman who had been for him the cause of both great joy and heartfelt grief. The rapture and excitement, warmth and affection, that he had found in the arms of Sarah Carter were unlike anything he had ever known. None of the women he had ever been with before came close to matching the tenderness he had experienced during his few brief encounters with Sarah. It was more, Anton told himself, than the secretive meetings that he arranged at a small inn on a side street of lower Quebec. Like a lovesick child, he would wait there for Sarah to come whenever she was called to work at Monsieur Bigot's lavish banquets. It was more than the patient, caring manner that a woman who is both mature and in love brings to an affair that drew him to her, again and again. It was much more, Anton told himself as he moved about from one circle of solemn soldiers to another.

The sudden snap of a sentinel halting and bringing his musket up to salute Anton shook him from memories and images that, even here, were sufficient to excite him. With a flourish of his hand, Anton returned the salute and turned quickly in an effort to hide the embarrassed blush that betrayed his most intimate thoughts of Sarah. After a shake of his head and a quick looking about, he continued his meandering, though his thoughts were now irretrievably shaken from his recollections of his lover's tender embrace.

The army assembled this year in and around Carillon was less than half that Montcalm had gathered on the very site a year before. Though it represented the finest fighting force France could muster in this part of the world, it was incomplete. To stand with the regiments of La Reine, Béarn, Guyenne, La Sarre, Languedoc, the Royal Roussillon, and the Berry under Montcalm's personal command, there were but a handful of Indians and very few militia and La Marine units. The unity of their combined effort that had assured them success the previous year was lacking. Rather than bringing all the colony's strained resources together at what Montcalm declared to be the critical point, the governor of New France had insisted on sending his Canadians and those Indians who had answered his summons this year on an ill-advised raid down the Mohawk Valley.

Even Anton, in the throes of his infatuation with the American captive, could not ignore the serious rift between the political and nominal commander in chief in New France, the governor, the Marquis de Vaudreuil, and his senior military commander, the Marquis de Montcalm. Though Montcalm was appointed to that post by the king himself, Vaudreuil felt no obligation to follow his advice. For his part, Montcalm, appalled by the graft and corruption of Vaudreuil's underlings, had as little to do with Vaudreuil and the colonial government of New France as he could manage. The bickering and backbiting, Anton's friend Pepin told him before departing for the Mohawk, "is a recipe for disaster. We can only hope that the English keep sending their most inept commanders to face us."

Anton approached a watch fire, tended by a pair of guards

lost in their own thoughts, and reflected upon Pepin's words. While fortune had indeed blessed New France with a steady parade of weak or incompetent English commanders, he doubted if they would be so lucky again this year. Already word had come from Cape Briton that Louisbourg was under siege. While nothing had come of the previous year's effort against the largest fortress on the continent and the gate to New France, few imagined they would be so fortunate again. There were also rumors of a new expedition being readied for a stab at Fort Duquesne. And then there was the massive army sitting little more than thirty miles away. Looking up, Anton peered across the burning embers of the watch fire, out into the darkness, as if he were looking for that army. Like all the professional officers gathered at the fort on the southern shore of the lake bearing the name of New France's great explorer and governor, Anton understood that the decision to divide what little Vaudreuil had to hold this vast wilderness empire for the king all but sealed their fate.

Downcast, Anton's eyes returned to the fire at his feet. In it, a log straddling the bed of coals snapped in two and fell. Its collapse sent a shower of sparks flying up into the black sky that surrounded them. It will be like that, Anton thought, when we are forced to yield this place. We will be thrown into the heart of the battle, be consumed, and, after a great shower of sparks, disappear into the darkness, never to be heard from again.

Looking up into the sky, he blinked his eyes. Catching sight of a few stray stars, he pushed all thoughts of the coming battle from his mind. Instead, Anton gave thanks for having been given an opportunity to enjoy the love of a woman such as he had known with Sarah Carter to the God whose most sacred commandments he had so cheerfully violated.

Along the Great Portage, on the Northern Shore of Lake George

WHAT had begun as a carefully planned and marvelously organized advance from their landing sites was quickly falling into a shambles. Thomas, moving with the middle column, saw that right off. It seemed that the confidence and enthusiasm that had been bountiful in their encampment on Lake George and during the trip up the lake melted away with every tentative step that took them into the forest. It had been a mistake to send the American Rangers of Robert Rogers off in a futile reconnaissance to the west and use, instead, Gage's light troops to lead the way north. Though good men, every one, Gage's soldiers didn't have a fraction of the knowledge of the area or the savvy needed to do the job right. Together with the painfully slow pace of the army and the intermixing of the three columns, the error of that decision was beginning to be borne out. Thomas wished he could have said something when the matter had been discussed. But as a junior officer, he didn't have a right to voice an opinion when it came to the conduct of operations in the field. His task during this campaign was to provide for its needs and do as he was told. So he held his tongue and hoped that all would work itself out.

But more and more, as the men trudged forward through the dense forest, over broken ground littered with numerous tree trunks, company commanders found it harder and harder to maintain order. It would take much more to pull this off, Thomas realized, than everyone merely doing their duties as they knew them. It would take everything they had, and, perhaps, more.

After clawing their way little more than a mile through the dark forest, a spattering of shots, echoing their way back from the head of the jumbled column, rang out. Instinctively, everyone looked up from the soggy ground they had been tromping upon for hours. Wide-eyed and nervous, each man tried to penetrate the dense undergrowth that covered the forest floor all about them. To those new to forest warfare, the rattle of musketry, now growing in ferocity as more and more of Gage's men joined in, brought to life the vivid stories of Indian savagery and mutilations that had been so freely discussed over campfires just days ago. Others, like Thomas and many of the Forty-fourth, felt a cold chill run down the length of their spines. For them, the memories of a day not unlike this one, under similar circumstances, three years before were all too real.

Among the staff, there was a nervous shuffling about. The commanding general, unaware of what exactly was going on, was not sure what to do. As Braddock had been, he was torn between going forward and seeing for himself what was going on and waiting where he was in the hope that his subordinates could handle matters and report quickly. Unlike Braddock, he waited, for he had great trust in the true leader of this army, Viscount Lord Howe. Around him, staff officers, waiting for direction, found they had nothing to do but look brave. Most alternated between keeping an eye on their commanding general, waiting for him to summon them, and nervously watching the woods for the first sign of a red savage. Thomas, unlike most of the others, found he could not stand by idly. Seeing that he was of little use where he was, he let it be known that he was going to make his way along the column until he came to the Forty-fourth Foot and left without waiting for anyone to grant him permission to do so.

Making his way up the line of men, Thomas was greeted by many stares and questioning expressions from wide-eyed soldiers waiting to go into battle. When he saw that many of the officers were also standing by, nervously milling about, Thomas took matters into his own hands. "No need to worry, lads," he started telling the soldiers as he went by. "It's the vanguard. They've bumped into the Frenchies and they're clearing the way for us. Tend to your muskets and be ready to follow your officers." To those who had come face-to-face with their fear of dying for the first time, the calm, steady tone of Thomas' words brought reassurance that they were not alone, that they were in the hands of trained, competent officers.

Some even managed a nervous smile as they realized how foolish they had been. Even officers who watched Thomas as he trooped past their men spreading calm as he went were galvanized to follow his example and reassert their own control of their skittish troops.

The real test for Thomas himself came just as he reached the Forty-fourth Foot's small staff. Without warning, a series of high, piercing shrieks echoed through the forests and all but drowned out the gunfire. No one knew who had raised the cry, but all assumed the worst. Thomas, like everyone else, was momentarily startled. He found himself peering anxiously first to the head of the column, looking for the first signs of flight, and then out into the forest, straining to catch the first sign of an Indian springing forth from the undergrowth, tomahawk raised, ready to strike him dead. The sweat beading up on his forehead seemed to make the scar from the previous year's campaign burn, so much so that Thomas was positive it was visible to all. In his embarrassment he glanced about from face to face of those gathered around him.

Yet, when he did, he saw that no one was paying him any attention. Instead, he noted that they, too, were shuffling about uneasily. Relieved that no one had noticed his own apprehension, Thomas chuckled. "Well, that's rather generous of the marquis." Confused by the cheerful tone of Thomas' remark, everyone who heard him turned and stared at him as if he were quite mad. Undeterred, Thomas' smile broadened. "Well, look at it this way," he explained. "He's doing us a great favor by bringing his army to us and saving us from having to wander about in this wilderness in search of him. With luck, we can finish things here and be at Carillon in time for a decent night's sleep."

Whether they laughed at the utter absurdity of what Thomas was suggesting or simply were glad to having something other than their own personal doom to reflect upon, a chorus of laughter rippled through those gathered about Thomas. This, in turn, caught the attention of the men in the ranks who, quite convinced that their officers were mad, shook their heads and somehow, for a moment, forgot they were supposed to be afraid.

Near Fort Carillon

IF numbers alone were the measure, then the skirmish between Gage's light infantry and the American Rangers, leading Abercromby's column, and a small French force was inconsequential. But often numbers alone do not determine who wins and who loses a fight. The death of Viscount Lord Howe, shot dead with a single ball to the chest, did more than kill an English officer. It took the heart out of the English army just when it needed encouragement. It dumped full command of the army into the lap a man who had, up to that point, been little more than commander in name. It also gave the French an additional day to decide where they would make their stand and prepare to do so.

The choice of defending Carillon forward, outside the walls of the fort, along the crest of the massive hill it sat upon, was, to Anton's analytical mind, a correct one. It would allow the Marquis de Montcalm to use all his troops, rather than pen them up uselessly within the confined spaces of the massive stone fort while leaving the fighting to the artillery. Of course, if the English refused to assault the strong position being prepared by the infantry and opted for a contest of artillery, they certainly had their pick of several exceptional pieces of high ground from which they could bring Carillon under fire with their guns. Rattlesnake Mountain, within easy cannon shot of Carillon to the west and on the east side of the river that flowed from Lake George past the very walls of Fort Carillon, dominated the fort. Across the southern tip of Lake Champlain itself, another promenade, even more commanding, lay to the south. A battery of heavy guns there, together with a battery on Rattlesnake Mountain, would expose every French position in and around Carillon to a devastating cross fire that no amount of earthworks or fortifications could long stand up to. With no means of denying these strategic points to their enemy, Montcalm would be forced to yield without a fight. So he deployed his vastly outnumbered forces where they could be of greatest service, and hoped for the best.

Since there was the need to deploy some of their guns forward, in support of the infantry, Anton made it known that he wanted, as he referred to it when he submitted his passionate plea to his commander, "the post of honor." It was not that Anton was being foolishly noble or brave. He had no more desire to die here than any man in his battery. Rather, it was eminently practical, as most things he did were. Like the majority of the officers under Montcalm, he knew that death, captivity, or worse was a strong likelihood if the English won. Even if he survived the battle, there was the very real possibility that the French prisoners would find themselves exposed to the cruelties of those Indians fighting with the English, just as their prisoners had been eleven months earlier just a scant thirty miles to the south. Given the choice of standing in the cramped confines of the fortress or enduring an around-the-clock battering that would accompany a protracted siege and fighting in the open, Anton had little difficulty in deciding.

All throughout the seventh day of July, Anton found himself side by side with his men, throwing up fortifications. Like most of his fellow officers, he put aside all pretenses of office, rank, and class and took up a shovel. In shirtsleeves, Anton worked with his faithful sergeant and gunners, digging and scraping under an unusually warm sun. He found the work good therapy. Rather than dwelling on his pending doom, he threw himself into his labors. Even his sweet, melancholy memories of Sarah Carter were pushed aside with the same ease that he moved dirt to where it would protect his guns and gunners.

What thoughts he did have were of the past four years of war. It was, he realized as he dug, just four days past the fourth anniversary of his first experience of battle, and two days short of the third anniversary of their great victory on the Monongahela. How different, he thought as he paused to rest and look about, the military affairs of New France were now in comparison to then. While this type of warfare, like the assault on Fort William Henry the previous year, was far more logical to Anton, it saddened him that the ways of the

Old World, even when it came to matters governing the killing of their fellow man, were beginning to rule the affairs of this continent.

"You are always thinking, monsieur," the old sergeant stated blandly as Anton realized that he had been caught leaning absentmindedly on his shovel instead of digging.

"Oh," Anton found himself mumbling apologetically, "I was lost in a few thoughts."

The old sergeant smiled, as much at his lieutenant's discomfort as at his admission that the sergeant was correct. "Well," the sergeant responded as he wheeled his pick in a high arc and brought it down with a thud, "if I had to leave a woman as lovely as that young creature of yours for this, I, too, would be thinking of other things."

With wide eyes, Anton stared at his sergeant. "You know of my affair with the, ah . . ."

"English girl?" the sergeant concluded for Anton. "Why, yes, of course, monsieur," he continued while he rested and wiped his forehead with his sleeve as he leaned on his pick. "We are not blind. Of course," he stated matter-of-factly.

Still reeling from the shock that his careful plans to conceal their meetings had been for naught, Anton shook his head and continued to stare at his sergeant.

"Oh, monsieur," the sergeant replied with a smile as he took up once more the high, powerful swings with his pick. "Do not feel badly that your secret was, well, something less than a secret."

With a slight chuckle, Anton looked down at the ground. "I've never had a woman such as Sarah. Nor have I had one return my affection as lovingly as she did."

The sergeant stopped, placed the head of his pick on the ground, and leaned over toward Anton on its handle. He gave Anton a wink. "Well, monsieur, that is not at all too difficult to understand. After all, it is well known that there isn't an Englishman alive who knows what a tongue is for. Besides," the sergeant added hesitantly as he straightened up and looked Anton in the eye, "the news of your adventures with the English girl came as a relief to me and the men."

Confused, Anton raised an eyebrow. "What sort of relief?"

"Well, monsieur," the sergeant said as he again leaned forward over the handle of his pickax until he was close enough to where Anton could hear his whisper. "There was great concern, among some of the men, that perhaps it was not women you were fond of."

Shocked, Anton pulled back and stared at his sergeant.

The sergeant, for his part, simply took up his pickax and prepared to give it another mighty swing. But before he did, he cocked his head and gave Anton an innocent smile. "Well, monsieur, what's a man to think when you spend so much time alone?"

For a moment, Anton stood and watched his sergeant as he went about swinging his pickax, all concerns about their conversation already past and his full attention returned to the serious work of preparing for the coming battle. It amazed Anton how little he knew of this man, a man who had shared dangers and deprivations with him for nearly four years. And in all those years, Anton could recall only twice, at most three times, when he and the sergeant had engaged in such frank, almost intimate conversations. Yet this man, and the other gunners working at his side, were ready to follow him, to the death if necessary. Perhaps, Anton thought, maybe far too much of his life had been wasted studying books and listening to the philosophical statements of professors. Maybe the real key to unlocking the mysteries of life and the secrets surrounding mankind was standing right there, in the person of a man whom he had commanded for so long. With a shake of his head he took up his shovel and turned his efforts and full attention back to the crisis at hand. But throughout the rest of the day, he found himself looking over every now and then, in awe and amazement, at his stalwart sergeant as he hummed while he worked, as if he didn't have a care in the world.

In Front of the French Works

THOMAS was there in the morning, together with the other staff officers, standing off to the side while a young officer of engineers rendered his report on his reconnaissance of the French works to Generals Abercromby and Gage. The young man was quite confident that the works he had observed could easily be carried by storm. This assessment, given to generals, one of whom was bold and the other rash, made for a quick decision. Rather than wait to emplace their guns on the commanding high hills that surrounded Carillon and conduct a protracted siege, the overwhelming weight of the English forces would be used to crush the French forces where they stood. To everyone who had heard the engineer's report, it all seemed so logical, so self-evident. "We've no need to piddle about there in these blasted woods and wait for the Frenchies to send reinforcements down to Montcalm," Fenton announced as he endorsed the decision. "We'll roll them up here, move north, take Fort St. Frederic, and be done with the lot of them."

"And then?" Thomas asked with an amused smile.

"Well, that, dear boy, will be where the general will have the really hard decisions to make," Fenton explained. "You see, he'll have to decide if it's in our best interest to go back to Albany to breathe some life back into that boorish community of Dutchmen or press on to Montreal, where we can demonstrate the superiority of good English stock to the cream of Canada's womanhood."

Finding little amusement in his friend's assessment of the army's future movements, Thomas made ready to leave. "And where, old boy," Fenton asked as he watched Thomas walk off, "are you going?"

"The general will have no need of me this afternoon to count blankets or supervise the comings and goings of his teamsters," Thomas explained. "I intend to watch this assault from a spot that isn't blocked by the hind quarters of our noble commander's horse." With that, Thomas made his way to the Forty-fourth Foot and took his place in their ranks.

•

Now, with nothing to do but wait, Thomas paced in front of the solemn soldiers of the Forty-fourth Foot. Like the men behind him, they were waiting for the troops of Gage's light infantry, with a number of provincials mixed in, to begin their advance. Behind this thin line that stretched across the entire front of the army were the combined grenadier companies of the regular regiments of foot. When their time came, they would follow the skirmishers. Then it would be the turn of the Forty-fourth to go forward. Arrayed in three ranks, the Forty-fourth Foot, the Fifty-fifth Foot, and the combined independent companies of regulars would provide the main weight for the center of three columns that would assault the French works.

Pausing, Thomas peered through the open woods that lay before him. Over the heads of the light infantrymen and grenadiers, he could catch glimpses of the French works that covered the high ground to their front. He could even see the heads of the French soldiers who stood there, waiting in their works, for Thomas and his regiment to begin their advance. From what he could see, the works were well laid out and soundly built. Yet, as daunting as those fortifications were, it was the abatis in front of those works that gave Thomas cause for concern.

Comprised entirely of trees cut at their base and left untrimmed, this row of obstacles covered the foot of the hill upon which the French works sat, creating a virtual jungle of intertwined branches that faced out. Taking a formed body of troops through that tangled mass would be difficult. Though it could be done, it would take time. During that time the enemy above, protected by stout fortifications, would be free to pour a devastating point-blank fire into the dense, slow-moving mass of attacking troops below. Many of the silent soldiers behind Thomas would perish between the spot where they now stood and the line of works that he could clearly see. Perhaps, Thomas thought, he himself would meet his own fate out there. Though he had always been lucky before, Thomas knew as well as anyone else that every man had only so much luck. Like in cards, Thomas knew that the more one played, the more chances one had of drawing a bad hand. Still, Thomas accepted the odds and waited patiently for the advance to begin.

In the French Works

SET back midway between the forward works, where the infantry stood, and the fort itself, Anton and his gunners also waited. With the aid of a telescope that had been a gift from his father, Anton could clearly see the movement of individual English soldiers along the edge of the woods where they were massing. Closer in, on the same large, flat hill mass where his battery was located were the breastworks where the infantry would make their stand. All but one battalion of the Regiment Berry were deployed there, three ranks deep, with each battalion's company of grenadiers held back in reserve.

Satisfied that nothing had changed in that part of the field, Anton turned quickly to his left. Slowly, he searched the mountain known as Rattlesnake Mountain for any sign of movement or work. It was, to his trained mind, inconceivable that the English would not plant at least a small battery of guns there to support an attack on the line of French works or the later siege. But try as he might, he was unable to detect any activity at all. Satisfied, he continued to turn about to the left, until he was almost facing the rear. As soon as he had the dominant promenade that lay across the southern branch of Lake Champlain in view, he subjected that piece of terrain to the detailed scrutiny he had given the other hill. Again, despite his best efforts, Anton could see nothing. Taking the spyglass from his eye, he lowered it but still continued to search in the direction of the last hill in an effort to see what sound military logic told him had to be there.

"It is not good to wish too hard for something you do not want," his sergeant told him as he came up next to Anton.

"I am sorry, my friend," Anton replied without taking his eyes from the distant hill, "but even the dullest Englishman has to see what magnificent positions those hills afford anyone willing to use them."

"You sound," the sergeant stated, "as if you wanted the enemy to be there."

Finished with his inspection, Anton collapsed the telescope between his hands and turned to face his sergeant. He smiled, and was about to say something, when the scattered firing that had been going on for the past several hours suddenly erupted into a steady roar. Instinctively, both men turned their heads in an effort to see what this development meant. Quickly, the same hands that had just closed the telescope now grasped the two ends and reextended it to its full length. Lifting it to his eye, Anton surveyed the line of works, where he could see the soldiers of infantry battalions now returning the English firing or reloading their weapons. Beyond them, through brief breaks in the clouds of white smoke that were being generated by the musket fire, he could see a long, thin line of red-coated soldiers making their way forward. Here and there, he could see one or two of them stop, drop to a knee, and fire before continuing on.

"Skirmishers," Anton informed his sergeant.

"A great deal of firing for skirmishers, is it not?" the sergeant asked.

Anton dropped his glass, surveyed the entire scene before him, and thought about that for a moment. Then, with a nod of agreement, he hoisted his spyglass back up to his eye and took a closer look at the woods from which the English light infantry had emerged. Suddenly, he caught a glimpse of a solid body of troops as they moved out from the shade of the trees and into the open ground that lay between the woods and the French works. The tall mitre hats of these men left no doubt as to who they were. "You are right, my friend," Anton stated without taking his eyes off these new additions. "The English are sending the grenadiers forward. It seems they have decided to take us by storm."

Impatient to join the fight, the sergeant grunted, throwing one arm out before him in frustration. "Were we but a couple of hundred toises closer, we would be able to do something besides stand here and watch."

Turning his entire upper body off to the left, Anton looked down at the river, where the right flank of the English army rested. "Perhaps," he stated confidently, "we will be able to enjoy a bit of sport from where we stand."

Noting where his lieutenant was watching, the sergeant

smiled. "Good! Let him try our open flank. We will smash his boats before he even has a chance to land."

Anton looked over at his sergeant, then at the nervous faces of his gun crews, who were watching and listening to them. Anton, too, smiled. "Yes, of course. That is why we are here. Now," he commanded, "prepare to load and prime the guns."

In Front of the French Works

WITH the skirmishers and grenadiers retiring, it was time for the three assault columns to go forward. Drawing his sword, Thomas waited for the drums to sound the advance. With the same high-pitched shout used on the parade ground numerous times, the regimental commander finally gave the order. All at once, the drummers of the nine line companies beat the tune that set the entire regiment in motion as one single mass.

After that, however, all semblance of parade-ground maneuvers and drill ceased. The Forty-fourth was in open woods, made up of thick, towering trees that made advancing in straight lines impossible. Thomas knew this, as did the army's second in command, Sir Thomas Gage. Yet the company commanders, and their sergeants, struggled to maintain the dress of their units as the regiment made its way toward the open ground. Incessant shouts by red-faced officers to dress to the left or to the right echoed above the pop of musket fire and the steady, uncompromising beat of drums that few soldiers were unable to keep in step with. Individual soldiers pressed together shoulder-to-shoulder found themselves time and time again confronted by great trees that demanded them to yield to one side or the other. This resulted in jostling, shoving, and pushing, as each man did his best to balance the demands of the frustrated officers to maintain his place in line and the need to go around the numerous obstacles he encountered as they advanced.

Thomas, assigned to go forward with the regiment's left battalion, was not disturbed by this. He understood the problems of moving through such terrain and felt confident that once they had cleared the forests, things would sort themselves out. Quickly, he found that such a hope was a foolish one. Even as the company officers were redoubling their efforts to realign their staggered ranks the moment they stepped out into the open ground before the French works, Thomas saw that these efforts would be in vain. For now, instead of whole trees standing upright, the advancing line of soldiers found themselves in the middle of a field littered with stumps of trees that had been hewed down and hauled away to be used in building either the abatis before them or the fortifications behind which the French stood. In many ways, this new threat was more infuriating to the soldiers, for now they were forced to watch the left or right in order to maintain their alignment, and simultaneously the ground, to ensure that they didn't trip over a stump. Added to this was the terrible fact that they were now fully exposed to French fire, fire that was beginning to have a telling effect.

For a few moments, Thomas, marching before the struggling line of musketeers, felt strangely alone. With only the steady, uncompromising beating of drums pounding in his ears, he fixed his gaze upon the line of French works before him. Slowly he scanned those fortifications, now partially hidden by a cloud of smoke that was punctuated by random tongues of flame jabbing out at him. Here and there his eyes captured the image of an individual soldier going through the complicated drill of firing and reloading, or an officer waving his sword as he pointed this way and that to show his men where to shoot.

Thomas tried not to dwell on the sight of these animated men who were doing their utmost to kill him. Nor did he allow the whine and whiz of bullets streaking past his head to alter his steady, unhurried advance. With sweat running down his face, and a tightness in his stomach that left it in a knot,

Thomas forced himself to turn his mind away from the dangers that threatened to end his life. He shut his ears to the cries of men behind him, just a few scant yards away, who caught bullets that passed within inches of his head but ripped into their bodies. Straining, he used every ounce of strength he could muster to keep himself erect and moving forward, at the same slow, deliberate parade-ground pace that had been drilled into him since his first day with the army.

Before he realized it, they were at the abatis. There, just as he had feared, the last vestiges of an orderly advance disappeared. But the forward progress of the Forty-fourth Foot was not arrested by this obstacle. While some men fought with the sharpened ends of the branches that snarled on every loose stitch of clothing, others tried in vain to walk over it. All around him men were snagged by the twisted maze of branches as legs slipped between tree limbs. Others simply fell to a steady, murderous fire that the French infantry, now less than fifty yards distant, continued to pour into them.

And still the Forty-fourth went forward. For the first time, Thomas paused in his personal struggle with the jumbled mass of limbs and branches to look back at the men following. "COME ON!" he screamed, jabbing his sword up, in the direction of the French works. "FORWARD, LADS, FORWARD!" His words, meant as much to embolden himself as those he was hurling them at, were being drowned out by the horrible clatter of musket fire in which the sounds of single shots were no longer distinguishable.

Foot by brutal foot, the fifty yards was soon narrowed to less than forty. Behind him, Thomas could see that the number of men endeavoring to keep up with him was diminishing. Farther back, laid across the same limbs and branches he himself had climbed over, were the corpses of those who had been struck down in mid-stride.

Suddenly, while his attention was elsewhere, Thomas felt his foot slip off the trunk of one of the trees that made up the tangled abatis. A sharp pain shooting up his leg caused him to shift his weight, more in a desperate effort to keep from causing more damage than from pain. Unfortunately, once he started, he had great difficulty retaining his balance. Only his doubling over and throwing his hands out before him onto two different tree trunks broke his fall, though he lost both his sword and his hat in the effort. For a moment he paused in this awkward position as the chaotic battle continued all about him.

Uttering a silent oath, Thomas caught his breath before he gingerly started to pull the foot that had given way up and out of the spot where it had become wedged. This effort caused further pain and resulted in another curse. Then slowly, carefully, he managed to move his foot free and plant it on another log. With great trepidation, Thomas began to put weight on the injured foot. And though it still sent spasms of pain up his leg and caused him to grimace, he found he could put weight on it.

Having satisfied himself that he could continue, Thomas recovered his sword and began to stand up. He refused to waste even a second in a senseless search for his hat, now lost somewhere in the twisted mass of tree trunks and limbs. This, he knew without even needing to consider the idea, was not the time or place for such foolishness.

To his surprise, when he lifted his head and looked to the front, Thomas saw that he was but a few yards from the French works. Startled, he hesitated as he looked at the faces of his foe, now close enough to see their every expression and grimace. Some wore the same wide-eyed look of fear that his own men behind him did. Others had no expression at all. With their eyes squinted until they were little more than slits, and their faces devoid of all feeling, they continued to work their muskets as quickly as their hands allowed them to. This, a voice inside Thomas told him, was the moment of truth.

Just as he steeled himself to cover those last few yards, Thomas again caught himself. As if warned, he looked over his shoulder and saw, to his utter amazement, the soldiers of the Forty-fourth retreating. They were not fleeing, panic-stricken and wild. They were not even hurrying. Rather, they were slowly melting away, like the outgoing tide on the shore that had reached its farthest point and found it could go no more. Even the few officers who remained standing were going back, picking their way through the same tangled mass that had so slowed their advance. In an instant, Thomas realized that they had done their best, but it simply hadn't been enough.

Looking back at the French works one last time, his eyes met those of a soldier, a grizzled old veteran with a black mustache. The French musketeer was also eyeing Thomas as he was bringing his piece up to his shoulder to fire. Thomas could imagine that through the deafening din of battle he heard the click of the musket's hammer as it was locked back into the full-cocked position. Thomas watched the Frenchman's eyes as they sighted down the barrel of his musket, took aim, and prepared to fire. Knowing there was little he could do, Thomas drew himself as erect as he could, threw his chest out, and defiantly planted the tip of his sword in the dirt at his feet as he waited for his end.

In a single moment, as if all the time in the world had slowed to a painful, leaden pace, Thomas saw the flash in the pan of the Frenchman's musket. He saw his foe reeling back from the buck of his weapon just before all sight of him was obscured by the cloud of dirty white smoke that erupted from the bore of the musket. And he felt the hot sting of the musket ball as it cut through his coat and creased the right side of his extended chest.

He stood there for a moment, as stunned by the fact that he was still standing as by the wave after wave of pain that rippled through his body. Only after he was sure that there had been no damage, and, more important, that he had demonstrated for all to see that he was not afraid to stand his ground, even in the face of death, Thomas turned sharply and walked off. In his wake he left a stunned French musketeer, and an enemy works that was unbroken. He also left a good part of his regiment there, dead and dying.

In the French Works

WITH the line of works to their front aflame from one end to the other, and the outcome very much in question, Anton found it difficult to keep an eye open to the flank that bordered on the river that led to Lake George. But he did. Within minutes of the opening of the main English assault, his vigilance was rewarded. As he and his superiors before him had anticipated, a number of troop-laden boats came slowly into view from behind the mass of land that had been masking them. "Well," he stated rather blandly, "at last we have a target."

While his gunners scurried about their pieces, preparing them to fire, Anton pulled the two ends of his spyglass apart and lifted the instrument to his eye. Leaning against the parapet of his own works, he braced his arms in an effort to keep the long telescope from wobbling.

He could clearly see now the figures in the boats, long boats and bauteaux. Sailors and men in civilian garb were pulling at the oars in a mechanical rhythm that was fascinating to watch. In the center of the boats sat the soldiers, all scrunched in tightly, shoulder-to-shoulder, holding their muskets upright and between their knees. Though he couldn't make out any details, Anton could see that the faces of some of those soldiers were looking up in his direction. Others, perhaps in fear, perhaps in silent prayer, kept their heads bowed low. Having participated in similar operations under somewhat the same circumstances, Anton had vivid memories of the feelings and sensations that he had experienced. For a moment, he imagined that he could hear the creaking of the oars, straining against the oar locks, as the boats' crews pulled with all their might. The grunts of those men mixed in with the quiet murmuring of a man in prayer. There was the soft, rhythmic splash and swoosh as oars dipped into the waters of the lake and then the gurgling sound of water stirred by those oars as they were pulled back in unison. He found that he could even conjure up the smells associated with the experience. The sweat of wet men, combined with the strange odor that nervous soldiers about to enter combat emitted.

"Lieutenant," the old sergeant of gunners announced firmly, "the guns are ready."

Having lost himself in his recollections, it took Anton a moment to collect his thoughts. When he was ready, he stood upright, collapsing the telescope as he did so. "Ah, the range," he announced in a clear voice, "is, I believe . . ."

"Fourteen hundred yards. I took the liberty of laying the pieces, monsieur," the sergeant announced hesitantly. "All is ready."

Looking beyond his sergeant, whose face betrayed no emotions despite the seriousness of the situation, Anton saw that his gunners were standing by their cannon, ready to fire. "Well, then," he announced as he stepped back from the parapet, nervously collapsing his telescope again for what seemed to be the hundredth time to his sergeant. Walking over to the rear of the gun line, Anton took post off to one side from where he was sure he would be able to observe the fall of each shot clearly. When he was ready, he began to give the orders to fire. "Number one gun," he announced, using the sharp, clear tones he used in all their gun drills. "Fire!"

There was no drama or excitement involved. Even before Anton's arm dropped, the match was mechanically applied to the first gun's touch hole, setting off the primer, then the charge. The heavy two-ton cannon roared to life, bucking up and back as flame and smoke spewed from its muzzle. Anton didn't bother watching this or the gun crew as it started the set drill of reloading by first swabbing the bore with a wet sponge to extinguish any burning residue. By that time, Anton had his telescope back up to his eye, watching with satisfaction as the first shot fell just short of the advancing barges.

"Number two gun," he ordered. "Fire."

This round, for whatever reason, was nearer the boats, landing right between two fully loaded barges. Though a miss, the geyser of water it sent up showered all the occupants in both boats with a heavy spray of water. The oarsmen, dedicated to their work, did little but bend over as one would in a rainstorm and continue their rowing. The soldiers, however, with nothing to do, leaned away from the cascading water, even though all danger had passed.

There was a problem with the third gun's aim. When it fired, its round was so far off the mark that Anton was forced to pull the telescope away from his eye to see where it went. Angered by such an error, Anton first looked at his sergeant, who was already turning his attention to the third gun's crew, and then to the gun captain of that piece. Their eyes locked only for a moment, but it was enough for Anton to convey, without saying a word, that another such miscalculation would not be tolerated.

When the fourth gun fired, Anton noted with satisfaction that, though the ball missed, landing just in front of one of the boats, it caused a great deal of concern and discomfort to both crew and passengers. Whether it was due to the waves created by the cannonball impacting on the water's smooth surface or the human tendency to shy away from danger, the boat began to veer off to one side. This put it on a course that caused a second boat's crew to panic as they, too, turned to one side to avoid the first boat, which was still seeking safety.

"We have the range," Anton announced, smiling for the first time in several hours. "Stand by when you are ready to fire."

In short order, all was ready. Again, Anton went down the line, firing one gun at a time and observing the fall of its shot. This time, all rounds fell somewhere near one of the English boats. In several cases, the ball snapped oars, forcing the crews to shift some from the other side in order to maintain proper maneuverability. It was during the third volley that the first direct hit was scored. At first, Anton thought the ball had been wild, like that of his number three gun before.

But then, as he watched in amazement, one of the boats lifted a few feet from the water, split in two, and spilled out crew and soldiers into the water. Everyone who saw the round hit, whether they were at the battery or elsewhere within the French works, took heart. Some even cheered. Anton, however, continued to watch as the boat, now reduced to splinters, disappeared. In the choppy waters where it had been, he could see the bodies of men, floating facedown, bobbing about as survivors struggled desperately to keep from joining their comrades in death.

"All right!" Anton snapped as he turned to his guns crews, some of whom were leaning forward over the earthwork's parapet to catch a glimpse of their handiwork. "We haven't won yet. Reload your pieces and prepare to fire again."

Sheepishly, those who had been the most enthusiastic gave Anton a look not unlike one he had often assumed himself when being scolded by a teacher or a priest, and returned to their posts. There, they resumed their task of loading, rolling out, aiming, and firing their guns as more and more Englishmen, both on the water and before the long line of French works, continued to die.

In front of the French Works

IT was late afternoon before the Forty-fourth Foot was reformed and ready to have another try at the French works. In the interim, other units, from the proud and impetuous Highlanders of the Forty-second Foot to regiments of provincials, many seeing their first battle, had tried their luck at storming the French works and failed. Thomas, one of the regiment's few remaining officers of grade, was far too busy to concern himself with those efforts. Like his regiment, other units that had gone forward had been roughly handled, but not broken. His fall in the abatis left him with a limp from a sprained ankle. The slight wound in his side, as yet undressed, continued to ooze blood that mixed with his sweat, leaving a dark, wet stain that ran from his chest all the way down his side. Even his old scar, partially visible along the length of his hatless forehead, seemed to burn as he went about the chore of reforming the ranks.

When all was finally set, he again took his place. Unlike the previous wait, when the attitude had been mixed and uncertain, a silent grimness descended upon the ranks, from the most senior surviving officer to the last man in the line. Turning, Thomas looked at the men behind him, some of whom were hatless, like him. Here and there, he could see a bloody head, crudely bandaged but held high. They were good men, Thomas saw, all of them. They were not given to the sudden panic or loss of confidence that had sent the provincials scurrying back through the woods without any thought of stopping or reforming. Some of these men had stood with him at the Monongahela, under a grueling fire for hours, without flinching. And these very same men had, just hours before, come to within yards of their objective. Even as he turned back to watch the latest wave of refugees fleeing from another failed attempt at the French works, Thomas told himself that there was simply no way his regiment would fail a second time. They would go forward as before, and they would seize the French fortifications there on the hill and, in turn, Fort Carillon itself. There was, in Thomas' mind, simply no other outcome.

When it was their turn, the drums of the Forty-fourth Foot again sounded the advance. Again, the soldiers stepped off and, as one, made their way out of the open woods into the dead zone between their starting point and the French, high up on the crest of the hill. Again, a devastating fire was hurled at them by the enemy, who stood three ranks deep behind their breastworks. Again, soldiers hit and wounded fell from the already thin ranks, forcing those behind them to step over or, if necessary, upon them in order to keep up. And again, the men of the Forty-fourth Foot came face-to-face with the terrible abatis, now littered not only with their dead from the previous fight but the bodies of men from other units.

With a determination that bordered on fierceness, Thomas began to pick his way aggressively through the blood-stained tree limbs and branches. Whenever a part of the abatis poked him or impeded his progress, Thomas took his sword and beat upon it with all his might. Though such efforts seldom did any good, Thomas was now beyond reason. Sound, analytical thinking had no place here. Sane, logical men would not be venturing back out into a place occupied only by those who were dead or would soon be and dominated by other men, aloof and well protected, who were doing everything they could to see that more joined the dead. There was no more need for generals to think, for engineers to plan, or for staff officers to confer. The battle had long ago degenerated into nothing more than a test of wills, one in which the participants literally bet their lives that the other men, equally obsessed and driven by pride, anger, desperation, and countless other emotions, would break first.

Forward, Thomas made his way. Always forward. He struggled to find decent footing and squeeze past the limbs and branches surrounding and confronting him. He desperately tried to ignore the hiss and whine of bullets as they flew by or smacked on a nearby piece of the very obstacle he was climbing over. He even managed to forget about the pain of his own injuries as he drove steadily on.

Unfortunately for Thomas and the English cause that day, the only thing he was unable to do was inspire the men in the ranks behind him to follow his lead. Again, as they had earlier in the afternoon, the soldiers of the Forty-fourth Foot had gone as far as they could go, but found that it was simply not far enough. In ones and twos, then in entire groups, they turned their backs on the French works and made for the safety of the woods where they had started from.

Thomas, finding himself momentarily stranded between the two lines, one of which was holding and the other receding, paused. In the twinkling of an eye, all the resolve that he had managed to muster in his effort to keep going disappeared. As had happened before, on the Monongahela, Thomas took his unit's failure as a personal defeat. This renewed realization that he had again failed crashed down upon him. With it came all the pains and aches, so long kept in abeyance by little more than his will and his determination to succeed. Dejected, and no longer seeing any need to stay where he was, Thomas slowly made his own way back to the rear. If he heard the whine of parting shots being taken by the French infantry, he paid no attention to them. His mind was busy closing itself to all that was around him as he reeled, physically and mentally, from his latest failed effort.

In the French Works

WHEN the fighting died down near sunset, Anton, as well as every Frenchman, from the marquis to the lowest private, believed that the seven assaults they had thrown back had been but the opening moves of the English. With few exceptions, they waited for the next dawn to see, if the English permitted them to do so, what their foe's next move would be. Few guessed right.

It wasn't until well after sunrise the following morning that they realized they had won. Together with the officers and soldiers of the line regiments, Anton stood atop the works that commanded the crest of the hill and looked down at the terrible execution they had visited upon the advancing English regiments. Every so often, a moan could be heard above the awful silence that lay upon the battlefield as an Englishman, wounded and abandoned, was overcome by pain. Back and forth, Anton's eyes swept, pausing every so often to inspect in greater detail one of the hundreds of corpses that littered the abatis and the open stretch of ground that lay before it and the woods where the English had been. Red-, blue-, green-, and brown-coated corpses, all mixed together, were all that remained of the English army that had come here to conquer them.

"It is amazing," one officer stated softly in awe.

"It is a miracle," another murmured with great reverence.

"It was to be expected," a captain stated firmly.

Turning, Anton looked at this captain of regulars for a moment before shaking his head and correcting him. "Nothing, my friend, in this life is certain."

The captain, as unbowed as the French army with which he stood, looked at Anton with narrowed eyes. "The English soldier is a good soldier. He marches well and can deliver a devastating volley again and again that only the bravest of the brave can stand up to. But his commanders are fools. They are, to a man, idiots, and cowards. Their efforts to break us here proves the first point. And their panicked flight in the night demonstrates my second. We have little to fear from any army led by such men."

Anton shook his head and gave his overly confident companion a sad smile. Looking out at the abatis, Anton caught sight of an English officer lying yards from where they stood and pointed to him. "They are not all cowards. If we were to walk the ground before us, we would find, I am sure, many like him, who died doing everything they could to reach us here." Dropping his hand, Anton again looked at the captain of infantry. "And if some are not cowards, then there are those who are not idiots. Given time, my dear captain, one will find his way to these shores, and then it will be our bodies, and not theirs, upon which the flies feast."

Stunned into silence as much by the conviction in Anton's voice as by his logic, the captain of infantry blinked, then looked away. The others who had been listening kept staring at this lieutenant of artillery who was foolish enough to predict gloom and doom at the moment of their greatest triumph. Only the appearance of their commanding general, trailed by his staff, broke the stillness that had descended upon this group as first one, then another, lifted his hat and joined the chorus of cheers that preceded the victor. Even Anton, who had moments before taken great pains to restrain his enthusiasm, found himself joining in.

CHAPTER TWENTY-FOUR

Western Pennsylvania
August, 1758

I T WASN'T UNTIL he had left Winchester, to join the main force moving against Fort Duquesne, that Ian McPherson discovered just how much he had come to depend upon the attention and company of Megan, his wife. "I didn't think it would matter as much as it has," he confessed to James McPike as the two sat perched where they could watch for trouble. "Just the thought that I can't walk out of the fort here," he lamented, "like I did in Winchester, and be with her in little less than a quarter hour is pure torture. We didn't even have to talk, you know. Just being in the same room was often good enough."

McPike, who had heard this same story on a daily basis now for the better part of two months glumly replied, "I know, Ian. You've told me all about this many, *many* times."

Lost in his own thoughts, Ian didn't pay any heed to McPike's bored tone. Instead, he continued to rattle on, telling his friend of his love for his wife as if it were the first time. "You know," Ian chuckled, "there're times we'll go on for hours without either of us saying a word. While she's tending to her bread and pies, I sit before the fire and smoke my pipe in peace, listenin' to her as she hums her tunes. The boy, of course, doesn't say a word. She claims he has, to her. But I've never heard a peep from him except, every now and then, when I'm still there and he's already asleep. On some nights he'll whimper a bit. Megan, the dear heart she is, only needs to lay her hand along his cheek, whisper in his ear, and the lad's off to sleep again."

"So," McPike interrupted, "you're plannin' on keepin' him?"

Ian turned and looked at his friend. "I'd as soon face a pack of bloodthirsty savages as tell Megan that we've got to give the lad up. Besides," Ian added with a hint of a smile on his face, "I've come to like the boy myself. Though he's small, he's tough, like a good Highland lad should be."

Turning his head from left to right, Ian looked over the wooded mountains that surrounded them. Back behind them, within easy running distance, he could hear the constant ringing of axes and, every now and then, the cracking of a tree as it began to fall and smash its way to the ground. There were times when Ian found himself wishing he was part of the detachment assigned to cutting the new road that would open the way to the French fort on the Ohio for Forbes' six-thousand-man army. Like Braddock, Forbes was hewing a wagon trail wide enough for his guns and provisions train. Unlike Braddock, he was building stout, defensible forts along the way. "If things don't go well again," Ian's commander had told him, "at least we'll have someplace to go to when it comes time to tuck tail and run."

That this expedition, Ian's third to the Ohio, might fail bothered him. Perhaps, he thought, that was the reason that he so missed his Megan. "James," Ian asked slowly as his mind turned to other matters, "have you ever thought of going back?"

Far more attentive to the dangers that lurked all about them, James McPike replied with a halfhearted, "Back? Back where?"

"Home," Ian replied. "Back to Scotland."

McPike looked over at Ian, stared at him for a moment, then shook his head. "It ain't my home anymore. The dragoons destroyed any feelings I had left for that sorry, miserable land. No, Ian, the thought never crossed my mind. Too many McPikes died there for naught. I'll not add another."

Ian looked out over the landscape for a moment as he collected his thoughts. "But it's our land, James," Ian responded. "*Ours.* Every generation has spilled its blood to defend what's rightfully ours. Doesn't that mean something?"

Now McPike's expression turned stormy. "Yes, Ian. By God it means something! It means it's time to stop shedding our blood in a fight we'll never win. It means finding a new life for ourselves, here, where a man is beholden to no one other than himself and his God. I've had enough of the clans, and the kings, and the English. And if there was an ounce of sense in that head of yours, you'd wash your hands of them, too."

Stunned by this outburst from a man who seldom raised his voice above a whisper, Ian fell silent. He was still trying to frame a response when, from out of the bushes that surrounded their high, rocky perch, a voice called out. "I've heard magpies that squawked less than you two," Captain Shaw said to them as he stepped from the shadows and into sight. "With as little concern as you two show for vigilance, I'm surprised that your hair isn't already decorating some brave's lodge."

Startled, both men instinctively grabbed for their muskets as they prepared to defend themselves. "Ah, well," Ian started to explain, "we were just discussin' . . ."

"I know what you were doing," Shaw answered for him as he continued to make his way up to the two men. Behind him another pair of soldiers from the company followed. "You were passing the day away with idle gossip and sad tales instead of keeping a sharp watch for the war parties that have been making Colonel Bouquet's road crews nervous."

Mention of the Englishman who served Forbes as his

second in command and was the individual responsible for opening the road made Ian smile. "By now I'm sure our darling Colonel Bouquet is regretting not having heeded Colonel Washington's advice and used the road leading up from Fort Cumberland," Ian stated.

Shaw, lifting his left boot up onto a rock, leaned forward, took off his hat, and folded his arms across his raised knee. Using the tip of his hat as a pointer, he thrust it at Ian. "All discussion over *that* issue," he stated, "is over and done with. Our English friends all accuse Colonel Washington of being far too concerned with colonial politics and not paying enough attention to his military duties. It's a sore subject, and I, for one, am tired of hearing about it. Now, sir, if you'd be so kind," Shaw continued, changing his tone of voice as he stood upright. "You and I have been asked to take a wee little walk."

Neither Ian nor McPike was fooled by Shaw's manner. Both knew that this was Shaw's way of telling Ian there was a particularly hazardous or unpleasant duty for him. Turning to face each other, Ian looked into McPike's eyes, then back to Shaw. "Is it to be both of us, or just me?"

Shaw frowned. "Good God, man, just you. I don't dare let the two of you go anywhere together where keeping one's mouth shut is a must."

Though he hadn't been looking for a clue as to what Shaw had in mind, this last comment left little doubt about what the nature of this pending mission would involve.

The "wee little walk" that Shaw had told Ian of turned out to be a scout of Fort Duquesne itself. Indians, sent off on their own, had returned with reports of French strength at the fort that Forbes and others suspected were inflated. All previous attempts by other provincials to reach the fort and provide accurate intelligence on the enemy had failed. "All we need to do, Ian, me lad," Shaw told him in what both knew was a gross understatement of the truth, "is go out there, count heads, make our way back as quick as we can, and tell the general what we saw."

"Oh!" Ian exclaimed, acting as surprised as he could. "Is that all? I thought you'd gone and volunteered us for something dangerous."

"Volunteered?" Shaw asked in surprise. "Who said anything about volunteers? Seems Major Lewis thought I'd be just the man for this particular task, so he threw his arm about me and said, 'Shaw, I need a favor of you.'"

"And you," Ian stated glumly, "decided to 'ask' me along?"

Shaw looked at Ian quizzically. "Strange! I don't remember asking you anything."

The two men would not be traveling alone. They would be accompanied to the forks of the Ohio by a band of Indians. This aspect of the scout was the one that troubled Ian the most. Indian loyalties throughout the entire region were in a state of flux. Efforts by English agents, priests, and some Indians themselves to wean tribes away from their traditional support of the French were having their effect. Together with the growing tide of French difficulties, including an inability to supply the Indians with trade goods and gifts, fewer and fewer natives were responding to French calls for warriors for their war against the English. This shift, of course, did not mean that the Indians were now solidly in the English camp. Many were more than happy to let the whites butcher each other in the forests that were still, as far as the Indians were concerned, theirs. Even those who did march with Forbes' column were regarded with great suspicion. "I'm sorry," Ian told Shaw. "I've buried far too many innocent women and children whose only sin was bein' in this country tryin' to make a life for themselves to place any faith or confidence in those people. If I had my way, we'd go out on our own."

Shaw, looking over at the Indians they would be traveling with as they prepared to leave, nodded. "Aye. I can't say that I'll be able to sleep without keeping one eye open myself while we're with 'em. But, we have our orders, lad. All we can do is place our faith in God and keep our wits about us. Now," he added in an effort to change the subject quickly, "let's finish up here and get moving."

They would travel light, taking only those things that they would absolutely need. Both wore a hunting frock, which was better suited to the wilderness than their regimentals and far less visible. On their heads they wore wide-brimmed, floppy hats that provided shade on those rare occasions when the sun did find its way through the forest, and kept the rain out of their eyes when the weather turned nasty. Leggings protected their shins, and moccasins provided both comfort and sure-footedness.

Though they were not looking for a fight, they needed to be ready if one found them. Each man carried a musket and drew thirty fresh cartridges for it. Rather than rely on bayonets, which Ian didn't much care for, they carried tomahawks tucked into their belts. The only difference in their choice of weapons came when Ian insisted on taking his ancient family broadsword. Shaw, who viewed a sword as little more than an encumbrance on such a mission, left his in the care of Ensign Flemming. "It'd be better," he advised Ian, "if you left that great bloody big sword of yours behind."

Ian, however, wouldn't be dissuaded. "It's more than a talisman to me," he tried to explain to Shaw. "I feel that when I carry this into battle, all my ancestors, long departed from this world, are with me." Having his own beliefs that were just as rooted to the mystical beliefs of his Irish homeland, Shaw just nodded and left it at that.

Besides their weapons, they each carried a blanket tightly rolled up and secured at the end of old cartridge box straps slung over one shoulder. From the other, a haversack containing several days' rations hung. Thus prepared, the two Virginians joined their Indian guides and departed without ceremony.

As always happened whenever he left the crowded, vile camps where too many soldiers loitered in their own stench like plump pigs in a sty, Ian found his spirits buoyed long before the small party made their first night's camp. With each step that first day, his attitude concerning his selection to accompany Shaw on this scout underwent an amazing transformation. Rather than shuffling along, shoulders slumped over and head hung low, Ian straightened up and took in the lush green landscape around him. It was more than the simple need to stay alert for danger. For only a blind man could travel through that world that was still fresh, still unspoiled by the despoiling hand of his fellow man, and not be awed by its beauty. The Indians, who claimed that these lands belonged to no man, left marks that were so light, it took only the passing of a single season to eradicate all evidence of their presence. Even traces of those few brave souls who had ventured west of the Susquehanna to establish trading posts or a farm and had fallen victim to the war were hard to discern.

Though his ancestral home couldn't boast but a fraction of the trees and greenery that the wilderness their tiny party was crawling through, the rocks underfoot, the fresh, flowing streams, and the quiet emptiness awoke old feelings. It wasn't long before Ian was lost in long-forgotten memories of his wanderings up and down the vast emptiness of the Scottish Highlands. "There would be days," Ian told Shaw that night, "when I'd be left on my own to tend the landlord's flock. I'd take the stick I used as a walking cane and pretend it was a sword. With a mighty battle cry, like those my grandfather had taught me, I'd charge the sheep and scatter 'em before me like so many leaves."

Shaw nodded and looked about to check on their Indian guides before he responded to Ian. "My landlord wasn't foolish enough to trust me with his sheep," he mused. "In fact, he didn't much trust any of us. Spent most of his time in London, where he could squander the money he collected from us, regardless of how bad the times were. In London, there were no famines, no droughts, no crop failures. I only saw the man twice before I gave up on laboring day and night with nothing to look forward to but an early grave. He was not at all what I expected, not the effete wisp that I had always imagined. He had a hard, cruel look about him, an image that stayed with me during all my years of service in one of the French army's Irish regiments of Wild Geese. I always hoped that someday there would be a war between France and England, one that would bring me face-to-face with the bastard, at bayonet's point." Lost in his own memories, Shaw thrust a stick he had been holding into the heart of the fire, as if he were stabbing his former landlord.

In time, Shaw realized that he had allowed himself to be carried away by his own passions, something he seldom did. Looking over to Ian, he smiled shyly. "Of course, I left the French army after the War of Austrian Succession without ever catching the old devil on the battlefield. Fact was, he wasn't the military type. He was just mean."

"And now," Ian chuckled at the irony of their situation, "here we are, two former rebels doing the bidding of a master we both took up arms to slay."

Shaw saw no humor in Ian's comment. Instead, his eyes narrowed as he leaned forward, closer to the Scotsman. "We're not doing this for him," Shaw snapped. "We're doing this for *us*. When this is all over," he whispered, "this land will be *ours*. There'll be no lords or ladies to profane this place with their presence. There'll be no absentee landlords who suck away the lifeblood of their tenants so that they can troop about a city as foreign to us as the sultan's palace. This land, this war, it's *ours*."

The viciousness with which Shaw stated his views surprised Ian. To see a man so worked up who was, under any other circumstances, rather reserved and calm was novel.

Ian's action broke the trance that Shaw had allowed himself to slip into. Turning back to the fire, now beginning to die, he took up a stick and began to stab at it again. "My time will be up when we finish this campaign. If all goes well, and we finally do manage to chase the French from the Ohio, the fear we've lived with in Virginia should lift like the morning fog." Glancing over to Ian, he studied his trusted sergeant for a moment. "A word of advice, if you don't mind?"

Ian shook his head.

"I overheard what you and McPike were talking about. You can believe me when I tell you, I understand that burning desire to go back to your homeland that you hid so well. For years I carried the same thought with me like a great bloody rock. And like a rock, it always held me back from starting a new life, finding a place where I could spend my days in peace. Ian," Shaw cautioned the Scotsman, "let go of it. Scotland and Ireland are not our homes anymore. Maybe," he added mournfully, "they never were."

Again, a silence lapsed between the two men as Ian tried, but failed, to find a way of arguing his point. Shaw, sitting across from the fire, watching Ian, allowed time for his words to set in before he continued.

"Ian, give up your foolish quest. Take that wife of yours, and the boy, too, if no one's claimed him yet, and buy that patch of land Megan's got her eye on. Turn your hand to the plow and raise a family. You're ready to, lad. Let the English and the French settle the rest of their affairs between themselves. Once we've burned Duquesne, the Virginia frontier will be safe, and our duty will be done."

Ian looked down, bowing his head as if in prayer. For the longest time he thought about his life, both past and present, and tried to reconcile the two. It was some time before he looked up at Shaw and nodded. "Captain," Ian started, using a reverent tone of respect to a man who had become more of a father to him than his own, "I always told myself that someday I'd go back. And yet, every step I've taken these past years has led me along a new trail that's so inviting, so promising. Still," he continued, turning his head from Shaw, "it's not within me simply to turn my back on something that's been a part of me for so long." Looking back at Shaw, Ian leaned forward, stretching out his right hand, palm up. "Surely you can understand that?"

"Ian," Shaw responded in a dour tone, "don't let the shadows of your past lead you to a miserable end. Close your mind to those sad chapters from your past and write yourself a new future, one that's free of the ways that have been the bane of our people."

It was some time before Ian, turning his attention to the fire that was slowly dying away, responded to Shaw's admonishments. "I will consider what you said, Captain." Then he looked over at Shaw. "It's not easy, you know, to cast away your past."

"I'm not asking you to cast away anything," Shaw countered. "But I am asking you not to squander your life in pursuit of a fool's errand. Take command of your life, and your future, lad. It's in your power to do so, if you will it."

Ian nodded, but said nothing.

Then, without preamble, Shaw reached out and laid his hand on Ian's knee. "Whatever your decision, lad, always keep that sword of yours close at hand."

With a quick glance, Ian looked over to where the Indians

sat, then back at Shaw. "Aye, that I will. I've seen what they can do. I'll not drop my guard, ever."

Shaw smiled again as a wicked glimmer began to shine in his eye. "It's not them you'll be needing to be on your guard against, Ian. In time, I dare say, we'll both live to see our fondest dreams come true, but only if we're willing to fight one more fight, one that we've both dreamed of for years."

Having lost track of where Shaw had taken the conversation, Ian thought about what he had just said. Finally, as if the woods were full of spies, Ian leaned forward and whispered, "You mean the English?"

"Aye," Shaw replied dryly. "There'll be a day when this land will feel their heavy hand, just as Ireland and Scotland did. Just be ready, lad, when that day comes."

When they were but a few miles from the French fort, the Indians halted. Gathering around, the chief warrior opened an otter-skinned pouch he had been carrying and began to pull out various packets of paint from it. With great care, the warriors dipped their fingers into the small packets and smeared their faces, bodies, and arms. Each created, for himself, his own particular designs and devices. When they were finished, the chief warrior picked up his packets of paint, stood up, and made his way over to where Shaw and Ian sat watching. Kneeling down before Shaw, the warrior looked into his eyes for a moment, then went fishing about with his fingers for something in the small otter-skin pouch. When his fingertips found the charm that he was searching for, he pulled it from the pouch. Without a word, he hung the charm about Shaw's neck. Then he turned to Ian. Pulling out a small packet of paint, he handed it to him.

For a moment, Ian looked at the warrior, then over at Shaw. Then, lifting himself until he was on his knees before the Indian brave, Ian dipped his fingers into the packet and began to color his face. His ancestors, he had been told, had painted their faces before going into battle. Perhaps, he thought, there might be something to it.

Only when Ian was finished, and indicated as such with a nod, did the warrior speak. "None of us can be shot," he said in a calm voice. "These things we wear will turn the French balls from us." Then, after shaking the hands of the two Virginians, he told them, "Go, fight like men."

Fortune smiled on the small party that day as they climbed a small hill covered with trees and brushes not far from Fort Duquesne. They didn't run into any Frenchmen, or any of the Indians who had gathered about the walls of the fort in huts and skin-covered lodges. Hidden from view, Shaw and Ian were free to survey the French works, a place whose destruction had long ago become a quest to many an English general and politician. It did not take Shaw long to determine that the number of defenders previously reported had been grossly exaggerated. "Perhaps this time," he quietly told Ian as they prepared to back away from their hidden vantage point, "we'll be able to see this thing through, to the end."

Ian, gripping his musket tightly as his eyes glanced from side to side, didn't reply. After having started the journey to this very point twice before, and being stopped cold at a terrible cost each time, he wasn't about to allow his hopes to run wild. Leaning forward, he whispered in Shaw's ear, "I'll not be satisfied till I see that place in ashes."

Though he was busy taking one last look at a party of French officers gathered about the open gate of the fort, Shaw nodded. "Aye. Nor will I."

CHAPTER TWENTY-FIVE

Western Pennsylvania
September, 1758

THE SUCCESS of the scout by Shaw and Ian was not greeted with anything near the joy or relief that Ian had expected. Instead, it created more disharmony among the senior officers of the expedition than it did satisfaction. Colonel Bouquet, commander of the advance party at Fort Loyalhanna, while pleased with the information that Shaw and Ian brought him, still had his difficulties. General Forbes, the nominal commander of the expedition, had been stricken with the curse of the soldier high and low, the bloody flux. Reduced to being carried about from place to place on a litter, Forbes was unable to carry out his full range of duties and responsibilities. That left Bouquet solely responsible for opening the road to Fort Duquesne, still some forty miles from Loyalhanna. With the advancing season now becoming as threatening as the growing number of Indian attacks on his road-building crews, Colonel Bouquet was fast reaching his wit's end.

Ian, who was constantly being charged with leading small parties out in the hope of finding and discouraging these raids, saw all the signs of a pending disaster. "It has been three years we've been at it," he complained to Shaw and Major Andrew Lewis after returning from an exhausting hunt that had taken him up and down the surrounding mountains. "Three years since Braddock was shot from his saddle. And still, the English send us gentlemen like Bouquet to lead us blindly into the woods like sheep."

Both Lewis and Shaw, experienced with the peculiarities of Indian warfare, shared Ian's feelings. Unlike Ian, they had to withstand the indignity of having their advice ignored and being told time and again by officers of the Crown that they were little more than amateurs who knew not what they spoke of when it came to the serious matter of war. "After all these years," Shaw muttered to Lewis and Ian, not caring who heard him, "I thought that the anger that colored Colonel Washington's cheeks when he spoke of his dealings with the English generals in America was due to wounded pride. Between the pompous politicians in Williamsburg and the arrogant laced and braided gentlemen sent by the king to save us, it's a wonder he's managed to keep his sanity."

Major Lewis agreed. "At least," he sighed, "this will all be over soon. With the road near completion, we'll be free to move the entire army forward and bring this campaign to an end." Then, with a note of regret in his voice, he added, "While it will be a shame to see both of you leave the regiment, I cannot say that I blame you."

Shaw, knowing where Lewis' comment was leading, quickly intervened. "If it's a speech you're planning on making about how much better the regiment would be if we stayed, then you're wasting your time, Andrew. I've got a small farm that I can almost hear crying for my attention and McPherson here has a lovely wife and a burning desire to find a place of his own, back in Winchester. We'll go with you to the Ohio, and see this thing out. But then you're on your own."

Lewis smiled. "What? You're leaving me all alone to deal with our English cousins?"

Without hesitation, Ian answered. "If ever there's a need to give 'em what they deserve," he whispered, clasping the hilt of his broadsword, "I'll be there, with you."

The coming of the first chilling winds of autumn increased the level of desperation among the senior English officers. The road crawled forward, but only slowly, painfully. The Indians continued their attacks, nibbling away at the expedition, doing far more damage to its morale than the number of scalps would indicate. And the expedition's forceful leader, still laid low by his painful malady, had little choice but to leave the day-to-day operations to his subordinates.

One of these men, a major in the Seventy-seventh Regiment of Royal Americans, came forth with a plan to solve many of Colonel Bouquet's problems. With the confidence of one ignorant of what he was speaking about, Major James Grant proposed that he be permitted to lead a large detachment of five hundred men, his own, of course, on a reconnaissance right up to the very gates of Fort Duquesne itself. Bouquet, desperate to try anything that would take the pressure off his road crews and expedite the completion of the campaign, approved Grant's scheme, not realizing when he did that General Forbes had already disapproved the same request when Grant had presented it to Forbes himself. Since both Bouquet and Grant were regular officers highly regarded for their professionalism but totally lacking in experience in the conduct of irregular warfare, neither man appreciated the dangers they were preparing to venture into.

Bouquet, seeing the possibility of doing more than scouting out the French fort, reinforced Grant's five hundred men with an additional three hundred. Together with these men, he tasked Grant to attack and destroy any Indian camps that they might manage to find. Grant, pleased that he had finally managed to secure an independent command and an opportunity to secure for himself glory and recognition of his military prowess, set off with that command on September 9. Part of this command was led by Major Andrew Lewis and consisted of several companies of Virginians, including Shaw's.

Whereas in their previous scout, Shaw and Ian had moved through the forests of western Pennsylvania with the deftness of a deer, Grant's column blundered forward like an ox. The baggage train, though small and composed of pack-horses, still required a guard. The Virginians, the most experienced of all of Grant's soldiers when it came to fighting in the woods, were assigned this duty. Except for putting up with the antics of a few of the horses and their smell, Ian didn't mind being in the rear. It kept him separated from the red-coated and kilted soldiers of the Seventy-seventh Regiment. Those few who did lag behind when they had problems with their feet and couldn't keep up knew to stay clear of Ian. All it took for most was a glimpse of Ian's broadsword at his side and the scowl that he wore to warn off any member of the Seventy-seventh who came close to him. "You know, Ian," McPike quipped, "they're on our side."

With an expression every bit as vicious as the one he flashed at the passing Highlanders of the Seventy-seventh, Ian turned on McPike. "Men like that betrayed us in '45. Given a chance, they'd do it again. They've sold their soul to the German devil who claims to be our king."

McPike, expecting such a reaction, surprised Ian by returning his friend's angry condemnation with a smile. "If they were traitors for following that king in '45, what does that make us? After all, in case you haven't noticed, the flag they're carryin' is the same as that which flew at Culloden. And when we finally do manage to throw the Frenchies off this continent, that's the flag that we'll all be livin' under."

Ian didn't respond at first. Instead, he looked down at the ground as his feet continued to carry him forward, toward the forks of the Ohio. As he did so, he thought about what Shaw had said before. He thought about his life as it had come to be. More important, he thought about what he hoped it would become. After a while, he looked up. At first, he didn't look over at McPike, who was still walking next to him, waiting to pick up the conversation where they had left it. Instead, Ian peered through the breaks in the trees, catching a glimpse, every now and then, of the forest-covered mountain across the valley from the one they were moving along. It was a beautiful country that his eyes fell upon. Though it would never have the hold on his heart that the Highlands still seemed to exert, Shaw had been right. This was their country, their home. Regardless of what had brought them here, all of them—Ian, Shaw, McPike, Megan, and countless others marching side by side with him now—had no other home than Virginia.

Finally, as the last rays of a fading day made their way through the dense, silent wilderness, it occurred to Ian that on the frontier it didn't matter what king finally claimed them as subjects. When all was said and done, what King George did or said would be of little importance. "Out here," Ian stated as he tilted his head back as far as it would go and looked up at the massive trees that seemed to reach heaven itself, "what will matter is what we do with our lives and this land."

"Then, you're going to take the land they give us, and settle out here," McPike replied.

Ian laughed as he shook his head and let it drop. "No, James, I think not. I'm too old for that sort of thing. Perhaps, if I were fourteen again." Then, as if a cloud passed over him, the joy on his face faded. By the time he looked over at McPike, he wore an expression of regret. "I was a foolish lad at fourteen, you know. Thought that being a soldier in Prince Charlie's service was the thing to do." He paused, looked around, and shook his head. "Well, I'm twenty-seven now. At times," he continued as he eyed two soldiers of the Seventy-seventh Foot resting against a tree on the side of the road, "I wonder if I'm any smarter."

Sensing Ian's melancholy mood, James piped up. "I wouldn't say that, exactly. Least you were bright enough to reach out and catch Megan when she came your way."

This caused Ian to smile. "I'm not sure if it was a case of me catching her, or the other way around. She's got to be the most determined, strong-willed woman I've ever known."

"And," McPike added, "a damned fine cook."

Ian chuckled, looked McPike in the eye, and nodded. His friend had reminded him that, despite the long and bloody roads he had taken in the past, this one would be different. This time, when the long march they were on was over, he would have someplace to go, where a person who loved him would be waiting.

Near the Forks of the Ohio, Western Pennsylvania September 13, 1758

LYING among the leaves flat on his back, with the fingers of both hands knitted together behind his head, Ian was enjoying the quiet, peaceful afternoon along with Major Lewis and the bulk of the Virginians. It had been hours since he, and practically every one of the two-hundred-odd men of Lewis' command sent forward by Grant to set up an ambush, had given up on the enterprise. Only Lieutenant Colesby Chew and fifteen men sent forward to "stir up some trouble" were not there to enjoy the restful afternoon. No one with Lewis' ambush party knew yet that Chew and his men had failed to find the French fort, let alone take shots at its defenders. Nor, as the late afternoon sun began to cast long shadows throughout the forest, did anyone much care.

McPike, who had been fast asleep next to Ian, woke up and propped himself up on his arm. Looking about, he let out a yawn. "Well, Ian, me lad, either they've come and gone without tellin' us, or our dear Major Grant's plan isn't workin'."

Ian grunted. "Couldn't have been here. Captain Shaw promised to wake me if anything exciting happened."

"Then, I fear," McPike replied mockingly, "we've been

had." In the same tone, he asked, "Ian, do you suppose our dear Major Grant knows what he's doing?"

Cracking one eye open, Ian looked up at McPike. "Don't be a fool." He sighed. "Major Grant's a professional. Why, he's one of the king's finest, didn't you know?"

With a more serious note in his voice, McPike replied as he continued to look about, "Aye, so I've been told." With nothing to do, and sensing that there was no imminent danger, McPike eased his body back down to the ground and did what most soldiers do when they're left to their own devices. Within minutes, he was sound asleep, letting his snores mingle with those of other men scattered about the peaceful woods around them.

By late afternoon even Major Grant himself had given up all hope of seeing this plan through. Moving with his main body of troops to where Major Lewis and his Virginians still sat, unengaged and undetected, he learned that Chew and his party, now terribly lost and stumbling about in the wilderness, had not returned. After several minutes of discussion with other English officers, Grant decided to move on with his entire force.

Into the early evening darkness, the column pressed on. The lazy, almost idyllic afternoon was replaced by a nightmarish march through the forest that left most wondering what was going to happen next. Only the incessant stumbling and tripping over fallen trees, roots, and, at times, each other kept the soldiers of Grant's small command from dwelling on their fears and apprehensions. After several hours, the entire column was brought to a halt. Ian, like many of the others, thought that their trials, at least for this day, were at an end. He was, of course, wrong.

After a brief halt, during which the noncommissioned officers and soldiers dropped immediately to the ground and made themselves comfortable, a new plan emerged. "We're leavin' the baggage train," Captain Shaw informed his officers and senior sergeants, "and going on. Tom Bullett and his boys will be staying with the trains." Shaw's words were met with a stunned silence. He himself was thankful for the darkness, for it saved him from having to look into the eyes of men whom he had just ordered to participate in what all now believed to be a dangerous folly. In the hope that their captain had another bit of information with which they could make some sense of what they were about to do, all of Shaw's leaders continued to stand about their commander as they waited for him to continue. Shaw, however, was not able to provide them with this or any other form of encouragement. With their immediate future as black as their very surroundings, the long column of English regulars and provincials pressed on, leaving Captain Bullett and his fifty Virginians behind to guard the train and count their blessings.

It wasn't till an hour before midnight that the column reached a hill Ian thought was familiar. Glancing off to one side, he caught glimpses of the Monongahela. Looking off in the opposite direction, he saw an occasional sparkling of light on the Allegheny. Though there was a sizable number of men in his way, Ian looked to the front, where the French fort stood. And though he couldn't see it, he knew it was there.

Again the column halted, and again new orders came down from Grant, through Lewis, to Shaw, and eventually to Ian and the rest of the company. "We're to go forward now, to attack the Indian camps outside the fort."

Again, Shaw's pronouncement met with a dead silence. Drawing in a deep breath, he continued. "We're to strip down to our white shirts, so that we don't become confused in the dark and shoot each other."

That the French also had white shirts, and would more than likely be wearing them, and little else if aroused in the middle of the night by an attack, occurred to Ian. But he said nothing. Somehow, he told himself, this all had to make sense. He couldn't make any of it, but surely . . .

"Major Grant and the main force will remain here, on this hill," Shaw continued. "When the shooting begins, they'll beat their drums and play the pipes to guide us back."

Although Ian, like all the other officers and sergeants gathered about, wanted to ask some very serious questions, none did. As Shaw had with Lewis, they trusted that their next senior commander had a better grasp of the situation than they themselves had. With little else to do but place their complete trust in the judgment of that commander, everyone carried out Grant's orders. "Neither Lewis nor Shaw," Ian responded to questions McPike felt no reservations about voicing, "would willingly take us forward unless there was a chance of succeeding."

McPike was not convinced. He continued to rant as he secured his hunting frock in the same roll he carried his blanket. "I'm not near as trustin' as you, Ian. And I'm a damned sight less willin' to go do whatever someone says simply because there's 'a chance' we'll make it through."

Ian, already exerting all his inner strength to suppress his own fears and doubts, snapped, "What are you going to do, then? Stay? Desert?"

Angered by Ian's innuendo, McPike gave the leather strap of his blanket roll one final tug and turned to face his friend. Surprisingly, his voice was calm, almost friendly. "Course not. Who's gonna watch out for you if I up and did somethin' like that?"

McPike's reply and tone had its desired effect. Ian calmed down and allowed himself, for the moment at least, to push aside his fears. How could he be afraid with good men like this all around him.

With four hundred men, Major Lewis went forward. Not all were Virginians. Some were Marylanders, some from Pennsylvania. All were exhausted, all frightened. Yet they, like Lewis, followed their orders. Fortunately for them, once he was away from Major Grant, Andrew Lewis was struck by a fit of sanity. Belatedly, he realized that it would be madness to conduct a night attack with so many men who had not worked together before, on bad ground that he was totally unfamiliar with, against a more numerous enemy. Using his own discretion, he ordered his men back and, without much of an apology, explained to Grant that what was required of them was simply beyond their ability.

Major Grant, however, was still under the belief that nothing was impossible. He would do more than harass the Indians and the French. *He* would seize Fort Duquesne, not to mention the honors that would follow in the wake of such a coup. Again, on the spot, Grant came up with a new plan. He started by sending Lewis back with 250 of his men to the supply train. In part, they were sent to guard it. In part, they were to serve as a reserve. But also implied in this decision was a punishment for Lewis' failure. While it may have been true that Grant was acting wisely in establishing a strong reserve, it was just as likely that he decided the Virginians would not have the privilege of sharing in the honor and glory that victory would bring him. With three hundred of his Highlanders, one hundred Marylanders, and one hundred Pennsylvanians, Grant remained on the hill, where he again set up an ambush. Sending fifty of his own Highlanders forward to "shoot somebody," Grant waited impatiently for the French to come boiling out of their fort in response to his prodding and march straight into the guns of his men.

By dawn, despite the torching of a barn the Highlanders had stumbled upon in the dark, the French continued to refuse to cooperate with Grant's plan, leaving the English commander desperate and with few options. With no darkness left to conceal his efforts any longer, Grant threw all caution to the wind and presented the French with an invitation that they could not ignore. With his entire command in formation, in full sight of the French force, he ordered his drummers and pipers to sound reveille.

This, of course, did the trick. The French commander, informed of the English presence only minutes before Grant's musicians struck up their peculiar call to give battle, responded immediately and decisively.

Before his very eyes, Major Grant watched in amazement as the gates of the dreaded French fort at the forks of the Ohio opened wide and disgorged its eight-hundred-man garrison with three hundred Indian allies. Amazement soon turned to shock when, instead of forming up properly and marching dumbly into his guns, the way a good European army should, the Frenchmen and Indians continued to run off on their own, around the flanks of the English formation. In a battle reminiscent of the one that had claimed Braddock's life three years prior and left the entire frontier of Virginia open to Indian raids, Grant's five hundred men were butchered where they stood. Were it not for the fact that discipline quickly collapsed under the devastating weight of enemy fire and most soldiers took to their heels, none of Grant's men would have survived.

Two miles to the rear, Andrew Lewis listened to the sound of battle as it quickly started to roll his way. Realizing what this meant, he reacted without hesitation and decisively. Taking all but fifty men, Lewis led his Virginians forward at a run in the desperate hope of saving at least a part of Grant's command. Unfortunately for Lewis and his Virginians, the refugees of Grant's shattered command didn't use the same trail they had used the night before. Fleeing every which way, except the way Lewis had chosen to come to their assistance, Lewis' column ran smack into a wave of French and Indians trying to catch up to Grant's routed command.

For several minutes, there was confusion and utter chaos as Frenchmen and Indians, running for all they were worth in the hope of catching their foe and finishing their destruction, collided with the charging Virginians, who were equally determined to save their fellow soldiers. In this wild melee no commanders were able to give orders in the beginning. There was, after all, no need to do so. Frenchmen and Indians fell upon Virginians, and the Virginians took up the challenge by seeking cover and opening as deadly a fire upon their foe as they could manage. The only command Andrew Lewis finally managed to issue in the course of that fight was one that was almost unnecessary. It was the order to withdraw. For while he still had no idea what had become of Grant and his men, Lewis quickly saw that to stay and fight it out would be suicidal. Fortunately for him and the fleeing survivors of both detachments, enough of his Virginians kept their cool and stayed with their officers and sergeants. With skill and a courage borne of desperation, this handful of men conducted a fighting withdrawal to the supply train, where Captain John Shaw and his small company waited, deployed and ready, to pick up the fight when it reached them.

Major Andrew Lewis had not even departed in his vain effort to save Grant from himself before the men of Shaw's company scattered to find themselves good positions from which to meet the oncoming French. As with Lewis' men, Shaw needed to give few orders. Everyone knew what was at stake. Some, like McPike and Ian, had seen this all before. They knew what was coming. So they prepared as best they could as quickly as they could. Together with two other men with whom Ian and McPike shared practically everything, they created a hasty fieldwork that offered them some protection in each direction. "They'll not come at us head-on," Ian told the other three as he posted one to each side. "Once they have a measure of where we're at, they'll go around and try to find where we're weak. Some will even manage to sneak up behind us."

Patting his musket, all primed and ready, McPike smiled. "That's what I'll be keepin' one good eye open for. So don't worry about what's happenin' back here."

Ian gave McPike a wary smile and nodded. "Once I can tell where their most dangerous fire is coming from, I'll shift myself to that side. The rest of our lads," Ian indicated as he pointed to the other clusters of men, "will be doin' the same. And from over there," he pointed, "Captain Shaw and the other officers will be watchin' us all. If need be, he'll use us to reinforce a weak point."

One of the two men was a young German lad who hadn't saved enough money to buy his own land yet. After looking about he asked the obvious question. "Vhat if ve cannot stop der savages?"

For a moment, Ian looked intensely into the wide, nervous eyes of the German in an effort to gauge if this boy would fight, flee, or freeze when the shooting began. When he had determined he would stand, Ian put his hand on the boy's shoulder and gave it a gentle, reassuring squeeze. "Lad, put your faith in God, make sure you take careful aim, and stay close to me."

For a moment, the German looked at Ian, half expecting him to say more. But then he realized that his sergeant wasn't going to say anything else. Ian's advice pretty well summed up everything he would need to remember in the coming fight. With a stiff nod, the boy acknowledged that he understood and turned to take his place.

The first to reach Shaw's small bastion of safety were the

fastest and healthiest of Grant's men who had been the first to break and run. Mixed with them without any rhyme or reason were Marylanders and those of the Pennsylvania regiment. Ian took little satisfaction in seeing the Highlanders of the Seventy-seventh, bare-headed, without their weapons, and with kilts flying, fleeing past him. Hardly a man among them paused long enough to return his stares. They were all too anxious to put as much distance between themselves and their godless foes as their feet would let them. That their salvation depended upon how well the Virginians they were ignoring did in the coming fight didn't matter to these men Grant had so boldly led to the slaughter.

Next came small knots of men. Like the others they were broken, but they were going back at a slower pace. Most of these men, unlike the first bunch, still had their weapons with them. A few even cast a wary eye back in the direction from which they had come. Many, Ian imagined, were as concerned with keeping away from their own officers, who might make them stand and fight again, as they were about their foes.

Following a short break, the last of them came. With them were those officers and sergeants who had survived, so far. Some of these leaders had even managed to keep a handful of their men together and under their control. Not that they did anything with this gift. After having survived their first shock of battle, few were prepared, at that moment at least, to face another trial by fire. Besides, Ian knew that most of the officers appreciated that if they tried to make their men stand, those few remnants of what had been a proud regiment would scatter before their very eyes. So the officers contented themselves with the knowledge that they, at least, would be permitted to salvage some semblance of pride from the fact that they hadn't run and had managed to behave as good English gentlemen were supposed to.

Again there was a break before the next cluster of fleeing men raced back through Shaw's positions. This time it was the refugees of Lewis' ill-fated command. Though there were far fewer Virginians fleeing in abject panic, their determination to survive at any cost was just as sincere as it had been with the men of the Seventy-seventh Foot. This time, there was no clear, discernible break as the French soldiers and the Indian allies came on. Lewis and his officers, struggling to hold their men together, were fighting as they withdrew. Drawing in a deep breath, Ian brought his musket up to the ready, scrunched down a bit more behind the log to his front, and cautioned his men, "Make sure you mark your targets, lads. Some of our boys are mixed in with the Frenchies."

None of those with Ian replied, at least not with words. As he kept an eye out to the front, Ian counted the clicking of hammers as his companions pulled them back to the full-cocked position. When he had counted three, he slowly eased his own back and waited.

To his front, a Virginian appeared. With his musket at his side and a tomahawk in his other hand, he was pumping his arms for all he was worth as he headed straight toward Ian. Behind him, two Indians came bursting out of the woods. One held a musket across his chest, swinging it wildly back and forth as he tried to catch up to the fleeing Virginian. The other, not more than a stride or two behind the Virginian, held his tomahawk over his head as he bore down on his prey. Though the wild flight of his bullet coming out of an unrifled bore had as good a chance of hitting the man he was trying to save, Ian did not hesitate. Bringing his weapon up to his shoulder, Ian fixed his eye along the barrel until the muzzle was on target. Only when he was ready did he squeeze the trigger. The flash, the kick, and a cloud of smoke from his musket's discharge obscured both the Indian and the Virginian for a moment.

Even before Ian had a chance to bring his weapon down and start to reload, the Virginian popped back into view. Realizing what had happened, the Virginian looked behind. As soon as he noticed that he had but one pursuer still chasing him, the Virginian stopped dead in his tracks and turned on him. The Indian, surprised by this sudden reverse, tried to bring up his musket in an effort to club his quarry. This move, however, served only to expose his chest to a strike by the Virginian, delivered with his tomahawk. With a single well-practiced swing, the Virginian brought the tomahawk around, smashing it into the rib cage of the shocked Indian. With a flick of his wrist, the Virginian freed his weapon from between the two ribs it had bitten into and turned to continue his flight even before the stricken Indian sank to the ground.

Ian was busy reloading his musket when the Virginian he had just saved leaped over the logs with a single, high leap. Though he landed on both feet, the newcomer quickly dropped to the ground next to Ian, and immediately set about reloading his own musket. By now, the German boy was up and aiming his piece, as was the lad on Ian's other side. Only McPike, to the rear, was unengaged for the moment. For that small blessing, Ian uttered a silent prayer as his nimble fingers ran the long ramrod down the barrel till its progress was arrested by contact with the ball and wadding. He gave the ramrod two quick shoves to seat the round, then withdrew it and made ready to fire.

Both Ian and the newly arrived Virginian popped up from behind their protective log at the same time. Ian, catching sight of a likely target, was quicker and fired first. The Virginian held his fire, giving Ian a chance to get started on his reloading so that they would have one weapon loaded and ready to fire at all times, just in case a foe got too close too fast. Only when Ian was returning his ramrod back into the holders under the barrel did the Virginian find a mark, aim, and fire.

Just how long they stood their ground was impossible for Ian to tell before he heard the loud, clear voice of Captain Shaw bellow out the order to withdraw. With the Indians and their French allies up close and on both sides, not all of Shaw's men could up and run at once. Turning, Ian shouted to McPike to take the others and go while he hung back a few seconds. McPike, he knew, would go back ten, twenty yards, stop, turn, and cover Ian's withdrawal. Whether the other two would stay with McPike was questionable. Though they had held so far, once a retreat started, the courage and determination in many men quickly melted away.

It took Ian a moment to realize, after McPike was gone, that the Virginian who had joined them had stayed with him. Looking up from his musket as he reloaded it, he locked eyes with the Virginian. Ian gave the man a nod, and he returned it with a nod and a smile of his own. Then he raised his weapon, took aim, and fired. "Reload," Ian shouted over the din of battle. "When you're ready, we'll go."

The Virginian didn't bother to acknowledge the order. He merely went about reloading and didn't look directly at Ian until he was done. Then he smiled again. "Ready," he shouted. Ian took a single, quick glance about the smoke-choked woods, now littered with dead and dying men as well as pack animals abandoned to the enemy. Only when he was confident that there were no foes bearing down on them or about to fire did Ian push himself up off the ground. Together, the two Virginians leaped over the log that had formed the rear of their tiny bastion and took off at a dead run. With muskets held at the ready, the two headed back, side by side, to where they hoped they would find McPike, and safety.

CHAPTER TWENTY-SIX

Albany, New York
October, 1758

THOMAS WASN'T greeted by his wife when he arrived at his home. A servant told him, as she was taking his cloak and hat, that his wife still had not fully recovered from the birth of his son. "She's been feelin' poorly since that day," the girl chatted on despite the fact Thomas paid her no attention. "Can't say that I blame her. What, with her father passing on the week before the boy came and all the bleedin' she suffered after the baby was delivered, I venture to say you're a lucky man to still have a wife to come home to."

Not surprisingly, the passing of the elder Van der Hoff was of little concern to Thomas. The old man had always been opposed to the marriage. His death simply meant that Thomas would no longer need to tolerate the old man's ridicule and scorn. And as far as Katherine's ill health, well, such problems, as far as he knew, were part of childbirth. It was the boy whom he was concerned with. Anxious to see him for the first time, Thomas took the stairs two at a time. It was only when he reached the top of the stairs that he realized he wasn't quite sure if the baby was with the mother or in another room.

From behind him a voice called up from the hall below, where the girl was still hanging up Thomas' coat. "Sir, the child's room is the second to the right, adjoining the governess's room. Her name is . . ." Having no interest in what the name of the woman charged with caring for his son was, Thomas headed for the appropriate room. Seeing no need to knock and wait to be invited into a room that was in his own house, Thomas barged in. It was only when he was actually there, standing in the open doorway, that he came to realize he had no idea what to expect. Having been raised virtually in isolation, with next to no contact with his own father and only an older brother to play with, Thomas suddenly found himself stymied as to what to do as he stared dumbly at the crib sitting before him.

Without a full-sized bed, the room looked almost empty. The small crib, resembling an ornate basket, sat in the center of the room. A rocker, a second chair, a simple set of drawers, and a small round table with a pitcher and bowl were the only other objects of note in the darkened room.

From the crib, a small cooing sound broke the silence. The baby, Thomas told himself, was awake. Perhaps it had heard him and was calling to him. Though that was a ridiculous thought, since the child had yet to lay eyes on him, everything else surrounding the baby was, to Thomas, somewhat of a mystery. What, he wondered as he slowly crossed the room, could babies hear? How did they act when they did hear something? When he reached the crib, lined and covered with rich, soft materials, Thomas looked down and saw his son for the first time.

The child, preoccupied with the laborious task of attempting to stuff his entire fist into his mouth, didn't notice Thomas at first. But when he did, all thoughts of his hand disappeared. Wide-eyed, the baby threw its chubby little arms out, opened his mouth as wide as he could, as if surprised, and looked up at his father. Thomas was, from that moment on, in love with the blue-eyed cherub that lay before him. That the feeling was mutual was, at least in Thomas' mind, beyond dispute. When Thomas' lips parted in a broad smile unlike any he had had occasion to wear in a very long time, the child returned the expression. Smiling, the bright-eyed baby began thrashing his arms about in excitement, adding a wild thumping of feet to his spasm of disjointed joy. Then he began to squeal with a loud, piercing shriek that caused Thomas to laugh.

"You're a lively lad, you are," Thomas chuckled as he leaned over. Slowly, ever so carefully, he brought his right hand up and inserted it into the crib. Pausing when the tip of his index finger was but an inch from the child's stomach, Thomas wondered if touching the baby there would hurt it. Though he had never touched a baby, at least not that he could recall, he remembered seeing many a small child being cradled in the arms of its mother at Fort Edward and Fort William Henry. He tried to recall what they had done to entertain their children, how they had handled them.

Unfortunately, in his quest to find an answer in this manner, Thomas' mind betrayed him. Rather than finding an answer to the question he was pondering, his memory flashed images that were far from those he had been searching for. In an instant, he was no longer in Albany. Instead, he was back there, on the shores of Lake George, reliving that terrible August day. There, in the midst of a field, surrounded by men cowering in horror as savages fell upon them, stood a woman, dressed in plain, simple homespun clothing, clutching a baby to her breast as she awaited her fate. In quick succession, Thomas' memory recalled the sight of a small child, not more than a year old, clawing at the body of her dead mother, freshly scalped and unable to respond to her daughter's needs because her head had been bashed in. Then, just as quickly, that image was replaced with the sight of a brave holding a baby not much bigger than the one lying before Thomas now upside down, by its leg. Thomas had watched helplessly as the savage swung the baby over his head and then smashed its tiny body against a tree.

Such memories, so vivid, so vile, so terrible, wiped away all traces of joy and happiness in Thomas. Slowly, sadly, he pulled away from his own son. Without thinking, he looked away.

As if he had felt the change in his father's mood, the baby ceased its cooing and excited squawking. Dumbly, the small boy stared up at the monstrously tall person before him wearing a bright red coat with shiny buttons and gold lace. Why this person didn't pick him up and feed him confused the baby. Everyone else who came by did. He wanted to be picked up. But this person, once so happy and fun to look at, was now sad. With no way of reaching out or stopping the brightly colored monster from leaving, the baby was left to watch helplessly as his visitor turned away and passed from sight. With nothing better to do now, the baby returned to the task of sucking on his own hand.

From the doorway, Thomas paused. In his heart, he wanted to return to the baby. He wanted to pick it up and hold it, to feel its warm body next to him. He wanted so badly to give it the love and affection that he, as a child, had never felt from his own father. But he found he couldn't, not for the moment at least. Not as long as the image of Drummer Jones, his face frozen in terror and fear as he was about to meet his death, hung before Thomas' eyes. Slowly, quietly, Thomas closed the door behind him and walked away.

Along the Banks of the Monongahela
November, 1758

IAN was surprised at how difficult it was to find where the great massacre had taken place. He had carried the images of that fateful day around with him, burned into his mind, for so long that he had been sure he would be able to return to that place blindfolded. But now, here among the falling leaves, he found that it was a most difficult task indeed.

As he wandered through the woods, a bit off from Captain Shaw and James McPike, who were also looking for the bodies of those they had left behind, Ian reflected upon how so many things in his life had not quite turned out as he had expected them to. He had left home in search of adventure, but found only death and horror at Culloden. He had left Scotland with the determination that he would return, but found that such a dream was little more than a fantasy that kept him from enjoying a new life that he had, quite by accident, discovered in America.

Even the campaign that was now at an end didn't finish the way he and the others had expected. Though Major James Grant's ill-advised foray had fit the pattern of blunders and disasters that seemed to characterize so many of England's efforts to subdue the French in America, the withdrawal of the French from the forks of the Ohio, without so much as a shot being fired, came as a surprise. Like many of the others, Ian had stood on the hill, still littered with the rotting bodies of Grant's Highlanders, and stared with disbelieving eyes at the smoldering ashes of Fort Duquesne. Shaw later explained that the departure of the Indians after their great victory against Grant had left the French commander with little choice but to flee with his troops or face defeat and surrender. "Despite all my years of soldiering, I still don't understand the way the English and the French fight their wars," Ian complained. Those in the company who had been with it from the beginning and stood on the hill gazing at a goal that had eluded them for so long nodded in agreement. "Ever since my own dear Prince Charlie made us stand under the English guns for an hour on that god-awful day in '45, I've had to wonder about the sanity of those who call themselves generals."

In his quiet, unruffled manner, Captain Shaw turned to Ian and responded. "It's not important that we understand, lad. It's not important." Though Ian didn't quite agree, he didn't argue. With the enlistments of the Second Virginia Regiment about to expire, the soldiers of the First Regiment would be left to deal with the many tasks that still remained at the forks of the Ohio. First, there was the need to put up some sort of defensive works. Though the French were gone, the threat of Indian attack, especially so close to the sites of two disastrous encounters with them, was still very real. Then there was the need for shelter. With the end of November but a few days away, snow was likely to come at any time. Already the bite of winter could be felt in the air.

In addition to these very necessary chores, soldiers of the First Virginia Regiment were drafted to find and bury the dead of the two battles fought by Braddock and Grant. Ian's fellow Virginians who had fallen while covering the flight of Grant's Highlanders were taken care of first. They were the easiest to find. Here and there, the severed heads of Grant's Highlanders had been stuck upon a stake on the spot where the soldier had fallen. Around the stake each man's kilt was wrapped, creating weird, grotesque markers the Indians had erected in an effort to insult the dead and demoralize the living. The bodies of the Virginians, already well decomposed and eaten away by wild animals, had not been abused like that, making their remains easier to deal with. Only after these had been tended to properly did Shaw and the others turn their attention to the recovery and interment of the remains of those who had died three years prior.

Coming to the rise where Captain Beaujeu of La Marine had first caught sight of Braddock's vanguard, Ian could barely see the field where so many Englishmen had died. Making his way down the hill, he came upon his first pile of skeletons. These were, of course, the converged grenadiers of the Forty-fourth and Forty-eighth Foot who had first met the French. The bones of these soldiers, mixed in with tattered remains of faded red cloth and bits and pieces of equipment abandoned by both the English and French, were covered with the leaves of three falls. Farther on, Ian, Shaw, and McPike came to the spot where St. Clair's road crew had ceased their labors. Some of the trees, half cut through, had died, while others had managed to heal themselves and continued to prosper, though they still wore the gashes made by axes so long ago. Once on the road, partially reclaimed by the forest, it was easy to trace the flow of the battle. At some points, it seemed every time someone kicked up the leaves, another skeleton was discovered. From off to one side, Shaw called out, "Over here, lads."

There was no need for Shaw to say anything further. Ian, McPike, and the small burial party knew what he had found. Only after climbing up the side of the hill they had fought on for so long, taking fire from both the Indians above them and the English below, could Ian finally begin to match the landscape he now saw with the images that had been burned into his memory so long ago. "Start over here, lads," Shaw told them, "and work your way across. I fear they're still here, where we left them."

There was a sadness to Shaw's voice, a sadness that told Ian that even now, three years later, his captain still mourned for the men who had served with him on that day. Ian would miss Shaw. He would miss him more than he had ever missed anyone else in his life. But he had to move on. Ian had become convinced that there was nothing more for him to do here, not after they finished today's work. He had set out four years ago with a young redheaded colonel of Virginia militia to establish a fort at the forks of the Ohio, and, as of today, that was a reality. While he had had no clear idea of where that adventure was taking him then, he did now. Now he knew exactly what he would do with the rest of his life. He knew what to expect, what role he would fill in this new country, and who he would share the rest of his life with. All was so very clear to him now. The only thing that still puzzled Ian was why it had taken him so long to figure it all out.

Sitting down among a circle of logs, he paused to take a short rest before starting his labors. After looking around, he noticed that the tree trunks were more than vaguely familiar. Reaching over with his foot, Ian stirred the damp, tightly packed leaves in one corner of the small enclosure created by the dead tress. After a few sideward scrapes of his shoe, he found what he was looking for. It was him, Ian told himself.

It was the poor, dear blond-haired boy with whom he had shared this small protected shelter. Dropping to his knees, Ian carefully pulled away layer after layer of decayed leaves. Slowly he exposed the remains of his nameless companion. When he had managed to clear all the rotted leaves away from the skull, he stopped for a moment and studied it. Though most of the skin and hair was gone, enough remained to tell Ian that this lad had been fortunate that day. His corpse had not been found and molested by the Indians who had swept them from the field. Easing back until he was resting on his heels, Ian sighed. This man had prayed that day, before going into battle. And though the Lord had not seen fit to save his life, He had watched over his mortal body and left it here, intact, for Ian to discover. Now, together with the rest of those who had fallen that day, Ian would be able to lay this poor soul's mortal body to rest. Perhaps then, Ian thought as he finished the task of clearing away the leaves that covered the body, he would finally be free to live his life in a state of peace and freedom that, until now, he had only dreamed of.

Fort Carillon, New York
December, 1759

DESPITE the piercing wind that cut through his cloak as if it weren't even there, Anton stood upon the parapet of the stone fortress and peered vacantly out over the frozen landscape before him. Wherever his eyes roamed, they were greeted with the same sight. Trees, stripped of their leaves, stood stark and naked against the glaring white snow that shrouded everything in sight. Even the calm, serene waters of the lake were hidden by a thick crust of ice that the snow lay upon like a smothering blanket. With his arms held tightly to his chest, Anton leaned upon the wall, silent and motionless. Except for the occasional shifting of his eyes from one desolate scene to another, and the clouds of vapor that he emitted with each breath, Anton did not move. Just as the sentinel who slowly passed back and forth behind him paid Anton scant attention, so, too, did Anton ignore the soldier. Anton's mind, like his heart, was elsewhere.

It had been a year now, he reminded himself, since he had met Sarah Carter, and almost seven months since he had last seen her. His repeated request to go back to Quebec with the bulk of the army when it came time to stand down for the winter had been denied. "You have been blessed each year," the fortress commander reminded the young officer of artillery, "by being permitted to make your winter quarters in Quebec. It is your turn, monsieur, to stand watch on the frontier. Perhaps next year good fortune will smile upon you again when it comes time to see who goes, and who stays."

Though it was meant to lighten the blow and provide Anton a measure of hope, the commandant's words served only to heighten Anton's sense of despair. In his mind, he feared that there would be no next year. With the fortress of Louisbourg in English hands and the forks of the Ohio abandoned, the victory here at Carillon in July seemed to have done little to stave off the pending doom of France's fortunes in America for a little while. Even their own king, in response to pleas for reinforcements, gave little cause for hope. "Monsieurs," he replied to his ministers, "one does not fight a fire in the stable when the house is burning."

Yet, as bitter as all these reverses were, nothing was more demoralizing to Anton than his winter exile at Carillon. When he realized that he would be unable to renew his friendship with Sarah Carter, Anton pined for weeks. He considered asking his friend Pepin to look in on the girl. He needed to reassure himself that all was well with her. After serious consideration, however, he decided not to. He felt uneasy about involving someone else in an affair that his Catholic morals, at times, left him feeling uneasy about. Then he thought of writing to her, at the convent. No one, he told himself, would see any harm in an officer in a far-off garrison corresponding with a friend. The fear, however, that the nuns might read his letters before passing them on, or even withhold them, gave Anton pause. The sisters, after all, were no fools. They possessed the unique ability to sense impropriety, even where none existed. It took little for Anton to convince himself that they would see the true meaning of his letters and destroy them. Unsure of what to do, Anton did nothing. For the longest time, he stood where he was, motionless, literally and figuratively frozen by indecision.

In the end, it was Sarah Carter who broke the impasse. From out of nowhere, a letter from Quebec for Anton arrived with the normal dispatches coming down from Canada. Knowing that there could be only one person who would make the effort to write to him, Anton had seized the letter handed to him by the fort's adjutant and retreated to the walls of the fortress, where he could enjoy his note from Sarah far from the prying eyes of his fellow officers. With hands trembling from excitement as much as from the cold, Anton had broken the seal that bound the letter and unfolded it as quickly as he could.

The momentary lift he experienced when his eyes confirmed that it was, indeed, from Sarah was dashed as soon as he began reading.

I hope this letter finds you safe and in good health. I think of you often, my love. I would have enjoyed seeing you, if only for one more time, but God has seen fit to keep that from ever occurring. I am to be returned to Massachusetts, soon. With the realization by the Sisters that I am carrying your child, I have become both a burden and an embarrassment to them.

The revelation that she was pregnant, together with her statement announcing that she was being returned to the English colonies, was doubly hard for Anton to take. Crushed, he balled up the paper, stuffed it in the pocket of his vest, and wandered over to the wall of the parapet where he could mourn his loss in private.

For the longest time, he stood there, doing nothing but looking out over a landscape that was as cold and barren as his heart felt at that moment. He had served in Canada for almost six years. He had enjoyed the experience of traveling to the fringes of civilization. To him, the early years had been little more than a great adventure, an escape from the oppressive rules and regulations that governed his nation and society. Even when his duties required him to participate in battle, exposing him to the brutal excesses of war, Anton was able to turn a blind eye to them, at least in the beginning. *It is the nature of our world,* he wrote soon after starting his diary, *that good exists side by side with evil. There is no changing that. Like great weights in a scale, they balance each other, providing a sense of contrast that allows man to measure all his actions against.* But slowly, Anton found that such philosophical drivel could do little to erase memories that haunted his sleep. As the war dragged on, year after year, slowly escalating from little more than skirmish warfare between small bands of soldiers and savages to full-blown battles between well-equipped and drilled European armies, Anton's ability to see beauty in the world he found himself in ebbed until it had all but disappeared. Only his brief affair with Sarah Carter had returned to his life a ray of hope and joy. Perhaps, his heart had told him as he had imagined his return to Sarah, *I will be able to come away from this brutal war with something upon which I can build.*

But now, like the leaves that had once hung from the trees before him, that hope was gone. In its place, there was only a cold harshness that was incapable of sustaining even the faintest of dreams. Though he knew that life, like the war, would go on, it was now little more than a play whose ending had already been written. *All that remained to be done by we fools who are its captives,* he wrote in his diary on the last day of the year, *is to wait for the curtain to rise on the final act.*

CHAPTER TWENTY-SEVEN

Fort Carillon, New York
July, 1759

Anton was not there to see the opening of the final act that took place on the Saint Lawrence before the very eyes of the governor of New France. It was a fitting scene, one that was both dramatic and spectacular. Above a chorus of panicked cries from the leading citizens of Quebec and the wailing of women, the governor, his aides, and the senior leaders of New France watched in stony silence as the crisp white sails of English warships appeared, as if by magic, out of the treacherous passage leading to Quebec known as La Traverse. Leading a procession of ships that stretched fifty miles down the Saint Lawrence River were big warships, ships of the line. Some of these were England's finest, mounting as many as ninety guns on three decks. Behind them came other ships of every description. In their hulls and on their decks they carried supplies, ordnance, ammunition, and 13,500 soldiers and sailors. They had everything that would be needed to conquer the new world for England, including a thirty-two-year-old commander who possessed both the determination and the skill required to do so. By the time the great pageant of tall ships finished anchoring in the great basin before Quebec, two hundred ships, all flying the Union Jack, lay poised to commence the serious business of destroying the last vestige of French power in the New World.

He did not witness the beginning of a siege that would last some eighty-five days. Instead, Anton was still at Carillon. There, he and a force of some three thousand French and Canadians waited for the English to come at them again. When they did, they came as Abercromby had come the previous year. From their winter quarters in New York and Albany, General Jeffrey Amherst gathered his army on the southern shores of Lake George, where English armies had gathered every summer since the summer of 1755. There the English piled up their supplies, built their boats, and launched their effort against Carillon. Though his army was not as large as Abercromby's had been the previous year, Amherst was determined to do what his predecessor had failed to.

Thomas Shields was among the officers who went up the Hudson to the sprawling encampment on the shores of Lake George. A major now, he had left his young son and pregnant wife in Albany, rejoined his regiment, and, as he had for the previous three years, gone north to do his duty, for king and country. But, unlike previous years, Thomas' heart was no longer filled with the same desperate urge to achieve glory, fame, and fortune on the battlefield. Four years of war in the colonies and defeat after defeat had slowly taught him that such dreams were little more than illusions. Like characters in a bad play, Thomas had watched a parade of officers come forth, stumble, and then slip away into obscurity, leaving the Americas as broken men. Because of this, Thomas' ambition of advancing on the coattails of generals catapulted into positions of authority and rank through good fortune and impeccable connections faded with each passing year.

Of course, Thomas was no fool. He had, after all, not been a total failure. His road to fame and fortune had merely taken him along a different path. In the place of his dreams of martial glory, Thomas had found a growing desire to become a country gentleman, divorced from the harshness of a world that had left him scarred in body and soul. "I think," he told Fenton over a glass of fine wine, enjoyed before the fire of his richly appointed home, "I shall leave His Majesty's service when we've finished our business in Canada. I've become fond of managing my wife's business affairs. What, with her health in such a poor state, I hardly am left with a choice in the matter. Besides," he added with a note of melancholy, "I yearn for the day when I will be able to lay aside my bitter memories and embrace my son as a loving father should."

Fenton, normally quick with a sarcastic remark, said nothing as he listened to Thomas. A year older than his married friend, Fenton simply stared into the fire, sipped his wine, and struggled to suppress the envy he felt for a man who he believed had found a happiness that still eluded him.

Hand in hand with Thomas' growing appreciation of the finer things in life was his mastery of a system that allowed one to profit from war. It seemed that it was the merchants and contractors who supplied everything to the soldiers, from the food needed to sustain them to the shovels required to bury them when they died, who gained from war, not the soldiers. With his prospects within the military fading, Thomas had moved, with the same methodical precision that had been drilled into him by the army, to seize any opportunity that presented itself, to secure more and more of a mercantile empire that he had once renounced. In time, he convinced himself, his own fortune and influence would eclipse anything he could ever have achieved in the service of his country.

First, however, there was still the war. Thomas had not, and could not, totally turn his back on those loyalties he owed to his king and his duties as an officer of the line. Before he could embark wholeheartedly upon his conquest of the Van der Hoff fortunes, the French needed to be humbled, once and for all. To this end, he followed the king's colors back to Lake George and took his place in the ranks.

From its encampments, the army moved north across Lake George, as it had the year before. Forward, through the same woods in which they had staged their bloody assaults the year before, the regiments advanced against the French fortress. Though few believed that Amherst would repeat Abecromby's fatal mistakes and allow them to blunder, headlong, into another pointless slaughter, no one who had been there the previous year ruled out the possibility. Far too many were like Thomas, men who had watched as certain victory was dashed before their very eyes. So it was not surprising, given this experience and Thomas' newfound ambitions, that when the drums sounded the advance, he complied, but with more trepidation and apprehension than he had ever felt before.

Even before they cleared the wood line and ventured forth into the open, Thomas' well-trained eye could see that the French had used their time well, improving already formidable works. Yet, unlike the previous year, all was strangely silent. There were no signs of the proud regimental standards of the French regiments of the line, flying defiantly above the works. Beyond the maze of abatis, there were no brightly polished barrels protruding over the log and earthen walls, aimed at the oncoming ranks of Englishmen. Even though every step took him closer without any hint of danger, Thomas could still feel the sweat running down his spine as his eyes darted nervously from one end of the line of works to the other. Could they really be that fortunate? he found himself asking. Or was this simply another trick, another invitation by the French to another surprise and more destruction?

As Thomas worked on these questions, another slowly emerged from the dark recesses of his mind. Was he becoming fearful of what might happen to him? Was all this apprehension he was feeling at that moment more than just professional concern over what would happen next? Had his life become so comfortable and his future so bright that his concerns about surviving the coming battle threatened to outweigh his professional conduct? Thomas found that he needed to think on this, for, in truth, he could not recall ever having felt such reluctance when going into battle.

A cheer raised by an officer in another regiment managed to drag Thomas' thoughts back to the matter at hand. With a shake of his head, he regained both his composure and his presence of mind. Looking up, he saw, again, the French works he had come within arm's reach of before. Unlike before, there was no one at them to contest him. Behind him, his own men took up the cheer and began to press to go forward faster, as if they were simply dreaming all this and needed to reach their goal before they awoke and found themselves faced with a terrible truth all wished to escape.

For a moment, Thomas let himself be carried by the excitement. Dropping all pretenses, he lengthened his strides and all but took off at a run. Without much effort, he scaled the earthen works, gained the top of the damnable fortifications that they had failed to reach the previous year, and stood tall and erect upon them as if posing for a painter. Thrusting his sword high over his head, he waved it about and let out a cheer that his adoring men joined as they swarmed over the works all about him.

Fort Carillon

FROM the walls of Carillon, Anton watched with his gunners as the red, white, and blue flags of the English popped up, one after another, over the crest of the hill Montcalm had so skillfully defended the previous year. That such a feat would not be repeated was already known. For even as Anton and his gunners loaded their guns and prepared to fire on the English, they knew that this battle was already lost. With events of far greater importance taking place to the north, the governor of New France had already determined that he could ill afford to squander a sizable force holding what had become little more than an outpost. In compliance with sealed orders from the governor himself, Bourlamaque prepared to abandon Carillon and blow it up, just as the commandant at Duquesne had been forced to do the previous year.

Still, resistance was to be maintained, at least for a short while. Even as some of the garrison were busy making all the preparations necessary to make good their escape and blow up the fort in their wake, Anton and his gunners prepared to fire on the English. With a keen, detached, professional interest, Anton watched as the red-clad figures milled about upon and behind the abandoned works. Given time, they would bring their own guns up and use the French field fortifications as the basis for their first siege line. From there, they would start digging trenches along a zigzag toward the walls of Carillon until they reached a spot where a second trench would be dug for a new battery position. It was, Anton knew, the same thing he had done two years prior at Fort William Henry. That they would be gone long before the English had an opportunity to play out that drama pleased him. He had no desire to sit within the walls of this cold, isolated fortress and wait for death or the humiliation of surrender. He had seen both and desired neither.

Besides, he had something to live for, something that gave him hope when all those about him sank deeper and deeper into gloom and despair. *News that my Sarah, carrying my child, had been taken from beyond my reach was, at first, devastating,* Anton noted in his journal. *But then, the idea that I had, in some small way, participated in the wondrous process of life filled me with awe. Here, I realized, I was no longer dealing with abstract thoughts or philosophies. Here, in this small miracle, all the mysteries of the cosmos were being combined with the reality of this world to create something that had never existed before, a new life.* That the child was his was never a question in Anton's mind. And that Sarah would somehow manage to protect it until fortune allowed him to behold his child was equally certain. *God,* Anton wrote, *despite the many cruelties that he visits upon us, is still a kind and benevolent shepherd. I must believe that after bestowing such a gift upon my Sarah and me, he will watch and protect it until such time as circumstances permit me to relieve him of that awesome responsibility.*

With the same patient cough that he always used to gain his lieutenant's attention, the old gunner made his presence known to Anton. "Monsieur," he announced when Anton turned to face him, "the guns are ready."

"Ah," Anton replied, making no effort to hide the fact that he had been preoccupied with other thoughts. "Then, let us find ourselves a target and open this battle." Turning, he opened his telescope, brought it up to his eye, and scanned the works newly occupied by the English. With an eye for range and opportunity, Anton caught sight of an English officer, standing defiantly upon the works, waving his sword as his men swarmed about him. Dropping his spyglass, Anton lifted his hand and pointed to the spot. "There," he ordered his senior sergeant. "Lay the guns using that fellow as your mark."

The old sergeant smiled. "Excellent choice, monsieur. We may have to turn our backs to them, but not before we teach them a little respect."

Anton smiled and nodded. While his gun captains received their instructions from the sergeant, Anton returned to his observation of the enemy. When all was ready, he left the honor of giving the commands to fire to his sergeant while he remained where he stood, watching for the effects of their work. He was not disappointed. Each gun, carefully laid by a gun captain as familiar with the range to the English-occupied fortifications as he was with the small, squalid barracks room of the fort they had wintered in, made its mark. One solid cast-iron ball after another slammed into the wooden and earth fortifications beneath the English officer whose arrogance had caught Anton's attention. Dropping his telescope from his eye, Anton turned to face his sergeant and gun crews, smiled, and saluted them with a slight, stiff bow. "Excellent work, men. Excellent."

The English Camp before Fort Carillon

FENTON arrived just as the surgeon finished his work. The staff captain ignored the bloody, wounded soldiers lying about on the ground outside the surgeon's tent, where they waited until their superiors had been properly tended to. They were of no concern to him. Only his friend mattered.

"Doctor," Fenton asked as he caught the surgeon by his arm, "what of Major Shields? Has he . . ."

"I've saved the leg," the surgeon replied dryly as he wiped Thomas' blood off his bare hands using a rag already turned deep red from the blood of others. "But there was nothing I could do to save the eye. God willing, he'll learn to walk with a limp and find one eye sufficient."

Though he was sorry to hear that his dear friend was to be disfigured and crippled for the remainder of his life, Fenton didn't dwell on it. "Well," he sighed, "I guess that our God is a merciful one, in his own way."

The surgeon, who had been looking down at the waiting wounded, gave Fenton a sideward glance. Catching the man's expression, Fenton explained, "Though I feel for the suffering my friend will have to endure, I can assure you the life he'll enjoy after all has healed will be the envy of both of us. It is we, my good doctor, who will be left to finish this sordid war, who need to be pitied."

The doctor merely grunted. "I'll tell you straight. I can mend the body, and Lord knows I've been handed many a body to mend. But I can do little to repair the scar that such wounds leave in a man's head. Your friend, should he survive the fever, will never be the same again."

With a blank expression, Fenton looked at the surgeon. "My good doctor," he asked, "can any of us be?"

Without waiting for an answer, Fenton turned and walked away, leaving Thomas to rest as best he could and ponder his own mortality and future.

Quebec,
September 13, 1759

UPON the open ground west of the city, a final, climactic drama, befitting a period known as the Age of Reason, was played out. After enduring eighty days of frustrations and failures, James Wolfe, the thirty-two-year-old commander of the English army besieging the city, threw his fortunes to the wind and set out on a last, desperate gamble. Under the cover of darkness he moved his army, by boat, past the guns of the great city and ascended cliffs that the French had felt needed no defenses. With a determination every bit as fierce as their commander's, the soldiers of Wolfe's army made the impossible ascent and assembled, by morning, on the Plains of Abraham before Quebec.

When, at dawn, the Marquis de Montcalm realized that the climactic crisis was at hand, he reacted swiftly and decisively. Though denied the use of much of the city's garrison and all but a few of the fortress's guns, Montcalm was determined to meet Wolfe's desperate stroke with one equally as desperate. Mounted on a black charger, with 2,900 regulars and militia arrayed in line of battle, Montcalm stormed upon the Plains of Abraham to confront Wolfe's 4,500 men.

Making little use of the 1,900 Indians and *coureurs de bois* who hovered impatiently on the flanks of the waiting English army, the French army marched to within canister range of the English and opened an ineffectual bombardment of their foe. Wolfe, equally fired up for the contest, moved back and forth behind his troops, deployed in two thin lines rather than the usual three. With the style that had won him the respect of all those who followed him, Wolfe moved among his men, encouraging them. With two balls loaded in their muskets rather than one, Wolfe warned them to lie down and avoid the mortal danger that he himself ignored while he waited for the French to come even closer.

On the French side, Montcalm was equal to the challenge. With the two small guns Wolfe had managed to bring up the cliffs with him, wreaking havoc on his troops, the marquis came to the conclusion that he could wait no longer. Placing himself between the Regiment La Sarre and the Regiment Languedoc, he raised his sword, dropped it till it pointed at the English line, and ordered the attack to commence.

With regimental flags unfurled and fluttering in the breeze, the French soldiers gave a long shout, took four quick steps forward, then began a headlong rush toward their foe. As they went forward, their neat and orderly lines began to disappear, with the center, where Montcalm was, surging ahead of those on the flanks. At a distance of one hundred yards, without orders, the entire line fired a ragged, disjointed volley that did the English no harm. At seventy yards from the enemy, another volley, equally erratic, was delivered. Though this one did manage to inflict some damage, the English waited patiently until the French were within forty yards.

Only when he was sure that his men's fire would be the most devastating did Wolfe finally give the order to shoot. After coming to their feet and realigning themselves, Wolfe's entire line took a few steps forward, turned to the side to present small targets to the foe, and prepared to fire. On Wolfe's own command, his musketeers brought their weapons up to their shoulders, leveled them at the mass of men bearing down on them, and fired.

In a single, thunderous volley, practically the entire front rank of the French army was knocked down. Staggering, the survivors reeled as French officers and sergeants struggled to close ranks and realign the survivors. Wolfe, sensing the moment, gave the order to advance three paces. Moving forward, the English soldiers reloaded and waited for the command to fire again. It took seven long minutes before the smoke of their first volley had cleared sufficiently for Wolfe to feel that it was time to unleash a second. When he did, its effects were equally devastating. This time when the smoke cleared, there was no French army left standing before them. Leaving the bodies of almost 1,400 of their companions dead and dying where they had fallen, the French army had turned and fled.

As battles go, it was quite brief and rather small. But its consequences were enormous. Together with the fate of the commanders who led the armies that day on the Plains of Abraham, the fate of an entire continent had been decided. Wolfe died there, on the field itself, stricken by a bullet from a Canadian. Montcalm would survive him but by a single day, shot twice as he was swept away from the battlefield by his routed army. The war in Canada would continue through one more long, bitter winter before the governor of New France himself capitulated with all his remaining forces at Montreal the following September. And though the war known in history as the Seven Years' War still had three more years to play itself out in Europe, the conflict that had been opened in the mountains of western Pennsylvania by a handful of poorly trained men, led by an inexperienced colonel of militia, was over in America.

Epilogue

Epilogue

Montreal, Canada
September 7, 1760

WITH THE ROYAL GOVERNOR set to sign the instrument of surrender the next day, there remained little for his soldiers to do but perform one last duty to their king and their regiment. In solemn ceremonies held that night, the color bearers of each of the line regiments of La Troupe de Terre burned their regimental colors. "They would rather this," Anton explained to his friend Pepin as they looked on, "than permit the standards they have followed so gallantly for so long become a trophy to be laid at the feet of the English king."

Pepin, never able to appreciate fully the finer points of the European art of war, merely grunted. "It will be a long, hard winter for us all." Turning to Anton, he regarded his young companion for a moment before continuing. "I imagine they'll be sending you back to France, eventually."

Anton, his eyes transfixed on a burning flag that sent a shower of sparks skyward, shrugged. "Yes," he replied half-heartedly. "Most of my fellow officers of La Troupe de la Marine will be going back to France also. Even many of those who were born here, in Canada, like you, have decided to return to a homeland they have never known."

Shaking his head, Pepin looked down. "There has been much I have not understood in this war. I freely admit that. You," he said, waving his arm over at Anton, "are not a Canadian. I can see why you go. But the others, those who are, I cannot conceive that. Turning one's back on this land is unimaginable."

With the last remnants of the regimental colors consumed by the flames, Anton looked over at Pepin. "Have you ever considered, dear Pepin, that some of your fellow Canadians are more French than they are Canadian?"

At first Pepin did not answer as he shuffled feet while thinking. Then, looking up till his eyes met Anton's, he leaned toward the young officer. "And have you, my friend, ever considered the fact that after seven years here, you have become more Canadian than French?"

For the first time since the combined force of more than eighteen thousand British soldiers had gathered around and lay siege before the fortress of Montreal, Anton smiled. "You know my mind, sometimes, better than I," he replied. Then, as his face settled into a more serious expression, Anton looked up at the night sky. For a moment, his mind turned away from the trials of war and the pending surrender. Instead, the image of Sarah Carter passed through his mind. "In time," he finally said, "I will return to this place. There is much that this land has to offer. Much," he continued as he looked over to Pepin, "that it has taught me, about myself, and about my fellow man. But first, I must carry that knowledge back, to France. Perhaps there I can be a humble instrument that will help my fellow countrymen discover the same sense of freedom that has been, for so long, the birthright of this land's inhabitants."

"You are an ambitious man," Pepin remarked as he stared at Anton.

"I am a dreamer," Anton countered. "Despite all that I have seen here, and all that I leave behind, I cannot turn my back on the fact that we are all placed here for a purpose and that, in time, God will let us find that purpose. Is that so difficult to understand?"

"No," Pepin replied with a smile as he shook his head. "You have your books to write and your stories to tell back there, in France. And, who knows, maybe someone will listen to what you have to say. Maybe the mother of Canada will be able to learn from her child."

Anton did not respond. Whether anyone in France would listen to him did not matter. What did matter to Anton was that the story of this land would be told, as he had experienced it, in all its striking beauty and terrible agony. In that way, he would preserve a collective memory that otherwise would fade away into the night, like the ashes of the burned regimental colors.

Albany, New York
September, 1760

WITH his first son seated on the saddle in front of him, Thomas Shields leisurely walked his horse through the fields where the tenant farmers of the Van der Hoffs' vast holdings were gathering for the annual harvest. Except for the black eye patch that covered the ugly scar where an eye had once been, Thomas looked no different than any of the other landholders of means. He wore finely polished riding boots over breeches that were immaculate despite hours of riding. His coat, custom-made by the best tailor in New York City, was faced with satin rather than the coarse wool that had been the mainstay of his regimentals. Under it he wore a fine vest upon which the crisp white ruffled collar of his shirt fell. Only his hat, a new tricorn, was conspicuously plain. Even the satin edging was black. But, like his breeches, it was spotless and looked as if it were new.

But there the similarities between Thomas Shields and his fellow Albany proprietors ended. While they, born to this land and their positions, were conservative and circumspect in their business dealings, Thomas was bold and ambitious. It was said that Thomas had inherited those traits from his wife, a woman whose health had been broken by the very child Thomas loved so much. But those who thought that hadn't known Thomas. They had never been afforded the opportunity to look into the soul of a man so driven by ambition that he would risk everything to obtain it, even his life. And though his well-concealed scars and faded memories of martial glories denied him sometimes cast a pall of sadness about him that infected his own son, his quest for fortune and power had never diminished.

Halting, Thomas looked out over a field waiting its turn to be harvested. "Look out there, boy," he commanded his son in the same manner he had used to send the men of his regiment into battle. "This is ours, all of it. From this land will come the crops you see, to be sold to the highest bidder. With the profit we make from that, we will buy new land, land that is yet to be claimed or cleared. Or perhaps we will buy another ship, in whose hull future crops from this field and the fields of other men will be taken back to England. Or maybe we'll buy a printing press and start a small publishing house in New York. There's always the need for good books." Looking down at his son, Thomas saw that the boy, wide-eyed and attentive, was slowly surveying all around him. "That's it, boy, take it all in. Though you'll never know the thrill of battle, the excitement that comes when a man risks all he is and all he has, you'll never find yourself beholden to another. You, boy," he emphasized with a squeeze, "will be the one wielding the power and influence that so long eluded me."

Thomas' son, delighted to be out and about with his father on the horse, didn't understand a word the man was saying. None of it made any sense to him, nor did he care. Though the hands of his father were necessary to keep him securely in place in the saddle, the younger Shields wanted to be free, free from his father's control and his boring lectures. In his young, fertile mind, unspoiled by the harsh realities of the world his father lived in, the young boy dreamed of the day when he would be old enough to have his own horse, to have the freedom to ride it out here, in the fields that so dominated so much of his father's attention. He cared not for what those fields represented. He had no concepts of wealth and power. All that the boy understood, and longed for, was the chance to go, on his own, and explore the land that was his by birth.

Near Winchester, Virginia
September, 1760

FAR too concerned about the welfare of his wife, Ian McPherson found he could not sit or rest. Instead, he paced outside the small cabin that was home to him, Megan, and the boy he had found two years before. Together with his friend and neighbor, James McPike, and the boy Megan had named Patrick, Ian listened, waited, and prayed. "It'll be fine, Ian," McPike told him again and again. "Women have babies all the time."

Tired of hearing this, Ian turned on McPike. "I don't care about other women, James. That's my Megan in there! She's the one in pain, not some other woman," he thundered as he pointed a shaking finger at the closed door of the cabin. "God knows what's happening in there. Perhaps she's inches from leaving this world. And I'm out here, as helpless as a bloody new calf."

"Oh, now, don't you worry, Ian. God knows what's happening," McPike replied, completely unaffected by his friend's outburst. "Between him and the old woman, who's a good midwife, everything will come out all right."

Off to one side, Patrick, watched every move Ian made. Though he seldom spoke to either Ian or Megan, he was devoted to them. If he wasn't with Ian, out working in the fields side by side with his adopted father, he was glued to Megan, watching her every move as she prepared their meals and tended to the hundreds of chores that life on the frontier demanded of her. He was always careful to stay within easy reach of them at night, when even the slightest sound from outside the cabin, unheard by either Ian or Megan, sent the boy into a cold sweat and into their arms. Unable to deny Patrick the warmth and comfort Ian himself often found needing as a result of terrible images he carried locked deep in his memory, Ian would allow Patrick to settle between him and Megan in their bed. This, of course, made life difficult for two people who were madly in love with each other and anxious to share their affections at every opportunity. Still, they found the opportunities, and, in the winter of 1760, while New France was teetering on extinction, Ian McPherson and Megan O'Reilly conceived their first child.

From the cabin Ian heard the high-pitched squeal of a newborn. Unable to wait to be invited in, he stormed through the door. His eyes were drawn to the midwife, busily cleaning the newborn on the table where Megan cooked her bread and the three of them shared all their meals. "Megan, is she . . ." he stammered.

From the bed in the corner of the room, his wife called out. "Don't be such a worry," she chided her husband in a voice that was weak but still very much alive. "I'll be up and gathering the crops with you by tomorrow."

Moving quickly to her bedside, Ian seized her hand and held it between his. "You'll do nothing of the sort," he insisted. "Patrick and I will tend to that. You and little . . ."

Suddenly, he realized that he had no idea what, exactly, his own child was. Turning, he looked at the midwife. With a smile, she announced that they had a new son. "We'll name him James," Megan announced as Ian turned to gaze in his wife's eyes, "after your father."

Lifting her shaking hands to his lips, he kissed them. "Bless you, lass," he whispered. "Bless you."

Megan smiled as she reached up with her other hand and touched it to the side of Ian's face, now moist with his tears. "He'll be a fine Highland lad," she whispered. "Just like his father."

Ian bent over, planted a kiss on his wife's forehead, then sat upright on the side of the bed. "No," he corrected her as he shook his head. With an expression that she could not quite understand, Ian looked over at the child, then at the door of their cabin that opened out onto their farm. After staring for several minutes, he looked back into Megan's eyes and shook his head again. "No, my love, he's an American." With that, he leaned over again, kissed her, and left her side to see, for the first time, the child who would inherit the freedom and prosperity that he had fought so long to gain.

Taking young James McPherson from the midwife's arms, Ian looked down at the red, wrinkled skin of his son's face. And while his tears of joy denied him the ability to look upon his son, nothing could blur the dream that James, and all his brothers and sisters, would inherit something that would be worth having: a chance to grow up free and in peace.

About the Author

HAROLD COYLE is the *New York Times* best-selling author of *Until the End, Look Away, Code of Honor, The Ten Thousand, Trial by Fire, Bright Star, Sword Point,* and *Team Yankee.* He lives in Leavenworth, Kansas.